GEMINI

Michel Tournier

GEMINI

Translated from the French *Les Météores*
by Anne Carter

THE JOHNS HOPKINS UNIVERSITY PRESS
BALTIMORE AND LONDON

Originally published as *Les Météores*
Copyright © 1975 by Editions Gallimard
Translation copyright © 1981 by William Collins, Sons & Company, Limited
All rights reserved
Printed in the United States of America on acid-free paper

Johns Hopkins Paperbacks edition, 1998
9 8 7 6 5 4 3 2 1

The Johns Hopkins University Press
2715 North Charles Street
Baltimore, Maryland 21218-4319
The Johns Hopkins Press Ltd., London

Library of Congress Cataloging-in-Publication Data

Tournier, Michel.
    [Météores. English]
    Gemini / Michel Tournier ; translated from the French Les météores by
Anne Carter.
        p.   cm.
    ISBN 0-8018-5776-7 (alk. paper)
    I. Carter, Anne.   II. Title.
PQ2680.083M413   1998
843´.914—dc21   97-18469
                                                           CIP

A catalog record for this book is available from the British Library.

CONTENTS

GEMINI

CHAPTER I

The Pierres Sonnantes

On the twenty-fifth of September 1937, a depression moving from Newfoundland to the Baltic sent masses of warm, moist oceanic air into the corridor of the English Channel. At 5:19 P.M. a gust of wind from the west-southwest uncovered the petticoat of old Henriette Puysoux, who was picking up potatoes in her field; slapped the sun blind of the Café des Amis in Plancoët; banged a shutter on the house belonging to Dr. Bottereau alongside the wood of La Hunaudaie; turned over eight pages of Aristotle's *Meteorologica,* which Michel Tournier was reading on the beach at Saint-Jacut; raised a cloud of dust and bits of straw on the road to Plélan; blew wet spray in the face of Jean Chauvé as he was putting his boat out in the Bay of Arguenon; set the Pallet family's underclothes bellying and dancing on the line where they were drying; started the wind pump racing at the Ferme des Mottes; and snatched a handful of gilded leaves off the silver birches in the garden of La Cassine.

The sun was already dipping down behind the hill where the children of St. Brigitte's were picking Michaelmas daisies and

chicory flowers to heap in untidy bunches at the feet of their patron saint's statue on the eighth of October. This side of the Bay
of Arguenon, facing east, got the sea wind only overland; and in
among the salty brume of the September tides Maria-Barbara
caught the acrid smell of the stubble burning everywhere inland.
She threw a shawl over the twins lying curled up together in one
hammock.

How old are they? Five? No, six at least. No, they are seven.
How hard it is to remember children's ages! How can one recol-
lect a thing that is forever changing? Especially with these two,
so puny and immature. In any case, this immaturity, this back-
wardness in her two youngest soothes and comforts Maria-Barbara. She breast-fed them longer than any of her other children.
She was thrilled to read one day that Eskimo mothers suckled
their children until they were capable of chewing smoked meat
and frozen fish—which meant to three or four years old. For
them at least, learning to walk did not inevitably take them
away from their mothers. She has always dreamed of a child that
would come to her, upright on its small legs, and deliberately,
with its own hands, undo her bodice and take out the gourd of
flesh and drink, like a man at the bottle. The truth is that she has
never been able to distinguish very clearly between the nursling
and the man, the husband, the lover.

Her children . . . A mother so many times over that she does
not really know how many there are. She does not want to. She
refuses to count them, just as she has refused for years to comprehend the increasing reproach, the veiled threat in the faces of
those around her. Sterilized. The birth of the twins necessitated
a brief period of anesthesia. Had they taken advantage of it to
commit the horrible act upon her? Had Edouard lent himself to
the conspiracy? It is a fact that she has had no more children
since. Her maternal vocation seems to have worn itself out with
that double birth. Normally she begins to grow restless as soon
as her latest-born is weaned. She is one of those women who are
never really happy unless they are pregnant or breast-feeding.
But her twins might be said to have given her ultimate fulfillment. Perhaps there are natural mothers of twins, each of

whose children is only half complete until matched by an identical brother . . .

A chorus of barking and laughter. Edouard has arrived. His trip to Paris must have been shorter than usual. Could he be losing his taste for jaunts to the capital as he gets older? He has gone up to La Cassine to change. Then he will come and greet Maria-Barbara. He'll come loping up behind her deck chair. He'll lower his face to hers and they'll look at one another upside down. He'll kiss her on the forehead and come and stand in front of her, tall, slim, elegant, good-looking, with a tender, ironical smile to which he seems to be pointing, stroking, his clipped moustache with the tip of one forefinger as though to draw her attention to it.

Edouard is Maria-Barbara's second husband. The first she scarcely knew. What did he die of exactly? It was at sea, certainly, because he was a second officer in the merchant marine. But by accident or disease? She can hardly remember. Perhaps he simply faded away because his wife was so absorbed in her first pregnancy that she forgot the fleeting author of it.

Her first pregnancy . . . It was the day the young wife knew she was expecting a child that her life really began. Before that was adolescence, parents, the waiting with the flat, hungry belly. Afterward the pregnancies did not so much follow one another as merge into a single one, they became a normal, happy condition, scarcely interrupted by brief, distressing vacations. The husband, the sower of the seed, the donor of the slight flick that set the creative process in motion, mattered hardly at all.

The twins stir and moan and Maria-Barbara bends over them, moved yet again by the strange transformation that awakening works in their faces. Asleep, reverted to their most private selves, reduced to what is deepest and most unchanging in them— reduced to their *common denominator*—they are indistinguishable. It is the same body entwined with its double, the same visage with the same lowered eyelids presenting at once its full face and its right profile, the one chubby and tranquil, the other pure and clear-cut, and both entrenched in a mutual rejection of everything outside the other. And it is like this that Maria-Barbara feels them closest to her. Their flawless similitude is the image of

the matrical limbo whence they came. Sleep gives them back the
original innocence in which they are as one. The truth is that everything which divides them from each other divides them from
their mother.

The wind has touched them and a single shiver runs through
them. They disentangle themselves. The world about them is
taking possession of their senses again. They stir and the two
faces, responding differently to the call of the outside world, become those of two brothers, Paul's confident, willful, autocratic,
Jean's restless, open, inquisitive.

Jean-Paul sits up and says: "I'm hungry." It is Paul who
speaks but Jean, nestling behind him and like him looking up at
Maria-Barbara, accompanies the cry, which thus becomes a joint
effort.

Maria-Barbara takes an apple from a wicker basket and gives
it to Paul. The child rejects it with a look of surprise. She takes a
silver knife and cuts the fruit in two, holding it in her left hand.
The blade crunches into the circle of five tiny shriveled petals
that lies in the hollow on the underside of the apple. A little
white foam froths the edges of the skin where the knife has cut
it. The two halves fall apart, still held together by the short,
woody stem. The moist, pulpy flesh encloses a horny, heart-
shaped chamber with two brown, shiny pips set in it. Maria-Barbara gives a half to each twin. They study their pieces intently
and, without a word, exchange them. She does not attempt to
understand the meaning of this little ritual, knowing only that it
does not spring simply from a childish whim. With their mouths
full, the twins embark on one of their long, mysterious confabulations in the secret language known in the family as Aeolian. Waking has divided them for an instant, wrenching them
out of the confusion of sleep. Now they are re-creating their
geminate intimacy by adjusting the direction of their thoughts
and feelings and by this exchange of caressing sounds which can
be heard as words, wails, laughter or simply signals, whichever
you like.

A red spaniel bounds across the grass and prances joyfully
round Maria-Barbara's "camp." An upside-down head looms
over her and a kiss lands on her forehead.

"Hello, darling."

Now Edouard is in front of her, tall, slim, elegant, attractive, his face alight with a tender, ironical smile which he seems to be stressing with his forefinger as he strokes his clipped moustache.

"We weren't expecting you so soon," she says. "This is a nice surprise. Paris is beginning to pall, it seems."

"You know I don't go to Paris just for fun."

He is lying. She knows it. He knows that she knows. This mirror play is their own private ritual, a reconstruction on a marital level of the great geminate game of which Jean-Paul is patiently laying down the rules, a trivial, superficial repetition, like the ancillary love affairs in plays which provide a comic echo of the sublime loves of the prince and princess.

Fifteen years earlier, Edouard made Maria-Barbara help him choose and decorate a handsome apartment on the Ile Saint-Louis. It was—he said—so that they could get away together—dine out, go to the theater. Had he forgotten—or was he merely pretending to forget—that Maria-Barbara did not enjoy going away, Paris and dining out? Out of good nature, or laziness, she fell in with the game, went, chose, signed, and decorated, but once the last workman had gone she never went near the Ile Saint-Louis again, leaving Edouard a clear field for his business engagements. These multiplied and lengthened rapidly. Edouard would disappear for weeks on end, leaving Maria-Barbara to her children and the weaving sheds of the Pierres Sonnantes—the Sounding Stones—to the foreman, Guy Le Plorec. On the surface at least, she accepted these absences, absorbed in her gardening, keeping an eye on the weather, the big aviary, her host of children, with some of the backward ones from St. Brigitte's always in among them, and most of all the twins, whose radiant presence was enough to satisfy her.

She rises and with Edouard's help gathers up the familiar things that are a traditional part of her afternoons in the deck chair. Her glasses, folded on top of a novel—the same one for months past—the basket in which she keeps her knitting, pointless now, since she is unlikely to have another child, her shawl, fallen on the grass, which she throws around her shoulders. Then, leaning on Edouard's arm and leaving the chairs, tables and hammock for Méline to put away, she trudges up the rough zigzag path to La Cassine with the babbling twins racing ahead.

La Cassine is a large, not particularly interesting building, like most of the houses of eastern Brittany, starting as a modest old farmhouse and elevated at the end of the last century by the owners of the Pierres Sonnantes to the status of a gentleman's residence. It retains from its humble past its cob walls—granite showing only on the corners, in the framework of doors and windows and in the cellar—a steeply pitched roof on which the thatch has been replaced by gray slate and an outside staircase leading up to the loft. This Edouard has converted to house the children and it is lit by four jutting dormer windows. Edouard has consigned all his offspring to these attics where he himself has not ventured three times in twenty years. It had been his dream that the downstairs should remain the private domain of the Surins, husband and wife, where Maria-Barbara might be willing to forget for a while that she was a mother and become a wife again. But those attics, all warm and untidy and privately ordered to suit the personality of each of their inhabitants and the mesh of his relationships with the rest, had an irresistible fascination for her. As her children grew up and escaped her, she would find them all again in this friendly muddle and lose herself in all their different stages of play or sleep. Edouard would have to send Méline to look for her before she would come down to him again.

On the other side of the road, St. Brigitte's, a home for handicapped children, shared with the textile factory the buildings of the old Charterhouse of the Guildo, dissolved in 1796. The children had the domestic offices—the old dormitories, refectories, workrooms, infirmary, and administrative offices—as well, of course, as having the use of the gardens which sloped gently downhill toward La Cassine. The factory workshops, for their part, occupied the abbot's palace, the cloister and surrounding officers' quarters, the farm, the stables and the church, whose spire, covered with golden lichen, is visible from Matignon to Ploubalay.

The Charterhouse of the Guildo had its finest hour during the disastrous uprising of the Whites in 1795. The landing of a royalist army at Carnac on the twenty-seventh of June had been preceded by a diversionary action in the Bay of Arguenon in which a party of armed men landed in advance, inflicted heavy losses on the republican forces and then retreated into the abbey, where the chapter was on their side. But Hoche's victory over Cadoudal and his allies sealed the fate of the Chouans in the Guildo, prevented by low tide from re-embarking in time. The abbey was taken by storm on the eve of the fourteenth of July and the fifty-seven White prisoners shot and buried in a mass grave in the cloister. The dissolution order issued in the following year only made official a closure of the Charterhouse which had been a fact ever since the departure of the monks.

The factory had put its offices in the chapter rooms. The cloister had been lightly roofed over to make a storeroom for bales of cloth and bobbin cases, while the recently installed mattress shop had been relegated to the old stables, which had been roughly restored. The heart of the factory dwelt in the nave of the church, where twenty-seven looms purred away, operated by a swarm of girls in gray overalls, their hair bound up in colored scarves.

Thus the factory, St. Brigitte's, and, lower down, on the other side of the lane leading down to the beach at Quatre Vaux, La Cassine, the home of the great tribe of Surins, together made up the Pierres Sonnantes, a rather disparate collection which only the force of habit and everyday living bound together into an organic whole. The Surin children were quite at home in the workrooms and at St. Brigitte's, and people had grown used to seeing the St. Brigitte's children roaming about the factory and mingling with the household at La Cassine.

One of these, Franz, was for a time the twins' inseparable companion. But it was Maria-Barbara who was fondest of the retarded children. She fought with what strength she could muster against the formidably powerful appeal this sickly, helpless flock, with its animal simplicity, had for her. Time and again in the house or the garden, she would feel lips pressed to her straying hand. Then, moving gently, she would stroke a head or a neck, not looking at the froglike face lifted worshipfully to hers. She had to fight against it, hold herself back, because she knew the

insidious, irresistible, implacable force that the hill of the innocents could exert. She knew it by the example of a handful of
women who had come, sometimes by chance, for a short while,
for a term, out of curiosity or a teacher's professional interest to
gain an insight into the methods being used with handicapped
children. There would be an initial period of familiarization,
during which the newcomer would have to struggle to overcome
the repugnance which, in spite of herself, the ugliness, clumsiness and sometimes the sheer dirtiness of the children inspired in
her, and which was all the more depressing because, however
abnormal, they were not ill, the majority being actually healthier
than most normal children, as though nature had tried them hard
enough and was exempting them from ordinary ailments. Nevertheless, the poison was acting unconsciously and pity, dangerous,
many-armed, and tyrannical, was enveloping its victim's heart
and mind. Some left, desperately wrenching free while there
might still be time to tear themselves away from the deadly hold
and in the future have nothing but well-balanced relationships
with normal, healthy, self-possessed men and women. But the innocents' formidable weakness would overcome this last spas-
modic attempt and they would return, defeated, obedient to St.
Brigitte's mute yet imperious summons, knowing themselves cap-
tives for life from that time on, yet still making the excuse of further training, additional research, projected studies that deceived
no one.

By marrying Maria-Barbara, Edouard had become the managing
director and principal shareholder of the textile works of the
Pierres Sonnantes, since his father-in-law promptly laid down
the burden of it. Yet it would have come as a great surprise to
him had anyone told him he was marrying for money, so much
was he in the habit of taking it for granted that his interests and
inclinations should coincide. Moreover, the business very quickly
turned out something of a severe disappointment. In fact, the
factory's twenty-seven looms were of an out-of-date type and the
only hope of rescuing the business lay in investing a fortune in
new machinery. Unfortunately, in addition to the crisis which
was affecting the whole of Western economy, there was also the

unsettling effect of profound, yet uncertain changes which were taking place within the textile industry at that period. In particular, there was talk of rotary looms, but these were a revolutionary innovation and their first users would be taking on incalculable risks. To begin with, Edouard was much attracted by a specialty of the Pierres Sonnantes called grenadine, a figured silk and wool mixture, a light, clear, transparent fabric manufactured exclusively for the great couture houses. He was entranced by the team of weavers and the ancient Jacquard employed for this luxury fabric and devoted all his efforts to the unprofitable line with its unreliable and not particularly rewarding outlets.

The firm's survival actually rested on the shoulders of Guy Le Plorec, once a working mechanic, who had risen to foreman and now acted as assistant manager. Le Plorec had found the answer to the Pierres Sonnantes' difficulties at the opposite pole from the grenadine, by combining with the warping and weaving sheds a mattress shop of thirty female carders which had the advantage of taking up a large part of the material manufactured on the premises. But this innovation had helped to make Edouard lose interest in a business which was full of hazards and pitfalls and now seemed able to survive only by a descent into vulgarity. Furthermore, the opening of the mattress shop had brought in an additional work force of largely unskilled girls, with no tradition of craftsmanship and prone to absenteeism and discontent, very unlike the disciplined, aristocratic body of warpers and weavers.

It was this aspect of Le Plorec's little revolution that Edouard felt most deeply. For such a ladies' man to become the head of a firm employing three hundred and twenty-seven women was at once galling and exciting. At first, whenever he ventured into the throbbing, dusty workrooms, he was embarrassed by the covert curiosity he aroused, which contained every shade of provocativeness, contempt, respect, and nervousness. To begin with, he was incapable of restoring the femininity to the gray-overalled figures in colored headscarves moving about the sizing machines and along the breast beams and felt as though an ironical fate had made him king of a race of specters. But gradually his eyes began to enjoy the sight of the women coming to work in the

morning and going home at night, normally dressed now, some
of them neat and even smart, their faces alive with chatter and
laughter, their movements light, graceful, and charming. After
that he would take trouble to single out in the narrow lanes that
ran between the machines some girl or other whose figure he
had noticed outside. The apprenticeship had taken him months,
but it had borne fruit, and from then on Edouard knew how to
perceive youth and beauty and prettiness underneath the working clothes and drudgery.

All the same he would have shrunk from seducing one of his
women workers, much less making one of them his regular, kept
mistress. Edouard had no principles to speak of and the example
of his brother Gustave strengthened him in his distrust of morality and his fear of the arid puritanism that could lead to the
worst aberrations. What he had, on the other hand, was taste, a
very strong instinct for what could be done—even in violation of
every written law—without disturbing a certain harmony, and
what, on the contrary, must be avoided as bad form. Now this
harmony demanded that the Pierres Sonnantes should be the
accredited sphere of his family and that the only proper place
for his extramarital affairs was in Paris. Besides which, the working girl remained for him a disturbing creature, impossible to as-
sociate with because she upset his ideas about women. Women
might work, certainly, but at domestic chores, or, if absolutely
necessary, on a farm or in a shop. To work in a factory must go
against their nature. Women might be given money, certainly—
for the home, for personal adornment, to amuse themselves, or
for no reason at all. A weekly wage was degrading to them. Such
were the beliefs of this pleasant, simple man who spontaneously
radiated around him an atmosphere of carefree gaiety without
which he could not live. But there were times when he felt
crushed with loneliness between his ever-pregnant wife, exclusively preoccupied with her children, and the gray, toiling mass
at the Pierres Sonnantes. "I am the useless drone in between the
queen bee and the workers," he would say with playful melancholy. And then he would drive to Dinan and take the fast train
to Paris.

To the provincial that he was, Paris could not be anything but a place of brilliant life and fulfillment and, left to himself, he would have looked for a flat near the Opéra and the Grands Boulevards. Maria-Barbara, having been duly consulted about this important undertaking, and taken to Paris several times, had made a choice of the Quai d'Anjou, on the Ile Saint-Louis, where the view of leaves and water and arched masonry suited her own calm, horizontal outlook on life. What was more, it meant that Edouard was only a few minutes away from the rue des Barres, where his mother lived with his younger brother, Alexandre. He settled into the place, for its dignity and prestige appealed to a basic conservatism in him, even while it bored the playboy who would have liked more noise and excitement.

This coming and going of Edouard's between Paris and Brittany was like the intermediate position he occupied between his two brothers, the elder, Gustave, who remained in the family home at Rennes, and the younger, Alexandre, who had nagged his mother into going to live with him in Paris. It was hard to imagine a more irreconcilable contrast than that between Gustave's almost puritanical austerity, aggravated by stinginess, and the blatant dandyism Alexandre affected. Brittany, a traditionally conservative and religious region, provides many examples of families where the elder brother has a rigid respect for the ancestral values and is opposed by a younger who is subversive, iconoclastic and altogether scandalous. The hostility between the two brothers was made worse by a practical consideration. For old Madame Surin, having her favorite son at her side and in constant attendance on her was a comfort, certainly, and one that no one could think of denying her. But she lived on a monthly allowance made by her two elder sons, and Alexandre, inevitably, reaped the benefit of it. This situation annoyed Gustave exceedingly and he missed no opportunity of making caustic references to it, accusing Alexandre of preventing his mother —for his own obvious reasons—from living in Rennes, in the midst of her granddaughters, as would have been only natural.

Edouard took care not to mention these grievances when he met Alexandre in the course of his little ritual visits to his mother, so that he came naturally to take on the role of family go-between. With Alexandre, he shared a zest for life and even for adventure, a love of things and people—although their tastes were different—and an inquiring nature which put a spring in their steps. But whereas Alexandre was forever reviling the establishment and conspiring against society, Edouard shared with Gustave an innate respect for the course of things he regarded as normal and therefore healthy, desirable and sanctified. Indeed, placed side by side, the conformist Gustave and the sanguine Edouard might easily have been confused with one another. But the thing that set the two brothers profoundly apart was the degree of feeling which Edouard brought to everything, his engaging cheerfulness, his good manners, and the innate contentment, radiant and infectious, that drew people to him and kept them there, as though they gained warmth and comfort from being with him.

The partitioned life he led had long seemed to Edouard a masterpiece of happy organization. At the Pierres Sonnantes, he devoted himself entirely to the demands of the factory and to caring for Maria-Barbara and the children. In Paris, he became the leisured, moneyed bachelor again, enjoying his second youth. But over the years even a man so little given to self-analysis was bound to recognize that each of these lives served as a mask for the other, blinding him to the emptiness and incurable melancholy which was the truth about both. Whenever the pangs of it seized him in Paris, when the end of an evening took him back to the loneliness of the big apartment with its tall, narrow windows reflecting all the lights in the Seine, he would turn with a wave of nostalgia to the warm, loving confusion of La Cassine. But at the Pierres Sonnantes, when he had got himself dressed for no purpose except to go to his office at the factory, he would contemplate the day yawning interminably ahead of him and be seized with a fever of impatience, so that he had to force himself not to make a dash for Dinan, where there was still time to catch the Paris express. At first he had felt vaguely flattered when the people at the factory called him "the Parisian," but the hint of disapproval and of doubts about his seriousness and competence which the nickname implied came home to him more fully year by year. In the same way, although he had long accepted with an amused smile the fact that his friends looked on him—on him,

the charmer, so long-practiced in the art of dalliance—as a rich
provincial, something of a sucker, ignorant of the big city which
in his eyes was decked with imaginary wonders, he was beginning to be irritated by the picture they had of him, as a Breton
caught by the fleshpots of Paris, a kind of country bumpkin in
clogs and a sailor hat with ribbons and a bagpipe under his arm.
The truth was that if the double life which had more than
satisfied him for so long was beginning to look to him like a twofold exile, a twofold uprooting, this disenchantment was a sign of
his helplessness in the face of an unforeseen problem, the ominous and unthinkable prospect of growing old.

His relations with Florence mirrored this decline faithfully. He
had seen her for the first time in a cabaret where she came on at
the end of the evening. She recited some rather esoteric poems
and sang gravely, accompanying herself skillfully on the guitar.
A Greek by birth and almost certainly Jewish, she put into her
words and her music something of the peculiar sadness of the
Mediterranean countries, not solitary and individual like Nordic
sadness but quite the opposite, a fraternal, even a tribal, family
affair. Afterward, she came and sat down at the table where
he was swigging champagne with some friends. Florence had
amazed him with her caustic, humorous shrewdness, a trait he
would have expected in a man more than a woman, and most of
all by the look she gave him, sardonic and yet full of understanding. There was, certainly, something of the bumpkin in the
image of himself he saw in her dark eyes, but he read in them
also that he was a man made for love, his flesh so deeply imbued
with heart that his very presence was a comfort and reassurance
to a woman.

He and Florence had very quickly agreed to "get together for
a bit," a phrase whose easy cynicism appealed to him even while
it shocked him a little. She never tired of getting him to talk
about the Pierres Sonnantes, about Maria-Barbara and the children, the Arguenon coast and his own boyhood in Rennes. It was
as though she, a nomad and a wanderer, were fascinated by the
music of the names that cropped up in his descriptions, names
redolent of seashore and moorland, like Plébouille, Rougerais,
the Quinteux brook, Kerpont, Grohandais, the Guildo, the Hébi-

hens . . . It was unlikely she would ever visit these remote country places, nor was such a possibility ever mentioned by either of
them. The apartment on the Quai d'Anjou, where she had ventured at the start of their liaison, made her uncomfortable but
she put it down to the chilly elegance, the rigid neatness and
lifeless beauty of the big, empty rooms with their patterned oak
floors reflecting the painted and coffered ceilings. She explained
to Edouard that the house corresponded neither with the family
in Brittany nor with any aspect of Paris, but was the unsuccess-
ful result, the stillborn child, as it were, of a hopeless blend of
the two.

Edouard answered her objection with arguments as contradictory as his own state of mind. The grand houses of the past,
he said, were usually empty. Whenever a table, chairs, arm-
chairs, even a commode was needed, servants would appear with
the desired object. It was the increasing scarcity of domestic servants that obliged us to live in a clutter which to the contem-
poraries of Molière would undoubtedly have suggested one was
on the point of moving out, or else had only just moved in. And
he would praise the spacious, noble beauty of sparsely furnished,
high-ceilinged rooms, whose chief and subtlest glory was in the
very way they gave one room to breathe and move about. But
then he would go straight on to say that if his apartment remained cold and unwelcoming it was for want of feminine influence. Maria-Barbara was glued to La Cassine and never came
to Paris, and if she, Florence, would not come to live with him,
then there was no hope of the place ever coming to life.

"A house without a woman is a dead house," he argued.
"Move in here with your things, spread your own clutter about
the rooms. Do you think I like living in this deserted museum?
Look at the bathroom even! I can't feel at home there unless I
have to hunt through jars of cleansing cream and astringents and
atomizers to find my razor. The whole pleasure of using a bathroom is the way one keeps coming across all sorts of feminine
nonsense hidden away. This one is as cheerless as an operating
theater!"

She smiled and was silent, and finally said that it was just like
him, setting out to defend an apartment that was too smart, and

ending up in the bathroom among jars of cream and powder puffs and curlers. But in the end it was always in her flat in the rue Gabrielle in Montmartre that they would meet, a red cavern, heavily curtained and stuffed with ornaments, made for living in by night, by the light of red lamps, and at floor level, on divans and poufs and fur rugs, amid a levantine bric-a-brac which Edouard extolled from the start for its "exquisite bad taste." In fact, he was attached to Florence and her chocolate box of a flat by very strong but complex ties which he felt in his flesh and in his heart. The flesh was captive but the heart had reservations. He could not conceal from himself that he loved Florence in a way. But the incredible paradox was that he loved her *un-willingly*, keeping back a whole side of himself—the Gustave side, Alexandre would have said, sneering. And that side of himself, he knew, was at La Cassine with Maria-Barbara and the children, and the twins especially.

His trouble, after twenty happy, fruitful years of marriage, was a kind of split in his nature, separating his thirst for affection and his sexual hunger. As long as this hunger and thirst were closely bound up together and merged with his zest for life and passionate consent to existence, he had been strong, balanced, sure of himself and his family. But now Maria-Barbara had ceased to inspire him with anything more than a great tenderness, a vague, gentle feeling which engulfed his children, his home, and all the Breton side of his nature and which was deep but not passionate, like those autumn afternoons when the sun emerged from the mists of the Arguenon only to sink back almost at once into the smooth, golden haze. His manhood he recovered when he was with Florence in her red cave full of dubious, primitive magic, which repelled him a little, even while they pretended to laugh at it together. This was something else that surprised and attracted him, the faculty she possessed of standing back from her Mediterranean origins, from her family, about which she would talk in a detached way, and ultimately from herself. The ability to observe, to judge and mock at things, yet without rejecting them, preserving intact her sense of fellow-ship and deep, unassailable love—that was something he was incapable of, and here Florence set him a shining example.

He himself felt torn apart, a defaulter and a traitor twice over. He had dreams of making a break, of escaping back to his old wholehearted contentment. He would say goodbye once and for all to Maria-Barbara, the children, the Pierres Sonnantes and begin a new life in Paris with Florence. The misfortune of such a man—of many men—is that they have it in them to become successful husbands and fathers at least twice in their lifetimes, whereas a woman is exhausted and ready to give up well before her last child is independent. For a man to marry a second time a new wife a generation younger than his first is in the nature of things. But there were times when Edouard himself felt tired, worn out, his manhood no longer spoke out so loudly when he was with Florence—was sometimes silent altogether. He would think, then, that his place was at home in Brittany, alongside his life's companion, in the state of physical and emotional semi-retirement that comes with the settled, tranquil affection of old married couples.

Wars might have been designed on purpose to break such insoluble deadlocks.

CHAPTER II

The Anointing of Alexandre

Alexandre

I think it is the effect of my age and that it is the same for everybody. My family and my family background, for which up to today I cared not one bit, now interest me more and more. There was certainly a basic hostility in the arrogant belief that I was a phenomenon unique among my own kin, inexplicable and unforeseeable. Now that the family circle in which I was so totally misunderstood is breaking up, its members dropping out one by one, my dislike is relaxed and I am more and more inclined to acknowledge myself a product of it. Dare I confess that I can no longer look on the big house in the rue du Chapitre in the old town of Rennes, where several generations of Surins have been born and died, without a degree of emotion? That is a new sensation, not so very far removed from filial piety and not so long ago the mere suggestion would have made me sneer ferociously.

This, then, was the home of Antoine Surin (1860–1925), who started life as a builder and demolition contractor and ended it dealing in textiles and ready-made clothes. He had three children. The eldest, Gustave, who was in time to be taken into his original business, remained faithful to the old house. His wife and four daughters live there still. The business which our father left in his hands has developed toward the recovery and "repurgation" of municipal waste. The second, Edouard, married the daughter of one of the suppliers of fabric to the paternal business who owned a small textile factory on the Côtes-du-Nord. Maria-Barbara, my sister-in-law, is—as so often happens with only daughters—so prolific that I doubt if she knows just how many children she has. True, she seems to have called a halt to childbearing for the moment, since the birth of the twins, Jean and Paul.

Which leaves the youngest of the Surin brothers, myself, Alexandre. I can't but laugh to think what any proper, right-minded family history would have to say about me. "Probably excessively spoiled by his parents, he showed no aptitude for any career but stayed at home with his mother while she lived and, after her death, gave free rein to his evil propensities, abandoning himself thereafter to the most frightful depravities."

Let us get the facts right. My father having engaged in just two lines of business—public works and textiles—my two elder brothers inherited the one and the other respectively. There was nothing left for me. Nothing but my own little darling whom I take after and who was never happy with that Antoine she married. Her coming to live with me in Paris was entirely her own choice: she no longer felt at home in the house in the rue du Chapitre, swarming with Gustave's daughters and regimented by the dragon he married. It is my pride and comfort that I gave her the only really happy years of her life.

On the twentieth of September 1934 an equinoctial storm of unusual violence ravaged Brittany with incalculable consequences for me. The fact was that on that day Gustave was killed on one of his own sites when a crane fell and buried him under three tons of household rubbish. His grotesque and disgusting end might have amused me but that it pained me indirectly because of my darling little Mama's grief. I had to go with her to Rennes for the funeral, shake hands with all the local worthies, and face up to my sister-in-law, made more formidable than ever by her widowhood, the dignity of head of the household and the black weeds it invested her with. But all this was nothing compared to the family conclave which had to be got through on the following day. I had been thinking that my brother's inheritance was no concern of mine and planning to go off and browse along the banks of the Vilaine—which is a misnomer because you can pick up some nice slips of boys there, and not too shy. Hm, well, yes, the widow must have got wind of my roving fancy because she buttonholed me that evening in front of the whole family and told me in that voice of hers, like someone murdering an old cello, "Tomorrow, Maître Dieulefit, such an old friend, is coming to preside over a family conclave. We are all relying on you, dear Alexandre. Your presence is *quite* indispensable."

The harpy must have known me very well to be so insistent!

I have never known whether the plot was hatched by the whole family beforehand, but all of a sudden I found myself, at the end of an hour and a half of stupefyingly boring chitchat, with an enormous and totally unexpected pit gaping before me. Out of the aforesaid chitchat, to which I had been paying only the remotest attention, it suddenly emerged with apodictic inevitability that Gustave's business interests were considerable, that they could not be left without anyone to run them, that that person ought to be a member of the family, and that I was the only eligible candidate.

I? I can still see myself, utterly flabbergasted, pointing with one finger at my chest and staring dazedly around at the ring of marble faces about me, all nodding repeated assent to an implacable fate. I? Step into his still warm shoes, that mean old devil who used to escort his dragon of a wife and his four ugly daughters to high mass in the cathedral of St. Pierre on Sundays? I? Take charge of that ridiculous, unsavory business? The indescribable absurdity of it choked me.

I got up and went out and tramped furiously all over town. But that evening, when I went up to my little boyhood room in the rue du Chapitre, I found on my bedside table a rather lavish booklet, soberly printed on art paper and bearing the enigmatic

title: *TURDCO and Its Task of Repurgation.* An invisible hand
was seeing to it that a certain idea should run its course.

Repurgation! The word might have come out of a medical
treatise on the digestive system or a study of theological cas-
uistry. That neologism—no use looking it up in any dictionary—
was Gustave all over in the way it conveyed his attempt to make
up for his horrible calling by putting on airs of intestino-spiritual
research. But what did I not learn on that night of September
26–27, 1934, a night only to be compared with that of the great
Pascal's nocturnal ecstasy!

I learned that until the reign of Philip Augustus—who was responsible for the capital's first public cleansing service—herds of
pigs, running wild through the streets, constituted the sole provi-
sion for the disposal of domestic refuse which people simply
dumped outside their doors. For several hundred years the ox-
carts trundled back and forth between the city and the public
garbage dump, which was the responsibility of the chief surveyor, the Grand Voyer of Paris. A retired guards officer, a Captain La Fleur (of all things!), in the reign of Louis XV, drew up
the first set of articles and conditions, laying down schedules and
times of collections, the size and shape of vehicles employed,
and also the composition of the gangs of workers, male drivers
and female sweepers, *jailloux* as these menial characters were
called here. A whole picturesque and odoriferous history opened
before my eyes, punctuated by such sensational events as the introduction by M. le Préfet Poubelle of that revolutionary article
the garbage can. But most of all, I learned that night that
TURDCO (The Urban Refuse Disposal Company) was a far-
reaching organization extending to six cities—Rennes, Deauville,
Paris, Marseille, Roanne, and Casablanca—with all of which it
had contracts for "repurgation."

Little by little I began to be attracted by the negative, I might
almost say *inverted* aspect of this industry. Certainly it was an
empire that spread through city streets and had its country acres
—the dumps—also; but equally it penetrated into people's most
intimate secrets, since every deed and every action left its mark
on it, the irrefutable proof of its doing—cigarette butts, torn-up
letters, vegetable peelings, sanitary napkins, and so forth. In fact,

it was a complete takeover of a whole community, and a take-over that came from behind, from the rear, reversed and nocturnal.

I also got a glimpse of the transformation that this diabolical dominion could work in me. Poor Gustave had undoubtedly had some inkling of the *duty of transfiguration* imposed by the noble order of the garbage can. But like a fool he had satisfied it by excessive respectability, striving to be godly and charitable and proclaiming himself a model husband and pelican-father. The silly ass! He deserved all those three tons of garbage he got on his head!

By next morning, my mind was made up. I was going to be king of TURDCO. I imparted my decision to my delighted family and, shutting myself up in Gustave's old office—which reeked of religious humbug—began going through the files of each of the six cities under contract. But that was not the most important part. Back in Paris, I acquired some very sharp outfits, in particular an ivory nankeen suit and a set of embroidered silk waistcoats. These waistcoats I had made with six fob pockets, three on each side. Then I got a jeweler to make me six gold medallions, each bearing the name of one of the six towns. I had decided that each medallion should contain a compressed sample of the refuse of its own city, and each should have its place in one of my waistcoat pockets. And thus hung about with relics, transformed into a refuse reliquary, armed with the sixfold seal of his secret empire, the emperor of dust should go forth to promenade the world.

For all the mystery that surrounds it, there is a quite ordinary logic about the mechanism which controls our destiny. What happened to me? A massive leap forward thrust me onto the path that I should follow—the path I was probably following tentatively already. All at once I was aware of all kinds of dormant implications making themselves felt, lifting their voices and taking charge. Now this happened in two stages. First a backward movement, going back to Rennes, retracing the steps of my childhood and adolescence and so on. What is generally called taking a run at it. Then a sudden identification with the one of my two brothers who was furthest removed from me, the one man in the world whom I had thought most alien. All this is fairly understandable. It is clear, for example, that a similar identification with my other brother, Edouard, although less paradoxical, would have been neither likely nor meaningful.

My brother Edouard. I must have had that elder brother's exemplary superiority dinned into my ears enough! They might have been doing their best to make me loathe him, and yet however much he may sometimes have annoyed me—especially when I was very young—I have never actively disliked him. With the passing years I am even coming to feel a kind of affection for him, strongly mixed with sympathy. Because all the obligations I suspected would come of every one of his "superior" qualities have not failed to materialize and burden him more heavily year by year. He will go under, for sure. Already, he is aging badly under the weight of honors, women, children, responsibilities, and money.

He has more or less my own build—or I have his—only he is some four inches taller, which is not quite the advantage it might seem. I have always thought excessive height a handicap which beyond certain limits could become fatal. As some secondary era creatures discovered to their cost. Certainly Edouard is taller than I am. In fact he is too tall. It helps him with women. I have frequently noticed that to be unusually tall is an undeniable asset with the ladies, whatever the defects that go with it. You may be shortsighted, bald, fat, with a hunchback and bad breath; but provided you are over six feet tall all the birds will be at your feet. Not that Edouard has any need of such crude attractions. As a young man he was handsome, he was more than handsome. He radiated a strength, a zest for living, a calm dynamism that came at you in warm waves. Friendliness. I can think of no better word to describe the sense of kindness and good manners he carried about with him. It worked on men. Was there any limit to his power to attract women? He had a way of looking at them, with an affectionate irony, a slightly sidelong glance, smoothing the ends of his clipped moustache with one forefinger at the corner of his lips . . . Good old Edouard! He really has swallowed the honeyed poison of heterosexuality by the bucketful! What an appetite! What bliss!

The result was not long coming. Edouard's charm is the—frequently irresistible—kind which belongs to weak men, lacking in character. He was married when he was scarcely out of his teens. Maria-Barbara's confinement followed hard on the honeymoon. Since then she has never stopped. She was no sooner up and about than she was promptly brought to bed again, so that it seemed as though she could get pregnant from the very air. I have not seen her very often, but never without her feet up. Beautiful, oh beautiful! The majestic alma genitrix in all her serene splendor. Behold the tender womb, teeming with fruitfulness, perpetually surrounded by flocks of children, like the Roman she-wolf. Then, as though the processes of gestation were still too slow for her, she had twins. Are there no lengths she will not go to?

I have gone on seeing Edouard, at lengthy intervals, in Paris. Our mother was the occasion for meetings which were not disagreeable but which we should not have sought, either of us, but for her. I watched exhaustion and then illness undermine that happy temperament. What with the grinding boredom of business and family life at the Pierres Sonnantes and his little trips to Paris which turned into increasingly protracted binges, his fine presence sagged, his confident talk ebbed, and the rather boyishly plump cheeks collapsed into unhealthy folds. His life was divided between the boredom of Brittany and the strain of Paris, encouraged by Maria-Barbara's excessive motherliness and the over-worldliness of his mistress, Florence. I heard that he was diabetic. His plumpness ran to fat which then hung in folds of flesh on what seemed suddenly a narrow, skeletal frame.

Really he is a most depressing case. There is a man, handsome, generous, attractive, hard-working, a man perfectly in tune with his age and environment, a man who has always said yes to everything, sincerely, from the bottom of his heart—yes to his family, yes to all the normal pleasures, yes to the pains inseparable from the human condition. His great strength has always been in loving. He has loved women, good food and wine, stimulating company, but just as surely his wife, his children, the Pierres Sonnantes, and, more surely still, Brittany and France.

In all fairness, his life ought to have gone up and up, a trium-

phal path, strewn with happiness and honors, culminating in an
apotheosis. Instead, there he is going downhill, turning to the
sere and yellow . . . I daresay he will come to a bad end.

While as for me, obliged from the beginning to take things
and people frankly from the wrong angle, moving permanently
in a counterclockwise direction, I have constructed a universe for
myself, crazy maybe, but coherent and above all one that suits
me, in the way that certain mollusks secrete about their bodies a
shell which, though misshapen, fits them perfectly. I have no illusions about the strength or soundness of my construction. I am
a condemned man under a stay of execution. Nevertheless, I can
see that my brother, having eaten his seed corn at a time when I
was little, ugly and wretched, must today be envying me my
good health and abounding appetite for life.

All of which proves that happiness should consist of a proper
mixture of the given and the manufactured. Edouard's was almost entirely *given* to him in the cradle. It was an unimpeach-
able and very comfortable store-bought garment which, since he
was a stock size, fitted him like a glove. Then, with the years, it
became worn and tattered and fell into rags, and Edouard
watched the ruin of it in grief and helplessness.

My case errs in the opposite direction. With me, everything
has been skillfully acquired and the part played by luck and accident proportionately reduced. The edifice is a fragile one. The
slightest disturbance in the environment will be enough to shat-
ter the too delicate shell. At least when that happens I shall
know how to make another. If I have time and strength. And
above all, if I still want to . . .

I never go back to Rennes without my footsteps leading me to
the Thabor College, next door to the gardens of the same name
which lie within the walls of the onetime Benedictine abbey of
Saint-Mélaine. Thabor! A name of mystery, wrapped in an aura
of magic, a sacred name, with its hints of gold and the taber-
nacle! All my adolescence trembles within me at the sound of it
. . . But whatever its promised ecstasies and transfigurations, I
was the only one of the three Surin children to be visited by the
light of the Holy Ghost within its aged walls.

I picture with pain and no little distress the boredom those college years mean to a heterosexual. What a grayness there must be in his days and nights, sunk body and soul in a human environment devoid of sexual stimulus! But then surely that is a fair training for what life has in store for him.

Whereas for me, ye gods! Thabor was a melting pot of desire and satiety all through my childhood and adolescence. I burned with all the fires of hell in a promiscuity which did not let up for a second in any of the twelve phases into which our timetable divided it: dormitory, chapel, classroom, dining hall, playground, lavatories, gymnasium, playing fields, fencing school, staircases, recreation room, washrooms. Every one of those places was a high spot in its way, and the scene for twelve separate forms of chase and capture. From the first day, I was gripped by an amorous fever as I plunged into the atmosphere of the college, saturated with dawning virility. What wouldn't I give today, cast out into the heterosexual twilight, to recover something of that fire!

My initiation came as a surprise when I was made the happy, willing victim of what the "Foils" used to call "shell fishing." Evening prep was just over and we were filing out to the dining hall by way of the recreation area. I was among the last to leave, but not the last, and I was still some yards from the classroom door when the boy assigned to the task put out the lights. I went on slowly in an obscurity relieved only by the lights from the playground. I had my arms behind my back, hands linked, palm outward, over my bottom. I was vaguely aware of something going on behind me, and I felt something obtrusive being pushed into my hands with a determination that could not have been accidental. Giving way to it as far as I could without bumping into the boys ahead, I had to accept that what I was holding in my hands, through the thin stuff of his trousers, was the erect penis of the boy behind me. If I unclasped my hands and removed them from the offering, I should be unobtrusively rejecting the advance being made to me. I responded, on the contrary, by taking a step backward and opening my hands wide, like a shell, like a basket waiting to receive the first fruits of love on the sly.

This was my first encounter with desire experienced, not in solitude, like a shameful secret, but in complicity—I had almost said, and it would be true before long, in company. I was eleven. Now I am forty-five and still I have not emerged from the daze of wonder in which I walked through that damp, dark college playground, as though wrapped in an invisible glory. Never emerged from it . . . How I like that expression, so right and touching, suggesting some strange country, a mysterious forest whose spell is so powerful that the traveler who ventures there *never emerges from it.* He is seized with wonder, and the wonder never lets him go and keeps him from recovery and return to the gray, unprofitable world where he was born.

I was so completely overwhelmed by this discovery that I had no idea which one of the schoolfellows behind me had put into my hands the keys of a kingdom whose wealth, even now as I write, I have not yet done with exploring. Indeed I never did know for sure because I found out later that the action had been the outcome of a little conspiracy among three of them who sat together at the back of the class, members of a secret society called the *Fleurets,* the Foils, who were in the habit of trying out all new boys systematically. I am only going to talk about two of the Foils here, because they are characters who shine with incomparable brilliance in my memory.

Thomas "Drycome" got his pseudo-patronymic from an amazing discovery which made him famous at Thabor and about which I shall have more to say later. All the boys had made the insides of their desk lids into miniature picture galleries of their dreams, memories, heroes, and private myths. So you would see family snapshots next to pages out of sports magazines and portraits of music-hall singers side by side with comic strips. Thomas' pictures were exclusively religious and devoted entirely to the character of Jesus. But this was not the infant Christ or the emaciated, suffering figure of the Cross. This was Christ the King, the champion of God, abounding in strength and vigor, "youth eternal," whose image formed a pyramid upon the small wooden square. This triumphant iconography had, as it were, a kind of signature in a tiny picture tucked away in the left-hand corner which might have passed unnoticed by the uninitiated. It was a crude portrayal of Thomas putting two fingers into the wounded side of the risen Jesus. To begin with, I saw nothing more in it than a reference to Thomas' own Christian name. But that was only a start. Its real meaning was not vouchsafed to me until later.

The little group of Foils used to meet twice weekly at the city's fencing school for the lessons that provided it with a respectable excuse as well as with a splendidly symbolic derivation. The fencing master's attitude toward us was ambivalent, unerringly strict when it came to passing judgment on a low feint or a stop hit in the high line, but turning a blind eye to any scuffles of our own we might engage in in the cloakroom or under the showers. We were quite sure that this retired cavalry officer, unmarried and fashioned from his grizzled head downward entirely of muscle and sinew, was really one of us, but he never gave us so much as a glimpse of what lay behind his fencing jacket and wire mask. When one of our number once hinted at having enjoyed his favors he met with such contemptuous disbelief that he abandoned the subject, but the attempt marked him in our eyes in a way that he never quite lived down. For there were among the Foils some things that simply were not done. No written law defined them, but we could tell them with an infallible instinct and the sanctions we imposed were strict and inflexible.

Because I was the youngest and the newest recruit, they called me Fleurette, a name I answered to quite readily, even from other boys who used it without knowing what it meant. To begin with I had been considered rather "unappetizing" because I was so skinny, but Raphael—whose word was law where matters of sex were concerned—had rehabilitated me by praising my penis, which at that time was relatively long and chubby. Its silky softness—he said—was in contrast to my skinny thighs and meager belly, stretched like a canvas across my jutting hip bones. "Like a bunch of juicy grapes hanging on a burnt-out bit of trellis," he declared rhapsodically, in a way that both flattered and made me laugh. I must admit that to these subtle charms I added a talent for sucking hard and thoroughly which derived from a liking I have always had for seminal fluid.

Thomas had the same liking, more than any of us, although he rarely satisfied it in our direct fashion by a straightforward head-to-tail. In fact, he did nothing like anyone else, but brought to everything a breadth, a loftiness which was essentially religious. Religion was the natural element in which he lived and breathed and had his being. For example, I could quote the kind of ecstatic trance he would fall into every morning in the dormitory as we made our beds before going down to chapel. The rule was that we had to give our sheets a shake before making up the beds. This simple action, performed simultaneously by forty boys, shook out the crust of dried sperm from the sheets and filled the air with a seminal dust. This vernal aerosol got into our eyes, noses, and lungs, so that we were impregnating one another as if by a pollen-bearing breeze. Most of the boarders did not even notice the subtle insemination. It was only to the Foils it gave a gay, priapic delight that would prolong the adolescents' early-morning erections. Thomas was deeply stirred by it. The reason being that, lacking the capacity to distinguish between sacred and profane, he had an intense awareness of the etymological unity of the two words "spirit" and "wind."

This vernal ecstasy, compounded of air and sunshine, was the luminous side of Thomas' spiritual life. But his burning eyes, always darkly circled, his tormented features, his brittle, flimsy body, said clearly enough to anyone willing to hear that he had also a darker side to contend with, one which he rarely overcame. This shadowy passion I witnessed only once, but the circumstances were unforgettable. It was one winter's evening. I had asked permission to go to the chapel to fetch a book I had left in my stall. I was just about to dash out again, awed by the dimly lighted spaces of the vaulted roof and by the dreadful echoes they gave back to every little noise I made, when I heard sobs coming apparently out of the ground. And indeed someone *was* crying underground: the sound was coming through a narrow opening at the back of the choir which led by way of twisting stairs down to the chapel crypt. I was more dead than alive and all the more terrified because—as I knew perfectly well— there was nothing to stop me from going down there to see what was happening below.

So I went. The crypt—as far as I could see by the flickering, blood red light of a single lamp—was a jumble of desks, chairs, candlesticks, prie-dieus, lecterns, and banners of all sorts, a whole assortment of religious odds and ends, God's lumber piled up in an odor of mildew and stale incense. In addition, there was the life-sized Christ from the Thabor garden lying on the flagstones, his worm-eaten cross in the process of being replaced with a new one. He was a splendidly athletic figure, a perfect physical specimen modeled out of some smooth, soaplike substance, stretched out in an attitude of acceptance with widespread arms, expanded pectoral muscles, his stomach hollow but powerfully molded and his legs thickly knotted with sinews. He lay there, stripped of his cross but nonetheless crucified for that, for presently I made out that Thomas was lying beneath him, reproducing his attitude exactly and grunting under the weight of the statue which was all but crushing him.

I fled in horror from a scene which so forcefully brought together the acts of love and crucifixion, as though Christ's conventional chastity had been no more than a long, secret preparation for his union with the cross, as though a man in the act of love were to be in some way nailed to his lover. However that might be, I now knew Thomas' dark secret, his physical, carnal, sensual love for Jesus, and I was in no doubt that this somber passion had something—although what precisely?—to do with the famous "dry come" of which he was the inventor and which earned him exceptional kudos with the Foils.

The dry come—as its name indicates—was the achievement of an orgasm with no release of sperm. It could be brought off by means of a fairly strong pressure of the fingers—either by oneself or by one's partner—on the furthest accessible point of the spermatic cord, i.e., just below the anus. It produces a keener, more unexpected sensation, attended by a sharp spasm—relished by some, abhorred, for reasons largely superstitious, by others. It causes a greater nervous exhaustion; but since the reserves of sperm remain intact, repetition is easier and more effective. To be honest, for me the dry come has always been an interesting curiosity but of no great practical advantage. Orgasm without ejaculation produces a kind of closed circuit which seems to me to imply a rejection of others. It is as if the man practicing the dry come, after an initial impulse toward his partner, were suddenly to realize that here was no soul mate or, more to the point, brother in flesh, and, seized with revulsion, break contact and withdraw into himself, as the sea, frustrated by the breakwater, sucks back its waves in the undertow. It is the reaction of a person whose choice is fundamentally for the closed cell, for a geminate seclusion. I am too far away—perhaps I ought to add, alas—from the perfect pair, I am too fond of other people, I am, in short, too much of a hunter by instinct to shut myself in like that.

This fierce piety and my disturbing discoveries surrounded Thomas with a somber distinction. The fathers themselves would gladly have done without their too gifted pupil, although, when all was said and done, he was a credit to them and it must be admitted that his excesses, which in a lay institution would have rebounded on themselves, found in a religious college a climate that favored their development. Drycome had distorted the meanings of most of the prayers and rituals on which we were nourished—but had they really any meaning in themselves, or were they only waiting, free and available, for someone with the wit to bend them, with gentle violence, to his own way of thinking? For instance, I need go no further than the Psalms which we sang every Sunday at vespers and which might have been written for him, and us. Thomas would crush us with his arrogant demand as our voices echoed his proud, enigmatic assertion that:

> *Dixit dominus domino meo*
> *Sede a dextris meis*

The Lord said unto my lord, sit thou at my right hand, until I make thine enemies thy footstool. And we would picture him with his head on Jesus' breast, spurning with his feet a groveling horde of humbled masters and fellow pupils. But we took completely for our own the Psalm's disdainful charge against heterosexuals:

> *Pedes habent, et non ambulabunt*
> *Oculos habent, et non videbunt*

Manus habent, et non palpabunt
Nares habent, et non odorabunt!

Feet have they, but they walk not. Eyes have they, but they
see not. Hands have they, but they handle not. Noses have they,
but they smell not.

We who walked and saw and handled and smelled would
bawl out that insolent indictment while our eyes caressed the
backs and buttocks of the fellow pupils in front of us, so many
young calves reared for domestic use and so paralyzed, blind, in-
sensible, and devoid of any sense of smell.

Raphael Ganesh was certainly a long way from Thomas Drycome's elaborate mysticism. He preferred the opulent, highly
colored imagery of the East to the iconographic traditions of
Christianity. He got his nickname from the Hindu idol whose
colorful picture covered the whole of his desk lid. This was
Ganesh, the elephant-headed god with four arms and a lan-
guishing, kohl-rimmed eye, the son of Siva and Parvati, always
accompanied by the same totem animal, the rat. The gaudy
colors, the Sanskrit text, the enormous jewels with which the idol
was decked were all there solely as a frame, to extol and set off
the supple, scented trunk which swayed with a lascivious grace.
That, at least, was what Raphael claimed, who saw Ganesh as
the deification of the sexual organ as an object of worship. According to him, the only justification for any boy's existence was
as the temple of a single god, concealed within the sanctuary of
his clothes, to whom he burned to render homage. As for the rat
totem, its meaning remained obscure to the most learned orien-
talists and Raphael was far from suspecting that it would be for
little Alexandre Surin, whom they called Fleurette, to unravel
the secret. This Eastern idolatry, crude and primitive as it was,
made Raphael the antithesis of the subtle, mystical Thomas. But
I have always thought the Foils were fortunate in possessing two
heads so diametrically opposite in inspiration and practice.

The cruel, sensuous society of the Foils, together with our encounters in the fencing school, have left me with a liking for
those weapons. But since it is no longer the fashion to go about
wearing a sword, I have provided myself with a secret array of

swords in the shape of a collection of sword sticks. I have ninety-seven at the moment and I do not mean to stop there. Their value depends on the fineness of the sheath and how perfectly it locks. The coarsest blades live in enormous sheaths—the civilian equivalent of a policeman's truncheon—and are simply jammed into them. But the best sticks are as supple as withies. There is absolutely nothing to show that they conceal a triangular blade, as light as a feather. The lock can be sprung either by pressing a button with the thumb or by twisting the knob halfway around. The handle may be of carved ebony, chased silver, horn or ivory, a bronze figure of a naked woman, or the head of a bird, a dog, or a horse. The best of them have two little steel bars that spring out at right angles to the blade when it is drawn to make a rudimentary guard.

My sword sticks are my daughters, my personal virgin army, for so far none of them has ever killed, or not in my service. I should not keep them by me were I not convinced that the time will come when it will be necessary to perform that act of love and death which involves two men and a sword. And so I never fail, before I set out for the nightly chase, to make my slow, ritual selection of a companion. My favorite is called Fleurette—like myself in my time at Thabor—and her blade of blued Toledo steel, triple-grooved, is as slim as a dart. I take her on my arm, like a bride-to-be, only on those evenings that are darkened by some foreboding. When the fatal night comes, she will be my only ally, my only friend, and I shall not fall until she has strewn the ground with the bodies of my murderers.

CHAPTER III

The Hill of the Innocents

In the twenty years that she had been in charge of St. Brigitte's, Sister Beatrice had ceased to make a distinction between her religious vocation and her dedication to the children. She was always secretly astonished—even shocked—that anyone could approach them in anything but an evangelical spirit. How could you respect and love them properly unless you realized that God has revealed to the simpleminded truths he has concealed from the clever and even from the wise? Besides, was there any remarkable difference between our poor intellect and the consciousness of a mongol when compared to the mind of God? She thought, moreover, that any progress made by the mentally defective must stem directly or indirectly from a religious inspiration. Their greatest handicap was their loneliness, their incapacity to form mutually satisfying relationships with another person—even someone as handicapped as themselves. She had invented games, round games and playlets in which each child had to become one of a group and model his behavior on that of his fellows—a laborious undertaking, demanding infinite pa-

tience, because the only human relationship they would accept
was that linking them to her, Sister Beatrice, so that her own
presence was constantly helping to break down the interde-
pendence she was striving to create among the children.

Nevertheless, success was possible and even assured with the
help of divine intervention. God, who knew each of the children
and had a special fondness for them just because they were simpleminded, embraced them all in the same love and sent the
light of the Holy Spirit to shine in them. So Sister Beatrice
dreamed of a Pentecost of the Innocents which would descend in
tongues of fire upon their heads, driving the shadows from their
minds and loosening the paralysis of their tongues. She said
nothing about it, knowing that her ideas had already caused
some uneasiness in high places and that she had very nearly
been found guilty in particular for the simplified version of the
Lord's Prayer which she had put together for the use of her
protégés:

> *Our Father greatest of all*
> *May everybody know you*
> *May everybody sing your name*
> *May everybody do what you like*
> *Always and everywhere*
>
>   *Amen*

The affair had gone all the way to the archbishop. In the end
he had approved the words, which, in his estimation, contained
the heart of the matter.

But this was not all. Sister Beatrice had convinced herself that
her innocents were closer to God and the angels than other people—and herself especially—not only because they were strangers
to the duplicity and false values of society, but also because sin
had, so to speak, no hold on their souls. She experienced a kind
of fascination in the presence of beings who—besides having a
very cruel curse inflicted on them—had also been gifted with
what was in its way a kind of original goodness, altogether loftier and purer than the virtue which she had been able to attain
from years of prayer and self-denial. Her faith was strengthened
by the glow of their presence and could not have forgone their

intercession without suffering a perilous setback. Thus she, too, was the children's prisoner (but more irremediably than her colleagues), because they had become the foundation and the living spring of her spiritual universe.

The institution of St. Brigitte's, which was made up of some sixty children with a staff of twenty, was divided theoretically into four sections like four concentric circles, each smaller than the last. The first three fell roughly into the classic categories of mild, moderate and severe retardation, as measured by the Binet-Simon intelligence tests.

But Sister Beatrice had enough experience of backward children to place only a relative value on such scientific distinctions. The test measured only certain limited aspects of intelligence, ignoring all other forms of mental activity, and disregarded the subject's degree of affectivity and cooperativeness, presupposing a passive child of unlimited willingness. For this reason the groups at St. Brigitte's fitted better into fairly flexible empirical categories defined by the degree of understanding that existed among the children themselves.

In the first group were those children who appeared normal—except when they exhibited personality problems or congenital feebleness—and who were educable, requiring only an unusual amount of supervision. The epileptic, the deaf and dumb, the overactive, and the psychotic could be seen getting on happily together. The second circle, however, had already ceased to have any outlet to the outside world. The children here could speak if they had to, but they could not read and would never write. Not so many years earlier, there would have been a place for them in some rural community where the village idiot was a traditional character, accepted, even respected, and able to do little jobs about the fields and gardens. Now the rise in economic and cultural standards of living was turning them into rejects, instantly recognizable compared to the general level of education and consequently rejected by the community, their wretchedness only increased by the gulf created around them. All that was left to them was to express by mumbling, stamping, head waving, hooting, squinting, dribbling and incontinencies of the bowels, their antagonism to a bureaucratic, rationalized, mechanized and aggressive society which they denied quite as strongly as it rejected them. The moving spirit of this group was a young student from the Conservatoire who had come to St. Brigitte's to gather material for a thesis on the therapeutic uses of music with backward children. She had formed a choir, then an orchestra, and finally, by dint of time and patience, had divided her group into an orchestra and a corps de ballet. It was a strange, grotesque and heartrending spectacle to see the small performers, each one incurably maimed in some way, but expressing themselves and showing off in spite of their physical and mental disabilities. At first sight there was something cruel, even indecent in their droll, awkward performances, but it did the children good, a great deal of good, and in the end that was the only thing that counted. Antoinette Dupérioux found herself trapped by her own success. How could she give up the work and nip such promise in the bud? She postponed her departure month by month, then stopped talking about it altogether, while still coming to no firm decision.

These at least had the possibility of speech. The severely retarded—those of the third circle—emitted nothing but inarticulate sounds whose meaning was reduced to the two extremes of like / don't like, want / don't want, happy / unhappy. Some attempts were made to raise their mental level by means of exercises of a practical or artistic kind which did not involve the abstract and symbolic function of language. They were set to drawing, modeling, making checkerboards by inserting strips of paper into parallel strips in a square of a different color, and sticking onto cardboard shapes of people, flowers and animals cut out with the aid of a pair of round-ended scissors. As a corrective to their clumsiness, lack of motor coordination and the problems of balance which had them lurching left and right at every step, they were made to ride little bicycles which were simultaneously their terror and delight. The overexcitable, the psychotic and the epileptic were not included in these ploys but the mongols loved them, and none more than stout Bertha and the seven others with whom she shared a dormitory.

It would seem sensible to have eliminated everything relating to symbols and verbal expression from these children's world.

Dr. Larouet, who specialized in linguistics and phonology, saw it otherwise. As soon as he could get himself put in charge of the third circle, he embarked on experiments aimed at introducing the concept of symbols. He was able to do this comparatively successfully by focusing his endeavors on the high spot of the severely retarded children's lives, the bicycles. One day the children were surprised to find the concrete playground where they rode their cycles marked out with lines of white paint and dotted with a number of boards like road signs: no entry, keep right, stop here, no left turn, etc. It was months before the number of mistakes—which were punished quite heavily by temporary confiscation of the bicycle—began to decrease. But then it fell away spectacularly all at once, as though the children had all understood and assimilated the dozen or so signs they had been given at the same time.

Larouet made a great deal of this fact, which he felt was particularly remarkable since the diverse nature of the selected groups of children ruled out the hypothesis of parallel development with no interaction. There must have been communication, some exchange of information among the children.

He therefore set out to analyze, with the help of a recording machine, the more or less articulate shouts and noises uttered by each child. He took a decisive step forward on the day he thought he had discovered that each employed the same number of basic phonemes, and that this phonetic armory comprised not only the basic sound material of French but also that of many other languages—the English *th*, the Spanish *r*, the guttural *r* of Arabic, the German *ch*, and so forth. For each child to have the same phonemes could not be explained away as mimicry. Gradually there emerged from Larouet's research a much more extraordinary theory which opened up fresh horizons within the human mind. This was that every individual begins by possessing all the vocal equipment needed for every language—and not merely for every existing language, past or present, but for all *possible* languages—but that as he learns his mother tongue so he loses forever the use of the unwanted phonemes—phonemes which he will require later on, whenever he comes to learn a particular foreign language, except that then he will never be able to re-

cover them as he had them originally but will have to build them
up again artificially and imperfectly by means of the inadequate
elements his own mother tongue makes available to him. This
would explain foreign accents.

That the severely handicapped should have retained their
phonetic stock intact was not after all so very surprising, since
they had never learned the mother tongue which isolated its
unused portion and precipitated its destruction. But what was
the nature and function of those linguistic roots whose retention
constituted an additional abnormality? It was not so much a language, Larouet thought, as the matrix of all languages, an ar-
chaic, universal linguistic base, a fossil tongue kept alive by the
same kind of anomaly as that which has preserved alive the
Malagasy coelacanth and the duckbill platypus.

Sister Beatrice, who had followed Larouet's researches earnestly, had developed an interpretation which she took care
to keep to herself, knowing that other people would see it only
as yet another piece of mysticism. Far more than simply a language, she thought, this might actually be the *original tongue*
which Adam and Eve, the Serpent and Jehovah spoke together
in the earthly paradise. For she refused to admit to herself that
the idiocy of her children was absolute. She was determined to
see it only as the bewilderment of creatures formed for another
world—for limbo, perhaps, a place of innocence—and uprooted,
exiled, cast into a world devoid of grace or pity. Adam and Eve,
driven from paradise, must all their lives have looked like idiots
to the cold, realistic eyes of their children who, having been born
to it, were perfectly adapted to this world where children are
brought forth in pain to toil until they die. Who shall say even
whether the language of paradise as their parents still spoke it
together, like exiles who never manage to assimilate the speech
of their adopted country properly and shame their offspring with
their accents and grammatical mistakes, did not sound like a confused babble to their earthbound ears? Similarly, if we failed to
understand the conversation of the severely retarded, it was because our ears were closed to that holy dialect through a degeneration which began with the loss of paradise and culminated in
the utter chaos of the Tower of Babel. This Babel state was the

present condition of mankind divided by so many thousands of tongues that no man could hope to master them all. In this way, Sister Beatrice came back to the Pentecost which for her constituted the supreme miracle, the ultimate blessing foretold in the Gospel incarnate in Christ.

But if Sister Beatrice found resources within herself to enable her to idealize her severely retarded pupils, she had to confess in her secret heart that she had more than once been tempted to despair when she went up to see those in the fourth circle, the last, the worst, nameless human deformities brought forth by the ravings of nature. Since they never went out or made any noise, a complete unit had been set up for them in the attics of the main building, including kitchen, sanitation, nurses' sitting room and a huge dormitory of twenty-five beds, more than half of which were, happily, generally unoccupied.

The profoundly retarded, those incapable of walking or even of standing upright, would sit slumped on commodes, round, bony knees drawn up to their chins, looking like skeletal mummies; and their heads, drooping like ripe fruit from their necks, would stir feebly and look up, darting at the visitor an unexpectedly bright, blank, baleful stare. Then the body would resume its interrupted swaying, sometimes accompanied by a vague, harsh droning noise.

The devotion these wrecks demanded was all the harder because not the slightest manifestation of affection, or even awareness, was to be expected from them. That at least was what the women teachers said who came to take their turns in this comatose atmosphere with its pervading sour, baby smell of stale milk and urine. Yet it was not what Sister Gotama believed, the Nepalese nurse who had been marooned in this fourth circle from time immemorial and, unlike her colleagues, went out scarcely more than her patients themselves. She possessed a capacity for silence that was more than human, but whenever visitors spoke in no uncertain terms about the patients her great dark eyes, huge in her thin face, burned with passionate protest. Yet she did not share Sister Beatrice's gift of a deliberately exalted vision and Sister Beatrice was always conscious in her presence of a feeling of mingled admiration and uneasiness.

Certainly Sister Gotama's totally secluded life, spent feeding, washing and nursing repulsive monsters, tirelessly and without disgust, was an incomparably saintly one. But Sister Beatrice was put off by what appeared to her a lack of any element of idealism, of anything otherworldly or transcendent in her life. One day she had said to the Nepalese, "Of course, these patients are not simply mindless brutes; if they were, surely they might as well be done away with? No, as well as the spark of life each of them possesses a glimmer of awareness. And if it pleased God to blow away the pillar of darkness he has erected about them, then they would begin at once to utter such truths as would set our minds reeling."

Sister Gotama, listening, gave a faint, tolerant smile and a slight negative movement of her head which did not escape Sister Beatrice. Perhaps it's the East, she thought, a little shame-facedly. The East, yes, the immanentism of the East. It is all given, it is all there. One can never take off. There is nothing elevated there.

At that time Sister Gotama was responsible for only about a dozen boarders and most of these were microcephalic and atypical idiots. The only noteworthy case was a hydrocephalic child of four, whose stunted body seemed a mere appendage to the enormous triangular head with its massive forehead overhanging the tiny face. The child lay flat on his back, scarcely moving, and regarding those about him with what the experts describe as a "setting sun" look, painful in its gravity and intensity.

But the files that filled the big cabinet bore witness to the barely human malformations Sister Gotama had had to care for over the years. The children she had reared included one with coelosomia, in which the viscera are exposed; two encephalocoeles, their brains developing outside the crania; and one with otocephaly, the two ears meeting below the lower jaw. But the monsters who made the deepest impression were those who seemed to have come straight out of myths and to provide a terrifyingly realistic illustration of them. Such were the cyclops, with a single eye set just above the nose, and the mermaid-child whose legs were fused into a single massive member ending in a fan of twelve toes.

Sister Beatrice did not rest until she had got the reticent Gotama to shed some light—however faint—on the vocation which made her stay with her monsters, and on what she had learned from this long and curious association. Evening after evening the two women would pace up and down the garden of the Pierres Sonnantes in earnest conversation. It was Sister Beatrice who did most of the talking, and the Nepalese would answer her with a smile which held a mixture of defensiveness, unhappiness at being kept from her charges, and the gentle patience with which she always met attacks from without. Sister Beatrice, who pictured the Indian pantheon in terms of a menagerie of trunked and hippopotamus-headed idols, was fearful of discovering some trace of these pagan aberrations in her subordinate's heart. What she did glean from their conversations surprised her by its novelty, its profundity, and how far it agreed with Dr. Larouet's conclusions.

First of all Gotama had reminded her of Jehovah's dilemma at the time of the Creation. Having made man in his image—that is, as a hermaphrodite, both male and female—and seeing that he was unhappy in his solitude, had he not paraded all the animals before him in order that he might choose himself a mate? A strange, almost inconceivable proceeding, which gives us an idea of the immense freedom that existed in that dawn of all things! It was only after this vast review of all the animal creation had failed that God decided to make the companion that he needed from Adam himself. So he took away the whole female side of the hermaphrodite and made it into an autonomous creature. And so Eve was born.

Alone with her monsters, Gotama never lost sight of those first groping steps of Creation. Her cyclops, her hydrocephalic, and her otocephalic, might they not have their places in a differently ordered world? More generally, she came to consider the various limbs and organs of the human body as bits having a great many possible combinations—although in the vast majority of cases one single recipe prevailed to the exclusion of all others.

This idea of the parts of the body being considered as a kind of anatomical alphabet capable of being put together in many different ways—as demonstrated by the infinite variety of the an-

imal kingdom—had an obvious affinity with Dr. Larouet's theory
that the various grunts of the severely retarded formed the
sound particles of all possible languages.

Sister Beatrice was not much given to speculation. She got no
further than the threshold where the two sorts of ideas con-
verged with their tendency to turn her institution into a repository of human origins. For her it all resolved itself into a charitable urge that passed unflinching through the darkness of
impenetrable mysteries.

There was another aspect of the Pierres Sonnantes which, however weird and apparently incongruous, was nonetheless welded
into an organic whole by a life of its own. The heart of this organism was the textile factory, humming with machinery and
human activity, the workers coming on and off, starting up in the
morning, pausing for lunch and stopping for the night, which
gave to the whole place a serious, grown-up, working rhythm,
while, alongside the works, La Cassine and St. Brigitte's lived in
the disorganized and sporadic noise and excitement of homes
full of children. All the same, the rank and file of the Pierres
Sonnantes mingled easily and some of the boarders at St. Brigitte's had the run of the factory and of the Surin household.

One of these was Franz, a boy of the same age as the twins,
who rose briefly to fame in the newspapers of the time as the
Child Calendar.

What struck one first and foremost about Franz was his brilliant popeyes, very wide open and staring with an intense,
haunted look in them. He was skeletally thin, burning with some
inner fire, and if you put a hand on his arm you could feel him
vibrating with a quick, light tremor that never ceased. But the
thing about him that attracted, disturbed and irritated was his
particular combination of brilliance and mental defectiveness.
The fact was that, along with a mental level very close to idiocy
—although it was not easy to assess the element of sheer un-
cooperativeness in the disastrous results of the tests he underwent—he displayed a stupefying virtuosity in juggling with dates
and with the days and months of the calendar from 1000 B.C. all
the way up to A.D. 40,000, which is to say far beyond the time

span of any known calendar. Professors and journalists of every nationality could be seen arriving regularly, and Franz submitted quite readily to interrogations which no longer aroused the slightest interest in the little community of the Pierres Sonnantes.

"What day of the week will it be on the fifteenth of February 2002?"

"A Friday."

"What day was August the twenty-eighth, 1591?"

"A Wednesday."

"What will be the date of the last Monday in February 1993?"

"The twenty-second."

"And the third Monday in May 1936?"

"The eighteenth."

"What day of the week was the eleventh of November 1918?"

"A Monday."

"Do you know what happened on that day?"

"No."

"Would you like to know?"

"No."

"And what day will it be on the fourth of July 42,930?"

"A Monday."

"In which years will the twenty-first of April fall on a Sunday?"

"1946, 1957, 1963, 1968 . . ."

The responses were immediate, instantaneous, and clearly not the result of any mental calculation or even of any effort of memory. The inquisitor, lost in the notes he had prepared to check Franz's answers, might venture into academic fantasies, to no avail.

"If George Washington was born on the twenty-second of February, 1732, how old would he be in 2020?"

The answer—288—produced without hesitation, still proved nothing since Franz was seen to be incapable of even the most elementary subtraction.

His first toy—at the age of six—had been a loose-leaf calendar, and that, it seemed, had influenced him for life. All those who came to study him noted this fact, which they found sufficiently revealing. Others who were not in quite such a hurry observed that the intellectual prison in which Franz had enclosed himself, which appeared to admit nothing from the outside world—for he rejected with equal scorn everything they tried to teach him, educational or otherwise—was nevertheless pierced by the extreme sensitivity he displayed to meteorological phenomena. If Franz's mind had been captured by the calendar, his emotions were slaves to the barometer; periods of high pressure—anything over 770 millimeters—induced in him a state of feverish excitement which frightened strangers and exhausted those around him. On the other hand, a drop in pressure would plunge him into a gloomy depression which at less than 740 millimeters expressed itself in the howls of a wolf in torment.

The twins seemed to have overcome his natural shyness and the three of them were occasionally to be seen together, absorbed in mysterious confabulations. Had Franz with his abnormal faculties penetrated the secret of Aeolian, the language of the wind that the twins spoke to one another? Some of the staff of St. Brigitte's who had eavesdropped on the gentle, wholly incomprehensible phrases that passed between them said unhesitatingly yes. The inquiry, later on, into his flight and his disappearance at sea shed no more light on his case and it was finally closed. Only Jean-Paul held the key to the labyrinth that was Franz.

Paul

Certainly that labyrinth was locked with numerous combinations one upon another, but it seems to me that with a little more patience and understanding it might have been possible to avoid the simplistic misconceptions by which the way was sealed forever. There was a dangerous but revealing experiment, for instance, which might have taught them something. It was clear that Franz was bound by every fiber to the environment of the Pierres Sonnantes, where he had grown up for several years. But —they asked themselves—was not this in itself perhaps a case of over-adaptation, and ought he not to be moved somewhere else so that he would be forced to break through his blockage and learn how to adapt to life with greater flexibility? They tried it when they sent him away to a special training school at Mati-

gnon. The startling degeneration of his personality which followed this uprooting necessitated his hasty return to the Pierres
Sonnantes, where things settled back to normal. The doctors and
teachers would have learned a good deal if this unfortunate attempt had led them to explore the nature of the lifelines binding
Franz to the Pierres Sonnantes. Yet his spiritual mechanism was
really quite simple. It is true that, when it comes to dissecting it,
I have—quite apart from the memory of having been close to
him—an instrument for grasping and understanding unique of its
kind in that *geminate intuition* not possessed by the non-twin.
Try not to be too hard on them!

Over-adapted to the Pierres Sonnantes, unable to become ac-
climatized to anywhere else, fixed, unmoving . . . yes, what
Franz hated more than anything in the world was change, being
required to adapt himself to new people and a new situation. He
had very soon realized that men and women were incurably restless, always on the move, running about and upsetting things,
forever demanding fresh responses from one another. And so he
had withdrawn into himself. He had fled from the society of his
kind into his own inner self, barricading himself into a fortress of
mute denial, huddled trembling deep down in his hole like a
hare in its form.

But then there was the question of time. Man was not the only
disturber of the universe. Time was his nightmare, time and the
weather: the inexorable onward rolling of minutes, hours, days,
years, but also the alternations of rain and sun. Many evenings
Franz ached with a gnawing anguish. He would fix his eyes stubbornly on the ground, feeling the light fading around him, already terrified by what he would see when he looked up at the
sky, the towers of foaming, billowing cloud going up to the dizzy
heights and subsiding slowly onto one another, like mountains
undermined and heaved up by an earthquake.

He had built up defenses against the irruption of change and
the unforeseeable into his desert island. The first and the most
babyish he had got from old Méline, from whom, when he first
came, he had been inseparable, almost like an adopted grand-
child. Like every peasant before her, Méline observed the seasonal round and the cycles of the weather very closely, with the

help of calendars, almanacs and a whole treasure house of proverbs and saws. Franz, who had always resisted with mulelike
stubbornness every attempt by his mentors to teach him anything, even to read and write, had assimilated with astounding
ease the gist of everything that came to hand which could be
used to capture the movement of time in a mechanical table in
which even chance and the future might seem fixed forever. He
began to talk, and could be heard now and then reciting the
days of some month or other, past or to come, along with its
high days and holidays, embellished with sayings invariably
relating to the state of the sky and laying down some rule about
when and how often it would recur. "When St. Lucy's day
comes around, days do lengthen with a bound." "March winds
and April showers bring forth May flowers." "Red sky at night,
shepherd's delight." "February fill-dike." "A warm Christmas
makes a cold Easter." "A little rain will drown a great wind."
"Rain in April, dew in May." "Rain before seven, shine before
eleven." This was the refrain Méline had lulled him to sleep by
and it would calm his fears. But he remained a prey to meteorological extremes and they knew at St. Brigitte's that they must
watch him more closely whenever a storm was threatening because he would be capable of any madness.

It was Méline herself who, with a casual word, thoughtlessly
uttered, destroyed the chronological and proverbial edifice her
adopted baby had built to shelter his obsession. One January
day, when a warm, bright sun was riding surprisingly high in the
blue sky, she said a thing that could only have been thought by a
woman and echoed ever after by all women in every latitude:
"It's downright unseasonable."

It was a commonplace remark. Because the pattern of the seasons serves as a frame for our memories, we think of our past as
being more strongly imbued than the present with the traditional
coloring attached to the months of the year, and the more so the
further back we go. Franz's system must have been strained already by incongruities too strong to be ignored. Méline's few
words fell on the child like a thunderbolt. He hurled himself to
the ground in convulsions. They had to take him away and give
him an injection to calm him.

After that there was a change in him which could have been put down to puberty, a kind of puberty in keeping with his eccentric and tormented nature. He grew away from Méline, to the point of seeming to avoid her. He dropped his meteorological sayings, proverbs and adages and seemed to give up the attempt to tame the heavens, suffering their humors with appalling violence. It was as though a rift had occurred for him in the whole equivocal concept of the times, which included such apparently diverse matters as the arrangements of hours, days and years, and the capricious alternations of skies blue and cloudy; chronology and meteorology, the one utterly predictable, and the other remaining irremediably unforeseen. This ambiguity may have its charm, for it charges with a concrete and abounding life the empty, abstract framework of time which shuts us in. For Franz, it was hell. As soon as Méline had uttered the magic formula that released the hold of the calendar upon the troubled atmosphere, he threw himself in his piercing terror into working out his gigantic calendar in which the days and nights of millennia were fixed for all time, like the cells in a beehive. But through the meshes of his calendar, meteorology was bespattering him with rain and sunshine, introducing the irrational and unforeseen into his immutable tables. His chronological genius, proliferating at the expense of all his other faculties, left him naked and defenseless in the face of atmospheric disturbances. And so this highly strung and terrifyingly delicate creature, in order to survive, had to fill the temporal space around him with an ordered structure which should have in it, in other words, no time that was slack and vacant. Time unfilled was an abyss on whose verge he tottered appalled; bad weather upset the calendar's ordered round by introducing elements of unreason, a joker in the pack.

(No one knows better than I do that fear of the chaotic upheavals which are part of everyday life, and that recourse to a sidereal equilibrium, sterile and pure. Entwined with my twin brother in an ovoid position, my head tucked in between his thighs as a bird hides its head under its wings to sleep, lapped in the warmth and smell that were my own, I could be deaf and blind to the unpredictable happenings taking place around us.

And then came the tearing apart, the cleaver that parted us, the dreadful amputation I searched the world to cure, and last of all this other injury tearing me apart for the second time and clamping me to this sofa, looking out over the Bay of Arguenon, where I can see the ebbing waters like a glistening sheet. I have survived that destruction of our geminate peace; Franz succumbed to the assaults mounted by winds and clouds against his chronological fortress. But I am better placed than anyone else to understand him.)

I do understand and I believe that I have penetrated the secret of his millenary calendar as of his fatal flight. Franz's mind was indeed the desert which all the intelligence tests he was put through indicated. But because that void was emotionally intolerable to him, he had managed to find two *mechanical brains* outside himself to fill it—one diurnal, the other nocturnal. By day, he lived plugged in, as it were, to the old Jacquard loom in the factory. By night, he was lulled by the lights in the Bay of Arguenon.

I can understand the fascination the great Jacquard exerted over Franz all the better because I was always conscious of it myself. The antiquated and imposing machine stood in the middle of the chancel of the old church and so had a kind of dome above it. This placing was justified by its unusual height. Whereas modern looms are built as far as possible horizontally, like their ancestors, the old Jacquard was surmounted by a huge towering superstructure like a baldachin, housing the square cylinder on which the perforated cards were hung, the vertical hooks, each controlling one neck card, to which were fastened all those warp threads acting the same way, the horizontal needles that came into contact with the cards, and of course the axle and transmission wheels that worked it all. Yet the old Jacquard was not so extraordinarily high that it could not have been put anywhere in the onetime nave. No, its privileged position in the chancel expressed precisely the sense of respect and admiration everyone at the Pierres Sonnantes felt for the venerable contrivance, a symbol of all that was noblest in the weaver's craft.

But it was for its music that Franz would haunt the vicinity of the Jacquard for days at a time. The Jacquard's song was a far cry from the undifferentiated clatter and rumble made by the modern looms. Its large number of wooden parts, comparatively slow action and complex but not after all very numerous movements—few enough at least for a trained ear to distinguish them —all helped to give the sound of the old loom an individuality not unlike speech. Yes, the Jacquard *spoke,* and Franz understood its language. The series of cards moving in an endless chain around the cylinder and commanding, by their perforations, the ballet of the warps and the design of the fabric made the machine as good as talk. But what was more to the point was that its talk, however long or complicated, would go on repeating itself indefinitely since the number of cards laced end to end was a finite one. Franz had found in the song of the great Jacquard the thing he needed urgently, imperatively, vitally, a progression so circumscribed as to form a closed circuit. His troubled brain was comforted and swept along, like a soldier in the ranks of a perfectly drilled battalion, by its manifold and strictly orchestrated clickings. I have even developed a theory for which I have no proof but which seems to me extremely probable. I think that the Jacquard's speech was to some extent the model on which Franz constructed his gigantic calendar. The seven days of the week, the twenty-eight, twenty-nine, thirty and thirty-one days of the months, the twelve months of the year and the hundred years in a century may not, as a system, have much obvious connection with the twilled pattern—woven on four or six threads—of the gros de Tours, which is obtained by adding a "pick" in the warp to the basic weave, or the gros de Naples, when the additional "pick" occurs in the weft, and so forth, but it does at least present the same kind of complexity and comparable regularly recurring patterns. Franz's confused brain, disintegrated by the vagaries of the weather, had made the great Jacquard into a blessedly reliable aid and, as it were, an extension of itself. For Franz, the Jacquard took the place of a cerebral structure. He thought through it and for it, and inevitably his thinking was monstrous in its monotony and complexity. Its only outcome was the millenary calendar.

There is some confirmation of this theory in the state of prostration Franz sank into whenever the humming of the weaving

58

Gemini

sheds fell silent. Deprived of his mechanical brain, suffering from a kind of lobotomy brought on by the stoppage of the works, the child shrank to a small, hunted animal listening in terror for a breath of wind or a patter of rain.

That left the nights.

It is already two hours since the line of green light laid by the setting sun upon the sea has been submerged with it. St. Brigitte's windows are darkened one by one. Deprived for two hours past of the song of the great Jacquard, Franz sinks into a solitude full of nightmares. The tiny cubicle opening off the mongols' dormitory is the quietest corner of the building they could find to put a child to sleep who was in constant danger of a fit of nerves. But although the phosphorescent square of the window commands a fine view of the sea, even that is still no help to him. He can only wait, wait in helpless terror for the rescue that will come when merciful darkness falls at last.

Franz lies rigid in his iron bed, his eyes staring at the white-painted ceiling of his cell. The saving phenomenon he is watching for makes itself felt by the faintest glow. It begins with a vague flickering but the complex structure of it becomes clearer minute by minute. There are red lights, white flashes, a big patch of green. Then nothing. Little by little the pageant takes shape and Franz feels the vise of terror that has been gripping him since dusk relax its hold.

Now the sequence starts with white flashes. A burst of three flares, then a dark pause, then a long green streak that seems to die away reluctantly. Another burst of white. And finally a thin red beam, this time treading hard upon the last white flash . . .

The bulging eyes, unblinking, never losing their look of frantic anxiety, are fixed on the pulsing screen and the spectral colors moving across it. From time to time a bony hand emerges trembling from the sheets and clumsily pushes back the clown's mop falling over his forehead.

The ghostly dance has settled into a new pattern. The white flashes move across the green field, breaking it up three times before allowing it to spread itself in peace. Then the red streak takes over the ceiling, suffusing it from end to end. Franz feels the calm happiness that had enveloped him ebbing away. This is because the three lighthouses in the bay revolve at different speeds and for a little while their beams are going to coincide, so that the room will remain in darkness except when it becomes briefly the scene of a confused melee. For Franz, the appearance of this lengthening *dead time* is unhappiness. Happiness is—or would be—a complex play of lights evenly distributed and following one another according to an immutable pattern, with no blackness in between. This ideal is approached but never attained, for always the three revolutions leave some yawning gap of dark.

The whole trouble comes from the headland of Saint-Cast, which separates the Bay of Arguenon from the Bay of La Frenaye and masks the great lighthouse of the Etendrée. Franz grew up at La Latte, in the shadow of the fort of the Goyon-Matignons, where the caretakers were friends. The child would slip into the castle of an evening and ensconce himself in a watchtower commanding the fabulous view. To the right could be seen the group of islands called the Hébihens, the beaches of Lancieux, Saint-Briac, and Saint-Lunaire, the Pointe du Décollé, Saint-Malo, Paramé and Rothéneuf, the Ile de Cézembre and the Pointe du Meinga. But the most important thing lay westward, in the direction of the cove of the Sévignés and Cap Fréhel, upon which there rose the white tower with the black top that was the lighthouse of the Etendrée itself. It is a sector light with two flashes. Its period is nine seconds, comprising a one-and-a-half-second flash, an eclipse of one and a half seconds, a one-and-a-half-second flash and an eclipse of four and a half seconds. Its sectors are divided in the following way:

- Red sector from 72° to 105° (33°), range eight miles.
- White sector from 105° to 180° (75°), from 193° to 237° (44°), from 282° to 301° (19°) and from 330° to 72° (102°), range eleven miles.
- Green sector from 180° to 193° (13°), from 237° to 282° (45°) and from 301° to 330° (29°), range seven miles.

In the luminous symphony played by the sea lights visible from the fort of La Latte, the tower of the Etendrée, eighty-four meters high, was the great organ with its stops, swells and basses. Now this royal instrument, obscured by the headland of Saint-Cast, is missing from the concert of lights that can be seen from St. Brigitte's. Franz thinks about it constantly. From the ruined tower on the Ile des Hébihens, which he can see from his window, he would be able to get the whole gamut of lights visible from the fort of La Latte, as well as the red flashing buoy and fixed white light marking the harbor entrance of the Guildo, a modest addition but by no means one to be despised.

Old Kergrist's fishing boat is drawn up out of the water but the tide is coming in and in an hour's time it will be only a few yards above the high-water mark.

Franz gets up and slips his feet into his old, worn-out espadrilles. He is locked in, as he is every night, but the key is still in the lock and there is a good half inch of light showing under the door. With the aid of a matchstick, he pushes the key out of its hole so that it drops outside. A sheet of blotting paper is there for it to fall on. Franz pulls it toward him and picks up the key.

He pauses, overcome with excitement. A convulsive shivering seizes him and he forces down the howl that rises to his lips. He sits on his bed, his face buried in his hands; he does not cry or laugh but waits for the nerve storm brought on by the nearness of the unprecedented adventure before him to pass. . . . He sags forward, head in hands and resting on his knees. He sleeps. An hour. Two hours. He wakes. What is this key doing on his bed? He looks up. The multicolored ballet is still evolving on the ceiling, the red streak like an arrow transfixing the big green target. On the instant, it is gone and the background fades out in its turn, the three white flashes follow faster than usual, it seems. Then, there is darkness. Etendrée! Etendrée! It is on this sheet of virgin blackness that you should be inscribing your variegated poem!

The door is open. Franz glides like a shadow past the glass partition of the mongols' dormitory. They too are locked in. The sister in charge sleeps in a little room at the far end of the passage. She is no longer young and is hard of hearing. That is why she has been given the easy children on this floor to look after.

Out of doors, the sky is glittering but in the west a dark mass

is slowly piling up. It is high tide and the fringe of phosphorescence along the waves that break with a swishing sound
shows up quite clearly. The three lighthouses spell out their
warnings tirelessly: the winking white light on the Pointe de la
Garde, the green revolving beacon on the Pointe du Chevet and,
a long way off, the small red flashing light marking the reef of
La Hache. It is in this direction one must steer to reach the Ile
des Hébihens, the largest of the group.

Franz braces his insect-thin body against the side of Kergrist's
small rowboat. He'll probably manage to shift it but he knows
that he will never have the strength to get it into the water. He
struggles on quite hopelessly, pushing, pulling, in desperation
even trying to dig away the sand under the boat's bow. In an
hour it will be too late. Already the tide is beginning to ebb.
Franz sinks down onto the hard, ice-cold ground and is shaken
by another fit of nerves. His teeth chatter, a little blob of spittle
collects at the corner of his lips and a harsh sob escapes them.
For a long moment he remains quite still, his big, bulging eyes
watching the friendly play of the lights out in the darkness. He
can go back to his room. The ghostly dance must still be going
on on his white ceiling. He is impatient to shut himself away
again in the closed cell where the outside world dwindles to that
subtle pattern of interlinking signals.

As he goes back past the glassed-in side of the girls' dormitory,
a beaming moon-face is watching for him and greets him with
an energetic pantomime. It is Bertha, the eldest of the mongols.
She has a passionate animal devotion to Franz which expresses
itself in unbridled displays of affection at every opportunity.
Franz has paused uneasily, knowing from experience that Bertha
is not going to stop at this first, mild demonstration. Already the
crooked little arms are waving, the slit eyes tearful and beseech-
ing and dribbles of saliva running from the triangle of a mouth
blocked by the protruding, fleshy tongue. She is going to make a
scene and wake the others unless Franz calms her down. He turns
the key in the lock and at once Bertha is hopping round him in
her thick, coarse nightdress. She tries to hug him and lunges at
him with such formidable strength that she almost knocks him
down.

Old Kergrist's boat . . . Perhaps Bertha might be able to launch it? Franz takes her hand and pulls her along. She squeaks delightedly and lollops after him like a great puppy. But when they get to the bottom of the steps leading to the beach he hears little footsteps and gruntings behind him. The dormitory door has been left open and the other seven mongols have come pouring after them.

Franz has a moment's panic. He feels himself teetering on the edge of hysterics. But the thought of the waiting boat calls him imperatively. Etendrée! Etendrée! He marshals his strange troop and leads it to the boat. He mimes pushing it into the sea. Immediately the girls swarm aboard and begin squabbling over the seats on the thwarts. He has to chase them out and make them understand that the boat must be put into the water. Bertha sets the example. Before the rush of stocky little bodies, their short, strong legs sinking deep into the sand, the keel grates and begins to slide down toward the strip of broken shells and dry seaweed that marks the tide line.

A wave breaks over the boat's bows, slips under its keel, and strokes its sides. It is done. The vessel is afloat, and once again the girls clamber aboard. Franz is sitting in the bows. He has no eyes for anything but the three lights as they continue their tricolored dance. In a moment Etendrée, the great light on Cap Fréhel, will overtop these lesser voices with her royal song.

The boat is without oars, sails or rudder, but the current of the ebb bears it swiftly out to sea, straight for the rocks of La Hache.

CHAPTER IV

The Quarry's Quarry

Alexandre

I sensed that the time had come to make myself a solitude again. Solitude is a fragile thing and one that ages fast. It starts out pure and hard as diamond but again and again it comes under attack. Slightly, in the smile of the waiter who has recognized you, a word or two about the weather from the woman at the fruit stall, and then more pressingly when they begin to notice this or that habit of yours—"The steak medium rare, just as you like it"; "Your paper hasn't come yet, they're late delivering to-day"—and finally there is the irretrievable outrage when they find out your name and eager tradespeople assail you on all sides with "Monsieur Surin" here and "Monsieur Surin" there.

But as a destroyer of solitude there is nothing to equal sex. For myself, if it weren't for sex, I really can't see that I should need anyone. An anchorite in the desert, a stylite standing day and night upon his pillar. Sex is the centrifugal force that drives you out of doors. Get out! Go and do your fucking outside! That is

what the ban on incest is all about. None of that in here! This is
Papa's preserve! And if you do go out, of course, it is not just to
walk about on your own. Sex only turns you out of house and
home so as to throw you into the arms of the first person you
meet.

Making myself a solitude again. And that consists of dumping
myself down in some dreary municipality, such as Roanne—virgin ground, utterly virgin, without so much as a memory or a
trace of me—taking a room in the Hotel Terminus and then waiting. Waiting for whom, for what? Happiness, to start with. With
the door closed behind the maid who brought me up and my
small suitcase resting on the luggage stand, I lie back on the
white crocheted bedspread.

I hear the distant murmur of the city, trams rattling and clank-
ing, the flow of cars moving past, voices, laughter, a dog barking,
all merging in a familiar murmur. There are so many of them,
and there they all are, I can hear them, I can feel their presence,
but they do not know that I exist. A one-way presence, a unilat-
eral absence. Happiness shines in my breast like the flame in a
dark lantern. Divine omnipotence! Is it not the privilege of God
to know all creatures without revealing himself? To be sure,
there are the believers, the mystics and the merely inquisitive
who think they have a right to swim against the tide and pry
into the divine secrets, but there is no risk of that in my case. No
one knows that I am on the trail. The hunt is on.

PORTRAIT OF A HUNTER

From head to foot, leanness prevails. Of bone and sinew, joints
and tendons. Of scrawny muscles, ropes and cables rather than
working masses. My profile aquiline, all skull and jawbones, my
general impression carnivorous, but more in the predatory than
the digestive sense. Do I digest? I am scarcely aware of it. Indeed, I wonder what becomes of the food, for I certainly put it
away in remarkable quantities. Because I am also inclined to
constipation. At all events, I lack the gift of defecatory euphoria.
I write this with a shade of regret. I like throwing away, casting
off, tearing up, cleaning out. In particular I think most houses

suffer from an inadequate waste-disposal system. If I had a big house, I should see to it that every month a large part of the furniture, carpets, pictures, crockery, linen and so forth was put out for the garbage men. For want of such regular purges our domestic surroundings become choked and congested and we have to wait until we move to make the clean sweep that is long overdue.

I know quite well what causes this leanness to persist, in spite of an ample diet. It is a kind of inward fire, a private forge, a nervous excitement, a quivering tension of mind and muscle which burn incessantly within me, so that even at night my sleep is light and broken. Mind and muscle. It would take a clever man to isolate the proportions of body and brain in the melting pot that is my life. Sex certainly has the lion's share, but sex is the whole man and with me I think its nature is largely cerebral.

Sex organ, hand, brain. The magic three. In between the sex organ and the brain come the hands, composite, intermediary organs, the small servants of both, caressing at the instigation of the sex organ, writing to the dictates of the brain.

OF MASTURBATION

The brain provides the sex organ with an imaginary object. This object, it is for the hand to create. The hand is an actor, playing first one thing, then another. It can become at will tongs, hammer, eyeshade, whistle, comb, primitive calculator, alphabet for the deaf and dumb and so on. But its masterpiece is in masturbation. There, it can become penis or vagina at will. To begin with, the meeting of the hand and the sex organ is the most natural thing in the world. Left to itself, the hand, dangling idly on the end of the arm, sooner or later—almost at once, in fact— comes in contact with the genitals. To touch one's knee or back or ear requires a specific muscular effort. For the genitals, none at all. One has only to relax. Moreover, the sex organ, by its size and shape, lends itself admirably to manipulation. Only think how many fewer and far less satisfactory handholds are offered by a head, a foot or even another hand. Of all parts of the body, the sex organ is undoubtedly the most maneuverable, the most manipulable.

To come to the point. The sexual object furnished by the brain and given shape by the hand can compete with that very object in its real form and outdo it. A man masturbating and dreaming about a partner would be put off by that partner's untimely arrival and would rather go back to his dreams, betraying him, as it were, with his own image.

So much for the belief held by the majority of heterosexuals that homosexual relations are to be seen as two people indulging in mutual masturbation. This is not the case. True masturbation is solitary and is symbolized by the serpent biting its own tail. All sexual relations—homo and hetero alike—involve offering something to a partner, a dedication of the orgasm to a particular person. True, that person may be far away, the dedication may take place at long range, and it is then that true masturbation asserts itself, unless the object presented by the imagination is personified.

This was what a little chum of mine meant to tell me once when he sent me a postcard saying simply: "Hi, pal! Just drained a tankard to your health!"

Roanne throws out an average of 30,773 kilos of domestic refuse every day. From this I deduce that the city must have a population of exactly 38,467. Five tipping trucks each doing two trips a day carry the stuff to a dump two kilometers out along the Digoin road, on the banks of the Loire. Since the trucks are not equipped with any crushing mechanism, I conclude that the economic status of the population is not high. In fact, I have learned from my observations that although the weight of domestic refuse does not increase greatly with a rise in the standard of living, its bulk, on the other hand, is rapidly doubled or trebled by a slight rise in average income. So that a cubic meter of household garbage in Deauville weighs only 120 kilos, whereas it goes up to 400 or even 500 kilos in Casablanca. Consequently my little Arabs will be able to make do for a long time yet with covered tipping trucks able to carry from twelve to fourteen cubic meters of waste.

After Casablanca, Roanne is the poorest of my six cities. It's like this. The garbage of the poor is very dense. They throw away vegetable peelings, jam pots, cheap household goods that fall to pieces at once and above all the inevitable buckets of clinkers and coal ash that weigh down the garbage cans. Deauville, the smartest of my towns, was the first to need the introduction of crusher trucks to evacuate its sophisticated packaging, its champagne corks, gilt cigarette ends, lobster shells, bundles of asparagus, dancing shoes and burnt-out Chinese lanterns. Frothy, tangled, shiny, lightweight, voluminous rubbish, needing expensive machines to squeeze, crush and compress it in order to carry it away, because the space all this nonsense takes up is no longer acceptable. Dead, it can have no more room than the garbage of the poor.

The refuse picture in Roanne is quite the opposite. Two members of the town council came to fetch me from the Terminus this morning and took me by car to the unauthorized dump hitherto in use which the municipality wants to close down—on account of a garden city which is to be built in the neighborhood —and replace with a controlled dump. They are looking to me to accomplish it.

I refrained from voicing my feelings in the presence of these good people, whose ideas on the subjects of beauty, creativity, profundity and freedom, if they have any, are bound to be entirely ready-made. But on being taken to the edge of the Devil's Hole, as they call it hereabouts, into which, with the aid of five trucks, Roanne discharges all her most intimate and revealing secrets, which is to say the very essence of herself, I was seized with an intense curiosity and emotion. I ventured alone into the "hole." I sank into a thick, whitish substance which I knew from experience was composed basically of chewed-up paper and ashes, but which was present here in an unusual density. In some places, the stuff became fibrous, stringy and felted and one of my guides explained, from a distance, that there were two textile factories throwing out bundles of wool shoddy which took a very long time to become absorbed into the general waste.

"There ought to be some way of recycling all that shoddy," he observed, with a note of censure for what he evidently regarded as wastefulness.

Middle-class cheeseparing! Always terrified to throw anything away, like a miser hating to let go of anything. With one obsession, one ideal: a society in which *nothing* would ever be thrown away, where things would last forever and where the two great processes of production and consumption would be carried on with no waste at all! It's the dream of a completely constipated city. Whereas what I dream of is an entirely disposable world where a whole city could be thrown on the scrap heap. But isn't that just what we are promised in the next war, with the aerial bombing they say we shall have? But never mind that. The fact remains that I like Roanne's shoddy. It gives its refuse a tweedy look and makes me think again about the status of the place. A gray, undistinguished refuse but of undeniably good quality . . .

A little further on my town councillors' indignation becomes altogether righteous when confronted by a heap of books, a whole library of them thrown out higgledy-piggledy. Soon every one of us is deep in one of the poor stained and tattered volumes. Not for long, though, because they turn out to be works of chemistry in Latin, come by what devious paths to end their scholarly lives here? Books, much sought after by rag and bone men, are not common on garbage dumps and I must say this was my first discovery of the kind. Now the funny thing was that my companions were incensed at the barbarism of people who could simply throw away books, the noblest of all things. I, on the contrary, marveled at the wealth and wisdom of a garbage dump where even books were to be found. There, in fact, is where we are at cross-purposes. To my town councillors, rooted through and through in society, the dump is an infernal place, no better than oblivion, and nothing is worthless enough to be thrown there. To me, it is a world parallel to the other, a mirror reflecting what makes the very essence of society, and every dump has its value, which may vary but is always positive.

There is another peculiarity I will mention. Naturally, the inhabitants of Roanne are no more in the habit of throwing away books than those of any other city. Yet the presence of those books struck me as interesting, revealing, instructive, and I straightway inscribed them in the coat of arms of the Roanne garbage dumps. I remember now that the same thing had already happened in more than one town. When I first set foot in Miramas, the awe-inspiring dump for Marseille—the largest in all France—I was struck by the presence of a whole truckload of spoiled hogfish with a host of gulls screaming and fighting over them, and ever since then the raw fish of the Mediterranean have been inseparably linked in my mind with the lunar hills of Miramas. The fact is that there is no such thing as chance or accident in these matters, everything is essential, the most ill-assorted objects are fated to meet here, from the very moment of their manufacture. What is so wonderful about garbage dumps is the way preferment is generalized, so that each item becomes a potential emblem for the city that produced it.

Roanne, then, a gray town and of good quality on account of its wool shoddy and its old books, was waiting for Alexandre Surin, king and dandy of garbage men, so that the Devil's Hole might be filled in according to the principles of controlled dumping and become a sports ground, a nursery garden, or a public park. It shall be done, your honors, but you will have to grant me the concession for the collection, removal, and treatment of your waste materials, along with a monopoly of all possible salvage.

PORTRAIT OF A HUNTER (continued)

Let us go back a bit. I picture myself, surrounded by the town councillors of Roanne, bounding about the refuse heaps, aiding myself here and there with my faithful Fleurette. There is a swashbuckling element in my character. That is to say, I oscillate between two extremes. At best, the soldier of fortune, at worst the goat. I like movement. Movement for its own sake—I loathe manual labor—and especially upward. A brief experience of the Alps has convinced me that, take away sex, I should only find real, blazing emotional satisfaction in mountaineering. When I called myself a goat I was doing myself an injustice. I should have said a chamois. Fencing and mountaineering. Two kinds of muscular thrill. One aims at overcoming an adversary, the other at the conquest of a landscape. But the mountain landscape fights back with weapons that are unsheathed and threatens to break your bones at any moment. A synthesis of the two is reached in the sublimest of all sports, the chase. For then the adversary/quarry is hiding in the landscape, is inseparable from it, so that the heart of the hunter is divided between love of the landscape and longing for the quarry.

My appetite is undeniably good, but selective, specialized. I have never understood why psychologists, psychiatrists, psychoanalysts, and other dispensers of mental laxatives pay so little attention to different people's nutritional likes and dislikes. Yet what a field for observation is there and what discoveries are to be made! How are we to explain, for instance, the fact that I have loathed milk and everything derived from it, such as cream, butter, cheese, etc., from my earliest infancy? When I was two, if they gave me a piece of bread to eat with even the tiniest morsel of cheese hidden inside it, I would be seized at once with uncontrollable vomiting. This is something which is not just a matter of taste but strikes right down into one's very vitals.

I like my food dressed, sophisticated, unrecognizable. I do not want a dish to declare itself crudely as tripe, tongue or calf's head. I detest the kind of barefaced victuals that seem to have jumped straight out of the farmyard onto your plate, and sit there staring at you. *Crudités,* shellfish, fresh fruit and such naturalia are not really for me. Talk to me of oriental cookery! I have a weakness for disguised foods: mushrooms, vegetables masquerading as meat; sheep's brains, meat got up as fruit; avocados, with flesh fat as butter; and most of all I love fish, that imitation meat which is, as they say, nothing without a sauce.

My long, inquisitive, aquiline nose, besides being the most notable feature of my face, also expresses my wit, my courage and my generosity. Truly, the sense of smell plays a major part in my life—not surprisingly when you think of my cynegetic vocation—and I would happily write a treatise on smells, had I the time and the talent. What I find most interesting is of course my own peculiar position in a society in which most people *have no sense of smell.* It is a well-known fact that man, like birds and monkeys, belongs to an animal species whose noses have atrophied as their visual sense has become more highly developed. Apparently one has to choose: either to see or to smell. Man, having opted for eyes, has no nose.

I could limit these generalizations in all kinds of ways. Here is one to begin with: I am gifted with remarkably keen sight, yet I also have an unusually good nose. Does that make me a superman? Well, yes, from one point of view I suppose it does. But not from that precise angle of sensitivity. Because with me this visual keenness is more a matter of a *glance* than of any broad, panoramic vision. Put a cat in a garden. Do you think he will appreciate the layout of the paths, the perspectives of foliage, the balance of lawns and fountains? He won't care for any of that, he won't see it at all. What he will see in one infallible glance will be the untoward tremor of a blade of grass that betrays the passage of a field mouse.

I am that cat. My eyesight is merely the handmaid of my desire. *Ancilla libidinis.* All about me is blurred except for the object of my desire and that shines with an unnatural brightness. Nothing else matters. In a museum gallery I yawn, unless the still life, the basket of fruit, is encircled by the podgy, bare arms of a Caravaggio youth, with pale, plump, crinkly head inclined above the grapes and pears. Women in particular have so little existence for me that I can scarcely tell one from another, like black people or a flock of sheep. Indeed, this little weakness of mine has played me more than one trick. But only let a young man come up behind me and I look around at once, warned by some secret instinct, and glancing at him with an apparent lack of interest, all in a moment I scent him, undress him, explore him inch by inch, I weigh him up, try him, fuck him. If he's a complete innocent, he won't even notice and his simplicity crowns my enjoyment. If he's a foil, he feels a kind of electric shock through every nerve. He has seen something like a flashlight turned on him, he has been warned and at the same time he responds by emitting a wave—either positive or negative.

This keen glance of mine, then, goes along with a pretty general myopia, and my private world is like a landscape submerged in a dim twilight in which only occasional objects and persons are endowed with an intense phosphorescence.

My ability to scent is a very different matter. My nose has *intelligence*. There is no better word to describe the power of selection, the interpretative capacity, the sagacity in picking up information displayed by my olfactory organ. All that other people get from their noses are vague impressions, a rough total of the ambient odors out of which only one signal more or less finally emerges. It smells good, it smells bad, it smells of nothing at all. That is all their wretched sense of smell can tell them. Now here is the paradox: the more of a nose you have, the less sensitive you are to good or bad smells. Perfumery owes its existence entirely to a public without a sense of smell. Because the more delicately the sense of smell can distinguish the composition of the olfactory sphere in which it finds itself, the more it dispenses with qualifications of good and bad. The more precisely it informs, the less it charms, the less it revolts, the less it arouses. This is a general rule which goes for all the senses. Shortsighted people who are bathed in a vague luminosity with no precise contours, with no firm outlines to provide something consistent for the mind to get a grip on, can only judge things as pleasant or unpleasant. While the clearsighted are so busy detailing and measuring that they forget the emotional overtones.

The smell of refuse is not, as most people think, a massive, undifferentiated, and universally painful stench. It is an infinitely complex cipher which my nose is never done with decoding. It distinguishes for me the burnt rubber of an old tire, the pungent, smoky smell of a barrel of herrings, the heavy emanations from an armful of dead lilacs, the sweetish taint of a dead rat and the acid note of its urine, the redolence of an old Norman cellar that comes from a load of moldering apples, the greasy exhalations of a cowhide, heaved up in peristaltic waves by an army of maggots, the whole stirred by the wind and shot through with sharp stabs of ammonia and musky, oriental breaths. How could anyone be bored amid a display of such richness, or so uncouth as to reject it out of hand as a bad smell?

Gray matter. The expression flowed quite naturally from my pen to describe the muck of Roanne, and I am delighted with the comparison it suggests. For this pinkish-gray waste, dense, rich and thickly felted by the wool shoddy, a compressed pellet of which is going to fill the medallion with the arms of Roanne (a crescent moon surmounted by the military medal) in the fifth pocket of my embroidered waistcoat, this fibrous substance with pearly lights in it has a certain affinity with the intricate synaptic substance of the human brain. Roanne, city of cerebral rubbish! It is the one thing my collection wanted, and after Rennes, Saint-Escobille, Deauville, Miramas and Casablanca, Roanne adds just the right finishing touch to my sextet. Even the old books—come here, surely, not through some wrongful eccentricity but as the result of a logical process—are where they belong. They are the inevitable flora of this intelligent midden, these ciphers; they have grown on it like mushrooms, they are their sublimated emanation.

I asked the employment office for ten men. Thirty turned up. By the end of the week there will probably be only six or seven. They are the usual dregs, tramps, Arabs, Piedmontese, Catalans and Frenchmen on the run from the police. As though it needed these castoffs of humanity to sift the refuse of society! I hire the lot of them. I am their brother—in spite of my fine clothes and smell of lavender water—like them, delinquent, antisocial and an enemy to law and order to the depths of my being.

A test bore of the Devil's Hole reveals a depth of between six and seven meters of refuse and a temperature of 80° C. That is higher than brain fever, it is a constant fire hazard. The only way to stop the fermentation is to cut off the intake of air, and to do that we must insert a bed of sand at least fifty centimeters thick in between every two and a half meters of refuse. I have had a floor of timbers laid up to the edge of the hole to prevent the wheels of the sand trucks, which are much heavier than the garbage carts, from sinking in. The men spread the sand as it falls at their feet. The clean, golden stuff contrasts with the rotten ground and the black men working in the hole. I can tell how low we have sunk by the almost painful wonder roused in me by this ordinary sand, because it is different from the filth in which we live. Sand, a beach, a desert island, crystalline waves breaking with a murmuring sound . . . Enough of dreams! Next week my screening truck will be in position and the refuse of Roanne

will be filtered through its great cylindrical jigger and sprinkled
on the edge of the hole, whence it will be gathered up for ma-
nure, while the coarser stuff is tumbled into the bottom of the
crater.

AESTHETIC OF THE DANDY GARBAGE MAN

The idea is more than the thing and the idea of the idea more
than the idea. Wherefore the imitation is more than the thing
imitated, because it is the thing plus the effort of imitation,
which incorporates the possibility of reproducing itself, and so of
adding quantity to quality.

That is why in the matter of furniture and works of art, I always prefer the imitations to the originals, imitation being the
original encapsulated, possessed, integrated and even multiplied
—in short, considered and spiritualized. The fact that imitations
are of no interest to the general run of collectors and enthusiasts,
and may also have a very much lower commercial value than the
originals, is only an additional advantage in my eyes. For that
very reason society will have no further use for it, and it is destined for the rubbish heap and so fated to fall into my hands.

Since it does not contain a single genuine object—except perhaps for my collection of sword sticks—my home in Paris is entirely made up of the second-rate. I have always dreamed of
elevating it to the third-rate, but if there are such things as
imitations of imitations they are so rare, and doomed to perish so
quickly from the fourfold contempt of the idiot mob, that I could
furnish my house with them throughout only by going to immense trouble. Nevertheless, I have found, in a modern furniture
shop called Le Bois Joli in the rue de Turenne, a cane chaise
longue copied from a West Indian model which itself was obviously inspired by the Récamier-style sofas of the Empire period.
Also I have on my desk a glass Buddha whose twin brother in old
crystal I once saw in an antique shop: the dealer assured me it
was modeled on the life-sized statue of the Buddha of Sholapur.
But these are exceptions. To multiply them and give myself a setting raised to an even higher degree—for there is nothing to stop
one from going from the third-rate to the fourth-, fifth-, and so on

—would take a time and patience I can only spare for another purpose. The truth is that I am not really interested in things or in decoration or collecting. They are all too static, contemplative and disinterested for my eager, restless temperament.

After all, what is rubbish but the great storehouse of things multiplied to infinity by mass production? The fancy for collecting originals is altogether reactionary and out of date. It is in opposition to the process of production and consumption which is gaining momentum in our society—and whose end is the rubbish dump.

In the old days everything was an original, made by a craftsman to last for ever. Its destruction only came about by accident. When it was worn out the first time it became secondhand goods (this was the case even with clothes). It became an heirloom and worth repairing endlessly.

Nowadays things are said to be worn out, useless, and are thrown away more and more quickly. And it is among the rubbish that the collector often comes to look for it. He rescues it, he takes it home and restores it, and finally gives it a place of honor in his house where its qualities can be displayed. And the rescued object, rehabilitated and glorified, rewards its benefactor a hundred times over. It imbues his house with an atmosphere of subtle peace, discriminating luxury and calm good sense.

I can understand this kind of activity and its charms well enough, but I take a different view. Far from trying to arrest the process of production-consumption-disposal, I pin all my hopes on it since it ends at my feet. The refuse dump is not an abyss in which the object is swallowed up but the repository where it finds a home after successfully passing through a thousand ordeals. Consumption is a selective process aimed at isolating the really new and indestructible aspect of production. The liquid in the bottle, the toothpaste in the tube, the pulp in the orange, the flesh of the chicken are all eliminated by the filter of consumption. What is left is the empty bottle, the squeezed tube, the orange peel, the chicken bones, the hard, durable parts of the product, the elements of the inheritance which our civilization will bequeath to the archaeologists of the future. It is my job to see to it that they are preserved indefinitely in a dry and sterile

medium by means of controlled dumping. Not without getting
my own excitement, before their inhumation, from the infinite
repetition of these mass-produced objects—the copies of copies
of copies of copies of copies of copies and so on.

His name is Eustache. Eustache Lafille. When he produced this
piece of information at the employment office I could not believe
my ears. He shall be forgiven his name on account of his excellent and extremely rare first name, which makes him close kin to
me, since Eustache and Surin are both French slang words for a
flick knife.

I had spied something tough and boyish in the distant figure
of the "gutter" working away in the bottom of the hole. The gutter stands at the foot of the slope, armed with a hammer and a
kind of machete, watching the bulky objects thrown out by the
jigger come bounding down to him. The first thing he has to do
is avoid them, like charging beasts, and then he moves in and
breaks them up. Bundles of rags and paper have to be ripped
open, carpets arriving rolled must be spread out carefully on the
ground, packing cases split and bottles smashed. The object is to
prevent the creation of spaces which can form air pockets deep
down. Eustache discharged his office of gutter with a kind of
athletic vigor that went straight to my heart and even further
down than my heart. His strong, supple body showed itself to
me in his every movement, and the thing that gave me a delicious thrill was the jerk of his hips after he had bent down and
hooked his prey that flung him back, opening out and bending
away in a beautiful backward curve.

At the end of the day I sent for him to come to the trailer
which serves me as an office and a temporary rest room. He
failed to appear and the next morning he had gone. It served me
right for employing the coercive methods of normal society,
which he probably cannot abide. I shall not commit the additional error of questioning his workmates. My only chance is to
scour every seedy hotel and coal merchant's café in Roanne to
try and find him. In a larger town, I shouldn't have a hope. Here
maybe, maybe . . .

Eustache, Eustache! No, with a name so sublime it is not possible that you should continue to elude me for long! All the same, I have had to find another gutter for the Devil's Hole, but I really have to force myself to take a shadow of interest in the business now. Yet it is healthy, sound, and of a kind to satisfy me, and the "gray matter" of Roanne is fulfilling its promise as my screening equipment arrives on the site. We have completed two layers of detritus in the bottom of the hole already, separated by a layer of sand, and we know where we are going.

But I shall not have peace of mind, of heart and sex—*nous, thumos, epithumetikon,* as our Greek teacher used to say—until I have found Eustache again. I am actually quite unhappy about it. An Alexandre unhappy because he hasn't got a Eustache! The cry might echo round and who would care? And yet isn't my unhappiness as good as anyone else's?

I like to imagine that every man is made up according to a particular formula—each one unique—tried out by nature, as one might buy a lottery ticket. Once the number has been selected, the individual thus designated is released into a particular environment. What will come of it? In the vast majority of cases nothing remarkable does come of it. But sometimes there is a winning number, one called J. S. Bach, Michelangelo, or Einstein. When all the possibilities of a number are used up, it is then eliminated to make room for another formula, since space is limited. So the time will come—soon, I hope—when Dame Nature will decide: "The Alexandre Surin experiment has gone on long enough. There is nothing more to be gained from it. Get rid of him!" And thereupon I shall die. And it will be very well. For the sentence of death will fall when my moments cease to be so many new attributes to enrich my substance and become instead merely successive stages in a translation without alteration.

I have him! The handsome black fish with the white arms is swimming still, but only in the room allowed him by my net. Thank you, Lord God of hunters, providence of fishermen!

I was at my last gasp. Or I thought I was, at least. Life is made up of last gasps. But truly, that night I was in a bad way. Unhappy. A lump in my throat. The feeling of having been walking for years through a barren desert. Dreary heterosexuality displaying its trumpery wares on all sides. An inhospitable, uninhabitable world. Now as for me, I am all of a piece, I'm a whole man! Love = sex + heart. Other men—most of them—when they go out hunting leave their hearts at home. Tied to their wife's or mummy's apron strings. It's safer. When love is sick or old it breaks down into its two component parts. Sometimes—it is the usual fate of heterosexuals—desire is extinguished. Only affection is left. Affection based on habit and knowledge of the other. Sometimes the reverse is true: the faculty of affection becomes atrophied. Only desire is left, fiercer and more demanding the more barren it becomes. That is the usual fate of homosexuals.

I am not threatened with these two kinds of degeneration. Physical desire and the need for affection are fused in me into a single ingot. That is the very definition of health and strength. Eros athlete. Yes, but a formidable strength, a dangerous health, an energy liable to explode and strike back. Because the absence of a quarry, which to others means only desire unsatisfied, rouses me to despair, and the presence of the quarry, which to others brings only the satisfaction of desire, in my case calls forth a display of all the panoply of passion. With me, everything always comes down to emotions.

Having gone the rounds of taverns, bars, brasseries, bistros, cafés, public houses, dives and other purveyors of rotgut, my stomach abraded by the shots of white wine I had been obliged to swallow in the prosecution of my quest, at about eleven o'clock I found myself in the vicinity of the Place des Prom-Populle where a fair was flaunting its colored lights and gaudy splendors.

I have always liked the tinselly atmosphere and full-blooded artificiality of a fairground. Everything bogus attracts me and I have always had an eye for trash like the Great Mogul's for the Koh-i-Noor. Besides which, of course, such places are happy hunting grounds. That alone is enough to draw me out of doors, as I have said already. The booths and merry-go-rounds attract crowds of youths, frequently in gangs—and so hard to come at—but sometimes, too, alone, unsure, short of cash and yet dazzled, lifted out of themselves by the heightened atmosphere onto a plane of perceptivity and adventure where everything is easier than when they are immersed in their everyday lives. The uncouth do not dream of their own accord. They need the violence of a show or a fair. Then they are more receptive to the miracle of Surin.

I had spotted one already, and his wan, peaky look, the whiteness of his thin face with a thick lock of black hair falling across it had moved me to pity, a new sensation for me and one which it occurs to me may be the most sophisticated and the most subtly virulent form of desire. I had seen him and I had seen that he had seen me see him, a deliciously dizzying reflection which makes a quarry of the hunter and a predator of the game.

It was then the dramatic event occurred which took my breath away and which I still cannot recall without a tremor of joy and surprise, and so crystal clear is the impression that I doubt whether its vividness will ever fade. Another boy, older and stronger, emerged from somewhere, went up to the pale lad, clapped him on the shoulder, and gripped him under the arm in a brief, powerful clasp that made him stagger. I had recognized Eustache at once and his appearance struck me twice over because it was enhanced by the glory of fairy lights and firecrackers sparkling around him and by the presence of the pale lad lending it an unexpected solidity. I have mentioned my fondness in the way of furniture and decoration not just for copies but for copies of copies and so on. I had no idea that my hunting grounds in their astonishing and sublime abundance were going to furnish me with the erotic equivalent of the idea of the idea, the copy of the copy: the quarry of the quarry. And I found in it a subtle similarity to Roanne's refuse picture, that gray matter so rich in abstractions that books grow in it like mushrooms.

The quarry of the quarry . . . This is something that makes a startling difference to the customary rules of my cynegetics. It makes everything more complex, more subtle, more difficult. To begin with, admittedly, it made things much easier. The actual approach was made very nicely thanks to the pale lad. Alone, Eustache would have been suspicious, and probably given the slip to the stranger whose designs on him were by no means

clear. But because he had the little one beside him he felt
bolder, more assured—one wonders why! That's psychology for
you! And besides, the little one was interested, curious about the
stranger that I was. What was more, they had every reason to be
surprised. Because Eustache clearly had no recollection of me,
while I knew his surname, first name, and that he had worked
for several days as a gutter in the Devil's Hole. I found out more
about them after I had invited them into one of the booths to eat
roast chicken and chips. The pale boy is called Daniel and he is
eighteen and looks fourteen. He is the son of the landlady of the
lodging house where Eustache is living temporarily. Temporarily,
like everything he does, everything he is. Everything is temporary with him—and always has been—in anticipation of a vague,
ill-defined future when, things being in their place and he in his,
all will become definite at last. I was not cruel enough to ask him
whether this definition of his might not resolve itself in the end
into a rectangle of earth in a cemetery, but I thought it—and, to
be accurate, with a rush of sympathy. I ended by telling him that
I worked on the site of the new municipal dump, and that was
where I had seen him. He broke into instant abuse of the dreadful hole, the rotten dump, and swore he was not going back
there. So if there was little chance of him coming back to me,
then I must go to him, which I began to do by inquiring of
Daniel what was the name and address of his lodgings and the
likelihood of there being a room vacant for me. All of which
promises some fairly juicy experiences.

We parted before midnight very good friends, but I felt a
slight pang at going off by myself and leaving them together, the
quarry and the quarry of the quarry.

I have a tapeworm. It is not the first time, nor will it be the last.
The solitary worm is the disease of garbage men. If, indeed, it is
a disease at all. I am not in pain, I am only a little thinner and I
eat with an even better appetite than usual. In other words, my
guest is pushing me in the direction of my own nature. Nothing
could be more apt. So I am in no hurry to take the ethereal extract of male fern with which I can easily rid myself of it. In
fact, I would resign myself to my private culture, if sir worm did

not now and then take it into his head to let go a very long piece of ribbon which emerges without warning. These uncontrolled escapes are supremely embarrassing in company, even in our business.

While still keeping my room at the Hotel Terminus, I have taken another at the Crane Driver's Rest on the bank of the canal. My window looks out onto the waterway and, more important, onto the slaughterhouse whose red brick mass rises up a few yards from the other bank. A dreary, brutish landscape, but sufficiently in keeping with the business of twofold seduction which brings me here. I smile pityingly when I think of the domestic exploits of Don Juans braving the noble father or cuckolded husband. All heterosexuality has something of the same kind of imposture as in those counterfeit corridas where heifers take the place of the bull. I, sir, I face real bulls, in the stern and joyful certainty that one day they will make an end of me!

It was Daniel who showed me to my room. Room number 11. Eustache, he informed me without my asking, is in 22, on the floor above. And you, little Daniel? He smiled faintly, pushing back the dark lock that falls over his face with one hand. He sleeps downstairs, next to his mother's room. So here I am, sandwiched in between the quarry and the quarry's quarry, and it is very well so.

This hotel is the same age and in the same style as the other, the Terminus. The most notable difference is in size. Everything here is smaller than in a better-class hotel—the rooms, of course, but also the stairs, the lavatories, the washbasins, the very windows, so that seen from outside the people who appear at them fill them entirely and seem monstrously big. The poor take up less room than the rich. They have to huddle together. But that is not all; the weird and at first sight almost unbelievable truth is that *the poor are actually smaller than the rich.* Comparative statistics drawn up by medical boards prove it. Indeed, in order to be convinced one need only look at the crowds on the Paris metro at the smart stations and at the working-class ones. The average traveler at Champs-Elysées–Clemenceau is ten centimeters taller than at Ménilmontant. Suppose one goes up in the social scale between one generation and the next, the children immediately top the parents by a head and shoulders. The son who carries on his father's trade, on the other hand, also stays the same height. It is absurd, it's even slightly disgraceful, but it's true.

So here I am installed in two places at once, the Terminus and the Cranes. At the Terminus, I am Monsieur Surin. At the Cranes, Monsieur Alexandre. Subtle difference. The politeness of the poor—quite as supercilious as that of the rich—takes in their fondness for first names, and even diminutives, because I am well aware that in a very little while I am going to be Monsieur Alex. This predilection frequently goes as far as a curious inversion which makes the surname into the first name and the first name into the patronymic. In fact, that was how Daniel's mother inscribed my name in the big black register, as Monsieur Surin Alexandre.

I have questioned Daniel as to the origin of the hotel's name. It seems there was once a coal depot on the canalside with a perfect forest of mobile cranes for loading and unloading the barges. But he never knew the cranes. When he was born, Roanne had already ceased to be the coaling port for the canal adjoining the Loire. It is a pity. It would have added rather a nice note to all the rest. Moreover, the very word "coalman" has a warm sound to my ears. When I was a child, one of my unavowable thrills came from the arms and shoulders of the coal delivery men, which took on an extraordinarily brilliant whiteness, like a paste, from their dressing of anthracite dust. Nothing remains of this period beyond a few grim and grimy abandoned warehouses adjoining the slaughterhouse buildings.

Frequenting the Cranes and its circle continued to provide me with all sorts of sidelights on that peculiar species which, for want of a better word, I shall continue to call *the poor*. In changing my hotel, I have already remarked on the reduction in the general scale of the interior which makes the poor a kind of miniature of the rich. Since then I have observed sufficient evidence to furnish an outline sketch of a

PSYCHOSOCIOLOGY OF THE POOR

1. The poor eat two or three times as much as the rich. At first I thought this was to make up for a greater expenditure of energy in laboring and manual work. This is not so, however, since the result of this diet is a general tendency to overweight and I live here surrounded by stout women and paunchy, heavy-jowled men. The truth is that the poor, even when not actually in want, are still not free from the inborn fear of starvation bred in mankind by centuries of famine. At the same time they have stuck to the aesthetic canons of penury which make fat women seem beautiful and desirable and big-bellied men virile and impressive.

2. The poor dress more warmly than the rich. After hunger, cold is the scourge that man fears most. The poor are still subject to the atavistic fear of cold and see it as the source of numerous ills. (To catch cold = to fall ill.) To eat little and to go unclothed are privileges of the rich.

3. The poor are born sedentary. Their peasant origins make them regard travel as an uprooting, a wandering and exile. They cannot travel light. They must surround themselves with preparations and precautions and encumber themselves with useless baggage. Their smallest move takes on the air of a migration.

4. The poor are forever ringing the doctor's doorbell. The third terror they have not outgrown is sickness. Doctors in working-class districts are always being badgered on account of colds and indigestion. The poor sometimes wonder how it is the rich are never ill. The answer is simple: they don't think about it.

5. Because their work is exhausting and unpleasant, the poor have two cherished dreams, which are essentially the same: holidays and retirement. It is necessary to belong to the ruling class to be able to ignore these two mirages.

6. The poor thirst after respectability. They are not perfectly sure of belonging to the human race. Suppose they are only ani-

mals? Hence the need they have to dress up, to wear a hat and take their place, however humble, in the body of society. Hence also their prudery. Respectability is easily defined: it is the degeneration of the code of honor which served for morals among the aristocracy. When the third estate replaced the nobility as leaders of the nation in 1789, honor yielded to respectability and its two pillars, prudery and propriety, both of which the aristocracy splendidly disregarded.

7. Politically, the poor are inveterate conservatives, since they accept society as it is and mean to make their way in it. They look no further than the middle classes to which they aspire to belong as quickly as possible. The result is that no revolution was ever brought about by the people. All the revolutionary elements in society are to be found in the young, in students, which is to say among the children of the aristocracy and upper middle classes. History provides frequent instances of violent social upheavals precipitated by the young of the most-favored classes. But revolutions that begin in this way are taken up by the working masses who use them to obtain better pay, shorter hours, earlier retirement, in other words to move one more step in the direction of the middle class. In doing so they strengthen and aggravate the social and economic system which has been temporarily shaken and help to support it by becoming more deeply involved in it. Thanks to them, revolutionary governments give way to tyrannical guardians of the established order. Bonaparte succeeds Mirabeau, Stalin follows Lenin.

I would have kept my solitude longer had I remained at the Hotel Terminus. By moving to the Cranes, on the trail of Eustache and Daniel, I plunged into the gutter world which is my true home. I know now that up to the present the practice of my horrible trade had only brought me halfway to the gutter. My private life, and my sexual life in particular, had remained apart from the refuse. I would pull off my garbage man's thigh boots and become once more the perfectly eligible Monsieur Surin, a member of a well-known and respected family in Rennes. It would have taken a sharp eye to discern that the studied elegance of my appearance, the choice of my invariable adornments —my six medallions and Fleurette—sprang, not from what might be called dubious habits, but from an overcompensation motivated by the abject nature of my daily work.

At Roanne, all this has changed. I found Eustache on my site and the inmates of the Cranes completed my involvement. So now my life is besieged by refuse on all sides. It was bound to happen, indubitably, and I am grateful to destiny for offering me at the same time some far from negligible compensations. It began with the gray matter of Roanne and the books that blossomed in it. Some basic element in me—my liking for the idea of the idea, the copy of the copy—had found an echo in the much-abused stuff amid which I work. Then Eustache and Daniel, those flowers of the muck, introduced me to a love veering back to abstraction through that curious thing, the quarry of the quarry. After all, it was no accident that Eustache should have landed in this cheap lodging, next door to the coaling wharves and the slaughterhouse. The Crane Driver's Rest is in truth a rendezvous for all the town's misfits, the nomadic or semi-nomadic casual laborers, seasonal workers, tramps, and, in particular, all those engaged in any way in the world of waste and salvage. My world, in fact, whatever I may say about it.

I have some experience of such unsavory spots. I have frequently encountered the odd, maladjusted species of human being to be found there, but as isolated individuals, or at most in pairs. For the first time I found myself faced with a little society, complex because its members, although closely knit together, are so particularized, so powerfully differentiated as to amount almost to caricature. This cohesive phenomenon no doubt arises from the existence of a center of attraction which appears to be Haon-le-Châtel and more exactly the somewhat mysterious owner of the "*châtel*" in question, Fabienne de Ribeauvillé. All of which needs clarifying. What does strike me is that all the riffraff that gravitates to the Cranes and its vicinity has spontaneously adopted me, despite the many differences between us—or is it arrant self-deception on my part to be always thinking myself fundamentally different from the rest of the world? The truth is that my carnal delinquency—which in no way prevents me from moving in high society—gives me access to and ensures me a place among those on the fringe. A homosexual is not out of place anywhere, that is his privilege.

(Delinquency may be of the mind, the flesh or the environment. The delinquents of the mind are heretics, political oppositions and writers, who disrupt the establishment in exact proportion to their creativity. Delinquents of the flesh are oppressed or massacred for biological so-called "reasons": blacks, Jews, homosexuals, madmen, etc. Lastly, the majority of convicted criminals have been brought to it by aggression suffered in childhood and early youth in the environments they were born into.)

Last night, as I was going upstairs in the hotel, I was buttonholed without warning by a hirsute individual—all hair and beard, with a blossoming red nose in the midst—who caught hold of my lapel and blew a gust of vinous breath into my face, with a flood of vehement speech borne upon it.

"Incineration! Incineration!" he kept repeating. "All very fine for your dead bodies! I've always been one for incinerating bodies. No profit in a body, so shove it on the fire, quick! It's clean, it's thorough, and what's more it gives him a little taste of where he's going to, eh! Isn't that so, Philomène?" he added loudly, addressing Daniel's mother. Then, suddenly serious again, he rounded on me once more with fury: "But burning rubbish! That's wicked, that is! You're a gentleman now, what do you think of it? Do you believe they'll really burn our rubbish heaps?" His voice grew suddenly suspicious: "But maybe that's what you've come here for?"

I swore to him by all my gods that, on the contrary, I was there to find a different answer to the treatment of domestic refuse and that the method of controlled dumping actually made the installation of an incineration plant unnecessary. He went off muttering to himself.

This is in fact the great subject which is furiously exciting the inmates of my hotel. When the problem of refuse disposal was raised at a recent meeting of the town council, burning was one of several solutions considered. The discussion was reported in the local newspaper and the little salvage world was in a ferment. Incineration, in fact, means the end of a hundred and one small businesses more or less directly involved in salvage work. But anyone in the trade knows that it is far worse than that. It is a savage, deadly blow to the very substance of the garbage man's world, a blow that is moral as well as material, for the fires of the incineration plants are akin to the fires of the Inquisition. To our eyes, beyond all doubt it is our bodies and our independent souls they are conspiring to cast into the flames. But we must wait and see, of course. A modern incineration plant is operating at Issy-les-Moulineaux, on the Seine. I must go there. To be honest, it is not that I've lacked the opportunity. The courage rather. I scent a whiff of sulphur which has made me hesitate. There's something to give the lie to brother Gustave's hints, right-minded Gustave who thought he saw the devil whenever I appeared. Hell isn't the place that scoundrels dream of, but the place the upright dream of sending them. A subtle difference. Never mind. Dante on the point of following Virgil into the next world must have shied very much as I am doing. But I'll go, I'll go because I must!

P.S. A strange, prophetic analogy! At the very moment we are talking of burning garbage, sinister rumors are coming out of Germany that Adolf Hitler is making his own arrangements. Homosexuals are being arrested wholesale, shut up in concentration camps—completely without trial—and allowed to die there from ill-treatment. Naturally, the heterosexual rabble hasn't a word to say against these mass crimes. Stupid swine! How can you fail to see that once he has taken this first step the tyrant will turn on another select minority, and send priests, university teachers, writers, Jews, trade union leaders and goodness knows who else to the slaughter? But then your silence today will muffle your cries. The memory of your silence today will belie your hypocritical gestures of indignation.

CHAPTER V

Heaven and Hell

Alexandre

I have not wanted to go back to the district near the church of Saint-Gervais where I lived for fifteen years with Mother. My small sorrow has not ceased, ever since the poor darling died. Small sorrow? Yes, for it is characterized as much by its moderation as its permanence. How hard it is to know oneself! A little experience and the sight of others had led me to think that Mother's death would provoke a violent grief in me from which I should recover in due course, as though from a serious illness, to become first convalescent, then restored to health with no particular aftereffects.

What happened was just the reverse. At first I felt nothing. It took weeks, even months for the dreadful news to penetrate, as though it had slowly and laboriously to overcome the disbelief in my heart. Meanwhile grief was settling in. A discreet pain, with no fuss, no piercing pangs, but it made no secret of its definitive, its irremediable nature. It is quite simple. Grieving in other peo-

ple is acute; with me it is chronic. My mother's death is like an
ulcerated wound, a place one learns to live with in the end by
day and night, but one that suppurates endlessly without hope of
healing. Even so there are some motions, some encounters that
are better avoided and I was not going out of my way to look at
her windows in the rue des Barres.

Leaving the Gare de Lyon, I strolled along, Fleurette in one
hand, a light overnight bag in the other. Being in a reflective
mood, I rather lost myself. I went down the Avenue Daumesnil
as far as the Place Félix-Eboué and came upon a little street
called the rue de la Brèche-au-Loup—the Wolf's Lair. The name
gave me a thrill of pleasure. Beyond a doubt, I had arrived.
Moreover, I discovered a small hotel on it of the same name. I
took a tiny room there and was led up by the proprietor, in
whom I instantly discerned a wolfish look. I went out again at
once, leaving my small bag on the bedspread as a sign of ownership. My hunting mood drove me to the Bois de Vincennes, because it was a well-known haunt of game. But a less frivolous
fate was watching over me and before I had gone more than a
few steps I was caught by the entrance to a brand-new and
rather impressive church. My feelings about the Catholic Church
are mixed. To be sure, I cannot forget that the delicious ardors
of my adolescence were bathed in the atmosphere of a religious
college and are inseparable from the prayers and rituals to which
they imparted their warmth and color. But since then I have
more than once been roused to anger by the infamous way some
priests stand up for the notion of a heterosexual God brandishing
his thunderbolt at those who do not fuck as he does. As for me, I
am like the Africans who want a black Virgin, or the Tibetans
insisting on a slant-eyed Infant Jesus, and I cannot picture God
as other than a penis rising stiff and erect from the base of its
two testicles, a monument to virility, the creative principle, the
holy trinity, the trunked idol set precisely in the center of the
human body, halfway between the head and the feet, as the
Holy of Holies in the temple is placed midway between the tran-
sept and the apse, a strange combination of silky softness and
muscular rigidity, of blind, vegetative, oneiric force and the
clear, calculating will to hunt, a paradoxical fountain dispensing

alternately ammoniacal urine, the quintessence of all bodily impurities, and seminal fluid, an engine of war, onager, catapult, but at the same time a trilobate flower, emblem of blazing life . . . I shall never come to the end of thy praises!

The imposing Church of the Holy Ghost, with its curious mixture of the modern and Byzantine styles, intrigued and attracted me immediately. The fantastic, frozen frescoes by Maurice Denis, the violent and moving Stations of the Cross, signed Desvallières, and above all the mosaics, that vast dome—made, it seems, to promote and crown the flight of the Holy Spirit—the rather exotic atmosphere of gladness and vitality, so unusual in Western churches, which are always dedicated more to the cult of death than to praise of life—all this delighted me, lightened my spirits and put me in what may have been something approaching a state of grace.

I was on my way out again when I came face to face with a priest whose mortified features and burning eyes struck me the more because he too seemed rooted to the spot by seeing me.

"Thomas!"

"Alexandre!"

His white hands, light as doves, came to rest on my shoulders.

"They haven't dealt too harshly with you," he said, staring at me so intensely that I felt as if I were being sucked up by his gaze.

"Who?"

"The years."

"They've been kind to you."

"Oh, me!" His hand fluttered up to the gilded cupola. "I am no longer the same person you knew at Thabor. Or even the same as I was a mere five years ago. I have come a long way, Alexandre, I have suffered a slow and a profound transformation. And you?"

I too had traveled, traveled—what else had I done since Thabor? And weren't my legs, thin and tireless like those of an old stag, the most notable parts of my body? *Homo ambulator.* But had I been traveling toward the light?

"We must have a talk," he finished. "Are you free tomorrow

evening? Come and have dinner here in the presbytery. I shall
be alone. Meet me in the vestry."

He threw back his head and smiled at me, then turning suddenly, fled lightly away and vanished like a shadow.

I went out thoughtfully, plunged back suddenly into the years
of my adolescence, into the strong wine that had intoxicated me
from my arrival at Thabor and which came back to me in melancholy waves that went to my head even now. Meeting Drycome
again with the promise of seeing him again tomorrow and
finding out about the ups and downs that brilliant, crazy
brother's path had followed widened my outlook, opened new
perspectives, roused up a power that was always present in me
but latent, as if it were slumbering.

A strange reversal! My friends at the Cranes, by dragging me
down into the world of household rubbish, had sent me rebound-
ing toward the abstract (the quarry of the quarry). Thomas, by
revealing to me for a moment the upward path of his choice, set
the scene for the maddest and darkest adventure I have ever
had. . . .

With my thin, tireless old stag's legs setting a cracking pace, I
crossed the Place de la Porte-Dorée and found myself on the
edge of the Bois de Vincennes. The Léo-Lagrange Stadium was
still bustling, despite the lateness of the hour. Some hearty, muscular young men were engaged in a peculiar ritual whose overtly
nuptial significance was not lost on me. They clustered together,
and each one promptly buried his head in the buttocks of the
one in front as hard as he could while holding on to his neighbors with both arms, so that the nest of males lurched and staggered to the thrusting of the mass of straining thighs. At last a
great egg was laid in the center of the nest; and as it rolled out
between their legs the men scattered to dispute its possession.

Thus the wood of Vincennes revealed itself from the start as a
thicket of love. I have always liked the play on the word "folly,"
which can mean both a sylvan meeting place for lovers and
the loss of common sense. The disturbing spectacle I had just
witnessed of the bare-legged men performing their nuptial rite
augured well for the evening. Dusk was falling. I turned down

one of the paths. I walked beneath tunnels of leaves. Seated on a
green bench, I listened to the quiet murmur of the city. A modern city is not as far as one might think from the copses and
hedgerows of old. Quite apart from the fact that Paris has its
woodcutters, and that I have often heard the owl's cry at night in
the rue des Barres, to a hunter like me there is nothing more like
a dense jungle, teeming with predators and their prey, than this
mass of houses and flats knit with streets and alleys. The "policed" state is a fraud, because the law and order the police are
there to protect is dictated by the dominant group, which is
defined by money and heterosexuality. This makes it something
which the strongest impose on the rest by force, who have no alternative but to go underground. In the "policed" jungle, the
cops are simply one species of predator among many.

I had reached this point in my musings when a figure came
and sat down on the bench beside me. Two men meet in a café,
at a party, an exhibition or some such place. The number of
points of attack and contact between them is practically infinite.
But if the meeting takes place at night in a wood, these points
are reduced to two, sex and money, the one not excluding the
other. All my senses, backed by all my experience, are mobilized,
straining toward the dark stranger whose breathing I can hear.
Call and be called. A whole art. To gauge quickly—and generally
in the dark—the reality of the call and its quality. Make no mistake. Mistakes are costly. An evening is at stake, but sometimes
also liberty, or life.

My neighbor rises, takes four steps forward. Halts. I see him
from the back. He spreads his legs. I hear him pee. It is the call.
Low quality, very low! Silence. He turns to face me. There is still
just enough light for me to see that his fly is undone, displaying
his sex. In any case, the exhibition follows so logically from the
situation that in complete darkness, with my eyes shut, I should
have known, I should have *seen* it. The intense nakedness of the
trunked idol exposed in its repository of garments as in a mon-
strance. In it all the nakedness of the world is concentrated. The
desire irradiating it is pure, absolutely pure, with no admixture
of beauty, tenderness, grace or wonder. It is strength, raw, brutal
and innocent. I am on my feet. My legs have pulled me up and I

go forward, as though drawn by a thread, to meet the phallus bearer. There is no resisting the pull which is anchored at a point somewhere deep in my entrails. I am about to kneel, to worship, to pray, to take communion, to drink of the milk of this root.

"Take it easy!"

The voice is common but it is young and lightened by a humorous note. Meanwhile, the trunked idol has vanished, engulfed in his fly. Of course, it was too easy. Raw sex is not for me. With me everything must always be packed with meaning, with promises and threats, hemmed in with echoes and premonitions. But over and above my desire, there is a flicker of intellectual curiosity, a hint of the imaginary efflorescence that will crown it. What shape is it going to take this time?

"Not here. Come!"

Held captive still by the spell, I walk after him like an automaton, except for Fleurette still swinging faithfully from the crook of my left arm.

"Bernard's my name. I work around here. What about you?"

What about me? What is my name, indeed? Come to that, what is my profession? Desire has simplified me, scraped me to the bone, reduced me to a core. How am I to hang the rags of civil status onto this elementary tropism? In these frantic moments I understand the fear that sex inspires in society. It baffles and negates its entire substance. So it puts a muzzle on it—heterosexuality—and locks it in a cage—marriage. But now and then the beast emerges from its cage, and even manages to tear off its muzzle. Immediately they all back away shrieking and calling for the police.

"Surin. Garbage man."

Once again my sordid trade has come to my assistance. I don't know what work Bernard does "around here," but it would surprise me if it outdoes mine for crudity. We are coming to a clearing bathed in a diffuse light. It is not a clearing, it is a lake, and the light comes equally from its metallic surface and from the phosphorescent sky. A wooden hut, a landing stage, a flotilla of little boats moored together with a rippling murmur running between them. Are we going to fuck in a gondola, rocked on the warm flood, beneath the compassionate gaze of the stars? No, to-night is not the night for me to experience the harmonies of Lamartine. Our walk continues around the edge of the lake. I can see my companion better now. He is wearing thin cycling shoes on his feet which give him that swift, supple walk. But am I seeing things or is he in a navy blue uniform? I have never had a cop—prickly game but much enjoyed by some. On the other hand, I have more than once had my pleasure of young privates and the rough serge uniform formed no small part of it. Bernard has no cap and for the moment his blond thatch is the golden plume I follow. He says he works here. As a park keeper in the Bois de Vincennes, perhaps?

We re-enter the wood and take a narrow path under the trees. The incomparable flavor of surprise, danger and fear! We come up against a new, high black wall, an impassable barrier. No! There is a small door and Bernard has a key to it. The door opens. My guide disappears. Straw, straw and more straw. We are inside a stack of straw. A bulb protected by a steel cage sheds a feeble light which we share with adjoining compart-ments, divided from us by a concrete partition. Even more than from the fragrant bales or the pitchforks hanging on the wall, the sense of being in the country, in a stable, comes to us from the adjacent gloom where sounds of breathing, small movements and a low mooing can be made out. My companion has vanished behind a stack of bales. Suddenly he reappears. He is stark naked but for his head which is adorned with a flat cap bearing a shield with the six letters MUSEUM. He stands to attention be-fore me.

"Bernard Lemail, keeper in the Zoological Gardens of Vin-cennes. Present arms!"

And in fact I see his penis come slowly erect. Hell, that's quite a trick, and as though to honor it a fearful bang shakes the build-ing and a terrifying cry, a bellow that re-echoes from the walls, makes me jump.

"It's Adèle. An elephant. In heat. She's got three weeks to go yet," Bernard observes.

An elephant, Raphael's trunked idol in all its literal enormity! So this is the gigantic jest fate has in store for me! But that first

cry is nothing, for it cannot go unanswered. The chorus it lets
loose is unbearable. A thousand devils pounding the walls with
battering rams, rattling tons of ironwork, trampling the ground
and raising an infernal clamor. Bernard remains unmoved. He
sinks back onto some bales arranged to make a couch, his cap
tilted over his eyes and his blond thighs spread wide apart.

"How many elephants have you got here?"

"Eleven, counting the babies, but they make the most noise."

The din has stopped abruptly. Two or three more squeals.
Then soft, wet slapping sounds, like an avalanche of slush, come
to us and at the same time our nostrils are filled with a honey-
smelling steam.

"And now they shit. All together, in unison," Bernard explains.
"That's all Adèle's love calls do for them. But I've got to admit.
The muck from the herbivores is bearable. Elephants, hippos,
giraffes, bison, camels, they're what I have to feed. I can't complain. But it's not so funny for my pals who have to cope with
the lions and tigers and panthers. For one thing there's the
carcasses from the knackers, and then there's shit that takes your
breath away. Well, I drew the obvious conclusions. I became a
vegetarian. Like my charges. So my crap smells like jasmine, just
you wait and see."

About the jasmine, I remain unconvinced. But how sweet the
hours I spent on that couch of straw with my nice little keeper,
watched over by eleven idols with life-sized trunks!

Animal triste post coitum. The ultimate heterosexual catch-
phrase. Speaking for myself, *post coitum,* I am on wings, I
am surrounded by heavenly music. In the solitude of the Bois de
Vincennes in the middle of the night, I was borne in triumph by
Ganesh, the elephant god, with a rat, the symbol of household
refuse, always at his feet—and he trumpeted fiercely in my
honor.

This royal progress was almost bound to have roused the
watch. But I was striding so swiftly down the darkened paths
that I failed to see the shadow standing motionless in my way.
At the last moment a beam of light sprang from it full in my
face, stopping me in my tracks.

"What are you doing here?"

He addressed me in a familiar way, which I loathe, and the pencil of light boring into my eyes made me very angry. Fleurette whistled through the air. There was a slight jerk, a loud oath and the flashlight landed in the lily of the valley, while the blessed darkness enveloped me again. Not for long, alas, because almost at once I saw sparks dancing before my eyes and felt my knees give way under me.

"The bastard! He's hurt me!"

I realized that I must have lost consciousness for a moment when I found myself face down in the grass with a hand brutally twisting my arm behind my back.

"Try and find your flashlight first, then the thing he hit you with. That's evidence! As for you, my night owl, get up on your hind legs!"

The tension relaxed. I got to my knees, then to my feet, causing a sharp pain in the back of my neck.

"Got it, chief! It's a walking stick. An ordinary walking stick. Too bad!"

Gallant Fleurette, humiliating this rotten cop with her seemingly harmless appearance! For two plainclothes policemen is what they are, no doubt about it, and what they're doing is hustling me roughly toward a police van which has been unseen in the dark until its lights blaze out suddenly.

Dear darkness, sweet friend, my accessory in the amorous chase, a warm belly filled with mysterious promise, dispenser of protection and secrecy, whenever ill-wishers assail me they begin by violating you, rending you with their flashlights and headlamps ... . We emerge from the dark into the Boulevard de Picpus. The poignant beauty of these working-class districts after dark. The darkness effaces the dirt, the ugliness, the teeming mediocrity of it all. Occasionally a fleeting pool of light snatches a wall, a tree, a figure or a face out of the night, but all simplified in the extreme, stylized, pared to essentials, a house reduced to an architectural design, a tree to a spectral sketch, a face to an isolated outline. And all is fragile, ephemeral, pathetically doomed to perish in oblivion.

I discover that in these rather extraordinary circumstances I am observing everything with an aesthetic detachment. Because

the long and the short of it is that I am being arrested—held for
questioning, as the official humbug phrase has it—and they are
taking me into custody in a police van. It is the first time anything of the sort has happened to me, although I have often
come within an inch of it. Despite the unpleasantness of my situation—my boorish escorts, the wet, muddy patch on my left
knee, and above all the dull ache at the back of my neck—I am
filled with an immense curiosity. And this curiosity is not just
about my experience with the police, it illumines and transfigures
everything around me.

We come to the Bel-Air police station in the rue Bel-Air and a
dismal room, smelling of stale cigarettes. They make me turn my
pockets out. I make sure that Fleurette is among my little personal belongings. It would be the last straw if these bums were
to filch her! They leave me my tie and my shoelaces. I'm disappointed that they don't make me take my trousers down and
bend over and show my asshole to the guard. I was promising
myself a certain satisfaction from that little scene, which I
thought invariably took place. I had even been keeping back a
nice ripe fart for more than half an hour, and then had to waste
it on the cells. For I recognized instantly the prison waiting room
with two crumpled figures there before me, huddled, shapeless
and colorless but not odorless, upon the bench running around
three of the walls. Indeed, it was all just as I had expected. Do
all law-abiding people have an equally clear and accurate picture of detention, or is it that, even without having undergone it,
I am the stuff that prisoners are made of? I select a corner of the
bench as far as possible from my two companions and settle
down to wait in a semi-doze, punctuated by brief periods of
sharp awareness. Twice the bars open and a wreck of humanity
is shoved inside, to come to rest one on my right, the other on
my left. I know, too, that the promiscuity in prison is worse than
the loneliness. In the end, the time passes fairly quickly.

Before seven, a uniformed policeman unlocks the bars and
beckons me out. Why me? Probably because I am better dressed
than my four companions. Obsequiousness to the bourgeoisie,
brutality to the lower orders, that sums up the social philosophy
of the guardians of law and order.

The police inspector is a bald, insignificant little man and his paltry looks—despite the air of the inveterate heterosexual—somewhat diffuse my belligerent mood. Nevertheless, I charge in.

"Last night I was attacked by two of your henchmen for no apparent reason. Then I spent a night in your filthy cells. What is the meaning of it?"

He regards me gloomily and, without a word, presses a button. A bell rings in the distance. We wait. The door opens to admit one of my cops from the Bois de Vincennes. He carries Fleurette in his left hand. I note with satisfaction that his right is hidden in a large bandage.

"In the matter of attacks, it was you who injured one of my men. I am going to charge you with assaulting a policeman."

"He was blinding me with his flashlight."

"What were you doing in the wood at night?"

"I am an entomologist. I collect butterflies."

"Hunting butterflies at one o'clock in the morning?"

"Certainly. I am the world's greatest expert on night-flying butterflies."

"You are trying to make a fool of me," he remarks wearily. Then, taking Fleurette out of his subordinate's hand, he waves her about, as though to test how light and supple she is, then presses the catch with his thumb and unsheathes the blade.

"A sword stick. An illegal weapon. Another potential indictment," he observes dispiritedly.

This puts me off slightly. I had been preparing to confront an angry bull. This bloodless creature refuses to take up my challenge. In order to regain my composure, I take the medallion out of one of my waistcoat pockets, flick it open, and put it to my nostrils. The inspector watches me cynically.

"What's that?" he asks at last. "Dope?"

I step forward.

"A compressed sample of the household rubbish of Roanne. I am the king of garbage men."

There is no curiosity in his face. He looks utterly appalled.

"What does sniffing that do to you?"

"The smell of it restores my self-respect and helps me to en-

dure whatever poisonous atmosphere I may fine myself temporarily captive in."

"Such as a police station, for instance?"

"Yes, for instance."

He gazes mournfully at his hands, folded on his blotter. Is he
going to burst into tears?

"Do you know anyone in Paris?"

I had foreseen that question and considered my answer. In the
end I had decided to call in Drycome if need be. I was not
averse to compromising my old fellow Fleuret a little and splash-
ing a bit of garbage over his immaculate dove's plumage.

"Father Thomas, of the church of the Saint-Esprit in the rue
de la Brèche-au-Loup. I am dining at the presbytery this evening."

The inspector makes a sign to the plainclothesman, who takes
me into an adjoining room. We wait. I suppose he is on the telephone to Thomas. He won't have had to wait long to see me—or
see me again—in my proper light!

The door opens and the inspector's startled face appears.

"You can go," he tells me.

In one bound I am outside. It is very early morning. The gutters are clear, singing streams along the newly swept pavements.
The street belongs to the garbage carts and the men who serve
them and feed them with multicolored offerings. I think of
Ganesh, of Adèle, Bernard's elephant in heat. There is an analogy between elephants and rubbish trucks. Someone ought to
design a truck with a trunk. It could use it to pick up the garbage cans and empty them into its back end. Only the trunk
would have to be in the form of a penis as well. Then there
would be no need of garbage cans. The penis would simply poke
into its own back end. Self-sodomy. That brings me back to the
dry come, to Thomas' *ejaculatio mystica*. It all fits, it all goes together, it all falls into place. But while I rejoice in the way my
universe comes full circle, I feel a pang when I remember
Fleurette is still in the hands of the police. I promise myself not
to go back to Roanne without her.

A wolf returning to the Wolf's Lair, I lengthen my stride so as
to reach my hotel before sunrise. The night was what it was, but

it will not impinge on my day. In a little while I am due at the incineration plant at Issy-les-Moulineaux. For the first time I am going to see this infernal city which arouses such horror in my firm.

The police station was purgatory. I have just come back from hell. Shattered, desperate, with reddened skin and eyes haunted by visions of horror, I shall be scarred forever by what I have been through.

The plant proclaims itself from a long way off with its tall chimneys, their exhalations naturally suggesting labor, productivity, and creative toil. Who would suspect that the facts are the exact opposite, and that what is carried on behind that traditional front is a work of diabolical destruction?

The first hint that something dark and mysterious is going on within those walls comes from the sight of a procession of refuse trucks, filled to overflowing with rubbish, winding up the long concrete ramp. Swollen with waste, the pachyderms crawl sedately upward, nose to tail, from the bank of the Seine to a weigh-bridge, where they pause briefly before proceeding to a kind of huge terrace. Moving onto it, all the vehicles engage in a kind of ballet—forward, back, forward, back—ending up thirteen at a time backed up to a trench big enough for whole houses to be toppled into it. The trucks are tilted, the rubbish slides out, the trucks settle down again and the thirteen vehicles reform in procession to make way for the next.

This trench is the mouth of hell. Gigantic steel grabs descend continually from above at a vertiginous rate and can be seen plunging into it, their eight hooked claws extended. They vanish into the soft white mass of refuse. Then the cables tighten, one senses the monster closing its jaws, and the octopus surfaces again, slowly now, clutching in its tentacles a shapeless mass out of which mattresses, cooking stoves, truck tires, and uprooted trees tumble back into the abyss. Under the control of a traveling crane, the octopus grabs glide toward the hoppers that feed the furnaces. The tentacles part and the outcasts drop onto a steep slope whence they go crashing head over heels, rushing down to the roaring fires. They slide into the flames along with their personalities, their memories, their words, their colors and halftones, their likes and dislikes. It is a furious, undiscriminating annihilation of every subtlety and shade, of everything inimitable and irreplaceable.

This hurling of everything human into that raging fire must appeal to some atavistic terror in me, some immemorial foreknowledge, for the sight of it to have dealt me so profound a blow. And to add the final touch of horror, the attendants on this funereal place are all clad in green overalls and hoods pierced with Plexiglas windows.

The explanations bellowed by my guide through the grinding, thudding, and roaring are graven on my passive and uncaring memory. That the capacity for combustion of rubbish increases annually—with the wealth of the population—and obviates the need for addition of coal or fuel oil. That the annual incineration of 740,000 metric tons of garbage provides potential sales of 850,000 energy units over and above the needs of the plant. That the process of incineration leaves tons of reclaimable clinker and provides winter heating for all the nearby districts. These wonders—and many more—only served to distress me further, because the mark of death was on all of them. The truth is that this inferno is the physical expression of the complete and final victory—unto ashes, unto obliteration—of the property owners over the social outcasts. With the destruction of household rubbish by fire, heterosexual society takes a great stride in the direction of uniformity, of leveling down, of the elimination of all that is different, unexpected, creative.

Once again I came back wounded, bruised and bleeding to my wolf's lair. I undressed, a basic act symbolizing the casting off of my social rags and the freeing of my body and sex organs. The reunion with my body is always a happy, reassuring occasion which revives my appetite for living for the whole day. The big, warm, familiar animal, faithful, docile and incorruptible, which has never failed, never betrayed me, the instrument of my hunting and my pleasures, accomplice in all my adventures, always in the forefront when it comes to taking risks and blows—all the time I am moving between my bed and my bath, naked as

Adam, I feel that it is with me, like a good dog, and I am invariably sorry in the morning when I must shut it into its prison of clothes to face the heterosexual desert. I do nothing for it, save to forbid myself those two great poisons, tobacco and alcohol, paltry vices, the pathetic comfort of those harnessed to the heavy tumbril of the propagation of the species. For me health is not merely the primary condition of my hunting and other pursuits. So far as I can trust myself—which is a very long way—I am confident that I shall escape the indignity of death from disease or old age. No, my dear, lean, sinewy carcass, tireless on the track of your prey, you shall not know the swollen obesity of the heterosexual, or the swellings of tumors or edema. You shall die a clean death, fighting an unequal battle forced on you by love, and by cold steel shall you perish . . .

I suffer from constipation but I should be cured if I could have the face of a heterosexual to cover with my dung each morning. To shit on a heterosexual. But perhaps even that is doing him too much honor? Isn't my shit pure gold compared to his baseness?

The loss of Fleurette, the frustration of my belligerent instincts by the lugubrious inspector and, as the last straw, the hell of Issy opening at my feet—these three things, originally fortuitous perhaps but arranged by my mind into a formidable logical sequence (myself disarmed, the inspector disengaging and then fading away before the gaping doors of hell), had put me in the blackest of moods, and the few hours of sleep I managed to snatch in the afternoon recharged my énergies. Which is to say that as I loped off to dine with Father Drycome I was spitting fire. In fact, I was so excited that the few yards dividing the hotel from the church seemed too short and I walked right around the block to allow myself to breathe a little.

I have always admired the capacity of churchmen to create their own particular atmosphere around them, which may be altogether at variance with their actual surroundings. Thus I happened once to wander into a convent of nuns right in the very middle of Paris. I thought I must be dreaming. The cloister, the garden, the vegetable plot, the colored statues of saints, the bells marking the time of day, all combined to re-create and maintain a piece of the countryside, a timeless piety, only a few yards from the metro. The presbytery of the Church of the Holy Ghost formed just such an original enclave on the Avenue Daumesnil, only the air one breathed upon entering was more rarefied and no less than two hours' conversation with Thomas would suffice to isolate the subtle balance of spirituality, Byzantinism and eroticism of which it was composed. The inside, opening on the ground floor onto a Paris street, certainly created an enclave of silence, devout and contemplative, but there was more between those white walls on which the icons and lamps made quavering patches of gold than in a simple village presbytery.

Thomas himself opened the door. If my nocturnal escapade and the police inspector's telephone call had made me remotely uneasy about his attitude toward me I should have been instantly reassured by his friendliness and the mild, affectionate cheerfulness in which he enveloped me.

"I have to set your mind at rest at once," he told me straightway. "It is here, waiting for you. A policeman brought it round this morning."

And he held out Fleurette. I must confess I almost wept at getting her back.

"My sword stick! Do you know what I call her? Fleurette! In memory of our secret society at Thabor."

"And in memory of the child you were when we nicknamed you Fleurette!"

"Yes, Thomas Drycome!"

We gripped each other's shoulders and laughed silently, but deeply and warmly, looking into one another's faces, and each saw in the other, at the end of a long, gray tunnel, the green paradise of youthful love. How good it was, after passing through a heterosexual desert full of smells and unpleasantness, to rediscover our old brotherly understanding!

The dinner, served by an apparently deaf-and-dumb old servant woman, was long and subtle and made up of the kind of food I love, pure creation of the utmost complexity, which is to ordinary dishes what abstract painting is to representational art. The maid set down the dishes in front of Thomas and then disappeared. He dealt with them thereafter, and there was in his movements such precision and at the same time such evident conformity to some secret rite that one was forcibly reminded of a priest engaged in sacrifice, but one who instead of cutting the throats of sheep or oxen might have been flaying entities or dissecting essences. He saw I was watching him curiously and paused for a moment, smiling, to say something which described him completely.

"Well, you see: I have never had any sense of the profane!"

We talked of Thabor and our little group.

"I have not kept up with any of the Fleurets," he told me, "and yet I can remember each of them extraordinarily clearly. I see us all at that all-important age when we were emerging from the limbo of innocence and opening fresh eyes on the world. I have an immense retrospective affection for us. Not having a child, I think of them as my children, those small boys of whom I am paradoxically one, and among whom I perceive a quite unmistakable air of kinship."

"We had just discovered at the same time who we were and that we had nothing to gain from a heterosexual society," I said. "Even the fathers at the college were wholeheartedly dedicated to such a society, however much their celibacy might cut them off from it. I wonder at how swiftly we formed ourselves into a caste, entrenched in secrecy and spiked with contempt. That secrecy and contempt I maintain to this day, and it is because of them that I am what I am and have even managed to attain a kind of happiness."

"This caste you speak of, I also have rediscovered it but in a very different way, through the monastic experience. I daresay I forgot the lesson of the Fleurets too quickly. I passed through a serious crisis and was cured of it by several years in a monastery. We will talk of that another time. On the other hand, I learned not to despise the mass of heterosexuals. Do not think I renounced any privilege. We are the lords of creation. If all men alive were to be classified according to their creative talents, we should get a vast pyramid with the abounding, unproductive horse at its base and the great creators at its summit. Now I am saying that the proportion of homosexuals in the base would be near enough nil, but that at the summit the proportion would be getting on for a hundred percent. Nevertheless, we must resist the temptation to pride. Our superiority over the heterosexual masses is not especially praiseworthy. The burden of procreation crushes women altogether, and half of heterosexual men. As light and gay as travelers without luggage, we are to heterosexual men as they are to women. Do you know what the word 'proletarian' means? It comes from the same root as the word 'prolific.' So that the proletarian is not defined by his trade, as is generally believed, but by his sexuality. The proletarian is the prolific man, harnessed to the heavy wagon of the propagation of the species. We are the salt of the earth. But he is the earth itself. We cannot do without him, if only to make love to. Because, you know, there is nothing to compare with the savor of making love to a heterosexual. Heterosexuals are our women."

I replied that homosexuals would probably think less about pouring scorn on the married man for being *domesticated* both in his work and in his sex life for social ends, if the heterosexual did not harbor such envy and hatred for them. "The slave rattles his chains noisily and calls for contraception, legalized abortion, and divorce by consent, all of which he thinks will give him the free, casual and lascivious loving of the homosexual's eternal spring. The married man demands absurdly that women should strain themselves unnaturally to be slim and childless, like boys, when their ingrained vocation for motherhood intends them to be fat and fecund. And all the time he is running after a homosexual model, he cherishes for homosexuals the hatred of the chained dog for the free, lone wolf."

"Those are mere revolts," Thomas said. "The heterosexual clods rise against their masters, burning castles and indulging in massacres like Hitler's followers today. But such unrest does not alter the basic fact which is tattooed in the flesh of both. One is either 'born' or one is not. The story of the *Bourgeois Gentilhomme* fits the case perfectly. Like the commoner, M. Jourdain, the heterosexual wants to lead the free, unattached life of the homosexual nobility. But the more he breaks out, the more firmly he is recalled to his proletarian condition. Some dabble in blood and filth and contraceptive drugs. Others stagger under the weight of wives and children of whom they have tried in vain to rid themselves throughout a lifetime's aberrations, but who never let them go and live off their substance. Take that little police inspector you were dealing with this morning! I can reveal his confidences to you, he did not tell them to me under the seal of the confessional. He brought about the death of a girl who was pregnant with his child, trying to procure her an abortion and now, after three divorces, he lives alone, dividing his meager salary among a whole tribe—who hate him into the bargain because they blame him for the poverty they suffer. He blamed sex for ruining his life and spreading misery around him. I taught him to see precisely that what had caused the damage was heterosexuality lived like homosexuality. In short, I showed him that the source of his errors was in a kind of imposture."

He broke off to make coffee with the aid of a miniature set of alchemist's utensils which the housekeeper had brought in to him on a tray.

"The animosity of poor wretches like that toward those as privileged and blessed by the gods as we are is all too understandable," he went on. "What is more, it may be good for us by compelling us to secrecy, obscurity, and irreproachable behavior in public. We must never betray our vocation as solitary, nocturnal hunters."

I objected that although this quite external physical constraint could certainly be turned to advantage, the constant moral pressure of heterosexual society could unfortunately have a dangerously corrupting and disintegrating influence on the homosexual. It was the same for all oppressed minorities who were hated by the majority. The majority manufactured a caricature of the minority man and compelled him to conform to that image. And the compulsion was all the more irresistible because the caricature was not wholly arbitrary. It was made up of some real characteristics, but enlarged out of all proportion and to the exclusion of all the rest. Thus the same pressure made the Jew a *yid*—little, hook-nosed and rapacious; the black American a *nigger*—lazy, ignorant and a drug addict; the North African a *wog*—a liar, a thief and a rapist; while the same pressure thrust the homosexual willy-nilly into the role of a pansy. What was a pansy but a homosexual who gave in meekly to the demands of the proletariat.

"And when that meekness is at its height," Thomas added, "it leads to transvestism. Transvestism is the ultimate triumph of the heterosexual over the homosexual, in which he is obliterated and swallowed up entirely in the other sex. It is Christ the King, crowned with thorns, a reed in his hand and a red cloak over his shoulders, being slapped in the face by the soldiery. But have you taken the measure of his revenge? For if the homosexual left to himself is a good deal more virile than the heterosexual—who is his woman—slighted, ridiculed, and travestied, his creative genius carries him beyond his pitiful model and he beats woman on her own ground. By putting all the power of his virility at the service of the feminine species, he becomes a woman so brilliant, elegant, delicate and aristocratic—such a superwoman—that he easily outshines all other real women rash enough to come near him.

"Homosexuality is a demanding business. It requires its elect to be strong enough to endure an unusual fate. And very often we behold the tragedy of the chosen vessel who is too weak, the second-rate man unwillingly promoted into the front rank. The heir apparent with no ability to rule, whose narrow shoulders sag beneath the purple folds of the kingly mantle, whose head is bowed under the gilded weight of the crown. Such a one will succumb to the atmosphere of heterosexual hatred. Crushed and trampled, there will be nothing for him but to drink to the dregs the poisoned chalice that is offered him. Nor can any one of us be sure that he is strong enough to reject altogether the poison which the proletarians mingle with everything he drinks, with everything he eats, with the very air he breathes. But the more he keeps his secret, the better he will manage."

"There is a negative proof of this form of poisoning," I put in. "In countries where homosexuality is normal and perfectly accepted—such as ancient Greece and Moslem countries today—such phenomena as the pansy and the transvestite do not occur. Just as, if the Jews were ever to gather themselves into a nation, they would immediately lose all the yid characteristics forced on them by anti-Semites. Then we should see Jews as peasants or craftsmen, Jewish athletes and soldiers, blond Jews, generous Jews, who knows, even homosexual Jews."

"I doubt if they'd go as far as that," he protested. "Because now, you see, we're touching on the religious sphere. Insofar as the Jews remain faithful to the Old Testament, they are closer to the third stage of spiritual development, which I have attained, than to the second—with which I began and which alone makes everything possible to homosexuality."

I asked him to explain himself more clearly, since it seemed to me that he had just compressed an entire system of theology into a few words. The meal was over. We had left the dining area and moved to the other end of the room where a big fire was burning in a massive stone hearth. I could not repress a grimace.

"Another fire! Do you know, this afternoon I made a real descent into hell? I went to see the refuse incineration plant at Issy-les-Moulineaux. It was Dante and Piranesi in one!"

As we sat down, our feet on the fender, he pointed out that fire had many avatars, of which hell was certainly the most unlikely.

"Fire has only been associated with hell by analogy with the burning at the stake suffered by heretics and witches under the Inquisition. Before that, fire, as a source of light and warmth, was a divine symbol, the sensible presence of God, the manifestation of the Holy Ghost."

When he had uttered these last words, he sat thoughtfully, his eyes on the incandescent structures in the hearth which seemed to be alive. At last he said that if Christ was the body of the Church, the Holy Ghost was its soul.

"Christ is the body of the Church, but the Holy Ghost is its soul. All through my childhood and a good deal of my adolescence, I committed the most widespread sin of the West: I stopped at the body. I was fascinated by Christ, by the naked, tortured body of Christ Crucified. I dreamed day and night of the ineffable joy that would illumine me if I were to lay myself down, naked, upon that body and put my mouth upon his like Elisha with the Shunammite's son. Yes, I loved Jesus as a lover. I was searching in two parallel spheres—my own body and Christological teaching—to attain some kind of union with him. Even my own name for a time shed light, although I wonder today whether it was not more dazzling than illuminating. You know St. Thomas insisted on being able to put his fingers into the wounds in the sacred body before he would believe in Jesus' resurrection. It goes without saying that the gesture must be seen as something very different from the flat positivism of a man obsessed with tangible, physical proof. In fact, the episode means precisely the opposite. Thomas is not content with a superficial perception of Christ. He does not believe his eyes. Any more than he believes his hands when they touch the cheek or rest on the shoulder of the resuscitated one. He needs the mystical experience of a bodily communion, a penetration of his own body into the body of the Beloved. That wound in the side, from whose opening there came forth not blood alone but also a colorless liquid which has been called water, Thomas demanded that his fingers—following in the wake of the Roman soldier's lance—should know it intimately.

"Haunted by the mystery of my patron saint, I stumbled for a long time over an enigma which no exegete has yet cleared up. In St. John's Gospel, Thomas is called Didymus. Didymus, from the Greek *didumos,* twin. Now although the Holy Scriptures never fail to indicate the family ties of such and such a person, nowhere is there any mention of Thomas' twin brother. I searched in vain for the alter ego of this unpaired twin who, it seemed to me, must be there, close at hand, similar and yet unrecognizable. Little by little, a daring, crazy but unexceptionable idea took possession of my mind: this twin brother of Thomas' was never mentioned because it was Jesus himself. So that Thomas was not the twin unpaired but the Twin Absolute, whose like was to be sought nowhere but in God.

"As this conviction grew on me, my appearance underwent a change which only those close to me perceived. Someone inside me would no longer be Thomas alone. I had to become Didymus as well. Before long people were shocked at the way I looked. My long hair, my blond beard, but still more the way I spoke and walked and above all an air of transparent gentleness, in spite of the angular thinness of my face—everything betrayed a blasphemous mimicry which, however, was very far from deliberate. I was reproached. People throught me crazed with pride and both my masters and my fellow pupils at the seminary strove to bring me back to humility. The worst came when I showed the first signs of the sacred stigmata. Then I sank into utter darkness.

"My masters were more than good to me. They behaved toward me with a clearsightedness which could not be explained purely by natural causes. They ordered me to go into retreat for as long as necessary at the monastery of the Paraclete, near Nogent-sur-Seine, the very same that Abelard founded and where he was buried in 1142. It is a huge collection of Romanesque buildings, modeled on the Abbey of Cluny, on the bank of a river with the musical name of the Ardusson. The prior, Father Théodore, was an old man, as fragile as glass, as white as ermine and of a diaphanous purity. He welcomed me like a son. I learned that there existed within the Catholic Church an oriental tendency—quite close to Orthodox theology—and that the Paraclete was one of the centers from which it spread. Rome naturally stands aside from this trend, which must remain within the limits of Catholicism, but she does not discourage it since she recognizes the value of a Byzantine wing, of a kind that could one day help to bring about a reconciliation with our Orthodox brethren. The years I spent at the Paraclete made me an unquestioning disciple of men who by word, writing and example preach a particular angle—which is none other than the Truth.

"When I came to the Paraclete, I was Christ-sick. Now the first thing Father Théodore taught me was precisely that examples of this particular kind of sickness are also to be found in secular spheres. Psychiatry and psychoanalysis describe certain neuroses as a more or less definitive fixation of the subject at a stage of development which is normal and even necessary, but which should be superseded by another stage, closer to maturity. I am going to talk to you frankly because you are a brother Fleuret and also because you are still a stranger to these theological questions. I should not say these things so crudely in the pulpit or in clerical circles. *Christ has to be superseded.* The great mistake made by Western Christianity is in too exclusive an attachment to the person, the teaching, even to the body of

Christ. We make ourselves guilty of Christocentrism, and even of Christomonism. No one was better placed than I to understand that verdict, because no one had gone so far into that error as I had. I had made myself Didymus, the Absolute Twin who found his own image—at once soothing and glorifying—only in the person of Christ. But Christ died on the Cross, mutilated and despairing, and Christocentrism is inevitably a religion of suffering, of agony and death. The emblem of Christ nailed to the Cross that is set up everywhere is a vision of horror we can only endure by reason of the deadening and anesthetizing effect of habit. But we have only to picture Christ dangling from a gibbet or with his head held fast in the lunette of the guillotine to be suddenly aware of the morbid ugliness of the crucifix. What we must accept is that Christ died because his mission was finished, and that mission was to prepare for the descent of the Holy Ghost among men. Certainly there was the resurrection. But it was very brief. And then Jesus' words are categorical: 'It is expedient for you that I go away,' he says to the unhappy apostles, 'for if I go not away, the Comforter will not come unto you.' It is as though most Catholics refuse to listen to those words. And it is true that they are heavy with meaning, too heavy perhaps. They mean that Jesus is a second John the Baptist. As the Baptist was only the precursor of Jesus, so Jesus himself was only the precursor of the Holy Ghost. Christ and the Holy Ghost are the two hands of the Father, one Eastern doctor has said. But the two hands act in succession and the second can only begin to work when the first has finished its task. Because it was necessary first for the Word to be made Flesh so that afterward we might be able to receive the Holy Ghost, or, as St. Athanasius said, God became sarcophorous in order that man might become pneumatophorous.

"So the great Christian festival whose resounding splendor shall eclipse all others is not Christmas or Easter, much less Good Friday, it is Pentecost. On the day of Pentecost, the Holy Ghost took the place among men which Jesus had prepared and which his ascension had left vacant. Pentecost is the beginning of the Church's history, it inaugurates Parousia and anticipates the Kingdom. The difference is considerable but too many men—

even the most fervent believers among them—refuse to admit it
and continue to worship Jesus. This rejection of the primacy of
the Spirit by the Roman Church is at the root of the Eastern
Schism. The quarrel over the *filioque* is not a matter of words.
The official symbol of the faith affirmed that the Spirit pro-
ceeded from the Father—and this fundamental dogma cemented
the unity of the Christian world. By adding the word *filioque*
(and of the Son) in the eighth century, Rome made the Holy
Ghost subservient to the Son and inscribed Christocentrism in
the heart of the faith. The Eastern Church, faithful to the revolution of Pentecost, could not accept this arbitrary act which
tended to make Christ the *begetter* of the Spirit whereas he was
only the *precursor*. Certainly during Christ's earthly ministry the
relationship between men and the Holy Ghost functioned only
by and through Christ. But Pentecost turned this relationship
upside down. Thenceforth it was the relationship to Christ that
functioned only by and through the Holy Ghost.

"The coming of the Holy Ghost inaugurated a new era of history, and there is a third Testament to fit this era in the Acts of
the Apostles, in which it alone is in control. The Old Testament
belonged to the Father. The Father's single voice rings through
it. But the creativity of the Father is so great that a thousand po-
tentialities are heard murmuring through his voice, some of them
so insistently that it cannot be doubted but that the future belongs to them. Each of the prophets foreshadows Jesus, and it
was in Bethlehem that David was born. But above all it is the
murmurings of the Spirit which make themselves heard in the
Bible, and the theologian David Lys has counted three hundred
and eighty-nine references to it.

"*Ruah* is the Hebrew word traditionally translated as wind,
breath, emptiness, spirit. In the old Semitic south, ruah meant
something vast, spacious, open, but it was also a scent, a per-
fume. Sometimes again it was a light contact, a gentle caress, a
sense of well-being in which one bathed. One of the first ruahs in
the Bible is the evening breeze in which Jahweh walks in the
Garden when Adam and Eve have sinned and hide themselves
from his sight. The Israelites, captive and oppressed, are said to
'lack ruah.' Anna, the future mother of Samuel, soured by her

barrenness, is 'bitter of ruah.' Koheleth teaches that it is better
to be 'long of ruah' (patient) than 'high of ruah' (proud). To
die is to lose one's ruah. Lastly, according to Ezekiel it is the
word for the four cardinal points, and according to Koheleth for
the endless circuits of the wind. So there is a close tie between
meteorology and ruah. There is a bad ruah which blows from
the east, dries up the plants and brings the locusts—and a good
ruah from the west and the sea, driving the quails to the Israelites in the desert. David, on becoming king, is visited by the
good ruah, while the bad overshadows the soul of the fallen
Saul. According to Hosea, God sends the ruah out of the east
upon men, the wind of prostitution, the mephitic atmosphere of
the orgiastic cults. Who sows the ruah of the east shall reap the
whirlwind. For Isaiah, it moves the trees, carries away the chaff
from the mountains, and it is by a ruah burning as justice that
the daughters of Jerusalem shall be purified.

"When one goes further into Holy Writ one finds the ruah
becoming milder, more spiritual, yet still without losing its physical associations and degenerating into an abstract concept. Even
at its highest metaphysical level—the miracle of Pentecost—the
Spirit manifests itself by a dry storm, and preserves its meteorological nature. Thus Elijah on Mount Horeb, waiting in a cave
for Jahweh to pass by: '*And a great and strong wind rent the
mountains, and brake in pieces the rocks before the Lord; but
the Lord was not in the wind; and after the wind an earthquake;
but the Lord was not in the earthquake. And after the earthquake a fire; but the Lord was not in the fire; and after the fire a
still small voice. And it was so, when Elijah heard it, that he
wrapped his face in his mantle, and went out, and stood in the
entering of the cave. And behold, there came a voice unto
him . . .*' (I Kings 19: 11–13).

"The Holy Spirit is wind, tempest, breath, it has a meteorological body. Meteors are sacred. Science, which claims to analyze them thoroughly and encapsulate them in laws, is nothing
but blasphemy and mockery. 'The wind bloweth where it listeth,
and thou hearest the sound thereof, but canst not tell whence it
cometh, and whither it goeth,' Jesus said to Nicodemus. That is
why meteorology is doomed to failure. Its forecasts are con-

tinually made to look foolish by events, because they are an attack on the free will of the Spirit. Nor should there be any surprise at this sanctity I claim for meteors. Truly, everything is sacred. To try to divide things into a profane, material domain and the sacred world floating above it, is simply to confess to a degree of blindness and to define its limits. The mathematical sky of the astronomers is sacred because it is the home of the Father. The lands of men are sacred because they are the place of the Son. In between the two, the confused and unpredictable sky of meteorology is the place of the Spirit and forms a link between the paternal heavens and filial earth. It is a living, sounding sphere which envelops the earth like a mantle, full of humors and turbulence, and this mantle is spirit, seed, and word.

"It is seed because without it nothing would grow on earth. Moreover, the Jewish Pentecost, celebrated fifty days after Easter, was originally the harvest festival and the offering of the first fruits. Even the women needed its moisture to bring forth children, and the Archangel Gabriel, announcing the birth of Jesus to Mary, tells her: *The Holy Ghost shall come upon thee, and the power of the Highest shall overshadow thee.*

"It is word, and the stormy troposphere with which it envelops the earth is in truth a logosphere. *And suddenly there came a sound from heaven as of a rushing mighty wind, and it filled all the house where they were sitting. And there appeared unto them cloven tongues like as of fire, and it sat upon each of them. And they were all filled with the Holy Ghost, and began to speak with other tongues, as the Spirit gave them utterance . . . the multitude came together and were confounded, because that every man heard them speak in his own language.* When Christ preached his words carried only a limited distance and only those crowds who spoke Aramaic understood him. After this, the apostles, scattered to the ends of the earth, become nomads and their speech is intelligible to everyone. Because the tongue they speak is a profound tongue, a weighty tongue, it is the divine logos whose words are the seeds of things. These words are things in themselves, the very things and not their more or less partial and lying reflections as the words of human language are. And because this logos expresses the common basis of being and humanity, men of every nation understand it instantly, so that, deceived by habit and inattention, they think they are hearing their own language. Now the apostles did not speak all the languages in the world, but a single tongue which no one else speaks although everyone understands it. Thus they speak to the divine part that is in every barbarian. And it was this tongue likewise that the Archangel spoke at the Annunciation, and whose words were sufficient to get Mary with child.

"I should be lying if I claimed to possess this tongue. The Pentecostal succession is a painful mystery. The supreme irony is that, as far as the logos of the Paraclete goes, the Holy Father himself has no more than Church Latin! At least they taught me at the Paraclete to give a broader, deeper meaning to the passion that was consuming me. I had transferred my unpaired state, from which I was suffering as from an amputation, onto Jesus—and that was right, and it was the wisest course I could have chosen, for all its apparent madness. Jesus is always apparently the maddest answer—in reality the wisest—to all the questions we ask ourselves. But it was wrong to remain a prisoner of the body Crucified. It was for Father Théodore to unfold the whirlwind of the Spirit to me. The flaming wind of the Paraclete devastated and illumined my heart. Whatever was still the prisoner of the body of Christ burst asunder and spread out to the ends of the earth. The common factor which I had found only in Jesus revealed itself to me in every living man. My didymy became universal. The unpaired twin died and a brother to all men was born in his place. But the passage through the brotherhood of Christ ballasted my heart with a loyalty and my eyes with an understanding which I believe they would have lacked but for that ordeal. I said to you that the Jews could probably move directly from the Old Testament ruah to the luminous breath of the Pentecostal Spirit. It may be that some miraculous rabbis whose radiance indisputably oversteps the bounds of Israel to attain a universal scope have accomplished that ultimate conversion. But because they have not passed through the era of the Son, they will always lack a certain depth of color, warmth, and grief. It is noticeable, for instance, that the Spirit does not encourage representational painting, drawing, or sculpture. This facelessness in the breath of the Spirit fits in very well with the curse placed by Mosaic law on the pictorial representation of living things. But how can one fail to see the immense riches which icons, stained-glass windows, statues and cathedrals, themselves teeming with works of art, have brought to religion? Now this brilliant flowering, cursed by the First Testament and emasculated by the Third—that of the Holy Ghost and the Acts of the Apostles—finds all its seeds and above all the climate it needs in the Testament of the Son.

"I remain a Christian, although converted unreservedly to the Spirit, so that the sacred breath does not sweep the distant horizons without being previously charged with seeds and humors by passing through the body of the Beloved. Before it becomes light, the Spirit must become warmth. Then it reaches its highest state of radiance and penetration."

CHAPTER VI

The Identical Twins

Paul

Kergrist's boat was spotted at daylight the next morning
smashed on the reef. The bodies of Franz and three of the mongol girls were washed up on the islands during the next week.
The other five girls vanished without a trace. The affair affected
everyone at the Pierres Sonnantes deeply but it was barely mentioned in the press and a hurried inquiry was quickly concluded.
If this had happened to normal children what an outcry would
have been raised throughout France! But for the mentally retarded, those remnants of humanity only kept alive at great expense by an obsessive scrupulosity, surely such an accident was
in fact a happy outcome? Of course, the contrast between the
scale of the tragedy as we lived through it hour by hour and the
indifference with which it was regarded by the world outside our
little community did not occur to me at the time. But I realized
it later on, in retrospect, and was confirmed in the idea that we—
the twins, with the innocents and by extension all the inhabitants

of the Pierres Sonnantes—were a tribe apart, obeying different
laws from other people, and therefore feared, hated and despised by them. Subsequent events have done nothing to dispel
this impression.

To begin with, the deep and unspoken understanding which
united Jean-Paul with Franz—and through him with the sixty innocents of St. Brigitte's—cannot be explained entirely by age or
physical association. That we were freaks, my twin brother and
I, is a fact which I managed to conceal from myself for a long
time, although I was secretly aware of it from my infancy. After
years of experience and reading many studies and reports on the
subject, it blazes across my life with a brilliance that twenty
years ago would have been my shame, my pride ten years ago
and which today I can contemplate unmoved.

No, man is not made for twinship, and as always in such cases
—I mean when you step outside the bounds of mediocrity (this
was what Uncle Alexandre maintained also about his homosexuality)—with exceptional strength you can rise to superhuman
heights, but capacities of an ordinary kind will land you in the
gutter. Infant mortality is greater among fraternal twins than
among non-twins, and greater among identical twins than among
fraternal. Height, weight, longevity, and even the chances of success in life are greater with non-twins than with twins.

But can one always be perfectly sure of distinguishing identical from fraternal twins? The books are quite definite: there is
never absolute proof of true twinship. At best one can only work
from the *apparent absence* of any difference which would throw
doubt on the twinship. But a negative proof has never been held
to establish certainty. In my view, true twinship is a matter of
conviction, a conviction strong enough to shape two lives, and
when I look back at my past, I cannot doubt the invisible but all-
powerful presence of this principle, so much so that I wonder
whether—except for such mythological pairs as Castor and Pol-
lux, Romulus and Remus, etc.—Jean and I are not the only really
identical twins there ever were.

That Jean-Paul was a monster was demonstrated in the second
place by what between ourselves we called the "circus." This depressing business, which repeated itself every time we had a visi-

tor, would start with exclamations of surprise at how alike we were and go on to the game of comparing, substituting and confusing. In fact, Maria-Barbara was the only person in the world who could tell us apart—except, as she admitted to us, when we were asleep, because then sleep erased all differences between us, as the rising tide obliterates all traces left by children on the sand at the end of the day. By Edouard, we were treated to a little piece of playacting—at least that is how I interpret his behavior today, for at the time it was painful and hurt us and, if we had had the heart to talk about it, we would have used a harsher word, lies or cheating. Edouard never could tell us apart, nor would he ever try to. One day he decided, half seriously, half as a joke: "One twin each. Maria-Barbara, you have Jean, since he is your favorite. For myself, I'll choose Paul." Now Maria-Barbara's favorite was me, at that very moment my mother was cuddling me in her arms, and it was Jean whom Edouard scooped up, startled and rather cross, from off the ground and pretended to carry off with him. After that, it became an established ritual and whenever either of us came within his reach, Edouard would seize hold of him indiscriminately, calling him "his" twin, his favorite, dandling him, giving him piggybacks, and having mock fights with him. The thing looked all right, because we were each of us his "favorite" in turn, but although he had sensibly given up calling us by our own names, and said Jean-Paul like everyone else, there was something fraudulent in his behavior that cut us to the quick. It was, naturally, when visitors were present that the pretense was especially upsetting. Because then he would display his assumed knowledge with complete confidence, confounding the baffled newcomer with assurances which half the time were wrong. At such times neither Maria-Barbara nor Jean-Paul would have dared give him away, but our discomfort must have been obvious.

"Monster" comes from the Latin *monstrare*. A monster is a creature that is demonstrated, put on show in circuses, fairs and so on, and we were not to escape this fate. We were spared the fair and the circus, but not the cinema, and in its most trivial form the advertising film. We must have been about eight years old when a summer visitor from Paris noticed us playing on the little beach at Quatre Vaux, which is where the Quinteux brook comes out. He came up to us, got us chattering, asking us how old we were, what we were called and where we lived, then went straight up the little stairway of eighty-five steps to La Cassine, whose roof was visible at the top of the cliff. Had he come by the road, he would have had to deal with a hostile Méline, who would undoubtedly have sent him packing. Emerging directly into the garden, he came upon Maria-Barbara surrounded by her "encampment" of deck chair, workbox, books, basket of fruit, spectacles, shawl, rugs, etc. As always when she was embarrassed or bothered, Maman concentrated on her work, paying only the slightest attention and returning evasive answers. Dear Maria-Barbara! It was her way of saying no, go away and leave me in peace! I never saw her go any further toward repulsing or rejecting anyone than this sudden absorption in some occupation, or even simply losing herself in contemplation of a flower or a cloud. Saying no was not something she was good at.

Edouard, who had seen from a distance, by Maria-Barbara's attitude, that she was stuck with an unwelcome visitor, came striding up to intervene. What the stranger had to say astonished him so much at first that he was temporarily speechless. The man's name was Ned Steward and he worked for a film publicity agency called Kinotop, whose business was mostly in making short advertising films put on in cinemas between the main features. He had noticed Jean-Paul on the beach and was asking permission to use him in one of his films. Edouard was highly indignant and let it show in his face, which always reflected whatever he was feeling as though on a screen. Steward made matters worse by mentioning the considerable rewards that we would certainly reap from the "performance," a word Edouard was to take up and produce ever after as though in quotation marks on the end of a pair of forceps. But Steward was shrewd and persistent and probably had some experience in such negotiations. He retrieved what seemed to be a hopeless situation by two masterstrokes. First, he offered to double the proposed sum and present it to St. Brigitte's. Secondly, he explained what kind of advertising he wanted to use us for. It was not, of course, for some commonplace product like shoe polish, salad oil, or puncture-proof tires. No indeed, the purpose he had in mind for us was a noble one, one for which we seemed, moreover, to be framed by destiny. Just before the holidays he had been put in charge of an advertising campaign for a brand of marine binoculars called Gemini. This was why he had been roaming along the North Sea coast in search of an idea. Well, he had found his idea. Why not put Gemini's reputation in the hands of twin brothers? There is a particular combination of silliness, humor and obtuseness by which Edouard was easily disarmed. I know it well because I am fairly susceptible to it myself. He saw in this business the germ of a good after-dinner story to tell his friends in Paris. Moreover, reading in his paper about the Dionne family in Canada and their quints who seemed to be a fairly profitable source of in-come, he had more than once teasingly asked Jean-Paul when he was going to settle down and make the family fortune. So he shut himself up with Steward and argued inch by inch the de-tails of a contract according to which we were to make three short, two-minute films for Gemini binoculars.

The shooting took more than a fortnight—the whole of our Easter holidays—and left us with an absolute horror of such "performances." I seem to remember that what we disliked most about it was a kind of absurdity which we felt very strongly, without being able to put it into words. They made us go over and over the same words, the same actions, the same short scenes ad nauseam, each time imploring us to be more *natural* than in the take before. Well, it seemed to us that we were more likely to be less and less *natural* because we were getting more tired, more irritable and more and more caught up in a meaning-less rigmarole. At eight years old we were to be forgiven for not knowing that naturalism—especially in matters artistic, and in this context we were actors playing a part—is something that can be acquired, worked up to, and is in fact nothing but the height of artifice.

The first film showed us one at a time, each with a telescope aimed at the horizon. Next, we were side by side, looking through the same pair of binoculars, one through the right lens, the other through the left. Finally we were standing three feet apart, this time each holding a pair of binoculars. The dialogue was made to fit the different stages. We had to say: "With one eye you don't see so well as with two . . . with two pairs of Gemini binoculars . . . you see even better than with one." There followed a close-up of the glasses, with our voices describing their various features. "The lenses—2CF—and prisms, made in England, are treated with a hundred percent magnesium fluoride for color correction and anti-glare. Ten times magnification. Fifty-millimeter objective lens. Don't forget those figures! Ten and fifty! Compare that with other makes! The eyepieces are curved for comfort, while the body is both light and very strong. It's made of aluminum. And they come in a grained-leather case, so your glasses are a luxury item, too."

This commentary was recorded separately but the difficulty lay in the precise timing needed to synchronize it with the pictures.

The second film put more emphasis on the wide angle of vision. We were seen scanning the horizon with opera glasses. Copy: "The sea is so big! You need to see a long way around to find what you are looking for. There's nothing more annoying than searching the horizon and never managing to catch anything interesting. Why? Because the visual angle of ordinary binoculars is so small. However powerful they are, they only show you a little bit at a time. With Gemini, there's no risk of that! They look wide! At one kilometer they have an angle of vision ninety-one meters wide. Like sailors, whose lives depend on it, look further afield with Gemini panoramic binoculars!" Then followed close-ups of the glasses and the commentary which was common to all three films.

The last film was in praise of Gemini's clarity. Two individual children—two child actors, a boy and a girl of about our age, were brought from Paris especially to do it—were seen walking in the country. The landscape around them was shown as though through their eyes, the picture, in short, of which they were the reverse angle. And this landscape was flat, with the unreal softness produced by compressing the perspectives on the screen. "We live in a neutral picture, without relief, in just two dimensions," mourned the commentary. "But things are not dull, like this. They have lumps and bumps, they go up and down and are sharp, pointed, hollow, interesting, exciting, alive, in fact." Meanwhile, the landscape was changing. There was a close-up of a flower, then of the remains of a picnic, and finally of the laughing face of a young peasant girl. And the flower, the food and the face were radiant with such a burning intensity of life that their immediacy and vitality burst out of the screen. This transformation was achieved mainly by altering the focal length of the camera. Whereas the individual children's vision had submerged everything in middling tones, with no differentiation, this time foreground and background alike were totally sacrificed, fuzzed into an indistinct blur against which the selected object of the close-up stood out with brutal clarity in its minutest details. Immediately afterward the reverse angle appeared. Jean-Paul had taken the place of the individual children and was pointing a pair of binoculars at the audience. "With Gemini binoculars," the commentary proclaimed triumphantly, "the third dimension is restored to you. With Gemini binoculars, things, landscapes, and women are visible in all their youth and beauty. You see the world in all its glory, and its glory warms your heart."

Then followed the usual technical details.

For a long time—and particularly during my adolescent years—I held it against Edouard that he had subjected us to the mortification of those film sessions which in some way set the seal on our "monstrousness." But with time—and especially thanks to the long, slow meditation on my whole past which my disability encourages—I see how much there was to be learned from that "performance," so that I have come to think that, for all his levity, insensitivity, and selfishness, Edouard was obeying our destiny in putting us through it.

To begin with, I find much food for thought in the continual alternation between the picture and its reverse angle, which seems to be the rule and the very rhythm of the cinematographic spectacle. The picture was a broader landscape, a deeper vision, a fruit, a tree, a face of incomparable, surrealistic brilliance. The reverse angle was the twins, and the glasses were no more than an attribute of them, their emblem, their equivalent in instrumental terms.

What did that mean if not that we were the possessors of a superior visionary power, the key to a better view of the world, a deeper insight, a better knowledge, possession, and penetration? All that playacting, in fact, had a premonitory value. It was a foretaste of that *geminate intuition* which for a long time was our strength and pride, which I lost when I lost my twin brother and which I am finding again, slowly now in solitude, having sought it in vain throughout the world.

As a bonus, Ned Steward left us a pair of Gemini binoculars. Only one. That was dead against the golden rule which decreed that we were always given two of everything, in spite of being twins. But Ned Steward was an outsider—worse than that, a clumsy oaf, because he might have arrived at that rule for himself, simply by watching us. The inequality did not matter, though, because only I was interested—and then quite passionately—in the optical instrument. I shall have more to say about that. Especially since Méline, who had put them out of harm's way, has just dug them out for me. So here I am again, scanning now the farthest horizon, now the long grass with the Gemini binoculars, just as I did twenty years ago. I still get great pleasure from it, all the more so of course by reason of my enforced inactivity.

I have said that Jean showed no interest in the glasses I loved so much. This may be the moment to mention the way his tastes and preferences differed slightly from mine even from our childhood. Many games and toys which instantly found their way to my heart were rejected by him, much to my distress. Of course, we coincided most of the time in a happy and harmonious unison. But there were times—and more and more frequently as we grew to adolescence—when he would dig his heels in and say no to something, even though it was in the direct line of twinship. It was in this way that he refused stubbornly to use a little battery-operated telephone with which we could have talked to one another from different rooms in the house. With no one to talk to, I did not know what to do with the toy, which I was delighted with and of which I had had such high hopes. But there was real anger in his rejection of one of those tandem bicycles that husbands and wives are to be seen pedaling out together on Sundays, got up in identical plus fours, roll-necked sweaters, and flat caps. It was true that he was willing to admit into our cell things which undoubtedly had a subtle bearing on our condition, but he could not bear too blatant references to our twinship.

He liked things whose function was clearly contradicted by being duplicated, but which we were given two of, against all apparent common sense, in accordance with our demands. For instance, the two little pendulum clocks to hang on the wall, imitations of Swiss cuckoo clocks, each with a little wooden bird that shot out twittering to mark the hours and half hours. Outsiders never failed to express surprise at those two identical clocks hanging on the same wall within a few inches of each other. "To do with being twins!" Edouard once told one of them. To do with being twins, in other words, one of the mysteries of twinship. But what no one realized, apart from Jean-Paul, was that Jean's clock persisted in chiming a few seconds *before* mine, even when the hands of both were in exactly the same position—seconds enough so that never, not even at midday or midnight, did the two chimes overlap. From a *singular,* which is to say a trivial point of view, a difference in the making is enough to explain the slight time lag. To Jean, it was something far different, what he called the "something or other," although he always refused to explain what he meant by it.

But even more than the clocks, he liked the barometer, of which we were likewise given two, as going further in the direction of twinship. It was a dear little wooden house with two doors and a figure to come out of each: a little man with an umbrella on one side and a little woman with a sunshade on the other, one forecasting rain, the other shine. But these, too, were slightly out of phase, so that Jean's little people were always ahead of mine, by twenty-four hours sometimes, so that occasionally they met, by which I mean that Jean's man would come out while my little lady was doing the same.

We had at least one passion in common, for things that brought us into direct contact with cosmic facts—clocks and barometers—but it seemed as if these only began to interest Jean

the moment they revealed a fault, some defect through which his
famous "something or other" could creep in. Presumably that is
why the binoculars—visually instruments of astronomically long
range but faultless accuracy—filled him only with indifference.

The phenomenon of the tides—which reach immense height in
our parts—was bound to divide us. Theoretically, it ought to assume a mathematical simplicity and regularity since it has its origin in the respective positions of the moon and the sun in relation to the earth: spring tides occur at times when the positions
of the moon and the sun are such as to counterbalance their respective attractions. When the solar and lunar tides are pulling
against one another, on the other hand, the rise and fall is only
slight. I should have found nothing more inspiring than to live
wholly in unison with this vast respiration of the sea—swimming,
fishing, walking along the beach—if only it had followed precisely the rational pattern I have just indicated. Far from it! The
tide is a clock run mad, suffering from a hundred parasitic
influences—the rotation of the earth, the existence of submerged
continents, the viscosity of the water and so on—that defy reason
and overset it. What is true one year is no longer so the year
after, what goes for Paimpol won't go for Saint-Cast or Mont-
Saint-Michel. It is the typical example of an astronomical system
of mathematical regularity, intelligible to the marrow, being suddenly warped, dislocated and fractured, and, while still continuing to function, doing so in an atmosphere of turbulence, and
troubled waters, with jumps, distortions and alterations. I am
convinced that it was this irrational element—and the appearance of life, freedom, and personality it gives—that attracted
Jean . . .

But there was something else which I can never quite explain to myself and which makes me suspect that there is one
aspect of the problem which still escapes me: it was the low
tides—and those alone—that drew him. Sometimes on summer
nights, at neap tides, I would feel him trembling in my arms. We
had no need to speak, I could feel—as though by *induction*—the
pull on him of the great, wet, salty expanse the ebb had just uncovered. Then we would get up and I would try to follow his

slim figure running over the ice-cold sands, then onto the warm, springy mud, newly uncovered by the tide. When we came back at dawn, the sand and salt and mud would be drying like puttees on our bare legs, like greaves that would crack and peel off as we moved.

Jean

On that point at least, Paul never got to the bottom of things. The capricious and unforeseeable aspect of the tides—in spite of their celestial springs—does not make up the whole of their charm, far from it. There is something else, not unrelated to that elemental force. What drew me so powerfully to the wet beach on the nights of neap tides was a kind of silent *cry* of helpless desolation that rose from the uncovered seabed.

The things that the ebb lays bare weep for the flood tide. The mighty glaucous mass fleeing toward the horizon has left exposed this living flesh, complex and fragile, which fears assault, profanation, scouring and probing; this batrachian body with its blistered, glandulous, warty skin, thick with papillae, with suckers and tentacles, shrinks before the nameless horror that is the absence of the saline medium, emptiness and wind. The thirsty foreshore, bared by the ebb, weeps for the vanished sea with all its streams, all its oozing pools, all its brine-swollen weeds, all its foam-capped mucosities. It is one vast lamentation, the weeping of the suffering shore, dying beneath the direct light of the sun with its terrible threat of drying out, unable to bear its rays except when broken, cushioned and fragmented by the liquid, prismatic depths.

And I run to them, moved by the mute appeal of those thousands upon thousands of thirsty mouths, and my bare feet recognize the seaweed, the banks of shingle, the razor shells, the pools of night sky traversed by unquiet ripples, the pounded shells embedded in the sand, the mudholes that send spirals of slime spurting up between my toes. The goal of my sprinting is simple but very far off, so that Paul, panting along behind me, is horrified at it. It is the thin line of phosphorescence shining there, a good hour's walk ahead, the slight surf of the low tide.

That is where one must go to find the living water with its murmured promise of infinity. I run into the wavelets, cooler than
the stagnant pools we have come through, with the winged spray
falling like heavy rain all about me. I am the forerunner, the herald of the marvelous good news. It spreads first deep down in
the sand where it is permeated by a subtle watery surge. Then it
is the waves that put out ever more invasive feelers toward the
shore. Rippling streams encircle the mud patches from all sides,
rounding ridges of pale sand, meeting, merging and gaining
strength from one another, creeping onward and onward, chuck-
ling to themselves as they join the pools into swirling arms. And
the covering of seaweed suddenly comes to life again and shakes
its green and black mane in the drag of a wave a little in advance of the rest.

The spring is returning. Far off, away beside the Ile des
Hébihens, where we were walking a short while ago, the sea
spreads confidently. We sit on the white sandy beach, both of us
splashed with mud and salted like herrings. Paul is happier now
that the familiar waves are breaking at our feet, licking us with
their frothy tongues. Paul is a man for when the tide is at the
full. Paul is the man for fullness of every kind, and for loyalties
too. He followed me, reluctantly, all the way to the horizon
where the ebb tide called me. Then we came back, like the Pied
Piper of Hamelin, drawing after us the myriad little wavelets of
the incoming tide. For the time being we are both of us calmed
and satisfied. In any case, fatigue sits heavy on us. Each of us
knows all that his twin brother is feeling. During those hours of
walking on the sands, each of us was being pulled in different,
almost opposite directions. Then we talked. Oh, not in the ordinary language in which two twinless people converse! We exchanged no remarks about sea horses and sea urchins. It was
simply that each expressed the way that he was being torn from
the common store. My cries, my groans and broken words indicated nothing more than the all-powerful attraction that the
great wailing emptiness of the shore abandoned by the tide exerted over me. Paul, on the other hand, mumbled and grumbled,
giving out waves of misery and boredom. Now that is over. Each
twin has dropped back into his mold—which is his twin brother.

But the beach is not the place for our oviform loving. We rise as one. Under our feet we feel the prickly tussocks of dry seaweed and when we stumble over one of those mats we lay bare its moist side with the sand fleas jumping out. The plank bridge. The path. La Cassine. Everything is still asleep, except that in one of the St. Brigitte's dormitories a faint light is burning. Our glory hole. Our clothes peel off. The egg. We curl up together head to tail, laughing to find ourselves so salty. Will we complete our seminal communion, or will sleep overcome our ritual?

P.S. *Laughing to find ourselves so salty* . . . Out of these last lines, only this phrase will, I think, be perfectly intelligible to the twinless reader. Because when two individuals laugh together—and only then—they come near to the mystery of cryptophasia. At such times they are using a pseudo-language, laughter, based on a common ground—stemming from a concatenation of shared experience—which, unintelligible in itself, has as its function to narrow the distance between their respective positions which divides them from that common base.

Paul

One of the nicest effects of our "monstrousness" was undoubtedly this cryptophasia, the unfathomable jargon we called Aeolian, which enabled us to talk together for hours on end without others present being able to understand a word we said. The cryptophasia which most real twins create between themselves constitutes for them a definite strength and source of pride in relation to other individuals. But in the majority of cases they pay a heavy price for this advantage since the geminate jargon can be seen clearly to develop at the expense of normal speech and so of social intelligence. Statistics have established that a rich, abundant and complex cryptophasia goes with an ordinary language that is poor, meager, and rudimentary. This imbalance is all the more serious because of the constant relationship that exists between sociability and intelligence on the one hand and the level of language development on the other. Here we put our finger on the drawback of exceptions, anomalies, and teratological forms which frequently possess some dazzling, superhuman gift, for this superiority has been purchased at the cost of some serious flaw on the most ordinary, basic level. I regarded myself for a long time as a superman. I still believe I am destined for something out of the common run. But I no longer conceal from myself—as how could I after my twofold amputation?—the terrible price I have had to pay for it.

The mistake made by all the psychologists who have dealt with the enigma of cryptophasia is to have considered it as an ordinary language. They have treated it as they would have done some African or Slavonic dialect, trying to amass a vocabulary and extract a syntax from it. This is the fundamental contradiction of translating a geminate phenomenon into individual terms. Geminate speech—wholly dictated and structured by twinship—cannot be equated with an individual language. To do so is to overlook the essence and retain only the incidental. For in Aeolian, *the words are incidental, silence is the essence.* That is what makes a geminate language a phenomenon absolutely incomparable to any other linguistic form.

Of course we had a vocabulary of sorts. The words we made up were of an original kind, at once more specialized and more general than ordinary words. The word *bork,* for instance. We meant by it anything that floats (boat, stick, cork, wood, foam and so forth), but not a generic term for all floating objects because the extension of the word was limited, relating only to a finite number of objects, those which we knew. What we were doing, in short, was to compress into one both the abstract term and all the concepts understood to belong to it. We were unfamiliar with the general concept of *fruit.* But we had a word— *grapple*—to describe apple, grape, gooseberry, and pear. A sea creature in the abstract had no place in our dictionary. We would say *crish* for fish, crab, gull or oyster and it may give a better idea of the way it worked if I add that one and the same name—Peter—would refer either to a particular one of our brothers and sisters or to all of them together as opposed to ourselves.

One does not have to be a philologist to understand that Aeolian, taking no account of either abstract concepts in general or the wealth of concrete terms, was only an embryonic, and psychologically very rudimentary language, such as might have been spoken by primitive men.

Once again, however, that was not the essence of Aeolian, and observers who got no further than its impoverished jargon were not merely unable to enter into the secret of our conversations but missed the whole principle of the phenomenon of cryptophasia.

In every dialogue there is an explicit part—the words and phrases exchanged which may be understood by anyone—and an implicit part which belongs to the participants alone, or to a limited group to which they belong. Moreover, the conditions of time and place common to both participants suffice to delineate one implicit element which is particularly superficial and easily shared. If, for example, I look up at the sky and say: "The weather's changing," I assume a familiarity with the preceding period of fine weather whose end I am predicting.

In its continual alternation between implicit and explicit—in varying proportions—a dialogue is like a floating iceberg in which the waterline varies from one pair of interlocutors to another, and in the course of one conversation. In the case of *individual* participants, the submerged part of the dialogue is comparatively small, while its visible part is large enough to form a complete and coherent whole, intelligible to the ears of a third party. Aeolian, on the other hand, is marked by an abnormally large implicit part, so that the explicit always remains *below* the minimum necessary to make it decipherable by outside listeners. But there, too, the iceberg's waterline is continually moving up and down as the twins approach nearer to their common base or move further away from it, drawn by their environment, the explicit part of Aeolian compensating for the distance from the common base and being proportional to it. But such fluctuations always keep on this side of the degree of explanation needed in *individual* dialogues. Aeolian starts from the silence of visceral communion and rises to the verge of the speech used by society, but without ever reaching it. As a dialogue, it is absolute, because impossible to share with a third party. It is a dialogue of silences, not of words. An absolute dialogue composed of *ponderous* words addressed to one interlocutor only, the speaker's

identical twin. The more people words are understood by, and
the more those people differ among themselves, the lighter, more
spontaneous, abstract and inconsequential they become and the
fewer sanctions and preconceptions are attached to them. What
individual people, antiphrastically no doubt, called our "Aeolian" was in actual fact a leaden language because every word
and silence it contained was rooted in the common visceral mass
to which we both belonged. A language without diffuseness, radiating nothing, the concentration of everything that was most
private and secret in us, shot out always point-blank and gifted
with a frightening incisiveness, I am quite sure it was to escape
its crushing weight that Jean fled. To that unerring bombardment, penetrating to the very marrow of his bones, he preferred
the minuets, madrigals, and gentle dalliance of a twinless society. How shall I blame him?

P.S. Human speech stands halfway between the wordlessness
of animals and the silence of the gods. But between that wordlessness and that silence there may exist an affinity, even a
promise of development, which the arrival of the word obliterates forever. The animal wordlessness of a baby might perhaps
blossom into a divine silence if his apprenticeship to the tumult
of society did not set him irrecoverably on a different road. Because there were two of us to share it, our original wordlessness
had exceptional, fabulous and divine opportunities to blossom.
We let it ripen between us, it grew up with us. What would have
come of it but for Jean's betrayal, but for the twofold amputation? No one will ever know. But tied to this sofa, it is that silence, teeming with significance, that I am striving to recover;
more than that, to bring to a perfection of greater brilliance even
than it had attained on that accursed day. That I should be alone
in undertaking it is the slightly crazy paradox of my venture. But
am I really alone?

Paul

You playing, Bep? I pronounce the childish injunction softly, the
incantatory formula, framed misleadingly as a question, which
was in fact a call to order, a formal summons to rejoin the gem-

inate ranks and play the great geminate game, perform its rites and respect its ceremonies. But those three words have lost their magic. I go over our history hour by hour, I search and search and I draw up a list of everything that happened to you, my twin brother, which was likely to have interfered with the game of Bep, everything that sowed in you the seeds of discord which later, years later, were destined to burst the geminate cell asunder.

In doing so I come upon the memory of that *baptism of the fair*, an encounter I would long ago have forgotten if it had not been so terribly important to you. My refusal, clear and decisive, straight from the bottom of my heart, would have put an end to it once and for all if only you, for your part, had not said yes, in a way: oh, not yes outright, in so many words, but what was no less serious an acceptance from your inmost self, the expression of your own inevitable bent.

It was some years before the war. So we might have been about eight years old. We had been spending a few days alone with Edouard in Paris and when the time came for us to go back to Brittany, the family car showed signs of breaking down on the western outskirts of Paris, at Neuilly, to be exact. Edouard turned to the nearest garage. I have forgotten the owner's name —I daresay I never even heard it—but all the same no detail of that evening or that memorable night escapes me. It was called the Garage du Ballon, after the grotesque bronze statue in the Place de la Porte des Ternes commemorating the part played by the balloonists at the siege of Paris in 1871. I have not seen anything more hideous than the owner of that garage. He was a giant of a man. Black hair was plastered over his low forehead. His sallow face was barred by a pair of glasses with lenses as thick as paperweights. But what impressed me most of all was his hands. The hands of a plasterer or a strangler—except that they were not white or red but black with engine oil. We watched him tinker with the engine of our old Renault, then give curt orders to some kind of Arab. I was seized with disgust, and with a vague terror too, because he seemed to be endowed with colossal strength, not merely physical, let alone moral—oh, no!— but a strength that lived in him, of which he seemed to be the repository and servant, but which did not belong to himself. It was, I think, what is called destiny. Yes, there was a fateful heaviness in him.

You seemed to find him funny. In a lighthearted way that appalled me, you seemed ready to laugh at anything unusual in his behavior. Which there soon was. A little Simca which had been badly parked got in his way and all of a sudden he seized hold of its rear end, lifted it up and put it by the wall. You looked at me as though to make sure of a complicity which I denied you, and then you started to splutter. But you laughed out openly the next moment when he spread his hands out wide, stared for an instant at his great greasy mitts and then did a horrible thing: he lifted them up to his face and smelled them. It was then most of all that the idea of his being fated impressed itself on me, because it really seemed as though the giant were reading his own dreadful destiny in his hands, like a palmist, except that it was not written there in fine lines but carved in thick grease, in power cables, black, brutal and irresistible.

When the three of us left the garage I hoped that we had done with the nightmare figure, although it had been arranged that we could not collect our car until noon the next day. We went to the post office and sent a telegram to Maria-Barbara. When we emerged onto the pavement again, Edouard was a changed man. Delight in the unexpected, in the evening before us, in our freedom, made him sparkle like a glass of champagne. Dear, simple Edouard! Having done his duty like a good husband by sending that telegram to the Pierres Sonnantes, he suddenly felt on holiday and in a mood to enjoy himself. He snuffed the air, stroking his small moustache with one finger, and smiled a knowing little smile.

"Darlings," he said, "the only problem we have to solve now is to find a restaurant worthy of us!"

He found one very quickly of course, specialist in good food that he was and accustomed to sorting out at a glance the truth from the lies in those menus put up outside eating houses. The dinner, to be quite truthful, was rather long—and a bit too lavish —but Edouard's enjoyment was so infectious that it did not occur to us to be bored, and we even forgave him on the spot for making us go through our hated act of the twins no one could tell apart, for the benefit of the headwaiter.

It was dark when we came out. Once again, Edouard snuffed the wind eagerly. He must have caught a breath of something because he held up one finger and said, "A fair! A traveling fair! Shall we go?"

He was already dragging us off gleefully. He was certainly out to enjoy himself that day!

I have always loathed fairs. They represent in their most violent form the separateness and exile which are the great problem of my life. On the one side is the anonymous crowd, merged into a screeching darkness in which everyone feels safer the more he conforms to the norm. On the other, stuck up on stands, bathed in harsh lights, are the ones who are on show, the monsters, fixed in their sorrow and loneliness, whether it is the little dancer in her faded tutu, her thighs marbled with cold, or the Negro boxer with the jaw and arms of a gorilla. And why not us, the twins no one can tell apart, an object of amazement, curiosity and laughter for every non-twin?

The answer to that question was spelled out to us harshly that night in a booth Edouard led us into, which was offering "some natural phenomena unique in this world." Alongside such clumsy frauds as a little girl with her lower half encased in a scaly corset sitting in an aquarium pretending to be a mermaid, was a sinister display of two or three genuine freaks—a Lilliputian couple, the fattest woman in the world, the human snake. But what drew Jean-Paul like a moth to the flame was a glass-fronted cupboard exhibiting a hideous collection of mummified corpses (or claiming to be, because I suspect now that they were really models made of wax and leather) of the most fantastic Siamese twins in teratological history. There to be wondered at were xiphopagi (joined at the breastbone), pyropagi (attached at the hips), meiopagi (connected by the forehead), cephalopagi (stuck together at the back of the neck) and as the culminating spectacle the famous Italian derodymi, the Tocci—with two heads, two legs and four arms attached to a single body.

Can Edouard possibly have failed to realize how hateful that exhibition might be to us? We stayed glued like flies to the glass and I like to think that his shoving us to get us to move on was as much from shame as ordinary impatience. But I still believe it was that encounter with the Siamese twins that first gave you, my twin brother, the idea that twinship might be nothing more than a disability, a deformity. The great test awaited you a few yards further on.

It was you who saw him first.

"Oh, look! The man from the garage!"

He had changed his dirty overalls for a pair of dark trousers and a thick navy blue shirt, the kind you always suspect hasn't been washed because it doesn't show the dirt. But his coal heaver's build and the thick glasses when he turned his head toward us were enough to identify him beyond the possibility of a mistake. Did he recognize us? I think so—especially since identical twins are not easy to overlook—but he chose to ignore us.

We were quite close to one of those trials of strength which consist in pushing a little cart loaded with a variable number of lead weights up a steeply sloping track. A ship which acts as a target at the top of the track tips over if the cart reaches it and hits it. The man from the garage slapped a note into the hand of the man taking the money and promptly made him put the maximum load on the cart. Then, with no apparent effort of his great arms, as thick as thighs, he sent it crashing noisily into the side of the ship, which toppled over. Having seemingly exhausted the interest of that mediocre amusement, he wandered off.

You had joined the little group surrounding the contestants in applauding the garageman's exploit. Edouard wanted to take us on the scenic railway but we had to go after you because you were following the garageman. That was how we came to a tall, circular booth, completely enclosed, bearing in enormous letters the short, mysterious word ROTOR. The Rotor had two entrances, a smart one with a ticket counter leading to a lot of wooden tiers, and another, humbler one at ground level which was free. It was this second entrance, rather like the passage for the wild beasts in a Roman circus, that the garageman was making for. He took off his glasses and slipped them into his pocket, then bent to go inside. You went after him, along with a few rough-looking youths.

I gazed up at Edouard in amazement. Were we going to follow you into that hole or let you venture in alone? Edouard
smiled and winked at me and led me up the steps to the official
entrance. I was temporarily reassured. He knew the Rotor and
knew that you were not in any danger. But then why hadn't we
followed you?

The greater part of the booth consisted of a huge, upright
cylinder. The paying customers looked down into this sort of
witches' cauldron and could see the others—the ones who had
gone in the little door—gathered at the bottom, who were the
show. So we were able to wave down to you. You looked all
right and were sticking close to the garageman. There were half
a dozen of you in the bottom of the pit, skinny youths for the
most part, so that you two attracted attention, you because you
looked so fragile and the garageman because he was so huge.
Then the agony began.

The cylinder started to whirl around at ever-increasing speed.
Very soon the centrifugal force was impossible to resist and was
forcing you to the side. Caught up as though by a whirlwind,
you were stuck there like a fly upon a wall, flattened by an invisible mass of ever-increasing pressure. Suddenly the floor beneath
your feet fell away to a depth of some six feet or so. But you did
not need it. You were suspended in space with a deadly, intolerable weight on your face, chest, and abdomen, growing worse
with every moment. To me, the sight was terrible because I felt
your anguish raised, as always, to geminate power. You were
lying on your back, crucified, not just by your hands and feet but
by the entire surface area, in fact by the whole volume of your
body. Not one atom of flesh escaped the torment. Your left hand
was pressed against your side, was one with it; your right hand,
up level with your face, was clamped against the metal, palm
outward, at an awkward angle which must have been painful for
you, but no effort on your part could have made it budge a fraction of an inch. You had your head turned to the right, facing
the garageman—and that was surely not by accident. You never
took your eyes off him, and admittedly he was something worth
looking at.

Slowly, with movements whose clumsiness betrayed the colos-

sal effort they were costing, he had bent his knees, brought his
feet up to his hips and was starting, by what miracle of willpower I dare not think, to get himself into a crouching position. I
saw his hands creep toward his knees, slide along his thighs, and
meet and clasp. Then his whole body came unstuck from the
wall and tilted forward as though he were about to fall headlong. But the centrifugal force held him back. The crouching
body was unfolding slowly and I realized to my utter amazement
that he was trying to get up, that he was meaning to stand and
was succeeding, and striving against the invisible, giant heel that
was crushing you all, back bent and pushing with his legs but
rising little by little, like Atlas bowed beneath the burden of the
earth but straightening slowly and thrusting it from his shoulders, he was now upright, straight as a die but horizontally, his
arms pressed to his body, feet together, being carried at nightmare velocity around that infernal drum. But this was nothing
yet.

Because he had hardly succeeded in this laborious maneuver
before he embarked on another. Slowly, he bent his knees,
leaned over, crouched again and, to my horror, I saw him stretch
out his left hand toward your right, grasp it, detach it from the
metal wall and pull you toward him, at the risk, so it seemed to
me, of tearing you apart. He succeeded in sliding his left arm
under your shoulders, then got his right below your knees, and
with an effort even more intense than before, began again to
stand upright. The most frightening part of it was his face, horribly distorted by the centrifugal force. His hair clung to his head
as though plastered down by a heavy rainstorm. His bluish eyelids, monstrously extended, stretched down as far as his high,
gypsy cheekbones, and worst, worst of all his distorted cheeks,
slackly distended, made pouches of skin flapping against his
neck under his lower jaw. And you, you lay in his arms, very
pale, with closed eyes, apparently dead, your death sufficiently
explained by the threefold ordeal you had just been through,
being crushed against the wall, then torn from its invisible hold
and now hugged in the arms of that prehistoric animal with its
rubbery gargoyle's face.

I realized that the cylinder was losing speed when I saw the other crucified figures slipping gradually down to the ground and collapsing, one by one, like broken dolls, prevented from rising still by the rotation which was sweeping them round. Meanwhile, the garageman jumped to the floor, astonishingly lightly, leaning forward to counteract the still noticeable effect of the centrifugal force. He did not take his eyes off the colorless, lifeless form of my twin brother cradled in his arms. When the cylinder had stopped completely, he set you down on the ground with a gentleness that was both tender and regretful.

He must have been among the first to leave, for we did not see him again when we went to meet you at the door below. You, however, seemed pretty perky, basically rather proud of your adventure. Edouard, who must have been somewhat anxious, expressed his relief by joking and exclaiming. Just then I saw everything around me start to swim. A sick dizziness swept over me. I collapsed in a faint at Edouard's feet. Poor Edouard! He could not get over it!

"Well, I never," he grumbled, "these two! First there was Jean . . . and now here's Paul. There's no understanding any of it!"

I think I can understand some of it now, but it has taken me years and a thousand trials to reach this glimmer of light. I have fought hard against the prejudice of blaming your defection on your filthy love affair with Denise Malacanthe. I knew that was taking too short a view, looking too near home, that the betrayal went further back, to a more innocent age, because everything is played out in the limbo of childhood and the gravest sins are always committed in all innocence. Thinking it over now, I am inclined to attach a decisive importance to that fair, to the meeting with that hideous giant and the way he tore you from the invisible suction of the centrifuge and carried you off.

Every word in that last paragraph deserves to be weighed and analyzed. The *fair*, for instance, from the Latin *feria*, a holiday, which is to say the rollicking temptation of a break from the geminate cell, bringing with it that sense of somewhere beyond, the something or other, that wonderful eagerness for far-off things that you have so often dinned into my ears.

But most of all it is the figure of the garageman, his stature and mysterious behavior, that I can read now like an open book.

That man, little brother, carried solitude, individualism, total, ruthless dedication to a particular destiny, everything, in short, that is the very opposite of ourselves, everything that goes against the very essence of twinship, to its ultimate conclusion. His behavior, his exploit are only too easily interpreted. He wrenched you away as a crab is plucked from its hole, as a child is reft from its mother's womb in labor, and raised you in his arms, took you over and made you share in that monstrous pose —*standing horizontally*—squeezed by a colossal force that annihilated gravity. That man was a slave, and not just a slave but a murderer, and I need no other proof than his gigantic size.

Now comes the solemn moment to let you into a brand-new, marvelous secret, and a joyful one too, which has just been revealed to me and which concerns the two of us, and us alone, and magnifies us. We have always been thought of as little, you and I. They said of us as babies that we were small but very lively. And we have never outgrown our supposed smallness. All through school we were top of our class for work and bottom for height, and by the time we were grown up our five feet six inches put us in the jockey class. Well, it is all wrong! We are not small, we are just right, we are normal, because *we are* innocent. It is the others, the twinless, who are abnormally large, because their height is their curse, the physical blemish befitting their guilt.

Listen to this wonder, and consider its vast implications: every man has a twin originally. Every pregnant woman carries *two* children in her womb. But the stronger will not tolerate the presence of a brother with whom he will have to share everything. He strangles him in his mother's belly and, having strangled him, he eats him, then comes into the world alone, stained with that original crime, doomed to solitariness and betrayed by the stigma of his monstrous size. Mankind is made up of ogres, strong men, yes, with stranglers' hands and cannibal teeth. And these ogres roam the world, in desperate loneliness and remorse, having by their original fratricide unleashed the torrent of crime and violence which we call history. We alone, you understand, are innocent. We alone came into this world hand in hand, a smile of brotherhood on our lips.

Unhappily, the world of ogres into which we fell instantly besieged us on all sides. Do you remember the half-buried anchor off a schooner, out beyond the Hébihens, which was only uncovered by the big equinoctial tides? Each time we would find it rustier and more corroded, more encrusted with weeds and little shells, and we used to wonder how many years it would be before salt and water got the better of that great creature of steel, forged to defy time and weather. Twins dropped from heaven are like that anchor. Their vocation is eternal youth, eternal love. But the corrosive atmosphere of the twinless condemned by their loneliness to dialectical loves attacks the pure metal of twinship. We ought not to grow old, did you know that? Aging is the deserved fate of the twinless who must one day make way for their children. As a sterile and eternal pair, united in a perpetual loving embrace, twins—if they remained pure—would be as changeless as the constellations.

I was appointed to guard the geminate cell. I have failed in my duty. You fled from a symbiosis which was not love but constraint. The twinless beckoned you away. The strongest of them took you up in his arms from the bottom of a witches' cauldron of a gigantic centrifuge. He held you over a grotesque and fearsome baptismal font. You received your baptism of the fair. From that time onward you were destined for desertion. Denise Malacanthe and Sophie after her only gave impetus to your flight.

Thou shalt love thy neighbor as thyself. I wonder what the twinless understand by that primary commandment of Christian morality. Because only the last two words are decipherable. As thyself? Is that to say that each person should love himself with a love that is true, generous, charitable, noble, and disinterested? An unintelligible paradox to the twinless who can only conceive of self-love as a limitation on outgoingness toward others, as a withdrawal, a miserly withholding in deference to the selfish claims of personal advantage. The twinless are all too familiar with that kind of self-love and they have some clever sayings to express it, which highlight its caricaturish ugliness. "Charity begins at home." "Blow your own trumpet." "God helps those who

help themselves." Like it or not, they are reminded of that caricature every time they look in their mirrors. How many of them
can feel a surge of delight when they wake up in the morning
and see the face in their glass all smudged and puffy after some
hours spent in the absolute solitude of their sleep? All the acts of
their toilet, comb, razor, soap and water, are so many pathetic
attempts to haul themselves out of the abyss of loneliness into
which the night has cast them and return honorably to society.

While we twins . . . The impulse that takes us out of ourselves, the surge of our youth, the gift of our vital force to those
around us, this fine, generous fountain is directed first and
foremost—and exclusively—to one another. Nothing is held back,
everything is given and yet nothing is lost, it is all kept in a wonderful balance between the other and oneself. Love thy neighbor
as thyself? That impossible bet expresses what is deepest in our
hearts and the law by which they beat.

CHAPTER VII

The Philippine Pearls

Alexandre

The Wolf's Lair, the nice little keeper, Bernard, and Adèle, his elephant in heat, the apologetic police inspector and the fiery hell of Issy-les-Moulineaux, Thomas Drycome and the ruah running through the three Testaments—I certainly did not waste my time during my forty-eight hours in Paris! And yet that welter of encounters and revelations is overlaid in my memory with a dreary, childish wail which goes so deep that it reduces all the rest to the level of pointless anecdote. I did not go near the church of Saint-Gervais, I did not look up at the darkened window in the rue des Barres which would let me believe that my poor darling was sleeping while I prowled the streets. Yet that return to Paris has exacerbated my small sorrow nonetheless, and overwhelmed me with fond, heartrending memories.

One of those memories is probably one of the earliest I have now, for it goes back to a time when I was two or three years old. A woman who is still young and has a little boy of that age lives with him in an intimacy more private and more exquisite than any she can experience with a sister or a husband. He is no longer altogether a baby. He no longer wets himself. He toddles like a bunny. The whole gamut of human emotions is reflected in his baby face, from pride to jealousy. Yet he is still so small! He is not yet a man, nor even a boy. He cannot talk yet, he will not remember anything.

I, however, do remember. When my father and brothers had left for the office or for school, we would be left alone, Maman and I. She would go back to bed again and I would clamber up onto the big double bed with shrieks of joy. I would launch myself at her, pushing my head between her breasts and trampling her soft, maternal stomach furiously with my chubby legs. She would laugh, breathless with surprise, and hug me to her to contain my frantic energy. There would be a loving tussle and in the end I would be vanquished. So much warm softness got the better of my eagerness. I would settle back instinctively in the same place into the fetal posture that still came naturally to me—and fall asleep.

Later on she would run her bath, and when she had turned off the taps would sit me in the water which came up to my chin. I would sit very straight and still, knowing from experience that if my behind slipped on the bottom of the bathtub I should get a mouthful of water. Then in a little while Maman would come and sit in it as well. This was no small matter because then the water would rise several centimeters and Maman would have to lift me up and set me on her lap before I went under. It is chiefly my fright as the water came up to my nose that has kept the memory so vivid and enabled it to survive so many years. It is not the kind of thing one makes up. For many years later I recalled the incident in front of the family and was surprised to see Maman, red with embarrassment, deny furiously that it had ever taken place. I realized too late that that memory was one of a secret store which I shared with her, and that I had just committed an unforgivable sin in betraying it. I ought never to have mentioned it, even alone with her. Between every couple there is some tacit and sacred reticence of the kind. If one of the pair breaks silence, something else is broken irretrievably.

Another memory, not so old, is just as close to me because of
its connection with my small sorrow. I must have been about ten.
One evening, Maman found me in tears, crushed by a cruel, inexhaustible misery. She tried to put her arms around me but I
repulsed her fiercely. "Oh no, not you! Not you of all people!"
She questioned me, anxiously, trying to understand. At last I
consented to explain.

"I'm crying because one day you're going to die."

"But of course I'm going to die, my darling, just like everyone.
But not now, later, not for a very long time perhaps."

My tears flowed faster than ever . . . "Of course, but later."
Of the two statements I was only prepared to take in the first,
which alone was true, unshakable, absolute. The other—"not
now, later"—was unacceptable, deceitful, evasive. It took all an
adult's frivolity to be able to forget that "of course" and remember only "later." To the child, living in the absolute, the "of
course" is timeless, immediate, and it is the only real truth.

I returned to my two hotels, the Terminus and the Cranes, with
the satisfaction of Ulysses returning to Ithaca after the Trojan
War and the Odyssey. My first night was, very properly, for the
Terminus, because I like a journey to end in just that kind of station hotel, which marks the end of one's travels quite as finally as
the buffers that the engine of my train ran up against. For a
wanderer like me, condemned to furnished rooms, there is something reassuringly final about a hotel called Terminus. One takes
what one can get.

The work has not made much progress during my absence—
actually very short, although it seems long to me because of the
incidents and encounters in Paris which have filled it, and of
course a good third of the men I had signed on at the beginning
have melted away. This brought me back to the Crane Drivers'
Rest, which suddenly proved a providential source of supply.
There I took on all the tramps I could find—starting with Eustache Lafille who is going to resume his post as gutter at the bottom of the pit—and including, in accordance with some vague
suspicion of a plan, Daniel, who is to help him in some way or
other. It doesn't matter. The main thing is that I have them both

together in my Devil's Hole, my quarry and my quarry's quarry. How they sing within me, they are so sweet in my mouth, those three words, the threefold repetition of those lovely sounds. The hotel has become my domain and its comical fauna "Surin's gang," whose daily comings and goings mutate into meetings or vigils every night. Work over, I look on from a distance, an approved spectator, before making my way back to the Terminus. The specter of the incineration plant continues to inspire terror, and I have not breathed a word about my visit to Issy because what I have to say would have horrified my men and also because that visit might have made them suspicious of me. (How could I explain to anyone the sort of curiosity which drove me to Issy?)

The idea of a strike is insinuating itself into the thick skulls of these men. Slowly but surely, one by one, they are coming around to the principle of some action aimed at extracting from the council a formal undertaking to abandon the plan for an incineration plant. But of course what is needed is to make an impact on people's minds, and the strikers' action—or rather inaction—will not be directed at my site. All hopes are pinned on the garbage men and the great accumulation of rubbish which their stopping work will produce throughout the city. Talks are in progress with their representatives. Their stumbling block is the disparity of objectives in a strike involving the whole of the corporation. The incineration plant holds no terrors for the garbage men who take their loads there as to any other depot. On the other hand, they are asking for wage increases, shorter working hours—at present fifty-six hours a week—free issue of working clothes—overalls, rubber boots, heavy-duty gloves, and cap—and lastly for the speeding up of the replacement of the ordinary trucks with crushers. The site workers have been obliged to accept this package of demands which is in danger of perverting their action against the incineration plant, because without it no garbage men! The strike is to be in ten days' time.

Last Sunday as I drew near the Cranes I was intrigued by a curious coming and going of men and women in slippers and dressing gowns between the hotel and a dirty brick building some hundred and fifty yards away down an empty side street. This was the municipal bathhouse and, upon my word, some of the inmates of the Cranes like to have a wash now and then and go along in their "morning dress" to this ablutionary soup kitchen.

I had an urge to try it, partly to complete my education in the ways of the working class and partly in the vague hope of meeting Eustache and Daniel there. So, deserting the Terminus for once, I slept in my room at the Cranes and this morning, swathed in an embroidered silk dressing gown, with green suede moccasins on my feet, I followed the grimy, straggling procession shuffling toward the squat brick building.

The baths on the ground floor are reserved exclusively for ladies—by what logic, I wonder? We buy a ticket—twenty-five centimes—and go up to the floor above, where the men go for their showers. At least a hundred customers are waiting patiently on hard wooden benches in a steamy haze. However, I make out several separate groups, some of whom are strangers to the society of the Cranes. Another trait to add to my picture of the poor: an instinctive tendency to form groups according to race, origin or even trade—but especially race, the great divider—which cease to ignore one another only in order to hate. But everyone is in pajamas or dressing gowns with hairy beards and seven days' dirt on their skins, already turning sticky with the steam. Of Daniel and Eustache, not a sign, and I am beginning to wonder what I am doing there. A one-eyed giant in an undervest and white trousers calls out a number each time a customer leaves a cubicle. Then he hammers on any doors that stay closed longer than eight minutes and threatens to drag out the dawdlers in their skins. From some of the cubicles doleful singing mingles with the rising steam, to be silenced at once by volleys of abuse from the adjoining cubicles. The sounds of water, the steam, the ragged, half-dressed crowd, all go to make up an unreal atmosphere, and it is as though in a dream that I suddenly see a door open and Eustache and Daniel come out, damp and pink, jostling one another with an air of complicity. That brief apparition takes my breath away. So one can share a cubicle with a companion? After all, why not, if that will speed up the backlog of customers? But I am reeling from the blow, I am suffering from

a two-edged jealousy—the foreseeable but unforeseen consequence of the quarry's quarry. I feel abandoned, rejected, betrayed, because it is quite clear there would have been no room
for me in that shower cubicle where God knows what has been
going on! There is definitely nothing more for me to do here.
Only how to get away? More than half these people know me, I
have certainly done myself some good by showing myself among
them; if I were to go away without going into one of the cubicles, there would be questions asked, they would think me peculiar, the unforgivable sin. Because in these backward, irregular
circles a gentle madness, eccentricity and originality are ferociously condemned. A piece of soap has slid out from under a
door. The door opens a crack and a bare arm reaches out and
gropes for the soap. It has almost reached it when a humorous
kick sends it a good yard away. At that the door opens wide and
a little man who would be stark naked except that he's as furry
as a bear pops out swearing, to be greeted by shouts of laughter
which are redoubled when he shows his behind bending over to
retrieve his soap. This little interlude restores my temper slightly
—it takes so little, just an asshole! I give up the idea of leaving.
Besides, five minutes later an amazing scene breaks out. The
tickets are numbered in six figures but the one-eyed man calls
out only the last three, which are all that change that morning.
Now what happens is that when number 969 is called two men—
a Jew and an Arab—get up simultaneously and start arguing and
waving their tickets. The giant rolls his eye at them and shrugs.
But by this time a third and a fourth customer are coming up,
shouting that they too have 969. In a few seconds all the men in
the room are on their feet, shouting and waving their arms. Then
a great roar is heard and they all fall back before a blind man
who shakes his white stick and demands to be told instantly the
number of his ticket. He is surrounded: "969!" several voices cry.
At that there is a rush for the stairs to demand an explanation
from the ticket office. Shouts, threats, abuse, stamping of feet
and muttering. In a little while they all come back again in a
sudden quiet, still broken here and there by growls of anger.
There was the explanation, elementary, obvious and irrefutable:
all this morning's tickets start with the figures 696, the first three

figures the one-eyed man never calls out because they are the same for everybody. But when it came to the number 696 969, each one had only to turn his ticket upside down to make it end in 969. Which most of the customers had managed to do.

For three days now the garbage men's strike has been strewing its splendors along every street in Roanne. In honor of what festival, one wonders, have these writhing, multicolored shrines been erected before every house, rising sometimes as high as the second-floor windows, so that pedestrians walk in a kind of trench between the building and a picturesque barricade. It is a new kind of Corpus Christi, Corpus Ganesh, the trunked idol whose totem is the rat. Because, of course, the rats from the depots, deprived of fresh food, have invaded the town and their black hordes are spreading panic in the side streets at night. Nor are they the only representatives of the dumps, for all my friends from the Cranes, in enforced idleness on account of the strike, stroll about in their Sunday best. We greet one another with knowing winks, we gather in admiring little groups in front of some particularly effective piles of rubbish, solid sculptures, still warmly redolent of the everyday life from which they sprang, which might be used with advantage to replace the dreary official statuary in the town squares. Even the cars parked alongside the heaps seem to fade and look dull and impoverished next to this riot of colors and shapes. I ought to be sated with refuse and to have exhausted its charms. Yet there are times when I am genuinely amazed at the exuberance and invention being displayed in the gutters. I think I see why. You can say what you like in favor of the crushers, and we could certainly not do without them considering how lightweight, voluble and voluminous is the rubbish of the rich. But that is just it! Those trucks are smotherers and extinguishers and the stuff they disgorge onto the dumps—admirable though it may still be—is battered, humiliated and robbed of its worth by this barbarous treatment. For the first time, thanks to this strike, it has been given to me to see and to praise rubbish in is primordial freshness and innocence, spreading its flounces unrestrainedly.

There is something far beyond mere aesthetic satisfaction in

the winged happiness that carries me about the town. There is a
sense of conquest, the satisfaction of ownership. For the centrifugal motion which drives urban refuse outward to the periphery
of the town, to the waste ground and public dumps, along with
stray dogs and an entire fringe society, that motion has been
stopped by the strike and has started to go into reverse. The garbage has taken over. That is the literal truth. But alongside it,
the refuse workers strut about the streets and by night the rats
carry all before them. The heterosexual middle class cowers in
terror. The city council is in constant session. It is going to capit-
ulate. That is inevitable. It is a pity. Because then everything
will go back to its execrable order. The garbage men will be a
little less badly treated. By a process of which history provides
more than one example, the beginnings of a revolution will be
forestalled by the damned of the earth being absorbed into middle class.

This memorable strike is still exciting the little world of the garbage men. Every night the common room of the Cranes is the
scene of noisy meetings at which I observe the keenest hostility
springing up between rival bodies. For some time, a man called
Hallelujah—in whom I have recognized the old blind man from
the municipal baths—has been figuring prominently. He used to
be a garbage man and has some standing in that field on account
of his experience, his loud mouth, and also his disability, gained
on the field of honor—which is to say by getting the contents of a
bottle of acid broken by the crusher full in his face. The strike
has given him status and he uses it unrestrainedly, in particular
to confound the ragpickers, who are the garbage men's natural
enemies.

Last night, he got the better of the most powerful of them, old
man Briffaut, a former coppersmith fallen on hard times who became a scavenger for spare parts in a used-car dump and then a
ragman. Briffaut and Hallelujah have always hated one another—
with a hatred derived partly from old scores and partly from loyalty to their own kind. For my part, what I recognize in Briffaut
is the all-around salvage man, able to be mechanic, old-clothes
man, dealer in junk, in paper, even in antiques. That he was also

able to turn his hand to blackmail and murder was something I was to learn that evening. He once expounded to me his theory of lost property: he looked on a thing without an owner as his rightful possession, by virtue of his job, even before he found it. Anyone who found it before him was guilty of theft. The fact is that in his old age nature has whimsically endowed this old rogue with a patriarchal beauty, with his snowy beard and fine-drawn, prophetic profile, so that he has the air of a redeemer. He believes he has a mission which requires him to rescue things that have been thrown away, restore them to their lost dignity—more than that—to confer upon them an even greater dignity: since, on being salvaged, they are promoted to the rank of *antique*. I have watched him at work on a rubbish heap. I have seen him extract a cracked porcelain coffee pot from the pile. With what priestly slowness he caressed the old utensil, turning it between his hands, running his finger over its scars and peering into its interior! That was the crucial moment! The coffee pot had been thrown away, it was no longer worth anything. Yet by an edict that depended on him alone, he could raise it to a value far above that of a similar brand-new object by sanctifying it as an antique. Abruptly judgment was delivered. His hands were still holding the coffee pot but by some imperceptible change they indicated condemnation—as surely as Caesar's downward-pointing thumb meant the death of the gladiator. The coffee pot fell and smashed to pieces on a stone. That was no accident. Briffaut could not bear the idea that another ragman might salvage what he had rejected. The day I discovered this thread in his philosophy, I quoted to him the passage in the *Divine Comedy* in which Dante says that the thing God can least forgive is pity for those he has condemned. Briffaut's eyes sparkled and he asked me who this Dante was. Taken aback, I answered that he was an Italian ragman whose business was salvaging souls from the circles of hell. He nodded earnestly and acknowledged that the Italians were prime scavengers.

The quarrel between Briffaut and Hallelujah was certainly based on professional rivalry, but there was also, as I was to learn, a body lying between them, the body of an adventurer of sorts who disappeared a quarter of a century ago. A regular fellow was this Bertrand Crochemaure, handsome as Lucifer and a mighty lady-killer, credited by gossip, of course, with ten times as many amorous exploits as he could ever have accomplished in several lifetimes. He lived alone, in a dilapidated farmhouse somewhere near Mayeuvre, and specialized, among a hundred other things, in training guard dogs. This was how he first came to have dealings with the Château of Saint-Haon, whereupon fantastic rumors began to spread at once about an affair between the lonely man and the Countess Adrienne de Ribeauvillé.

It was just before the 1914 war. The Château of Saint-Haon was going through a period of great splendor and provided the ragmen with the most distinguished rubbish in the entire region. For the Ribeauvillés entertained lavishly. It was nothing but receptions, midnight parties, and fancy-dress balls and the numerous servants busied themselves spreading scandalous rumors about them throughout the countryside. The Countess Adrienne's enigmatic features and provocative elegance set people's imaginations working, and everyone talked about her lapses without being sure if it were spite or calumny. True, the psychology of women is a bottomless well, and Crochemaure's farm was isolated enough for comings and goings to pass unnoticed.

One morning, the Saint-Haon demesne rang with shrieks and wails. One of the Countess's finest pieces of jewelry, a pair of earrings, had vanished in the course of a particularly uproarious night. The nature of these earrings has an important bearing on the case. They consisted of two Philippine pearls mounted on clips, so cunningly that they appeared simply to rest on the earlobes. Now, of course, Philippine oysters—so named because they are fished up off the Philippine Islands—contain two baroque pearls of no great size but fitted together in such a way as to resemble twin sisters, and also angled, so that you can tell the right from the left. Such pearls, not especially valuable on their own, become priceless when united in a single piece of jewelry or made into earrings.

The château, outbuildings and gardens were searched with a fine-tooth comb. The lake, fishponds and ditches were dredged. The garbage men were alerted and promised a thousand-franc reward if they should find the lost jewels. To no avail. Then one day Briffaut appeared at the lodge gates. He spoke to the porter, to the servants and then to Adrienne de Ribeauvillé herself, who finally agreed to see him alone. What passed between them will never be known. But a housemaid said later that as he entered the scented boudoir into which the Countess, dressed in a filmy negligee, led the way, anyone would have sworn that Briffaut had put himself out to look even dirtier and hairier than usual. She added that the interview lasted for three quarters of an hour and that when Briffaut emerged with an air of triumph, Adrienne looked as though she had been crying.

The earrings were not recovered, and the outbreak of war a few weeks later helped to throw a blanket over the affair. The château was first requisitioned and turned into a military hospital, and afterward shut up until 1920, when, Adrienne having died abroad in circumstances as obscure as her whole personality, the Count retired there with his daughter, Fabienne, then aged about ten. Meanwhile hardly anyone had taken much notice of a disappearance so quiet that no one could agree just when it had taken place: that of Bertrand Crochemaure. True, he was in the habit of slipping away quite frequently for varying lengths of time, only to reappear again suddenly. It was not until four of the six dogs he had at the time had been seen a number of times about the woods and fields that a gamekeeper became curious enough to go and knock on the door of his farmhouse. Getting no answer, he broke in. It was quite deserted, but the other two dogs were dead, probably of starvation, shut up in a makeshift kennel. Brutal though he was, Crochemaure loved his animals. He would not have abandoned his dogs deliberately.

It was this affair—this tangle of obscure affairs—that Hallelujah brought up a quarter of a century later in the common room of the Cranes to confound his old adversary. The crosscurrents of noise and argument among the tramps died away at once as he rose and thrust his leonine old muzzle, with its dead eyes, at the ragpicker.

"You're a liar, ragman! You're here, but you're not one of us. You've always gone all out for your own rotten ends and hard luck on any that got in your way! We're all of us borne on the same tide, only you swim against it. You dig things up and sal-

vage them, redeeming them, you call it. And too bad for any garbage man that goes against you!"

The blind face swung to right and left.

"Listen to me, all of you! You think you know old man
Briffaut. You don't know him! Me, the blind man, I can see a
white flash, a little pearly glint in his left ear. And what does it
mean, that pearlikins in a ragman's ear? A dead garbage man,
that's what it means! You listen to me!"

Still with his face fixed on Briffaut, he continued now amid a
prodigious silence.

"Near the end of the morning, it was, March 1914, you got inside the château. You almost had to break the door down but
this time you've done it, and you're in! White, she is, that
Ribeauvillé, and smelling of scent. There you are, all black and
stinking from the day's work you've just done. Begin at five and
finish at eleven, on the dot. You're reveling in your filth, in your
strength and coarseness, face to face with that woman worn out
with fear and exhaustion. You stand there in her little chocolate-
box room, all silk and swansdown. Take your greasy hand out of
your pocket and there, on the end of your finger, what is it? A
flash of pearl, the little earring. Ribeauvillé shrieks for joy and
starts forward to take what's hers. You stop her. 'Not so fast, little lady! Suppose we have a little chat?' You come clean, to start
with. You've only got one of the pearls. The other? You don't
know anything about that! As to the reward, you've no truck
with that. What? Ten thousand francs for one pearl? When with
its sister the two of them are worth five hundred thousand!
You're not letting go of your prize for less than a hundred thousand francs.

"Ribeauvillé, she thinks you've gone mad. She hasn't got that
sort of money. She never will have. You'd an idea of that. It was
a risk to be run. Who can tell with women? She says, 'I'll have
you arrested!' You wag your finger, like this, no, no, no, half
playfully, half nasty. 'No, no, no, little lady, because this pretty
jewel, you guess where I found it, and when? This morning,
you'll say, in the château garbage. Well, you'd be wrong! I found
it the day before yesterday, in the Mayeuvre dump. See what I
mean? Oh, I'm not saying it was in Crochemaure's garbage. No,

that would really be too much! Only that it's funny, all the same, first that it should have got to Mayeuvre all by itself, and second that you waited two days before reporting it missing. So there we are: either you give me the other earring—because mine isn't worth a light without it—or else I'll take my find to the police and tell them where it came from. The Count's the one who's going to be surprised if he finds out you spent part of the night before last with that devil Crochemaure!'

"That, Briffaut, was when you gambled for high stakes. Gambled and lost! Because, of course, Adrienne might have had the other jewel. Then she would have given it to you to buy your silence. That was what you were counting on. But there was another possibility, that Crochemaure had his hands on it. Oh dear, dear! Crochemaure is no pretty lady in tears and a dressing gown! He's tough and strong and mean, Crochemaure is! You'd lost, ragman. And you knew you'd lost when Adrienne asked you to wait twenty-four hours. You had to agree! You beat it! It was all up. Worse than that, Crochemaure would be paying a little call on you. Very soon. Because Adrienne, she went right off to his place and poured out the whole story to him. Now Croche wasn't going to hand her back the other earring for her to make you a present of it, that was for sure! Began by swearing to all his gods he hadn't found a thing! Now that wasn't true. And then he went on to say he was well able, not just to silence you, but to get the pearl away from you. And that was true. After that I daresay they had another go at it, he and Adrienne, but he wouldn't have had his mind on the job. He was wondering what was his quickest way to make you cough up.

"What happened after that, I'm not too sure. You must have got together, each of you with your pearl. It should have been quite a party between the two of you. But what I do know is twenty-five years later you're still here, in one piece, while Crochemaure vanished without a trace not long after the affair of the pearls. Of course you'll say he had the pearls and made off to enjoy them undisturbed. But I'm not with you there, ragman! I'm not with you on account of the dogs. You didn't finish the job, you see. After Crochemaure, you ought to have seen to the dogs. Get out, Briffaut! You stink of death!"

Briffaut is suddenly alone, facing a hostile crowd. They are
garbage men, contemptible creatures, and he scorns them. But
he finds it reassuring that the door is not far off, three strides at
most, one bound and he is out. He looks at the men and women
muttering among themselves. Is he thinking of Crochemaure's
dogs? He does not feel that he is one of them. The redeemer, the
man who swims against the tide, he can only be a messenger
from on high, a passer-by among these rooted in the mire. He
tries to speak but the black crowd is muttering more and more
excitedly. He shrugs. He starts to edge back. But he is a gam-
bler, and besides, he despises these wood lice. Then he has a
crazy inspiration and makes a gesture of defiance. He lifts his
long hair, uncovering his left ear. And they can all see something
white and pearly glimmering amid the grime and hair. He is
sneering silently as he backs toward the door. A gust of increasing hostility, more and more violent, pursues him out of it.

The old iron stove, rusty, broken, and black with soot, which
happened inexplicably to have got into the truck, may have been
to blame. I saw it tumble down the slope into the Devil's Hole,
bounce off a truck tire, and go bounding and whirling with a terrible force like a drunken bull toward the two motionless figures.
Eustache and Daniel were standing precisely in its path—naturally, since it was their job to retrieve and crush all bulky
items. But these were supposed to consist of rags, carpets,
mattresses, bundles of paper—soft, harmless things they need not
fear to see coming at them. I tried to shout out, to warn them.
To my shame, no sound came from my throat. I have frequently
been irritated by the kind of woman who, in any crisis, always
manages to screech idiotically to no purpose. An anguished silence, though more discreet, is, I feel sure, evidence of a lack of
self-control every bit as reprehensible. By the time the stove
reached the two boys it had hidden them from my sight and I
missed what followed. I only saw Eustache leap aside and Daniel rolling in the refuse. I got down to them as fast as I could. I
gathered that Eustache, having avoided the missile by a hairs-
breadth, had given Daniel a violent shove out of the way. The
younger boy was just getting shakily to his feet. His back was to-

ward me. Eustache, speaking to him, had his face to me. That, too, played a decisive part in what came after. Eustache was wearing a pair of tight black trousers, tucked into his boots, and a cotton undershirt, also black and sleeveless or with very short sleeves. On his hands he had huge padded leather gloves, proof against all the sharp edges, nails, and other things like broken glass that lurked in the rubbish like snakes in the grass. His bare arms were the only fleshy things contained in the picture of pale sky and landscape of refuse. Their rich musculature, perfect modeling, and floury whiteness were in stark contrast to the wretchedness all around. Soon I could see nothing else, they filled my vision, dazzling me and flooding me with desire. Eustache stopped talking to Daniel and looked at me with a smile whose cynical complicity said clearly enough that he had understood my feelings and accepted them as his due. Daniel still had his back to me, a slim back in a baggy jacket in which his thin shoulder blades made scarcely a bulge, a weak spine, attracting misfortune and enduring it in pain and humiliation. The stab of desire Eustache's baker's arms had just given me was nothing in comparison to the pity roused in me by Daniel's back. A demanding, violent pity that brought tears to my eyes and doubled me up, an anguish that rent my heart. I had just discovered a new passion, more devouring and more perilous than any other: the love that comes of pity. Eustache's arms played their part in the alchemy of this novel love philter. But for them, I should probably have seen Daniel with quite other eyes, seen him *entire* —as a stallion is said to be *entire*—with desire and tenderness equally commingled and giving birth to a fine, strong, healthy love. The subtle and perverse workings of the quarry's quarry would not have it so. Eustache's arms acted like a kind of philter on my awareness of Daniel's back. They retained for themselves everything strong and joyous in it, the cheerful greed that surrounds and celebrates good healthy flesh—and let through only a low, plaintive call toward Daniel's back. By the power of the quarry's quarry, love fell apart, and affectionate desire degenerated into compassionate cruelty. Even as I experienced with terror the vehemence of which pity is capable, I was tasting all its virulent poison. No, pity is certainly not an honorable feeling. It

is a dreadful perversion; because all the loved one's faults, failings and weaknesses feed and aggravate instead of discouraging
it. If virtue is strength and vice weakness, then pity is the vicious
form of love. It is a fundamentally coprophagous passion.

There was a silence traversed by a breath of wind. Some
papers flew about and I thought, I don't quite know why, of
Thomas Drycome's ruah. Perhaps it was fitting that it should
preside over the defining of those feelings that were henceforth
to unite me to the two boys? Daniel looked around and with a
painful jolt I saw his pale cheek and forehead, like an isolated
profile, barred with a lock of dark hair. He radiated the un-
wholesome glamor of the underprivileged. We all three looked at
the now harmless stove. The monster was embedded in the refuse with its two short, absurdly convoluted back legs sticking
up in the air. In spite of the black hole of the oven gaping in its
side and the brass tap of the hot-water tank, it looked like a bull,
landed there at the end of its furious charge, wedged head and
shoulders deep in the yielding ground.

The thing that makes my life so delightful is that, even at my
ripe age, I can still surprise myself by the decisions I make or the
things I choose to do, and all the more so since these are no
whims or sudden fancies but, on the contrary, fruits long nur-
tured in the secrecy of my heart, a secrecy so well kept that I am
the first to be astonished by their form, substance and flavor. Of
course, it takes the right circumstances to bring them out, but
these are so often forthcoming as to make the resounding word
"fate" spring readily to mind.

But everyone gets the kind of fate he asks for. To some I think
fate gives subtle, private signals, half smiles and winks that only
they can understand, a ripple on the mirror surface of water . . .
I am not one of them. For me there are huge farces, coarse,
scatological, pornographic jokes, mischievous, clownlike gri-
maces, like the faces we used to make as children, distending the
corners of our mouths with our little fingers—tongue sticking out,
of course—and our two thumbs stretching out our eyelids Chinese fashion.

All that preamble simply in order to get around to this ap-

parently harmless piece of news: I have a dog. Yet there was no
reason why I should be destined to join the company of doggy
lovers whose mindless adoration of their quadrupeds has always
irritated me. I hate any kind of relationship that does not contain
a modicum of *cynicism*. Cynicism . . . To each as much truth as
he can bear, as he deserves. The weakest of those I speak to are
the greediest for lies and make-believe. They are the ones who
must have everything disguised to help them live. I can only tell
everything in the bluntest terms to a being endowed with infinite
generosity and intelligence, in other words to God alone. With
God, no cynicism is possible, if cynicism consists in dishing
someone up *more* truth than he can bear or in terms *more*
forthright than he wants to hear. So that it seems to me that
friendly relations are only bearable if they are accompanied by a
certain mutual *overesteem*, so that each is continually shocking
the other, and by that very fact obliging him to rise above himself. Then if the dose be really too strong, the other will be hurt
and break contact—sometimes for good.

Can one have cynicism in one's relationship with a dog? The
idea had not occurred to me. And yet! I ought to have been
warned by the etymology of the word "cynicism," which comes
precisely from the Greek *kunos*, a dog . . .

This morning, not far from the hotel, I was watching the behavior of a handful of curs around a bitch who must have been
in heat. Needless to say, the obscenely heterosexual scene—with
its sniffings, threats, nuzzlings, pretended combats and couplings
—aroused simultaneously my curiosity and disgust. At last, the
little group disappeared along the canalside and I forgot all
about it. Two hours later, going out to buy a paper, I see them
again a few yards on. But by now one of the dogs has achieved
his object and, glassy-eyed and with lolling tongue, is energet-
ically mounting the bitch, who responds with a wriggle of her
hindquarters to every thrust. Little by little, the other dogs drift
away, all but one, like a fair-sized, long-haired griffon, the kind
generally to be seen rounding up flocks of sheep or cows. What
is he waiting for? Is he hoping to follow on after his more fortunate rival? That would surely be the ultimate in baseness, though
no more than might be expected of hetero trash. I am sorry I've

come out without a stick. I might have waited until he was
clamped to the bitch in his turn and then let him have it. Perhaps he guesses what I am thinking, because he is watching me
sideways, under the gray hair hanging over his eyes. Or is he
making sure that I am looking at him and not going to miss his
next move? For now he approaches the coupled pair. He seems
to be most interested in the male's anus, which is admittedly the
only accessible part. And he gets up on his hind legs. He mounts
him. I distinctly see him insert his red, pointed barb, like a chili
pepper, under the other dog's tail. Upon my word, he's buggering him! The muzzle of the laboring male evinces a sudden
disquiet. He turns his head a little toward my sheep dog. But he
is too much occupied elsewhere to be able to do much about it.
He relapses once more into his rhythmic bliss. As to the griffon,
he is going to it with a will. He parts his jaws, then turns and
looks at me. Indubitably there is a twinkle in his eye. The damn
tyke is actually grinning! It is then that the word "cynicism"
comes to me. For this is cynicism! But of the right kind, a cynicism going my own way and getting there faster and further
than I could have done, so that I am satisfied but also outclassed,
jolted a little and uplifted in consequence. The devil! Buggering
a hetero in the act of performing his marital duties just like that,
right in the middle of the road . . . To be honest, I'd never have
dared even to think of it!

I went up to my room again in a state of euphoria brought on
by the invigorating sight. I read my paper. Not very attentively.
Clearly I was waiting for something, or someone . . . I went
down again. There he was, on the doorstep. He, too, was waiting
for me. He lifted his great hairy head with its perpetual grin to
me, as though henceforth the memory of his exploit would
create a complicity between us. And it was true that the animal
had won me over! More than that, he had *edified* me, in both
senses of the word, augmenting my moral virtues but also as it
were adding a floor to the castle of my dreams by that act of
love in the second position he had shown me, like a commentary
on the dilemma of the quarry's quarry and an encouragement to
find the *cynical* answer to it.

I put out my hand to him and he responded with a flick of his tongue in its direction, but without touching it, because we were beginning to make contact but the final exchange had not yet taken place. I came back two hours later and found him still sitting there, as though guarding the hotel which was my house. It warmed my heart, no point in denying it. I turned back instantly and went and bought a kilo of calves' lights from the nearest butcher. I had intended to open the newspaper parcel of spongy, purplish meat and leave it spread out on the pavement. Then I was ashamed. I thought of the little old ladies feeding cats like that in the park. The sheep dog grinned at me. I gave him a wink and he followed me upstairs quite naturally. The advantage of this disreputable lodging house is that no one would think of taking exception to the presence of a dog in my room.

I have a dog. I must find him a name. Robinson Crusoe called his native Man Friday, because it was on a Friday that he adopted him. Today is Saturday. Samedi. My dog shall be called Sam. "Sam!" I call, and he lifts his hairy head with its two bright brown eyes to me at once. I have a dog, a *cynic* friend who shocks me by going further in my own way than I myself, who *edifies* me . . .

Underneath its apparent banality, the world is decidedly full of barely concealed wonders—just like Ali Baba's cave. Passing by a bookstall, I picked up a book at random and dipped into it. It was an etymological dictionary of the French language. A brief glance taught me that the word for buttocks, *fesse*, comes from the Latin *fissum*, an opening. What a difference it makes! No one has more than one *fesse*, dividing the two fleshy parts of his posterior. But because they are so outstandingly positive they have unfairly taken over the word *fissum*, which made the mistake of designating something wholly discreet and negative.

Sam never leaves me now. Philomène, the landlady of the Cranes, feeds him in the kitchen. The rest of the time, he is at my heels. There are times when I tell him he must leave me alone. Then he wanders about the house, where everyone is glad to see him. It is not quite the same at the Hotel Terminus, where they reminded me sharply that dogs were not admitted. Such is

the price of respectability! Because they want to be "proper,"
these vulgar people who grew up among pigs and chickens put
on airs like sergeant majors. Well, I am growing daily less inclined to put up with having my four-footed friend abused and
shut out. I was tempted to give up my room at the Terminus immediately but I thought better of it, first because it is a principle
of mine never to do anything drastic in the heat of the moment,
and then because I could not like the idea of finding myself
quite beleaguered in the Cranes. I like to keep a bolt hole, somewhere beyond the Cranes—and, let it be said, quite simply a
bathroom . . . So let it be. Monsieur Alexandre possesses not
merely a quarry and the quarry's quarry, but also a dog—in addition to his picturesque ragpicking friends from the rubbish
heaps. Monsieur Surin is a steady single man, enjoying the respect of the worthy tradesmen of Roanne. Is it necessary to add
that Monsieur Alex, the writer of these lines, would dearly love
to strangle Monsieur Surin?

Sooner or later I was bound to meet this Fabienne de Ribeauvillé who enjoys such mysterious respect at the Cranes, and
whose mother, Adrienne, probably once had a soft spot for the
terrible Crochemaure. Indeed, who can say whether or not this
Fabienne isn't the dog trainer's daughter? But that's enough of
romantic speculations!

The introduction was not without its piquancy. It was not far
from the Devil's Hole, at a place known as the Sign of the Ass.
There is a ruin there of what was once a tavern standing weirdly
in open country. And alongside it, a hollow whose bottom, eight
months out of twelve, is a stagnant bog full of rushes. I should
long ago have set about filling it in with controlled dumping but
for the fact that I have sort of been forestalled—by a couple of
decades, from what they say. Over twenty years ago, the three
hundred hectares round about, which had been divided among
some twenty or so smallholders, were bought by a wealthy
farmer and combined into one estate. The first thing he did was
to rip out the miles of fencing around the various plots. The
barbed wire was rolled roughly around the stakes that had sup-
ported it and chucked indiscriminately into the hollow. The hol-

low, the bog, and the terrible thicket of metal, tangled and eaten
away with rust, make a fearsome trap for living creatures and
each year it claims some victims.

This morning, then, someone came to me at the site to tell me
one of the Saint-Haon horses had thrown its rider and plunged
into this hornet's nest. Could I come and help get it out? I went,
my old Sam at my side. I could see from some way off a figure in
riding dress standing on the edge of the hollow with his back to
us. We were soon at his side. It was a terrifying spectacle. The
thing that was struggling in the maze of barbed wire no longer
resembled a horse in anything but shape. For the rest, it was a
flayed carcass, the anatomy of a horse streaming with blood
which nevertheless went on struggling desperately, absurdly,
dragging coils of wire from every leg, rearing heavenward a
head from which one eye had been plucked out. A young groom
was climbing slowly back up to us, gesturing helplessly. Certainly there was nothing more to be done now, nothing but to
shoot the poor beast. The groom had reached us when the whip
cracked, making a weal across his face. He recoiled, flinging up
an elbow to protect himself, tripped and fell backward. Then the
horseman was on him and the whip rising and falling with mechanical regularity. The absolute silence in which the horse's
death throes and this ghastly chastisement took place enveloped
us in an atmosphere of solemnity. I was interested. I would have
been more so had I known the truth, that the rider was a woman
and the little groom another . . .

When Fabienne de Ribeauvillé turned to me, her curiously
round, rather childish face was bathed in tears.

"Can you shoot him?"

"One of my men shall bring a gun."

"Quickly."

"As soon as possible."

"When?"

"A quarter of an hour perhaps."

She sighed and turned back to the thicket, where the animal
had fallen onto its side and was struggling less violently. The little groom had got up without apparent resentment and, oblivi-
ous of the purple weals crisscrossing her face, was staring, like

us, at the huge crater with its hellish riot of metallic vegetation.

Fabienne spoke again. "When you think of the gentleness of the refuse dumps, why must this place be such hell? It's as though all the wickedness of the whole countryside had been collected in this pit."

"I'm going to have it cleaned up," I promised. "By next week I shall have another gang."

The vigor of her reaction took me by surprise.

"Do nothing of the sort! I will see to it. After all, you haven't any animals to protect."

Then she turned her back on me and walked off, followed by the groom, her face striped red by the whip, toward the dirt track where a small sports car was waiting for her. The horse was put down that afternoon with a bullet through the head and a knacker was present to take the carcass away at once.

Watching Sam, I find out one of the reasons which must surely explain the animal cults there are in some civilizations. Not that I idolize this tyke of mine, but I am aware of something restful and soothing emanating from him, and it is quite simply that his adaptability to the outside world is contagious. Animals provide us with the spectacle of an adequacy in the face of their immediate surroundings which is inborn and effortless. Primitive man must have admired and envied the strength, speed, skill, and effectiveness of the animals he saw, while he himself was shivering in his ill-fitting skins, hunting with weapons that possessed neither range nor accuracy and with only his bare feet to get about on. In the same way I observe with what ease Sam has insinuated himself into my life, with what happy, straightforward philosophical cheerfulness he takes everything, me included, which is no small credit to him. I observe, I appreciate and I am not far from taking him for my model.

Come to think of it, I have experienced this feeling of slightly envious admiration before, but that was for heterosexuals and in moments of weakness. Yes, there have been times when I have been momentarily dazzled by the heterosexual's wonderful adjustment to the society into which he has been born. He finds in it, laid out, as it were, at the foot of his cradle, the picture books

which will provide his education, sexual and emotional, the address of the brothel where he will lose his virginity, a composite
sketch of his first mistress and of his bride-to-be, along with a
description of the wedding ceremony, the wording of the marriage settlement and the hymns to be sung, and so on. He has
only to put on, one by one, all these tailor-made garments which
fit him perfectly because he was made for them as much as they
were made for him. Whereas the young homosexual wakes to a
desert bristling with thorn bushes . . .

Well, from now on, this miracle of adaptability is not portrayed
in my life by the heterosexual but by my dog, and with how
much more wit and generosity!

Sam, my good angel, you are in the process of proving to me
the marvelous, incredible, unheard-of fact that it is possible to be
happy with Alexandre Surin!

The sun is rising over the vineyards of Roanne and their props
look like an army of black skeletons against the light. They are
the source of the lively though rather heady little rosé which is
drunk hereabouts and which suits the "gray matter" of the region very well. I have left my car at the Terres Colombar, a big,
squat, blank-walled farmhouse, and am walking upstream along
the Oudan. I have been living here for more than six months
now and the pleasant countryside has grown familiar, so that I
am not looking forward to the prospect of having to leave it
when I have finished with the Devil's Hole. My five other dumps
run themselves, thank God, but there is no reason why I should
go on staying here. My hundred hectares of dumps at Saint-Escobille—fifty kilometers or so south of Paris—fed daily by a train
of thirty-five trucks coming from Paris, could probably do with
rather closer supervision, and the vast site at Miramas, where
Marseille discharges its refuse, likewise awaits a visit from me.
When I first came to Roanne, I congratulated myself on setting
up my tent on virgin soil and enjoyed my renewed solitude.
Roanne for me was a snowfield unsullied by any footprint. We
have come a long way since then, and now here I am surrounded
by such a host as I have never known before. Eustache and
Daniel, Sam and now Fabienne—all of them have forced their

way into my life and I wonder how I am going to be able to say
goodbye to the region of Roanne and shake its dust from my
shoes so as to embark, naked and receptive, on a new adventure.
Will I have got so covered with heterosexual slime that I can no
longer go anywhere without trailing a whole crowd after me?

Like an illustration of my thoughts, two riders come prancing
to meet me. I recognize Fabienne and her little groom whose
swollen face is enough to frighten the horses. She pulls up short
in front of me and brandishes her crop in a way that may be
read as either a threat or a greeting.

"I've sent some men to the Sign of the Ass to cut up the
barbed wire," she tells me. "Are you coming?"

I shake my head sullenly, not caring for her lady-of-the-manor
air. But perhaps I am only mortified at being spoken to by someone on horseback when I am on foot? There is something of that
in it, certainly, but it also comes of having a completely new and,
for me, disconcerting relationship with a woman.

At school, we Foils used sometimes to talk about girls. We
knew, of course, that their bellies were mutilated by nature so as
to end simply in a velvety triangle with no apparent sexual organs, and that painful disgrace was enough to justify our
indifference. Nor did the breasts our heterosexual classmates
made so much of find any more favor in our eyes. Our admiration for the pectoral muscles which in a man form an arch above
the hollow of the thoracic cavity and are the motor, the power
house of the most beautiful of all gestures—the act of hugging
and embracing—was too great for us not to be put off by the
slack, bulging caricature presented by the female chest. But our
curiosity was aroused and our imaginations set to work when
they came and told us that the sexual organs whose lack we had
been deploring were more complex than they seemed, being
made up of two mouths, set one above the other, whose four lips
—two large and two small—could open like the petals of a flower.
And then there was some tale about tubes—two tubes—calculated to intrigue worshippers of Ganesh, only hidden inside,
inaccessible. No matter. For us, all this belonged to some exotic
sphere and the female sex intrigued without occupying us for

long, in much the same way as the Bororos of central Brazil or the Hottentots of South-West Africa.

And now here on this plain by Roanne is a woman taking the liberty of addressing me in a tone whose insolent familiarity piques me, with a mixture of conscious attraction and annoyance. What adds to my annoyance is that the effect it has upon me is quite certainly calculated and intentional on her part. I feel manipulated.

Here on my left are the buildings of La Minardière, already with a suggestion of the landscape of Forez in their steep ridge roofs tiled with slates and their massive chimney stacks, each with its small wooden pipe alongside, like a child clinging to its mother. Sam hurries ahead, suddenly interested in all the living smells the outskirts of a farm have to offer. He expresses his joy by skipping on his left hind leg, and the small action gives a slightly comical elegance to his gait. Why not admit it? I, too, am drawn to these great toilsome, fecund dwellings where men and animals share in the same warmth and together bring forth their young and their grain. The stars in their courses, the seasons' round, the progression of days and toil, menstrual cycles, calving and childbed, births and deaths—all are so many wheels in the same great clock whose tick-tock throughout a lifetime must be very soothing, very reassuring. While I, tilling mountains of refuse and wasting my seed on boys, I am doomed to sterile gestures, to a today with no yesterday or tomorrow, to an eternal barren present in which there are no seasons . . .

Sam, who had slipped through the archway leading to the farmyard, comes out again full tilt, pursued by a couple of mongrel curs howling with rage and hatred. He flattens himself against me and the farm dogs halt, still barking but at a respectful distance. No doubt their instincts warn them that Fleurette has secret powers, and that even a light touch from her on the left side or between the eyes could be lethal. Come, Sam, my old pal, and learn once and for all that between those sitting down and us, who are upright, there can never be any relationship but that of force, an occasional equilibrium—unstable and uncertain—but peace never, and much less love!

I swing around to the south, deciding to return by way of the

Sign of the Ass, where Fabienne and her men must be laboring
to clear the hollow of its thicket of steel brambles. A tough job
and one I am curious to see, and relieved not to be responsible
for. A strange girl, Fabienne! What was it she said before about
the rubbish that was so profound? Oh, yes! "When you think of
the gentleness of the refuse dumps!" she said, and sighed. What
a devilish creature! The gentleness of those vast, white, softly
undulating plains where sheets of paper lift and glide and flutter
like insubstantial birds at the slightest breath of wind, the yielding ground that swallows up your steps and yet retains no trace—
I thought that was my own private secret. She has had eyes to
see it! Has she also understood that what is there is a civilization
pulverized and reduced to its first elements, whose functional
relations with mankind have now been broken? The repository
of the everyday life of the moment, made up of objects which,
because they are useless, are thereby elevated to a kind of abso-
luteness? A site for archaeological excavation, but a very special
one because it concerns the archaeology of the present and so
has an immediate bearing on present-day civilization? A society
defines itself by what it throws away—which instantly becomes
an absolute—domestic refuse and homosexuals in particular. I
picture again the little groom Fabienne was thrashing so enthusiastically. I am sure it is a girl, my instinct could not be mistaken.
Could it be that Fabienne has a feeling for refuse because she is
a lesbian? It looks like it. But I cannot conquer my considerable
skepticism in the matter of female homosexuality. To put it in al-
gebraic terms:

$$\text{male homosexuality: } 1 + 1 = 2 \text{ (love)}$$
$$\text{heterosexuality: } 1 + 0 = 10 \text{ (fertility)}$$
$$\text{female homosexuality: } 0 + 0 = 0 \text{ (nothing)}$$

Untouched, immense, eternal, Sodom stares down from on
high at its paltry counterfeit. I do not believe that anything can
come of the conjunction of two nothings.

The little tarred road that leads to Renaison and Saint-Haon
rings hard and firm beneath my feet. Sam, whose paws are beginning to have had enough, has stopped going off up the banks.
He is trotting by my side, head down. But I can see his interest

gradually reviving as we come up to the Sign of the Ass, where a cluster of men are busy: men from the Cranes almost certainly, brought to the job in an old truck which is parked on the side. Not only does their height indicate the scale of the mound of barbed wire, but the finicky work in which each is engaged, armed with a pair of wire cutters, shows the immensity of the task. It will take them three weeks at the very least to cut up and clear away that huge, rusty, spiky mat. Their way of going about it intrigues me. Instead of setting out to reduce the wire systematically, starting from the outside, I see that each is cutting his own way in separately, in a kind of tunnel, so that they are moving deeper into the thicket, making for the center. Anyone would think their object was not so much to clear the hollow as to explore it in all directions, to find something that was lost or hidden in it. Then I remember Fabienne's energetic rejection of my offer to put one of my gangs of workmen on the job. And that is enough to set me dreaming childishly of hidden treasure, guarded by terrible, romantic obstacles. The thicket suddenly takes on a grim poetic quality. The cruel agony of the horse caught in this tangle of barbed wire like a fly in a spider's web has already become simply a spectacle. Now there are little men with scissor fingers turning the galvanized forest into a mole run, but a mole run with a difference, not dark, soft and earthy now but light, airy and ferocious. I am at one with them. I feel their dread. I know that they are moving into those steel galleries with a tightening of the heart and of the buttocks, their scalps and spines creeping, wondering whether these jaws with their thousands upon thousands of rusty teeth are not going to close on them as they did only a few days since upon a horse, as they have done always, for as they go in deeper they come upon the torn remains of dogs, cats, badgers—one even calls out that he has found a boar half swallowed in the muddy bottom of the dell —but for the most part so fragmented and decomposed as to have become unrecognizable, shreds of fur with a few bones sticking out.

Fabienne is there, of course, still in riding boots and breeches, the little groom as always at her side, her blue and swollen face looking like a clown's mask. Fabienne greets me with a jerk of her head.

"What are you looking for in there?"

I cannot help asking the question even though I know at once that I have no hope of getting an answer to it. Fabienne is without her crop today. Her fingertips are playing with a little pair of silver scissors, a proper lady's toy—for a certain sort of lady, naturally.

"Come on, if you want to know," she tells me. And she heads for the thicket and plunges into a tunnel deep enough for the man cutting it to be out of sight.

No, I am not going after her. This place makes me more than uneasy, it fills me with a real revulsion. I take the road to the Terres Colombar, where my old Panhard is waiting, with Sam going ahead, apparently in a hurry now to be home.

No one at the hotel, of course, can talk of anything but the Sign of the Ass, and I have already noted more than one desertion among the men who were working at the Devil's Hole. When the occasion presents itself, I shall point out to Fabienne that she is leading my men astray, but our usual work force is so unreliable in the ordinary way that I shall say it more to tease than in earnest. In any case, it is curiosity and the hope of finding goodness knows what that attract the men to that particularly unpleasant site. I shall be surprised if it lasts and the Devil's Hole doesn't get its work force back again before very long. I have not had to make a move to keep Eustache and Daniel, who have stayed meekly in their places ripping and crushing, apparently deaf to the Ass's siren song. That is lucky, because their desertion would have put me in a very awkward position. Not that it would have lost me Eustache's favors, or Daniel's company—for we have come to that, the quarry's favors and the quarry's quarry's company—but I should have had to give up paying them for their work, and I cannot like the idea either of paying them for anything else or of giving them nothing at all. In Daniel's case it is particularly delicate. Because to tell the truth it is not to him—a mere apprentice—but to his mother that I give the money, and if there is an element of excitement in paying a boy, to pay his parents for him is a rare experience indeed.

Well, in short neither of them has stirred and I remain as before, sandwiched in between the quarry and the quarry's quarry. Sometimes I go up to the next floor. The door of Eustache's room is never locked. I find him naked in bed, but with the sheet drawn up to his nipples. Most of the time I ask nothing more, for by a whim of my appetite it is his arms that continue to arouse me. I have never felt flesh fuller, more generous, and at the same time more controlled, more closely obedient to the power of command. Not one gram of that superabundant whiteness is wasted (whereas women's bodies no sooner go from being lean and skinny than they run to excess which quickly ends in chaos). At first, as they lie quietly at his side, they are two great skeins of milky flesh anchored in the oval mass of his deltoids. But in a little while he arches them above his head, and then what a difference! It is like the lifting of a curtain. Stretching, the pectoral muscles lose their roundness and become cables, powerfully welded to the smooth, resonant thorax. The undersides of the arms are whiter still, betraying their tenderness, and become granular toward the armpits, whose light, venial, sensuous down is a pleasant change from the fathomless, luxuriant depths of the pubic forest. The arm is really a little leg, a trifle misshapen and bony but more eloquent and ironical than the leg, no doubt owing to its proximity to the head. Only if it is to communicate intelligibly, the rest of the body must be covered up, and it is this that dictates my conduct with Eustache. For if I lay bare his torso, his belly and his sides, the cartography at once simple and infinitely varied of hips and genitals, groin and perineum in between—then the chorus rising from an assembly of such numerous and powerful parts muffles the gracious but by comparison rather fragile duet of the arms, lusty though they are.

As for Daniel . . . I have a tenderness for him, no use trying to pretend otherwise. The passionate pity he inspires in me softens and gentles the hardened solitary that I was, tempered, like my little Fleurette, in the flame of desire alone, flexible but stainless and impermeable. Love equals desire plus affection, and its health and strength depend upon how closely those two ele-

ments are fused. But for one thing Eustache creams off the better part of my desire for himself. As to the affection I feel for
Daniel, that is of a particular kind, the pitying affection that suits
ill with desire, which may even be wholly inimical to that combination. So I have made a bad start, or at least I don't know
where I am going. All the same, the situation has novelty in its
favor.

Daniel. He made his official entry into my life three days ago. I
had just been paying his mother his month's wages. He had been
a witness of the performance and was still bemused by it. I shall
have to cure him of his stupid fascination with money. In the
meantime, I make the most of it, for there is no doubt that
money and I are synonymous in his eyes. I shall have to . . . I
shall have to . . . We are to travel a little way together, whether
it is a little way or a long way fate will decide. And that is
enough to set me spilling over with plans for him. With plans
and happiness. I am twenty again and life is just beginning! My
lovely brand-new love is a gold mine and we are going to exploit
it together. For a start, I took him to the Terminus. I wanted
him, alone among the people at the Cranes, to see the other side
of my life, as M. Surin. He knew the Terminus, of course—from
the outside—as the poshest hotel in town. Entering, he was quite
stiff with awe. The room, with its high ceiling and pile carpet on
the floor, completed his bedazzlement. I took him over to the
window which looks onto the square outside the station. A neon
sign—the hotel's own—threw a red glow over him. I put out my
hand to the nape of his neck, then I unfastened his shirt collar. I
was trembling with happiness because it was my first act of possession. The childish fragility of his neck. I shall have to wean
him from the inevitable undershirt, but I have long been familiar
with this working man's version of the peasant's flannel undervest. My fingers catch on a thin gold chain on which hangs a
medal of the Holy Virgin. He has evidently forgotten this relic of
his pious infancy, in the same way as a puppy will struggle
furiously to rid himself of the collar that has just been put on
him and then forget it in an hour, and for the rest of his life. He
had forgotten it, his medal of the Virgin, but I, Alexandre Surin,

the dandy garbage man, I caught the pure and secret little thing full in my stomach, and once again my eyes were scorched with a passion of pity. I buttoned up his short collar again and retied his tie, a faded, greasy string. I shall have to buy him some ties. I shall have to . . . I shall have to . . .

The cry broke from the center of the thicket on June 15, at 5:10 in the afternoon precisely. Having, as I foresaw, gotten back nearly all my deserters, I had gone along to the Ass to see how the work of clearance was progressing. By now there was only a handful of men clipping away without method or conviction, and the "light, airy and ferocious" mole run seemed scarcely affected by what had been done so far. I just had time to notice the little groom holding two horses and draw the conclusion that Fabienne must be somewhere nearby.

Then the shout rang out, a bellow of pain and anger, a fierce, furious yell, murderous and threatening. And almost at once a man appeared, bursting out of one of the tunnels cut into the thickness of the wire, a man running and screaming still, with one hand pressed to the left side of his head. I recognized Briffaut and he must have recognized me too, for he plunged toward me.

"My ear, my ear!" he bellowed. "She's cut off my ear!"

And he stretched out his left hand to me, smothered in blood. But it was not the hand that startled me, it was the change in his head, unbalanced by the loss of an ear, making me wonder uncomfortably for a moment whether I was looking at it from the front or in profile.

I wasted no time on the old fool with his one ear. I left him to his moaning and ran toward the thicket. I dived into the tunnel from which he had emerged and found to my surprise that I was in a labyrinth complicated enough to arouse a real fear of getting lost. The fear was probably unnecessary, for the thicket was not particularly large, but the impression of ferocious menace emanating from those thousands and thousands of strands of barbed wire, and the sense of being entombed beneath them, undoubtedly had a good deal to do with it. I walked on, turned a corner, walked on, turned again and found myself face to face with Fabienne. She was standing quite still, not smiling, although I seemed to read an expression of triumph on her round, plump face. I looked down at her hands. Both of them were splashed with blood. The right one was still holding the little silver scissors I had seen her with at our last meeting. She lifted the left and opened it: in it I saw a pair of earrings, two Philippine pearls mounted on clips. She stood aside to let me see the ground. The first thing my eye was drawn to was a twist of red flesh, and I thought of Briffaut's ear. But that was nothing yet. Looking closer, I made out a human shape half buried in the soft earth. A skull, capped with a shred of felt, was grinning widely among the clods of freshly dug soil.

"I suspected Crochemaure must be in here with one of the pearls," Fabienne explained. "What took me by surprise was when the other pearl turned up in Briffaut's ear. A strange meeting, wasn't it?"

She had reverted to her tone of worldly irony, which grated particularly in the circumstances.

I had no wish to see or hear more. I turned my back on Fabienne without a word and left the labyrinth. As yet, we can only guess what happened there a quarter of a century ago, but the pieces of the puzzle fit together well enough. At that time, the Sign of the Ass was in its heyday and was used as a base by the ragpickers in these unsavory parts. There it was that Briffaut and Crochemaure met, each with his pearl, for one last bargaining session. Presumably, having run out of arguments, they agreed to play cards or dice for them. The game degenerated into a quarrel and the quarrel into a knife fight. There is some evidence that Briffaut was nursing a severe stomach wound at about that time, and that it kept him in bed for some weeks. It seems likely that Crochemaure, after leaving the tavern, also wounded, got lost in the dark among the long grass and died in that marshy bottom. It was not long after this that tons of barbed wire were thrown in. When Briffaut was on his feet again and went to search the spot for the body and the pearl, he had a shock to find that thicket of wire on top of his old enemy, like a fitting monument. He waited his chance, forgot, and remembered suddenly about the pearl when he saw Fabienne's men cutting passages into the wire. The affair of the earrings came to life again, and Hallelujah may have been obeying its dictates when he uttered his accusations. Briffaut watched the progress of clearing the hollow with passionate interest. He had to be the first to find Crochemaure's remains. He was only the second, and he left behind both his pearl and his ear. . . .

He has that gold chain and the medal of the Virgin around his neck. Also, on the third finger of his left hand, he has a large ring made of aluminum in the shape of a skull. Those are his two ornaments. I shall take care not to touch them. On the other hand, I must think about getting him some clothes. If only the better to divest him of them later. What kind of clothes? A delicate problem, exciting and delightful. The prudent, wise and peaceful course would be to efface him, to blot him out, make him into a gray shadow hidden behind me. I do not want that. I do not want to clothe him in garments the direct opposite of my own. I want him to look like me, even to my "bad taste." Daniel shall be a dandy, like me.

Like me? Why not *exactly* like me? My perfect copy? The more I entertain the idea, the more I like it. So shall I meet the sneering throng head on, I'll stop its sneers with wonder, I shall rouse in its dull brains dim theories of brotherhood, or fatherhood . . .

Brotherhood, fatherhood? Oh, how strangely that wrings my heart! I have stumbled inadvertently against the running sore of my "little sorrow." And in the lightning flash of that momentary pain, I ask myself whether the pity that draws me to Daniel may not be another incarnation of my little sorrow, the same compassion that I feel for the little orphan boy that Maman left behind. Narcissus bending over his own image and weeping for pity.

I have always thought that with the coming of evening every man and woman experiences a great weariness of existence (to exist = *sistere ex*, to sit outside), of being born, and to console themselves for all those noisy, drafty hours they set about reversing their births, becoming *unborn*. But how may one re-enter the mother's womb one left so long ago? By always having a pretend-mother at home, a pseudo-mother in the shape of a bed (on the same lines as the inflatable rubber dolls that sailors cuddle at sea to beguile their enforced chastity). Make all dark and silent, then slip between the sheets and, naked in the steamy warmth, get into the curled posture of the fetus. I sleep. I am no longer there for anyone. Naturally, since I am not born! That is why it is logical to sleep in a closed room, in a confined atmosphere. Open windows are very well by day, in the morning, for the muscular energy demanded by hard physical activity. By night, such activity should be kept to a minimum. Since the fetus does not breathe, the sleeper ought to breathe as little as possible. The atmosphere that suits him best is heavy and maternal, like a stable in winter.

So my Daniel, naked as the day he was born, shall be unborn, slipping into my big bed. And what will he find there? Me, of course, as naked as himself. We shall embrace. The hetero riff-raff imagines that penetration is necessary, some play with orifices in imitation of their own mating. Poor fools! For us, all things are possible, none obligatory. Your loves are clamped within the reproductive process, ours are open to all innovations, all inventions, all discoveries. Our penises, taut and curved as saber blades, engage, clash, beat against each other. Need I say outright that the fencing I have practiced since my boyhood has been wholly because of the way it echoes that virile discourse? It is the equivalent of dancing to heterosexuals. At fifteen, I used to go to the fencing school as my brothers at the same age went to the Saturday-night hops. To each his symbolic accomplishments. I never envied their vulgar amusements. They never tried to comprehend the meaning of our fraternal bouts.

Fraternal. The big word slipped from my pen. For if the bed is the mother's womb, the man who comes, becoming unborn, to join me there can only be my brother. My twin brother, of course. And that is really what my love for Daniel is all about, purged by Eustache's arms, moved to pity by my little sorrow.

The Bible tells us that Jacob and Esau, the rival twins, struggled together even in their mother's womb. It goes on to say that, Esau coming first into the world, his brother took hold of his heel. What does that mean but that he wanted to prevent him from leaving the maternal limbo where they dwelt entwined together? Those movements of the double fetus—I picture them as slow, dreamlike, irresistible, halfway between a peristalsis and a vegetable growth—why interpret them as a struggle? Ought they not rather to be seen as the soft, caressing life of the geminate pair?

Little Daniel, when you become unborn and slip into my bosom, when we two try our swordplay, when we know one another with the marvelous understanding that comes of an atavistic, immemorial, and as it were innate awareness of the other's sexual parts—in contrast to the heterosexual hell where each is *terra incognita* to the other—you will not be my lover—a grotesque word that reeks of heterosexual couples—you will not even be my younger brother, you will be myself, and in that state of aerial equilibrium that belongs to the identical pair we shall sail away aboard our great, dim, white maternal ship.

I have come a long way from my plans for a new wardrobe. Yet not further than the distance between night and day. For if by night we shall be communing in our mother's womb, by day Daniel, wearing my embroidered waistcoat—with the six pockets empty as yet, as befits one so young and not yet settled to his trade—and my nankeen trousers, will walk into restaurant or hotel on my arm, a strange sibling, a clear generation away from me, my twin son, myself thirty years ago, raw and innocent, ill-assured, guard lowered, open to every attack. But I shall be beside him, whereas thirty years ago I had no one, I walked out with no guide and no protector into the fields of lust, strewn with snares and pitfalls.

I roll them in the hollow of my hand, the two beautiful Philippines, so luminously orient that it is as though a phosphorescent spot wandered over their small, rounded iridescent surfaces. Was it not fitting that they should end their strange history in the ears of the dandy garbage man, these twin sisters, symbols of the absolute pair? But by what a grotesquely roundabout way they have come there!

It all started last week when I was overseeing two bulldozers which were leveling the surface of what was the Devil's Hole. That surface is so beautifully smooth, so firm and finely graded—

a real masterpiece of controlled dumping, my masterpiece—that when the town council came in full force to inspect the completed work they could not conceal their enthusiasm and decided unanimously to carry on the good work by voting funds for the erection of a municipal sports stadium, complete with covered stands and heated locker rooms. I stood back modestly before this bevy of small tradesmen, each of whom was visibly taking to himself the credit for the future sports center. Then I cast an arctic chill over their self-satisfaction by suggesting diffidently that the stadium might be called by the name of Surin. The sight of their suddenly disapproving stares reminding me that at the Cranes I was known chiefly as M. Alexandre, I conceded that the first name, Alexandre, would do just as well, being equally reminiscent of the great Macedonian conqueror and of the line of Russian tsars. I was not serious, of course, since nothing is further from my mind than to set myself up as a famous man in a hetero society, albeit the recollection of the Léo-Lagrange Stadium at Vincennes and of a certain cluster of young men with naked thighs engaged in a nuptial rite about a leathern egg was still sweet to me and inclined me to look kindly on such places of manly recreation.

Like a hairdresser giving one last touch of the comb to a head he has just brushed and trimmed, I was sending my bulldozers over the flawless acreage of the Hole just one more time when I saw Fabienne's little groom trotting toward me. She halted some ten feet away and addressed me clearly and with almost military precision, like a staff officer carrying an order to an advance post from GHQ.

"Mademoiselle Fabienne is holding a reception on Friday evening at the château. You are cordially invited."

Her horse wheeled impatiently and before galloping off again she added this astonishing piece of information:

"It's to celebrate her engagement!"

Well done, Fabienne! She'd managed to take me by surprise again! So that was what came of lesbian affairs! Hadn't I been right to suspect that aping of male love affairs from the first? Engaged! Then I recalled that I had not seen her since the business of the severed ear and that there had been some talk at the

Cranes of a mysterious ailment which confined her to the château. My first, somewhat naïve thought had been that she had been upset by her dealings with Briffaut, in spite of their triumphant outcome, but now I inclined to the belief—every bit as naïve—that it was the prospect of this engagement, no doubt agreed to under inescapable financial pressure, which had upset her. I blame myself now for judging hastily. I am well aware that my view of women is crude, cold and detached but even so it might have occurred to me that if financial need there had been, then the recovery of the Philippine pearls would have remedied it. As for what ailed her, I was to learn under almost incredible circumstances what that was, and it had more in common with my trade of refuse disposal than with the romantic vapors of the fair sex.

It is a sartorial principle of mine always to be so well dressed in the ordinary way that there is no more I can do for a party. It is the only way to avoid the kind of dressing up gone in for by oafs of heterosexuals. I do not possess either tails or a dinner jacket, leaving such livery to waiters and gigolos, nor would it occur to anyone to find fault with me even at the stiffest party, since that would be to require a *lesser* distinction of me. It was therefore in my customary nankeen trousers, carmagnole jacket, loose cravat, and above all my silk waistcoat with the six pockets, each with its own medallion of refuse—that is to say, precisely as I had appeared for the past six months about the refuse dumps of Roanne—that I presented myself at the Château of Saint-Haon on Friday, July 7, to celebrate Fabienne's engagement.

Even though I had been prepared for it, the sight of her as an elegant young woman, with lacquered hair, silk dress and high heels, took me aback, and it was several seconds before I could recover. She noticed it, of course, and said to me as I bowed over her hand: "It's lucky I put on my earrings or I doubt if you'd have known me!"

I, at all events, have not yet gotten over my own doubts concerning the diminutive person at her side, whom she introduced to me simply by her Christian name.

"You know Eva, of course."

Was it the little groom? Probably. I am not absolutely sure.

Admittedly her face had healed miraculously fast, but that was not impossible at her age. I had scarcely seen her the week before when she had flung Fabienne's invitation to me from the saddle. She greeted me with downcast eyes and bobbed like a little girl. Then I was let loose into the château's reception rooms like a tropical fish in a carp pond. The native breed, in fact, typical of the locality. Except for the servants, in knee breeches, blue jackets and red waistcoats, the whole select company outdid one another for dullness. Restraint. Worse than that, nihilism. Search out the precise color of fog, dust, so as to fade still more completely into the background. Those are the iron rules of good taste among the poor beetles in these parts. The hetero off-loads onto his womenfolk any attempt at elegance, any sartorial enterprise, any innovation in matters of dress. Sex, for him, being entirely subordinated to utilitarian purposes, it cannot exercise its primary function of transforming, glorifying and uplifting. I move forward through the groups preening myself. What a pity I left Fleurette in the cloakroom. Didn't Louis XIV carry a cane as he paraded among his courtiers in the Hall of Mirrors? Talking of mirrors, there is one now, gathering the succession of rooms into its spotted surface. How beautiful I look! I believe I am the only male in this barnyard, a golden pheasant amid a flock of ash-colored partridges. A dais has been erected in a recess formed by what was presumably an alcove and on it six musicians are tuning their instruments. Of course, there is a ball at the château tonight. The ball for the engagement of Mademoiselle Fabienne de Ribeauvillé to . . . to whom precisely? I grab at a passing partridge and inquire in a confidential tone where the young man is? Could someone introduce me? The partridge is flustered, gazes about distractedly and stands on tiptoe to try and see over the crowd. At last it spies the buffet and makes a push to lead me there. We find ourselves before a small, stout young man, as soft and rosy as a whitlow. His hair is crimped and I could swear his face is painted. From the outset, I am aware of the negative vibrations of a strong antipathy. There are introductions. His name is Alexis de Bastie d'Urfé. I place him. Noble old Forezian family. Historic château on the Lignon, a tributary of the Loire. But then my memory takes a greater leap and fragments of old scholarship are thrown up. Honoré d'Urfé, author of *L'Astrée,* the first of the "precious" French novels. What was the name of the lace-clad shepherd who was dying of love for Astrée? Céladon! That's it! And instantly I recapture the instinctive dislike which as a schoolboy I felt for that scented popinjay, that pansy ladies' man—what a mixture!—and it comes to me that it is the same as the other, that roused in me by Alexis de Bastie d'Urfé. I, who never open a book and don't give a damn for literature, find this confusion of the real and the imaginary both surprising and entertaining. We exchange a few cautious remarks. I feel bound to congratulate him on his engagement. Fabienne is so strong and lovely! He contradicts me with a look of distress. No, indeed, she has not been well for some time. But now they are to be married next month and will be leaving at once for an extended honeymoon which will, he hopes, restore her. It can do Fabienne nothing but good to get away from a district where both the climate and still more the people are bad for her, and where she associates—associates with those who . . . in short, most unfortunate. That, I feel, might be called an insult! Fleurette, Fleurette, where are you? I really think I shall have to take my pellet of Roannaise refuse out of pocket number five and stuff it down that damn fool of a Céladon's throat! And where are you going for your honeymoon? I simper. Venice, he tells me. That was all it needed! Gondolas and mandolins by moonlight. Really, Fabienne is going too far. I turn my back on Céladon and cleave my way through the flock of partridges to find her. She is outside on the steps, where she has been receiving the guests, all by herself. But everyone seems to have arrived by now and the beautiful bride-to-be is lingering there for nothing—or from a reluctance to join the partridges perhaps—in the growing coolness of the night air.

Hearing me approach, she turns toward me and in the harsh light that falls from the lamps above the perron staircase I can see that her round cheeks have indeed melted away and her eyes look larger and deeper. But the Philippine pearls only shine the more luminously in her ears. What disease has my slicer-off of ragmen's ears caught from her "unfortunate associates"? I shall certainly not ask her because that is not the sort of question

she will answer. This marriage, on the other hand, and that
Alexis . . .

"I've just been introduced to your fiancé, Alexis de Bastie
d'Urfé," I observe, in a tone that mingles questioning with a hint
of reproach.

She understands it so.

"Alexis is a childhood friend," she explains with an apparent
readiness belied by the note of irony in her voice. "We grew up
together. Like an adopted brother, in fact. Only you were not
likely to have met him. He has a horror of horses, of dumps and
of those who work there. He practically never goes out. A family
man, you see."

"You'll make a perfect couple. No one will wonder which one
wears the breeches."

"Do you think I could put up with a man as virile as—"

"As me? What about him? How will he put up with you?"

She turns her back on me pettishly. Takes three steps in the
direction of the door. And stops.

"Monsieur Alexandre Surin?"

"Yes?"

"Have you read *L'Astrée* by Honoré d'Urfé?"

"To be honest, no. But I do seem to recall that it's a trifle on
the long side?"

"Five thousand four hundred and ninety-three quarto pages,
to be exact. But you see, for us Forezians it's our national epic.
Not for nothing when I was a little girl did I paddle with bare
feet in the clear waters of the Lignon."

"So you are marrying Alexis because he is Céladon incarnate?"

"Incarnate? It's more than that, you know!"

She comes close to me and whispers, as if it is a complicated
and important secret.

"Céladon is one side, Alexis is the other. Céladon quarrels
with his sweetheart Astrée. She sends him away. He goes in despair. Soon after, a ravishing shepherdess comes to Astrée. She is
called Alexis and she has a knack of making herself agreeable to
ladies. Astrée quickly forgets her grief in the arms of her new
friend. But who is Alexis really? Céladon, disguised as a shep-

herdess! As though sometimes one only has to change sex for
everything to be all right!"

At that point, I should have demanded an explanation, asked
detailed questions, and unraveled the tangle. I hadn't thought I
was a prude. Well, I drew back. My head reeled in front of those
eddying skirts and trousers. A sow would never have found her
piglets among them. Meanwhile, the problem of Alexis remains—
so to speak—entire. That little devil Fabienne would be quite capable of marrying a woman, or even a man she had dressed up
in a wedding dress and veil. She is stronger than I. Like Sam,
she shocks me and enriches me in the process. The things she
says are cynical and edifying.

Complete silence had fallen suddenly on the rooms and the
guests had cleared a space in the middle.

"I must open the dance," Fabienne sighed. "And Alexis
dances so badly!"

I followed her as she made her entrance, greeted by discreet
applause. She wore a dress of pink tussore molded to her figure
here and there and short enough to show her strong, horse-
woman's legs. The impression was of an active young woman,
Diana the huntress, willing to accede to a betrothal, yes, but as
to marriage, not yet irrevocably committed. While she bravely
took her place opposite the plump, flabby little person with
whom she had to dance, I tried to insinuate myself into the confused background of guests. I jostled against an old bag in a hat
of violet tulle who was engrossed in clearing a dish of petits
fours with great chompings of her lantern jaws. The plate gave a
frightful lurch and steadied but the edifice of violet tulle had
acquired what was evidently a hopeless list. She must have been
taught as a child never to be rude to anyone with her mouth full
because she merely slew me with her eyes and jerked her long
chin at me.

Fabienne stood facing Alexis without moving. Six feet lay between them. There was a striking contrast between the straight,
well-built boy-girl and the girl-boy, bulging everywhere and
only held together by his good dark suit. The band leader raised
his arms. The violinists tucked the ends of their violins under
their left ears.

That moment of silence and stillness has acquired in my recollection an aura of unbearable suspense. For in fact, the party ended then. The thing that happened next put a full stop to the party which included the bourgeoisie of Roanne and the aristocracy of the Forez and ushered in a celebration of a different, private and intimate kind in which the only two real participants were Fabienne and myself, surrounded by a ghostly audience.

There was a soft, moist plop and something slithered over Fabienne's shoes and slapped onto the polished parquet. At first sight it looked like a mass of flat, whitish spaghetti, but alive, animated by slow, peristaltic movements. I recognized that tangle of coiled ribbon at once as the garbage man's *Taenia solium.* So the malady which had been blamed obliquely on the "bad company" Fabienne had been keeping was nothing but a harmless tapeworm after all? The moments that followed were of rare density. All the partridges had their eyes fixed on the five or six yards of sticky thread writhing in slow motion, like an octopus on the sands. My profession as a refuse collector would not allow me to stand idle any longer. My neighbor, who had noticed nothing, was still chewing at her little cakes. I snatched the plate and a little spoon out of her hands, stepped forward two paces, and knelt at Fabienne's feet. With the help of the little spoon I scooped the tapeworm onto the plate, a delicate operation, for the damned thing was as slippery as a handful of eels. An extraordinary sensation! I worked away all alone in the midst of a crowd of wax dummies. I got up. Glanced around me. Céladon was standing there like a melting candle, gazing at me with an appalled expression. I put plate and spoon into his hand. I'll swear I did not say: "Eat it!" I will not swear I did not think it. The thing was done. That page was turned. Now it is up to us, Fabienne! Our left hands clasped. My right arm went around her waist. I looked at the band. "Music!" The "Blue Danube" swept us away on its lilting waves. The amazon of the trash cans and the dandy of the rubbish dumps, each of them having left their sex in the cloakroom, opened the ball. "Mademoiselle Fabienne, Comtesse de Ribeauvillé, what a strange couple we make! Will you take me for your husband? Suppose we set out together for Venice? I have heard it said that every morning the refuse men go out in gondolas and tip the Venetian garbage into a shallow place in the lagoon, and that a new island is growing up on the spot. Shall we build a palace there?"

So my dreams ran on and all the while we circled and circled, never seeing the rooms emptying. For the gray crowd was streaming slowly out of doors. It was not a rout, a panic flight, it was a discreet defection, an evanescence that left us face to face and breast to breast. "Vienna Blood," "The Gypsy Baron," "Artist's Life," "Roses from the South," the whole gamut. In a little while only one violin remained, sobbing its long-drawn-out wail. Then the violin too was gone . . .

That was the day before yesterday. This morning, I received a note. "I am going away, alone, on my wedding trip to Venice. I tried to reconcile them all, those I loved and the others, habits and customs, and last of all myself. The pyramid was fragile. You saw the result. Happily you were there. Thank you. Fabienne."

Accompanying the letter, the Philippine pearls made the envelope appear to be pregnant with twins.

The summer is ending and there is the threat of war. Hitler, having completed the massacre of German homosexuals with the connivance of the world at large, is seeking further victims. Need I say that the massive heterosexual conflict which is brewing interests me as an onlooker, but is no concern of mine? Except perhaps for the last act, when Europe and the whole world will probably be reduced to a single heap of rubble. Then it will be the day of the demolition men, salvage operators, street sweepers, garbage men, and all the rest of the ragpicking fraternity. In the meantime, I shall keep a close eye on events, saved from participation by a hernia long recovered from and forgotten, at the age for military service.

It is different for my brother Edouard. He has asked me suddenly to go and see him. He is one who clings to the body of society with every fiber, with his enormous wife, his mistresses, his innumerable children, his textile works and I don't know what else! From what I know of him, if war comes, he will want to fight. It's logical and absurd at the same time. Absurd in the absolute. Logical in relation to his identification with the system.

Why does he want to see me? Perhaps to make sure of someone to take over if the worst happens. Wait a moment! They've already burdened me with my brother Gustave's inheritance, these six towns and their refuse. I have had the genius to direct this empire of garbage into the way I want it, to my greater glory. That sort of achievement doesn't happen twice in a lifetime.

So I shall take a trip to Paris to see Edouard before going down to Miramas to have a look at the big Marseille rubbish dump. I shall take Sam. On consideration, I am leaving Daniel. What would I do with him during the two days I am to spend in Paris? Solitude is so ingrained in me that the mere thought of a traveling companion puts me off. He shall come and join me at Miramas. To add a touch of romance to our assignation—as well as a slightly sordid incentive—I have left him one earring. "These earrings are yours," I told him. "The two of them together are so valuable that you need never work again for the rest of your life. But separately they are worth hardly anything at all. So here is one, and I shall keep the other. You shall have that too. Later on. But first you must come and find me at Miramas. In a week's time."

We parted. I should not have trusted myself to watch him go. The narrow, slightly rounded shoulders in a jacket too big for them, the thin neck weighed down by an excess of flat black hair. And then I pictured his thin, grimy throat, with the gold chain and the medal of the Virgin . . . Once again my heart was wrung with pity. I had to force myself not to call him back. Shall I ever see him again? Can one ever tell in this wretched life?

CHAPTER VIII

Wild Strawberries

Paul

Certainly I had a great deal to do with the failure of his engagement and I am not trying to minimize my responsibility. Nevertheless, one must be careful not to put a non-twin's interpretation on the business—which ought properly to be read in a geminate sense. From a *singular* point of view, the thing is simple, but that simplicity is a quite superficial and mistaken way of looking at it. Two brothers loved one another dearly. A woman came on the scene. One brother wanted to marry her. The other was against it and by a treacherous ruse succeeded in getting rid of the intruder. It did him no good because the brother he loved promptly left him forever. That is our story reduced to a two-dimensional, non-twin's viewpoint. Restored to their stereoscopic truth, those few facts take on a very different meaning and fit into a much more significant picture.

It is my belief that Jean was not destined for marriage. His union with Sophie was doomed to certain failure. So why did I oppose it? Why did I try to put a stop to a plan that had no hope of success? Wouldn't it have been better to let matters ride and wait confidently for the breakup of a marriage which was against nature, and the prodigal brother's return? But that again is a non-twin's approach to the situation. In practice I had neither to put a stop to it nor to wait trustingly. Events took their inevitable course, as they were fated to do, from a constellation in which the places were assigned in advance and the parts already written. Nothing in our world—the geminate one I mean—ever comes about by personal choice, purpose and free will. As indeed Sophie understood. She entered just far enough into our game to assess the inevitability of its workings, and to realize that she had no hope of finding a place in it.

Jean did not really want the marriage after all. Carder-Jean is a divisive, disruptive creature. He used Sophie to smash the thing he found most restrictive and stifling, the geminate cell. His plan to marry was simply a piece of playacting which only Sophie was taken in by—and she not for very long. To be sure, the comedy would probably have gone on rather longer if I had been willing to enter into it. I should have had to pretend to ignore our twinship and treat Jean as a non-twin. I admit I refused to go along with that mummery. There was nothing to be gained by it. It was doomed to failure from the start, quite hopeless, and reduced to nothing by the one undeniable fact that *when one has experienced the intimacy of twinship, no other intimacy can be felt as anything but a disgusting promiscuity.*

Carder-Jean. That nickname, which he earned at the Pierres Sonnantes, indicates the fatal, destructive aspect of his personality, the dark side of him, as it were. I have said how ridiculous it was of Edouard to pretend to have one of us for himself and give the other to Maria-Barbara ("one twin each"). Yet the staff of the Pierres Sonnantes had achieved precisely this division without even trying, by the mere attraction of opposites.

One of its two poles was the small staff of the warping room, three tall, very neat and rather austere girls who moved silently about the sloping pigeonholes that held the three hundred bobbins which fed the web of warping threads. Directing the warpers with a firm, though unobtrusive authority, was Isabelle Daoudal, whose flat face and high cheekbones betrayed her Bigouden origins. She was, in fact, a native of Pont l'Abbé, right on the other side of Brittany, and had only come here to the north coast on account of her highly specialized professional skills, and also perhaps because, for some unexplained reason, this splendid girl had never married. Whatever had prevented her, it was certainly not the slight halt in her gait, a thing fairly common around the Odet estuary and as characteristic a sign of "breeding" as the Savoyard herdsman's odd-colored eyes.

Even more than in the sizing passage, where the great drying cylinder breathed out intoxicating odors of beeswax and gum arabic, it was in the warping room that I loved to idle whole afternoons away, and my liking for the mistress of the place was so obvious that I was sometimes referred to in the workrooms as Monsieur Isabelle. Of course, I did not analyze the attractions that drew me to that part of the factory and held me there. Certainly Isabelle Daoudal's calm, gentle authority must have had a great deal to do with it. But in my eyes the tall girl from Pont l'Abbé was inseparable from the magic of the warping machine as it purred busily, unreeling its shining web. The creel—a huge, semicircular metal frame—partly obscured the tall window whose light filtered through the three hundred multicolored bobbins it contained. From every bobbin came a thread—three hundred glistening, quivering threads converging on the reed that gathered them together and merged them into a silken web which shone as it was wound slowly onto a huge cylinder of polished wood five meters around. This web was the warp, the basic longitudinal part of the cloth through which the shuttles flew, driven by the sword strokes, to insert the weft. The warping was by no means the most subtle and complicated part of the weaving process. After all, the operation was fast enough for Isabelle and her three helpers to be able, with a single warping machine, to keep all the Pierres Sonnantes' twenty-seven looms supplied with warps. But it was its most fundamental stage, the simplest and most luminous, and the symbolism of it—several hundred threads converging into a single web—was heartwarming to one who loved the act of coming together as I did. The muffled purr of the spools, the threads running out smoothly to meet one another, the oscillation of the gleaming web as it wound itself around the tall mahogany cylinder furnished me with a model of a cosmic order whose guardians were the slow, dignified figures of the four warpers. Despite the fans which were fixed above the heck with the object of blowing the dust onto the floor, the vaulted ceiling of the room was covered with a thick white down, and nothing contributed more to the magic of the place than those intersecting ribs, arches, soffits and groins all lined with cotton wool down, as though we were in the middle of a gigantic hank of yarn, inside a downy sleeve as big as a church.

Isabelle Daoudal and her companions were the aristocrats of the Pierres Sonnantes. The brawling, squalling herd of thirty carders were the plebs. When Guy Le Plorec decided to set up the mattress shop, one of whose uses would be to take up some of the ticking turned out by the weaving sheds, no better place had been found to house it than the old stables, a good-sized building but in a very bad state of repair. The first ten carding machines set in a row against the rotting walls were of the most primitive type. The women sat astride a kind of wooden saddle and with their left hands kept in motion a swinging curved plate, its underside studded with hooked nails which passed directly in between a crop of similar nails set in the bottom plate. Their right hands plucked handfuls of wool or horsehair and stuffed it in between the two jaws of the carding machine. At first, not a month passed without one of the workers, whether from fatigue or carelessness, getting her right hand caught in between the two plates. Then it would mean a long struggle to free her, fearfully lacerated, from the horrible trap which held her captive. Soon there would be murmurs of revolt in the stables. There was talk of a strike, and threats of destroying the sinister, out-of-date machines. Then the women would put back the wisps of cotton wool they stuffed into their nostrils to protect them from the dust and gradually, amid the din, work would be resumed. For the mattress shop was permanently submerged in clouds of acrid black dust which escaped from the musty, filthy, worn-out mattresses as soon as anyone touched them, and even more when they were slit open with a knife. This was not the pure, airy

white down of the warping room. It was a foul soot that covered
floor and walls and became ingrained in the cob walls of the old
stables. Some of the workers wore masks over their faces to protect themselves from the ill effects of the thick dust that could be
seen dancing in the sunbeams, but Le Plorec was against this
practice, which to his mind increased the risk of accident. Revolt
was always expressed through the mouth of Denise Malacanthe
who, by her vigilance, her ascendancy over her fellows and the
unfailing belligerence which seemed to be a part of her character, was in fact establishing herself as spokeswoman for the mattress workers. She succeeded finally in obtaining the purchase of
a big circular carding machine, its drum and cylinders run by an
electric motor. Thanks to this machine, the fatigue and the risk
of accident were considerably reduced; on the other hand, the
dust churned up by its moving parts escaped through every ap-
erture and made the air in the stables altogether unbreathable.

The social unrest of the thirties found favorable soil here and
the Pierres Sonnantes had its first strike on Maria-Barbara's
birthday. Le Plorec came in search of Edouard to beg him to go
and speak to the carders who had been out since the morning
and now, in the early afternoon, were threatening to occupy the
weaving shed and warping room, whose uninterrupted humming
constituted, they felt, a provocation. Edouard's sense of responsibility was too great for him to shirk intervention, deeply as he
disliked it. He tore himself away from the candles and champagne and went alone to the factory, having sent Le Plorec
home and requested him not to show his face until the morning.
Then he went to the weaving shed. He had the machines
stopped and gave the workers the afternoon off. After that he
went in among the carders, smiling and affable with his gleaming moustache. The silence that greeted him was more startled
than hostile. He made the most of it.

"Listen," he said, holding up a finger. "You can hear a bird
singing, you can hear a dog barking. What you cannot hear is
the looms. I have had them stopped. Your fellow workers have
gone home for the afternoon. You are going to be able to do the
same. I am going back to La Cassine, where we are celebrating
my wife's birthday."

Then he went from group to group, talking to each girl about her family and her little problems and promising changes, reforms, his own intervention at every level. Seeing him there in flesh and blood, the dazed and awestruck workers had no doubt that he would do his utmost and would bend over backward to improve their lot.

"But remember, there's a depression on, my dears!" was his repeated cry.

Denise Malacanthe, temporarily defeated by this attack of paternalism, as she later described Edouard's intervention, withdrew into a hostile silence. The factory, closed for the day, was working again at full stretch the next morning. Everyone congratulated Edouard. He alone was convinced that nothing had been solved and the incident left him with a feeling of bitterness which helped to alienate him from the Pierres Sonnantes. Le Plorec became increasingly the master, and after this false start future labor relations were conducted under the auspices of the Federation of Textile Workers.

However deplorable the urge that drove Jean to seek the carders' company, it was still nothing compared with his predilection for the old coach house where the mattresses were stacked until needed. Naturally, the peasants who made up the majority of our customers did not send a mattress to us until it was absolutely finished. Consequently, the piles of disgusting, shapeless objects that sometimes rose as high as the skylights of the coach house were what immediately came into my mind the first time I heard about the towers of silence where the Indian Parsees heap the bodies of their dead, offering them to the rapacity of the carrion birds. Vultures apart, it was of those infernal censers that I was reminded by the heaps of palliasses slept on by generations of men and women and imbued with all the sordid blood, sweat, sperm and urine of their lives. The carders seemed barely conscious of these odors; on the contrary, to judge from their chatter, it was dreams of fortune that they sought in the bowels of the mattresses, for not one of them but had some tale of a mysterious book of magic found in the stuffing of wool or horsehair, or a treasure in bank notes or gold coins. But it was hardly treasure hunting that made Jean hang about the shed so often. He would usually end up there, after dawdling about the carding room, and I believe he even used to clamber up the piles of mattresses and curl up for a nap in that pestilential place.

Later, when, back in our geminate intimacy, he would nestle up to me for the night, I would need all my powers of conviction and exorcism to overcome and drive away the musty reek that clung about his body. This kind of exorcism was both a ritual and a necessity because after going our own ways all day long we needed an effort of purification, stripping away all external influences, every alien accretion, in order that each of us might return to the sheet anchor that his twin brother was to him, and this effort, if we performed it together, at one and the same time, was directed chiefly toward the other, each one purifying and cleansing his twin, to make him identical to himself. So that even as I worked to detach Jean from his carding room for the geminate night, I am bound to admit that he was himself busy separating me from everything that was most alien to him in my life, the warping room with its three blameless madonnas, led by the fair Daoudal. Those opposites, the warpers and the carders, probably did more than anything to divide us from one another, and long efforts at smoothing over and reconciliation had to take place every evening before we celebrated our reunion for the night. But the fact remains that that effort came more naturally to me because it fitted in with the warping itself—which is composing, combining, bringing together hundreds of threads to lie close on the beam—whereas carding is a tearing apart, discord, dislocation, carried out brutally with two opposing plates studded with hooked nails. Jean's fondness for the carder Denise Malacanthe, if it means anything at all—and how should it not?—betrayed a quarrelsome spirit, a spirit of dissolution, a sower of discord and strife, and an ill augury for his marriage. But, as I have said, that supposed marriage to Sophie was really nothing other than a divorce from me.

Jean

You playing, Bep?

No, Bep is not playing. Bep will never play again. The gemiinate cell? Geminate intimacy? The geminate prison, yes, and slavery! Paul adapts to our parity because he always calls the tune. He is the leader. More than once he has made a show of dealing the cards fairly, without seeming to take everything on himself. "I am only the Minister of the Interior. Foreign affairs are your domain. You represent the pair in relation to the unpaired. I shall take note of all the information, all the impulses you pass on to me from outside!" Hot air! What good is a foreign minister without the rest of the government? He took note of what he felt like doing. I could only bow to his loathing of everything belonging to the world of individuals. He always looks down on everyone who is not a twin. He thought—probably still thinks—that we were creatures apart, which is undeniable, and superior, which is by no means proven. I am not repudiating all the things that went to make up my childhood: cryptophasia, Aeolian, stereophóny, stereoscopy, geminate intuition, ovoid loving and its preliminary exorcism, praying head to tail, seminal communion and the many other inventions that comprised the Game of Bep. It was a wonderfully privileged childhood, especially when one adds, standing on the horizon, those tutelary gods, radiating kindness and generosity, Edouard and Maria-Barbara.

But Paul is wrong, he frightens and suffocates me when he tries to perpetuate that childhood indefinitely and turn it into something absolute and infinite. The geminate cell is the opposite of being, it is the negation of time, of history, of everything that happens, all the vicissitudes—quarrels, weariness, betrayals, old age—which those who set out on the great river whose tumbled waters roll on toward death accept as the entry fee and, as it were, the price of living. Between unchanging stillness and living impurity, I choose life.

All through my early years, I never questioned the geminate paradise in which I, with my twin brother, was enclosed. I discovered the non-twin's aspect of things by watching Franz. Poor boy, he was torn between the yearning for a certain peace—such as was given to us in the form of twinship and such as he had recreated for himself with his millenary calendar—and fear of the furious, unpredictable assaults the elements could inflict on him.

As adolescence set up ferments of opposition and denial in me, I came little by little to side with the elements.

In this I was helped in a decisive fashion by Denise Malacanthe and the girls in the mattress shop. My rebellious heart delighted in contact with all that was most disreputable in the Pierres Sonnantes. There was an element of challenge, of provocation, in my declared liking for the dirtiest workshop, the coarsest work, the roughest, most undisciplined workers in the factory. Of course, I suffered every night, when Paul made me undergo an interminable and exhausting "exorcism" to bring me back to geminate intimacy from such a distance. But what I endured helped of itself to ripen my secret decision to make an end of this "ovoid" childhood, tear up the pact with my brother and live, live at last!

Denise Malacanthe. There were two conventions standing between me and the staff of the Pierres Sonnantes. One, because I was a child. The second because I was the boss's son. For that graceless girl this twofold barrier did not exist. From the first word, the first glance, I realized that for her I was a human being like the rest—better still that by some process of selection which appealed to her persistently impertinent mind, she had chosen me for her accomplice, her confidant even. Her impertinence . . . It was not until later that I learned the secret of it, and that it was in no way an expression of a working-class demand for middle-class privileges, but quite the reverse. A mysterious expression used by my family in connection with Malacanthe intrigued me for a long time. *Déclassé*. Malacanthe had come down in the world. A peculiar, shameful disease which made her different from the other workers and meant that she was allowed to get away with more because it was not easy to sack her. Denise was the youngest daughter of a Rennes haberdasher. She had been educated by the Sisters of the Immaculate Conception, first as a boarder, then as a day girl—when the sisters would have no more of her disruptive presence in their dormitories. Until one day she ran away with the Romeo of a company of actors on tour. Since she was only sixteen, her parents had been able to threaten the seducer with legal proceedings, whereupon he had made haste to send his embarrassing conquest packing. Next,

Denise had been picked up by an itinerant distiller, who hawked his still around the farms and initiated her into the taste for Calvados before abandoning her at Notre Dame du Guildo. She had found work at the factory where they soon identified her as the wayward offspring of a respectable customer in Rennes. Denise's impudence was therefore not that of the worker demanding the supposed dignity of the middle class. It was that of an upper-middle-class girl demanding the supposed freedom of the proletariat. Impudence on the way down rather than the way up.

Hence her attitude toward me stemmed from common social origins and a common rebellion against the constraints of our respective childhoods. She had sensed the need in me to make a break and thought that she could help me—if only by her own example—to escape from the charmed circle, as she herself had done. She did help me, in fact, a very great deal, not, as she thought, to free myself from the family circle but from a stronger, more secret tie, the geminate bond. Denise Malacanthe had escaped from her family by means of itinerant lovers. Twice she had joined her fate to wanderers, first a traveling actor and then a distiller. That was no accident. It was her response to the imperious call of the exogamic principle which prohibits incest— love within the circle—and requires that the sexual partner be sought at a distance, as great a distance as possible. This call, this centrifugal principle, she made me aware of. She helped me understand the feeling of uneasiness and dissatisfaction that was tormenting me in my geminate cage, like a migrant bird imprisoned in an aviary. Because it is only fair to admit that Paul is not always wrong: from that point of view, certainly, non-twins are pale imitations of twins. They are equally well aware of an exogamic principle, a prohibition against incest, but what kind of incest is it? The union of a father with his daughter, a mother and her son, a brother and his sister. The number of possibilities is enough to show how second-rate this kind of incest by non-twins is, and that it really consists of three pathetic imitations. Because true incest, the union incestuous beyond all others is, of course, our own, yes, that ovoid loving which unites like with like and arouses by cryptophasic understanding a sensual passion which multiplies itself, instead of being content with mere contiguity like the loves of non-twins—even when they are most successful!

It is true, I cannot deny it, the twinless passion such as Malacanthe taught me on the mattresses in the coach house pales, fades and wilts in relation to the geminate, like an electric light bulb in the rising sun. And yet there is a something or other, I don't know what, in that twinless loving which, to my twin's taste, has a savor so incomparably rare that it makes up for what it lacks in intensity. (*Intensity*, tension within, contained, energy turned inward upon itself . . . To describe the carder's kind of loving would need an opposite word, expressing a tension that is centrifugal, eccentric, outward-going. *Extensity*, perhaps?) It is a savor of vagabondage, of marauding, of loitering with intent, full of vague promises that are no less exciting for being meagerly fulfilled. The massive pleasures of the geminate embrace are to the acidulated joys of twinless coupling like those fat, sweet, juicy greenhouse fruits compared to the little, sharp wild berries whose tartness contains all the mountain and forest. There is marble and eternity in ovoid loving, something monotone and unmoving which is like death. Whereas twinless loving is the first step in a picturesque maze, no one knows where it leads, or if it leads anywhere, but it has the charm of the unexpected, the freshness of spring, the musky flavor of wild strawberries. The one is an identical formula: $A + A = A$ (Jean + Paul = Jean-Paul). The other a dialectic formula: $A + B = C$ (Edouard + Maria-Barbara = Jean + Paul + . . . Peter, etc.).

What Malacanthe taught me by getting me to tumble with her on the mattresses in the coach house was the love of life; and that life is not a great big linen cupboard full of neat piles of spotless, well-ironed sheets, scented with lavender bags, but a heap of dirty mattresses on which men and women have come into the world, where they have fornicated and slept, where they have suffered and died—and that it is well that it should be so. She made me understand, without telling me but simply by her living presence, that to be alive is to be involved, to have a wife who has her periods and who deceives you, children who get whooping cough, daughters who run away from home, sons who defy you, heirs who watch for you to die. Paul might regain possession of me every night, shut me up with him as though in a sealed bulb, wash me, disinfect me, anoint me with our common odor, and, finally, exchange seminal communion with me; but after the business of the triple mirror I no longer belonged to him, I felt the imperative need to live.

The business of the triple mirror which set the seal on the breaking of the geminate bulb marked in a way the end of my childhood, the beginning of my adolescence and the opening of my life to the outside world. Even so, the way had been paved for it by two minor, rather humorous episodes which deserve to be recorded.

When the time came for us to have our first identity cards, Edouard put forward the idea that it was pointless for us both to be photographed since the "authorities" we would have to deal with would never be able to tell one from the other. Only one of us need sit for both. This proposal met with instant agreement from Paul. But it revolted me, and I protested fiercely against the ruse. Thinking to satisfy me, Edouard immediately proposed that I should be the one to be photographed for both, and once again Paul agreed. But I would not hear of that either. Indeed, it seemed to me that by sticking the photo of only one of us on both cards they were setting the seal officially—and so perhaps irremediably and forever—on a confusion between us which in that moment I realized I no longer wanted. One at a time, therefore, we went into the automatic cabinet which had recently been installed in the booking hall of the station at Dinan, and each came out with a still-wet strip on which we were seen grinning six times over in the light of the flash. That evening, Edouard cut out the twelve little portraits, muddled them up idly and then pushed them over to me, asking me to sort out my own. The color mounted to my cheeks and at the same time I felt a special tightening of the heart, like no other, an anguish I had encountered recently for the first time. I could not sort out those pictures between Paul and myself except at random. What had happened was that I was being faced for the first time, unexpectedly, with a problem everyone else around us came up against several times a day: how to tell Paul and Jean apart. Everyone, that is, except us. Of course, we did not have everything in common. We each had our own books and toys and above all our clothes. But while we could tell them by signs imperceptible to the rest—a special shine, a worn patch and, more than anything, by their smell, which for clothes was decisive—these criteria did not hold good for photos which looked at the pair of us from an outsider's point of view. I felt my throat swelling with tears but I was too old to burst out crying and so I did my best to carry it off. Confidently selecting six pictures, I drew them toward me, pushing the others across to Paul. My confidence deceived no one and Edouard smiled, stroking the tip of his small moustache with his forefinger. Paul said merely, "We were both wearing shirts. Next time I'll put on a sweater. Then there can't be any mistake."

The other occasion was when the new term began in October. Traditionally we children went to spend a few days in Paris, to shop for winter clothes in the big department stores. Two of everything was bought for us twins, partly for convenience and partly out of respect for a kind of tradition which seemed natural. That year for the first time, I rebelled against the custom and insisted on buying clothes to make me look as different from Paul as possible.

"Besides," I added, to everyone's stupefaction, "we don't like the same things, and I don't see why I always have to have what Paul wants."

"Very well," Edouard decreed. "We'll split up, then. You shall go with your mother to the Bon Marché to buy your things, and I'll go with your brother to the Galeries Lafayette."

What Bep liked, in such a situation, was to fool the non-twins who claimed to tell us apart and make a surreptitious switch. For Paul, this was a matter of course and he was not a little shaken to hear me declare, "Bep's not playing. I'm going to the Bon Marché with Maria."

In this way I was working furiously to break up the geminate cell. Yet that very day I was to suffer a stinging defeat. I was the first to unpack my purchases. Paul and Edouard roared with laughter as they watched me bring out a tobacco-colored tweed suit, some check shirts, a dark green V-necked jersey, and a black turtleneck sweater. I understood, and felt again the same

anguish that gripped me every time the geminate cell closed in
on me in spite of my efforts to escape it, when I saw the same
tobacco-colored tweed suit, the same check shirts, and the same
black turtleneck sweater emerge from Paul's parcels. Only the
V-necked jersey was a lighter green than mine. All those around
me laughed a lot and Edouard more than anyone because the
"geminate circus" he clung to for the amusement of his friends
had been enriched with another entertaining anecdote. All the
same, it was he who pointed out the moral of the episode.

"You see, little Jean," he told me, "you didn't want to be
dressed like Paul anymore. But in choosing the clothes you liked
you forgot one small thing, which is that, whatever you may say,
you and Paul do like the same things. Next time, take one simple
precaution: choose only the things you hate."

Unfortunately there was a lot in what he said, and I have confirmed its harsh truth more than once since then. What sacrifices
haven't I had to make simply in order to distinguish myself from
Paul and not do as he did! If only we could have agreed to go
our own ways, then we could have shared the cost of our mutual
independence. But Paul never wanted to be different from me—
far from it—so that every time I took the lead or chose first I was
sure to find him following me or agreeing with my decision. And
so I always had to let him go first and be content with second
choice every time, a doubly unsatisfactory position because at
the same time I was forcing myself to accept decisions that went
against my instincts.

There were times when I weakened and gave in, letting myself slip back with no more resistance than in the days of our
childish innocence into the warm, familiar darkness of our geminate intimacy. Paul would welcome me with a joy which was
naturally infectious—everything is infectious within the cell, that
is the very definition of it—and would lap me in the joyous solici-
tude which is the prerogative of the prodigal brother returned.
The ritual exorcism would be exceptionally long and laborious
but that only made the seminal communion the sweeter. Yet it
would only be a truce. Once again I would tear myself away
from my twin brother and resume my solitary way. If I had had
any doubts about the necessity of what I was doing before the

business of the triple mirror, that horrible experience would have convinced me once and for all that I must carry it through.

If I am still hesitating on the brink of telling it, it is not just because it was a fearful, brutal shock and the mere recollection of it is enough to make me break out in a cold sweat. It is because it is much more than a memory. The threat is still there, the thunderbolt may fall on me at any moment, and I fear to challenge it by rash words.

I must have been thirteen or so. It happened in the shop of a tailor and outfitter in Dinan who used to "make a special price" for us because we were his wholesalers. It was not long after the affair of the department stores and I was still fighting to prevent Paul and me from ever being dressed alike again. Consequently I was alone in the shop, an important fact since if Paul had been with me the incident would probably never have happened. Paul's absence, which at that time was quite a novel experience, filled me, in fact, with a peculiar mood of exhilaration and dizziness, a somewhat mixed feeling, though rather pleasant on the whole, and not unlike that which pervades the kind of dream in which we believe we are flying through the air naked. Indeed, it has been with me ever since I parted from Paul, although it has changed a good deal in several years. Today I feel it as some power displacing my center of gravity and forcing me to keep going forward to try to regain my balance. In a way, it is a recognition of the nomadism which has always been my secret destiny.

But I had not reached that point on that fine spring Saturday as I was trying on a navy blue cloth cap in Conchon-Quinette's shop. I can still see the shop with its glass-fronted shelves, the heavy table piled with lengths of cloth and a brass-based measuring rod made of light wood standing on it. The cap seemed to suit me but I was trying not very successfully to make out my reflection in the glass cupboard doors. The shopkeeper noticed and invited me to go into a fitting room, where a triple mirror with the side panels moving on hinges let you see yourself full face and from both sides. I walked forward unsuspectingly into the trap and instantly its reflecting jaws closed on me and mangled me so cruelly that I shall carry the marks with me always. I felt an instant's shock. Someone was there, reflected three times over in that tiny space. Who? No sooner was the question framed than the answer came back thunderously: *Paul!* That rather pale boy, seen full face, from the right and from the left, fixed in that threefold photograph, was my twin brother, come there by what means I knew not, but undeniably there. And at the same time, a terrible emptiness grew within me and I was chilled by a deathly fear. For if Paul was there, living within the triptych, then I, Jean, was nowhere, I no longer existed.

The salesman found me unconscious on the carpet in his fitting room and, with the help of the owner, got me onto a sofa. Needless to say, no one—not even Paul—knows the secret of this incident, although it changed the whole course of my life. Has Paul ever had the same experience? Has he ever happened to look in a mirror and see me in his place? I doubt it. I think that for the illusion to occur there must be that *intoxication with emancipation* which I was describing earlier, and which Paul has certainly no idea of. Or else if he did one day see me looming up opposite him in a mirror, he would not be shocked as I was, but on the contrary delighted, charmed by the magical encounter, coming just at that moment to calm the uneasiness which, as he once confided to me, he felt at my absence. As for me, it has left me with a rooted grudge against all mirrors, and an insurmountable horror of triple mirrors, the presence of which I can sense anywhere in evil waves that are enough to make me stop and run the other way.

Paul

The twinless man in search of himself finds only shreds of his personality, rags of his self, shapeless fragments of that enigmatic being, the dark, impenetrable center of the world. For mirrors give him back only a fixed, reversed image; photographs are more deceptive still, and the comments he hears are distorted by love, hate or interest.

While as for me, I have a living image of myself of absolute veracity, a decoding machine to unravel all my riddles, a key to which my head, my heart and my genitals open unresistingly. That image, that decoder, that key is you, my twin brother.

Jean

You are absolute otherness. Twinless persons know of their neighbors, friends and family only the various particular qualities, faults, idiosyncrasies, personal characteristics, quaint or outrageous, by which they differ from themselves. They lose their way among these accidental features and fail to see—or to see correctly—the person, the human being underneath.

Now it was precisely to the presence of this abstract person that, over the years—the years of our childhood and adolescence —my twin brother's presence at my side had accustomed me. For none of the quaint or outrageous ornaments which are a stumbling block and a source of fascination to the twinless in their relations with one another had any weight, color or consistency for us, since we were both the same. The many-colored cloak of personality which halts the twinless gaze is colorless and transparent to geminate eyes, allowing them to see abstract, bare, disconcerting, vertiginous, skeletal, frightening: otherness.

CHAPTER IX

Fur and Feather

Alexandre

My lovely solitude—unified, virginal, and sealed like an egg—
which Roanne had so picturesquely shattered, is now miraculously re-established here in this white, undulating lunar landscape, the three hundred hectares of the rubbish dumps of
Miramas. It is true that out of that Roannais spring and summer
I retain a dog, Sam, whom I would now find it hard to do without. Also an earring—which I wear sometimes out of mischief—
that symbolizes the whole seething little world, Briffaut, Fabienne, the Cranes, the Château of Saint-Haon, Alexis, and
above all, above all, my little Daniel, to whom it is pledged and
of whose coming it gives me the promise every day and every
hour.

Fifteen kilometers before Salon, Route Nationale 113 is
crossed by a secondary road, Route 5, going south toward the
village of Entressen. After that, the desert of stones and gravel of
the Crau is broken only by a collection of low, windowless build-

ings, all identical and surrounded by enclosures of barbed wire. This is the munitions factory of Baussenq, sited in this deserted spot for safety reasons. Around here they have not forgotten the disaster of 1917 which laid waste the country like an earthquake or a bombardment. One of our people, young Louise Falque, who works on the dumps at Marignane, hurried up on her bicycle after the first explosions and no longer recognized her familiar landscape in that scorched earth with its torn-up trees and ruined houses. Despite the fires and continuing explosions, she tended the dreadfully burned and mutilated men she managed to pull from the debris. The general commanding area 15 is said to have praised her conduct in his dispatches.

To some extent these munitions dumps mark the border of my strange realm. After that, though the empty landscape continues as drear and stony as before, signs, more and more numerous, proclaim its next metamorphosis from the pure, barren plain to a pestilential chaos. It takes a good eye to make out from afar the first scrap of soiled paper fluttering in the wind among the branches of a sparse plane tree. But in this mistral country such unclean foliage sprouts with unusual luxuriance. As you go further, the trees—fewer and fewer of them, it is true—become laden with shavings, streamers, glass wool, corrugated cardboard, wisps of straw, tufts of kapok, and lumps of horsehair. Then all vegetation ceases—as in the mountains above a certain altitude—and you enter the land of the hundred white hills. For the refuse here is white, yes, and the pellet in my medallion with the arms of Marseille on it is like a little block of snow. White and sparkling, especially in the setting sun, no doubt because of the bottle tops, celluloid boxes, chips of galalith and panes of glass dotted about them. A strong, musty smell pervades the valleys; but it takes less than an hour to grow accustomed to it and after that you scarcely notice it.

The white hills would be cut off from the world but for the Paris–Lyon–Marseille railway which crosses them. This gives us two trains night and morning. They roar past, sealed up like strongboxes, drawn by thundering, whistling engines. Some quirk of the timetable makes the two trains, one from Paris, the other from Marseille, pass one another in our vicinity like contrary meteors, bringing noise and violence into our pale, silvery half-world. I cherish a hope that some day or other one of those meteors will be obliged to stop here. Windows will be lowered, heads poked out, startled and frightened by the strange, bleak terrain. Then I shall make a speech to those visitors from another planet. The dandy garbage man will inform them that they are newly dead. That they have been wiped from the face of the earth and passed over to its underside. That it is time for them to adapt their habits and ideas to this negative side of life to which they now belong. Then the doors will open and one by one they will jump out onto the embankment, and I shall encourage them, I shall direct their first, timid, faltering steps amid the discarded refuse of their past lives.

But that is a dream. The trains pass, spitting and screeching like dragons, and not a sign of human life is vouchsafed to us.

I am myself living in a converted railway carriage. Impossible to get back to a decent place to stay every evening. I sleep on a wide mattress laid on a board stretched between the seats of one of the compartments. I have water, heat and light—furnished in primitive style by an acetylene lamp that hisses like a cobra. It is a new experience for me and one more step toward my absorption in the refuse. The site workers who come every day in a truck from Entressen, where they live in barracks, bring me what I need from a list I give them the night before. The first evening I did not pay enough attention to the advice I had been given to keep every entrance to the wagon hermetically sealed. A terrified Sam woke me in the night. At first, hearing the faint, hurried pattering all around us, I thought it was raining. I lit the lamp. The rats were everywhere. They were running in black waves down the corridor and through the open compartments of the coach. They must have been galloping up and down on the roof. Fortunately, my own compartment was shut. Even so, I had to fight one huge female for twenty minutes before I finally ran her through with Fleurette. How had she got in? I shall never know. But I am far from forgetting the monster's squeals while her squirming bent Fleurette's blade like a fishing rod. Ganesh, Ganesh, trunked idol, how I prayed to you that night to call off your totem animal! After that, I immured myself in my compartment with Sam and my dead she-rat, fearful lest her open belly should spew forth a whole host of ratlings, while the rats outside besieged us with their infernal sabbath.

Just as the crowing of the cock brings the witches' revels to an instant end, so the rumble of the morning trains gave them the signal to depart. In less than three minutes they had all vanished into the thousands of holes that riddle the white hills. I understood the reason for this precipitate flight when I tipped the body of my victim out of the window. No sooner had the bloated corpse bounced off a heap of rotting potatoes than it was pounced upon by first one, then two, then three sea gulls, dropping out of the sky like stones. They were common gulls, clumsy and unfinished-looking, like albino crows, and they tossed that bloody rag about between them until it burst apart, strewing the guts and the fetus all about. Moreover, I could see that this was no unusual occurrence. Here and there, belated rats were being pursued, cut off, run down and torn apart by forays of gulls. For the daytime belongs to the birds and then they are sole masters of the silvery hills. The passing of the evening trains is the signal for this state of affairs to be reversed, because night is the kingdom of the rats. The gulls in their thousands take flight to their roosting places on the shores of the Etang de Berre, those that do not go to the Camargue to ravage the flamingos' nests. Woe to the slow or injured birds that linger on the rubbish dumps after the passing of the evening trains! Hordes of rats surround them, bite out their throats, and tear them to pieces. This is why, as you walk the hills, you come at every step upon shreds of fur or tufts of down, the leavings of a diurnal and nocturnal rhythm by which the hills are divided between the rule of fur and feather.

Twice a year, the little world of the tramps who work on the dumps receives a visit from men in white suits from the Cleansing Department of the city of Marseille. Armed with spray guns and carrying poisoned bread, they set about the business of disinfecting and clearing the rats from the hills. They are not particularly welcome. The men laugh at their masks and rubber gloves and their thigh boots. Look at the sissies! Frightened of dirt and germs! As for their task, it is both useless—for the immensity of the rat population defies all their efforts—and ill-omened, because their path is strewn with the corpses of rats and still more of gulls. Of course, it has been pointed out that these creatures are, after all, merely scavengers and help in their fashion to keep the dumps clean. But the truth is that the tramps feel a sense of solidarity with the animals and resent the activities of the men from Marseille as an infringement of their territory. Like the projected incineration plant at Roanne, the Marseille corporation's attempts at disinfection have the appearance of an attack by the central authorities upon the fringes.

(With the best of intentions, the men in white have left three buckets of poisoned paste in my wagon. "All-purpose," they assured me. But they warned me that the premium which the Marseille corporation used to pay rat catchers had been discontinued ever since one enterprising rogue had the idea of breeding rats in a van, killing them with acetylene gas and selling the resulting corpses in truckloads to the horrified public servants. The composition of the deadly paste is written on the buckets. It is lard thickened with flour and seasoned with arsenic. Out of curiosity, I left one of the buckets underneath my carriage all night with the lid off. The rats not only left the paste untouched, although they seemed to devour everything else indiscriminately, but they appeared to have avoided the very neighborhood of the receptacle. Which says a good deal for the efficacy of the poison!)

The work I am endeavoring to organize here is on a completely different scale from the controlled filling in of the Devil's Hole. Now that the Petite Crau to the north has been made fertile and transformed into olive groves, vineyards and pastureland by bringing the waters of the Durance to it by way of the Craponne Canal, the Marseille city council is cherishing the ambitious plan of making the Grande Crau fertile too by using the refuse of Miramas. What is now the shame of the great Mediterranean port, spread out for all the travelers on the Paris–Lyon–Marseille to see, would then become an object of pride. To do it, I have five bulldozers and a gang of twenty men, a pathetic force in relation to the transformation to be wrought. The way to do it should be to remove the more recent layers of refuse down to a depth of at least four meters in order to lay bare the old stuff underneath which has been turned into humus by long fermentation. But then the moisture stored and conserved at that level would be dissipated by the deep digging and there would be no way of replacing the essential irrigation.

Nevertheless, I have begun digging into one of the hills with a team of two bulldozers. The effect was terrifying. A cloud of gulls descended on the fresh-cut black trench that opened in the wake of each machine and the drivers needed unusually cool heads not to lose them in that whirlwind of beaks and wings. But this was nothing yet, because inevitably my machines ripped into tunnels inhabited by whole colonies of rats. Instantly battle was joined with the gulls. A number of gulls certainly had their throats bitten out in the fray, because a big rat can beat a sea gull in single combat. But the infinite number of the great birds overwhelmed the rats, driven out of their holes into the broad light of day. The worst part, though, was the sick terror and revulsion of my men, faced with this apparently endless task, aggravated by the pitched battle between fur and feather. One suggested fetching shotguns to drive off the birds. But someone else pointed out that only the gulls were keeping the rats at bay and that our position would become untenable if the rats became masters of the field by day as well as by night.

I have shared with Sam a can of cassoulet heated up on a small gas stove. In a few minutes the sun will be setting and already clouds of gray birds are rising and drifting away seaward, wailing. One by one I close all the entrances to the carriage, despite the stifling heat of the Provençal late summer. I have had the windows of the compartment I sleep in covered with wire netting so as to be able to keep them open all night. Although I am tormented by desire and nostalgia, I am glad that neither Daniel nor even Eustache is here to share such a weird solitude. Because the memory of their flesh is precious to me, I endow it with a delicacy incompatible with this terrible landscape. The rumble of the trains shakes the hills. They greet each other as they pass with piercing screams. Then silence falls again, enlivened gradually by the countless running feet as the rats pour out. My carriage is covered by the living tide but at least it pro-

vides as safe a refuge as a diving bell. The oblique light of the
setting sun gleams on a flock of simulated sheep, the effect
created by some bundles of glass wool scattered over the side of
the nearest hill. Why not admit it? The strangeness and horror of
my situation intoxicates me with a glorious joy. Any hetero
would think a man must be a saint, with a leaning toward mar-
tyrdom—or have murdered both father and mother—to endure
living as I am. Purblind fools! What of the strength, then? What
of the exhilarating sense of my own uniqueness? A few yards
from my window is a disemboweled mattress, losing its stuffing
through a hundred holes, and it is shaken by a kind of hiccup
every time a rat pops out of one of them. They generally emerge
in threes and fours—and the sight becomes increasingly comical
since it is evident that not all these creatures could be in the
mattress at the same time. Involuntarily, one looks for the catch,
the conjuring trick.

I am made of an alloy of steel and helium, absolutely changeless, unbreakable, rustproof. Or rather, alas, I was. . . . For that
little wretch Daniel has infected the angel of light with humanity. The passion of pity he injected into me still gnaws at my
heart. It was when I watched him sleeping that I loved him best
—and that alone betrays the dubious quality of my feelings for
him; for a strong, healthy love, I believe, implies a mutual clearsightedness and a giving on both sides. I would wake in the middle of the night and go and sit in the big high-backed armchair
by his bedside. I would listen to his regular breathing, his sighs,
his stirrings, all the business of the little sleep factory he had become. The mumbled words that occasionally escaped from his
lips belonged, I thought, to a secret and at the same time a universal language, the fossil tongue that all men spoke before civilization. The mysterious life of the sleeper, close to insanity,
which becomes obvious in sleepwalking. I would light the candle
that stood on the bedside table in anticipation of my visits.
Evidently he knew of this nocturnal habit of mine. He would
have been able to tell in the morning how many times I had
gone down to him by counting the used matches, how long I had
stayed in all by measuring the amount the candle had gone
down. He didn't care. I could never have tolerated being taken

unawares like that. Because I know—as he did not—with what
fervent vigilance I would watch over his slumbers in those fevered minutes. Incubus, my brother, succubus, my sister, how I
sympathize with you, you sly, lascivious imps, for waiting until
sleep delivers up to you the men and women you covet, naked
and unawares!

I must have been asleep for several hours. The moon has risen
over my lunar landscape. Those ragged, translucent clouds, like
thin slivers of crystal, just touching the lower edge of the milk-
white disk, probably herald the mistral. The site workers have
assured me it has the power of maddening my gentle creatures
of fur and feather alike. The white hills, spangled and glittering,
undulate as far as the eye can see. From time to time a section of
grayish carpet with rippling edges detaches itself from the side
of one of them and slides down into a valley, or else sweeps up
out of the dark depths and comes to rest upon a crest. A horde of
rats.

Daniel's face. His pale, hollow cheeks, his black forelock, his
lips, somewhat too full . . . Perfect love—the perfect fusion of
physical desire and affection—finds its touchstone, its infallible
sign in the rather rare phenomenon of *physical desire inspired
by the face.* When to my eyes a face has come to contain more
eroticism than all the rest of the body put together . . . that is
love. I know now that the face is really the most erotic part of
the human body. That man's true sexual parts are his mouth, his
nose and above all his eyes. That true love makes itself felt by a
rising of the sap all through the body—as in a tree in springtime
—mingling the come with the saliva in the mouth, the tears in
the eyes, and the sweat of the brow. But in Daniel's case, the
unhealthy pity he inspires me with—in spite of himself and of me
—insinuates its dross into that pure metal. Flushed with health
and bubbling with happiness, I have to confess that he would
lose all his noxious charm.

Another hour or two of dozing. This time I was awakened by
something banging against my wagon. A sudden, violent blow
which shook the long chassis resting on its two wheelless bogies.

A glance out of the window. The hills are placarded with a hurricane of papers and packaging. The mistral. Another invisible onslaught on my carriage which groans in the voice it used to use as it moved slowly out of a station. Sam is visibly uneasy. Has he noticed as I have the carpet of rats now rolling over the sides of all the hills? It is as though they are possessed by some furious madness. Is it the effect of the fiercer and fiercer gusts which are shaking our wagon and whirling masses of refuse high into the air? I am reminded of sand dunes moved slowly, a grain at a time, by the wind. Are the white hills of Miramas equally prone to wander? If so, it would explain the panic among the rats, for all their tunnels would be disturbed. It is impossible to see out of the windows on the north side of the carriage because they are blocked by the accumulation of refuse like snowdrifts carried by the wind. The terrifying thought occurs to me that if the hills do move we might find ourselves covered over, buried under one of them. Strong as my nerves and stomach are, I am beginning to find my situation here unhealthy. If I were to follow my inclination, I should seize the first excuse to take myself off to a more welcoming spot. Wouldn't I, Sam? Wouldn't we be better off elsewhere? I was expecting flattened ears, a flick of the tongue toward my face, a quickly beating tail. But no, he lifts a miserable face to mine and paws the ground. The dog is sick with terror.

An excuse to get out? Suddenly I have more than that. An imperative reason, an absolute necessity! In between two of the gusts of flying refuse which continually block my view in assorted clouds, I caught a glimpse of a figure out there, a long way off, on the crest of a hill. One arm was raised as though signaling, signaling for help, perhaps. I measure the horror of being lost like that in the livid light of dawn, amid the buffeting of the mistral, the bombardment of refuse and worse, worst of all, the black battalions of rats! Out. I open a door. Three rats, taken by surprise—as though they had been spying on what I was up to inside—glare at me suspiciously out of their little pink eyes. I shut the door abruptly.

First, Sam shall stay here. There is no reason for him to go out with me. Next I must find some protection against rat bites.

What I need, in fact, is armor, especially for my legs. Failing that, I don a pair of workman's overalls which are lying in the wagon. And I have the idea of smearing my shoes, my legs and thighs and up to my stomach with the deadly paste which the rats seem to hate. It takes time. I am reminded of the old women on the beach, anointing their skins with disgusting oils. It is to go bathing in moonlight and garbage that I am administering to myself this new kind of extreme unction.

I order Sam peremptorily not to stir. He lies down without protest. I slip outside. The same three rats fall back before my menacing feet. The deadly paste is working wonders. On the other hand, a crate launched with the speed of a cannonball hits me full in the chest. If that had got my face I should have been out for the count. Beware flying objects! I long for the masks and breastplates of the Foils' fencing school. I advance slowly, clumsily, leaning on a stick which could also be useful as a weapon. Not a cloud in the pale sky which is beginning to turn pink in the east. This is the sky of the Lord Mistral, dry, pure and cold as a mirror of ice, with terrible squalls skating over it. I put my foot into a nest of brown snakes with large, greenish heads which, on closer inspection, turn into a tangle of trusses with horsehair pads on the ends. I pass under an overhang of rubbish, instinctively quickening my pace. As well I did, for I see it collapse behind me, releasing a swarm of frightened, angry rats. I keep to the dips because there the wind and the missiles are not so much to be feared, only the rats are doing the same for the same reasons, and sometimes I see a running carpet part before my feet, to close in again behind me. But I am compelled to climb a hill to get my bearings. A backward glance shows the wagon half hidden under the refuse that has come up against it in its crazy flight. I find myself wondering whether it won't be covered over and buried, and indeed its oblong shape, seen slightly askew, does give the impression of a huge coffin lying in the snow. Sam. I must hurry and get him out of there. Ahead of me the hummocky plain that stretches as far as the eye can see is strewn with a wild cavalry of refuse, all charging southward. I believe I can spy the crest where I saw a human figure wave and then disappear. Forward! I set off downhill. My right leg plunges into a crevice and there I am writhing, flat on my face on a bed of jam pots. Scratched, but nothing broken. Only I can't get up fast enough to avoid being swarmed over by a wave of rats running in the other direction. I lie still for fear of crushing or injuring one or two who would fight back with their teeth. Now, up and on, keep walking! I scramble up the last hill, strewn with a quantity of small woolen objects, rotting baby clothes, the whole layette of a disinterred stillborn infant. At last I am looking down into a kind of crater. The horror of what I see there is indescribable.

In the month that I have been here I have seen many rats. Never in such a compact horde, activated by such a furious frenzy. They are seething like some viscous black liquid in the bottom of the hollow and around its edges. At the center of this boiling mass is a human form, stretched on its face with outflung arms. The skull has already been laid bare, although a few tufts of dark hair, half torn away, remain. That thin, narrow back, that knobby spine . . . I know, without seeing more. Daniel! What had been no more than an unspoken guess becomes an agonizing certainty. He came to me. He has perished. How did he fall? As if in answer, a gust of wind, followed immediately by a furious onslaught of empty baskets and boxes, has me staggering on the edge of the crater. Go down into that witches' cauldron? I must, I have to. Perhaps something may still be done for him. But truly my heart fails me. I hesitate, but gather my courage. I am going down, I am going to plunge into that horror. And then comes the reprieve: the double whistle blast of the two trains passing one another back there on the level. The rats will go away. They are going already. The black battalions with their hundred thousand feet are retreating. No, I do not see them running, moving away. They vanish, no one knows how. It is as if the viscous liquid were absorbed into the depths of the white ground. I wait now with a clear conscience. Patience, little Daniel, I am coming, I am coming! Another minute and the last rats will be gone.

I take a leap into space and land on a steepish slope. The ground goes from under my feet. A landslide, an avalanche. This is what must have happened to Daniel. I reach bottom close by him, upside down amid a huge collection of soiled dressings and empty medicine bottles, presumably the detritus of a hospital. Forget it. Daniel is there, at my feet. The wounds inflicted by the rats are much worse than I was able to see from a distance. It seems as though they went for the neck primarily. It has been cut into deeply, as if by an ax, as if by a saw, a saw with millions of tiny, nibbling teeth, so deeply that the head is barely attached to the trunk and falls backward as I turn the body over with my toe. They have gone for the genitals, too. The neck and the genitals. Why? The lower part of the abdomen, the only part where the clothes have been ripped away, is all one bleeding wound. I stand lost in contemplation of the poor disjointed puppet which has no more humanity now than the obscenity of dead bodies. My meditation is no finespun, considered reflection, it is a stunned silence, a mindless stillness in the strange calm of this hole. My poor, battered brain is incapable of more than the one, very simple, very down-to-earth question: the little gold chain and the medal of the Virgin? Where are they? Up above, the gusts are nibbling at the rim of the crater and sending lumps of refuse toppling down into it. Down here, there is the peace of the deep. The ruah . . . The wind charged with spirit. The wind with the wings of the white dove, the symbol of physical passion and of the word . . . Why is it that truth can never be revealed to me except in a grotesque and hideous form? What is it in me that always attracts this grinning masquerade?

For some seconds I had been watching a fat white rat panting up the side of the crater. Was it gobbling Daniel's genitals that had made it so heavy? What was that about the pure, symbolic dove? A meteor of claws and feathers has just fallen on the big rat. It turns bravely, lays back its little ears, and bares a row of teeth as sharp as needles. The bristling gull, made huge by its outspread wings, hisses at it furiously but keeps at a safe distance. I know from experience that, contrary to appearances, the fight would go in the rat's favor, but that it will not take place. The rat is cornered, immobilized, concentrated on its adversary. That is foreseen, expected. Another gull swoops on it, covers it briefly with its wings and soars skyward again. The rat is writhing on the ground, its neck sliced through. The same death as

Daniel's. And the first bird finishes it off, shakes it, tosses it in the air like a bloody rag.

A distant clamor reaches me. I look up at the circle of sky limned by the crater. A silvery cloud is undulating majestically up there, it elongates and then, on the point of dissolution, comes together again and grows with terrifying speed. The gulls, thousands, tens of thousands of gulls! Flee, before my tattered body goes to join the rat's! Dani . . . For the last time I bend over what was his face, over his empty eye sockets, his cheeks so lacerated that the teeth show through, his ears . . . A glint of pearl beside that mask of horror. I bend lower. The earring, the Philippine pearl whose twin is in my possession. Little Daniel had put it on to come to me! And I actually wonder whether it was that magic earring that drew him to my wagon, by the ear like a naughty schoolboy. Now the gulls are raining down all around. Flee . . . flee . . .

P.S. Dani, you knew that this hard, tense, unfeeling face I show to other people is not my real face. It is only shadowed by loneliness and exile. Thus it is when my face is naked and my body clothed. No one who has not seen me completely naked knows my true face. For then the warm presence of my body comforts and softens it, and brings back its natural goodness. I wonder even whether desire is not a kind of madness, the special madness brought on by exile, the wandering madness of a face dispossessed of its body. It is because it is orphaned of my body that my face seeks eagerly, hunts keenly for the body of another. It is because it is alone, naked and afraid at the top of a dressed-up dummy that it requires the hollow of a shoulder for its forehead, the hollow of an armpit for its nose, the hollow of a groin for its lips.

No one who has not seen me happy knows my true face. For then the ash that covers it glows and burns, its dead fish eyes light up like lamps, its lipless mouth is outlined in rosy flesh, a whole cinema of colored pictures passes across its brow . . .

Both these secrets and some others have died with you, Dani . . .

When none of my site workers turned up, I thought at first it was the mistral that had put them off, an unlikely theory but I could think of nothing else. I went with Sam to Entressen. When we arrived, before noon, it was to learn that the order for a general mobilization had gone out the night before and that war was going to break out at any moment. I went to the gendarmerie to report finding a body in the white hills. No one wanted to listen to me. With a mobilization order on their hands, they had other things to think about! In the white hills? That's a place that the police steer clear of. Outlaw country. The body probably belonged to a ragpicker, a secondhand dealer, a garbage collector or some tramp. The settlement of a score between Arabs, Piedmontese, or Corsicans. I understood that we were outside society, and I thanked my stars I was not liable for military service. Well, let them carve each other up, these respectable, heterosexual citizens. We, the outcasts, will stand by and watch them.

I whistled for Sam and made my way to the station. The train to Lyon. Then Fontainebleau, Saint-Escobille. There I'll be on my own ground and on the edge of Paris at the same time. A front-row seat for the arrival . . .

CHAPTER X

Almond Turnovers

One of the chief reasons for having wars is undoubtedly to provide men with holidays. Even a period of military service is delightful to them in retrospect. It forms a break of enforced idleness between the end of school and the beginning of their careers, devoted to entirely novel and useless tasks, dominated by preposterous, artificial disciplinary rules which take the place of morality and decency, but above all released from any sense of responsibility and all concern for the future. Edouard had nothing but happy memories of the long holidays he had had during the last part of 1918, which were brightened by the explosion of November 11. Fresh from the barracks at Rennes, he had set his victorious boots ringing on the streets of Paris without any fighting, and being a handsome lad, full of good fellowship, and free with his money, had enjoyed great popularity with men and women.

But the war did more than restore to him some of that free, lighthearted youth. It not only swept away the cares of the Pierres Sonnantes, of Florence and Maria-Barbara. It filled him with a happy exhilaration, a slightly intoxicated eagerness made up of a curious mixture of the love of life and a presentiment, almost a desire for imminent death. Added to the urgency of the ordinary duties his patriotic nature prescribed, there was an aspiration to sacrifice which secretly appealed to a bitterness and a world-weariness in him. His age, his indifferent health, his family responsibilities would have exempted him from military service. He made use of his extensive connections at the War Ministry to get himself enlisted as a volunteer.

He joined on September 15 at Rennes, with the rank of captain in the 27th Infantry Regiment, which was moved, ten days later, into a position on the Belgian border. Then began for him —and for several million others—the long, wintry wait of the "phony war."

The area was important because of the possibility of the Germans making a dash through Belgium, and large numbers of troops were stationed there. But facing them on the other side of the border they had only a friendly population, and the troops were reduced to leading the peaceful, carefree life of a garrison town. The public places in Saint-Amand, which had closed after the precipitate departure of those taking the thermal baths when war was declared, reopened their doors one by one before an influx of uniformed customers quite as numerous and with even more leisure than their civilian clients.

The church tower, which had been turned into a campanological museum, was the first to be reopened to the public, to whole companies of hilarious private soldiers, for whom the bells were the subject of unprintable witticisms. Then it was the cinemas, the tennis courts, the municipal concert hall, where the regimental band played overtures by Massenet, Chabrier, Delibes and Charles Lecocq. The officers went hare coursing on the plateau of Le Pévèle and boar hunting in the Forest of Raismes.

Edouard felt as if he were living a life of dreamlike happiness, he was so lighthearted and free from the trivial pressures of everyday life. Maria-Barbara, his children, Florence were all in their proper place, safely behind the lines. The questioning, the doubts and anxieties which had darkened his recent years, the uncomfortable awareness of approaching age—the war had post-poned all these for a long time, perhaps forever. He had a nice room at the Blue Inn beside the Scarpe, so close that he could have fished for trout from his window. A few yards further on, at a baker's shop named the Golden Croissant, he had noticed a splendid girl behind the counter and started laying siege to her. She was called Angelica—Angi to her friends—and she was very tall, very straight and very fair, and smelled agreeably of bri-oches and the *chausson amandinois* for which the place was famous. Edouard's courtship went through an initial pastry-eat-ing phase which consisted of twice-daily purchases of *chaus-sons*. But he very soon tired of the Flemish pastries, spiced with cinnamon and thickly encrusted with blanched almonds, and took to giving away his purchases to the first children he met. He was on the way to gaining a local reputation as an eccentric when the fair Angelica put an end to his maneuvers by agreeing to go with him to the dance which was to follow a performance of Marivaux's *La Surprise de l'amour* given by the Army Theater Company. Afterward she showed her good sense by steadfastly refusing to prolong the evening any further; the next day being *chausson* day she had to begin work at the Golden Croissant at six o'clock. But two days later, Edouard was learning to know the ways of the big, strong, awkward body which, although ad-mittedly somewhat slow to arouse, was powerful and sustained in its responses.

After a brief hiatus, the casino and thermal baths situated to the east of the village on the outskirts of the Forest of Raismes were once again in full swing. Inactivity made its douches, baths and massages a diversion which officers, NCOs and enlisted men alike took full advantage of. Edouard, who was suffering from back pains, consented for the first time, thanks to the "phony war," to do something about them. Having tried douches of ra-dioactive mineral water gushing out at 26° C., he made up his mind with the onset of the first cold weather to experiment with the mud baths from which he had hitherto recoiled.

He put his hesitation down to a very natural reluctance to im-merse himself in a slimy, semi-liquid substance full of noxious chemicals. He discovered by experience that the truth was something altogether different and profoundly more significant and disturbing. When he found himself up to his chin in the warm, quaking brown mass with traces of green in it and giving off fumes of sulphur and iron, his eyes turned to the walls and the sides of the plain cast-iron bath as the one solid thing to cling to, a rampart, a plank for a drowning man—and he clutched it, what is more, with both hands. Yet even the cast iron was eaten away, spotted and corroded by the sulphates, chlorides and bicarbonates that were poured into it. Surely it was the image of a coffin doomed to turn to dust along with the body it contained? Edouard was not prone to philosophical meditation but during those long, solitary minutes in the mud bath he found himself falling into a morbid reverie to which the mephitic vapors gave an infernal twist. The airy happiness he had been floating in since his arrival at Saint-Amand-les-Eaux certainly sprang from the severance of the ties, family, sentimental and professional, which had been growing consistently heavier, year by year, and in the end were suffocating him. But this release was not unlike the naked state to which extreme old age and the act of dying reduce a man, before easing him into the next world. In short, Edouard thought he recognized the winged joy that sometimes shines about the dying when their bodies have given up the struggle against illness, the happy remission which can look like a sudden rallying but which is merely the approach of death. A presentiment he had felt when war was declared returned to him with absolute clarity: he was going to die. The war was going to bring him the premature end—at once fitting and worthy of him, and unexceptionable if not heroic—which would spare him the decay of old age. After that the mud baths became spiritual exercises, periods of thought and contemplation, a novel experience for him and one he found enjoyable and also a little frightening.

So it came about that a succession of ideas and images hovered about what he thought of privately as his "metaphysical bath," surprising him by their serious and original turn. He recalled that slime was the primordial matter out of which man had been fashioned by God and thus the ultimate end of life returned to its absolute beginnings. That the starting point and destination of life's great adventure should be a dirty and gener-

ally despised substance filled him with amazement, and it set
him thinking of his brother Alexandre who had become a garbage man in spite of himself, dealing with all the nastiest, most
disgusting aspects of society, urban waste and household rubbish. Suddenly he looked at the dandy garbage man with new
eyes. He had always regarded this hostile, secretive younger
brother of his, who emerged from behind his mother's skirts only
to fling himself into unsavory escapades, with a mixture of fear
and contempt. Upon becoming the head of a family, he had kept
at a distance the shocking uncle whose example—and even his
business—constituted a danger to his children. Later on, Gustave's death and the problem of who was to succeed him had
given rise to the family plot aimed at placing the direction of
TURDCO on the shoulders of that idle libertine. True, Edouard
had stood aside, as far as he could, from these maneuverings and
negotiations. But how much of his reserve was caution and how
much selfishness? And in the end surely it was dreadful to have
pushed Alexandre into a job and an environment, into just those
grubby fringes of society which were most likely to encourage his
bad habits? Edouard, Edouard, what have you done to your little
brother? He promised himself to try to do something for him
when the occasion arose, but would it ever arise? Alexandre, the
refuse man, refuse himself, living refuse . . . Edouard, up to his
neck in mud, thought vaguely of the other living refuse with
which his children were surrounded, in the persons of the children of St. Brigitte's.

Was it because he was going to die? Amid the sulphurous
fumes of his mud baths, whole episodes out of his past life came
back to him with intense vividness.

November 1918. He was twenty-one. Having been called up
three months earlier, he had just had time to grow accustomed to his private's uniform when the Armistice was signed.
He was in Paris at the time, having gone there to say goodbye to
his mother and younger brother before undergoing a course of
intensive training behind the front line. The news burst like a
bombshell, a bombshell packed with confetti, streamers and
chocolates. Edouard looked so nice in his uniform—puttees em-
phasizing shapely calves, belt fitting neatly around his waist, im-

pudent little moustache on his young face which still retained its round, boyish cheeks, and as clean as if he were straight out of a bandbox—he fitted the civilians' dream of "our soldier boys" so perfectly that he was instantly taken up by the crowd, cheered and made much of, carried shoulder high and adopted as a mascot, the symbol of victory, he who had never heard a shot fired. He yielded with good grace to the general madness, drank at a score of tables, joined in the improvised dances that were springing into being at every street corner, and collapsed in a wretched hotel in the small hours of the morning with a girl on either side. He stuck to the one on the left for six months—while awaiting his demobilization. She was a chubby little brunette, a manicurist by trade, with a sharp tongue in her head, and having known from the beginning how slender was Edouard's military record, she introduced him everywhere as "my soldier boy who won the war." He allowed himself to be pampered and petted—she did his hands for him—and looked after with the clear conscience of the returned warrior. In the spring he had to hand in his uniform. The war was over. The boredom was about to begin.

"What it comes down to," Edouard sighed, moving his legs gently in the viscous mass that enveloped them, "is that I ought to have made the army my career."

September 1920. His marriage to Maria-Barbara. The church of Notre Dame du Guildo was crowded because people had come from far and wide to see the new master of the Pierres Sonnantes, and for Maria-Barbara's sake. She was a widow and a mother, but that first marriage, that first pregnancy had served to ripen her in the way that suited her type of beauty. What a couple they made, bursting with youth and health! It was a union of two great flowers, two divine beings, two allegories, Beauty and Strength, or Wisdom and Courage. There was one thing which had struck more than one guest. How alike they were! They might have been brother and sister! In fact, they were not alike, they had not a single feature in common. She was very dark, with a low forehead, big green eyes and a small, though full-lipped mouth. He had light brown hair which had been fair in childhood, a high forehead, mobile lips and a general air of innocent vanity, whereas Maria-Barbara gave an impression of reserved but friendly alertness. But the apparent likeness came from the happy confidence and speechless joy that radiated from both equally and enveloped them like a single being.

Brother and sister, indeed? That night in their bridal chamber they had laughed at the memory of that comment, which they had heard more than once during the day. Their relations, in the six months they had known each other, had been hardly those of brother and sister! And yet, once the light was out, lying on their backs in their twin beds, they had simply held hands and remained gazing up at the ceiling in silence, struck by the depth and seriousness of the echoes which that idea of fraternity had woken within them. Surely marriage created a kind of relationship between husband and wife and, since the two belonged to the same generation, wasn't the relationship analogous to that between brother and sister? And wasn't marriage between real brothers and sisters forbidden precisely because it was absurd to try to create by an institution and a sacrament something that existed already in fact?

They felt this incorporeal brotherhood hovering over their union like an ideal, weighing on it like an obligation, and if it was a pledge of fidelity and eternal youth it also implied a stillness, a perfect balance, sterility. And so they spent their wedding night, unmoving, sliding into sleep side by side and hand in hand.

The next day they left on their honeymoon, for Venice of course, since this was the Surin family tradition. But it was in Verona, where they went on a day trip, that they came across another allusion to that strange ideal of fraternal lovers. The orchestra and singers of La Scala, Milan, were giving a special performance there of Hector Berlioz's dramatic symphony *Romeo and Juliet*. Even more than Tristan and Isolde, the lovers of Verona stand apart from the image of the real married pair, even though they are one of the chief models of it. They are children —he is fifteen, she fourteen—and it is, besides, quite inconceivable that they should found a family and turn into mother and father. Their love is absolute, eternal, immutable. Romeo can no more leave Juliet than Juliet can deceive Romeo. But they live in an environment subject to all the vicissitudes of soci-

ety and history. The absolute is a prey to corruption, eternity to
change. Their deaths follow inevitably from that contradiction.

In fact, it was the image of a young brother and his younger
sister that Edouard glimpsed superimposed upon that of this impossible married couple. And he discovered—this time from outside—the same paradoxical resemblance that the people at Notre
Dame du Guildo had seen between Maria-Barbara and himself,
who were actually not at all alike. Romeo and Juliet were quite
unlike each other also, so far as details of face and figure went,
but they were brought together by a deep affinity, a secret similarity which prompted the notion that they were brother and
sister. In short, a couple joined by an absolute, immutable and
unchanging passion, suspended in an eternal present, is bound to
take on a fraternal form.

The form in his case was certainly a fleeting one, lasting no
longer than the trip to Italy. For Maria-Barbara was no sooner
back at the Pierres Sonnantes than she announced that she was
pregnant and she was to be so almost continually for the next
eleven years. They had come a very long way from the long-for-
gotten sterile and fraternal little pair in the arena at Verona one
September evening in 1920.

These successive pregnancies were to continue until 1931, the
year the twins, Jean and Paul, were born. By some curious quirk
of nature, Maria-Barbara never became pregnant again after this
double birth and no one could ever quite rid her of the suspicion
that she had been sterilized during the brief period of anesthesia
her labor had necessitated.

Now, amid the radioactive fumes of his bath, Edouard amused
himself by drawing comparisons between the pair of twins and
the lovers of Verona. He and Maria-Barbara—being totally un-
suited to it—had missed the invitation to the absolute which had
been offered them that night through Berlioz's music. Was it not
conceivable that they had made up for their failure eleven years
later by bringing those two children into the world? But while
they themselves had remained very much on this side of the
ideal of Verona, the twins were going very far beyond it, provid-
ing the literal, pure and original version of the fraternal couple,

so that now it was Romeo and Juliet who looked like a rough compromise by comparison.

There was one small point whereby the affinity between the two pairs was enriched and surrounded in mystery. Edouard, like everyone else who came in contact with Jean and Paul, had been struck by the Aeolian, the cryptophasia with which they communicated with one another secretly amid the public voices of those around them. He recollected now that in Berlioz's *Romeo and Juliet* only the outward events of the tragedy are expressed by the chorus in human language, while the intimate feelings of the two lovers are suggested solely by instrumental passages. The tender dialogue between Romeo and Juliet in the third section, for instance, is contained entirely in an adagio for alternating strings and woodwind.

The more he thought about it, the more illuminating he found the comparison between Aeolian and a kind of music, a secret music, attuned to the rhythm of the same living stream and understood by the twin brother alone, unintelligible to others who seek in vain for a vocabulary and syntax in it.

October 1932. In early autumn Edouard was obliged to take notice of some ill health which he had previously treated with contempt. He had put on a great deal of weight in the past two years and that could have explained his breathlessness after any exertion, his sudden bouts of exhaustion and lack of enthusiasm for life. But he was also complaining of his eyesight which was showing a galloping presbyopia, and his gums, which were soft and bled when he brushed them, were receding, exposing the roots of the teeth.

After a tentative suggestion about consulting a specialist, Maria-Barbara gave up and did not mention it again, and it was Méline who took him firmly to the doctor in Matignon. He agreed, laughing, to please the women, he said, convinced beforehand that he was perfectly well and also that in spite of this the doctor would find him to be suffering from every disease under the sun.

The only thing he did find was sugar diabetes, slight, certainly, but still worrisome in a man of thirty-five. He must give up smoking, drink as little alcohol as possible and try to cut

down on rich food. Edouard was triumphant. His forecasts about
the pointless consultation were entirely justified. But he was not
going to lend himself to the process which, with help from his
doctor, his pharmacist, and his loving wife, could turn a normal
man into an invalid. He was not going to alter his life at all. Of
course he had various minor ailments. But they were part of the
ordinary background of life and the wisest thing to do was to
leave them there, scattered, vague and diffuse, marring the general picture, certainly, but not adding up to a focus of morbidity
in which their virulence would be increased to form a coherent
whole.

The doctor's role was precisely to tease out as many little
weaknesses and assorted ailments as possible, to build them into
symptoms, group them into a syndrome and so raise a monument
to pain and death in the life of a man, classified, named, dock-
eted and organized. Of course, this initial action was in theory
only the first stage. It was directed toward isolating the malady,
setting it up as a target the better to shoot it down. But more
often than not that second stage went awry and the man, having
been elevated to the dubious rank of invalid, was left alone to
confront the black and green idol of his disease, with nothing
left to do, since he could not overcome it, but to serve and try to
placate it.

Edouard would have none of this dreadful game. In contrast
to the doctor, he was always trying to drown the unhealthy erup-
tions, the insalubrious islets that force of circumstances created
in his life, in the waters of everyday existence. He had been
wrong to give in to the women and take the first step along that
fatal road. He would go no further. Had even the word "diabetes" so much as reached his ears? If so, he had forgotten it at
once. He had cast out the kernel of that abscess of fixation instantly, by a reflex, before it could feed on the offerings of the
still untouched body on which it would have grown.

Smiling ironically, smoothing his moustache, he consigned pre-
scriptions and advice to the devil and when Maria-Barbara asked
anxiously about the outcome of the consultation, he replied,
"Just as I expected, it was nothing. A little overtiredness, per-

haps." And he had resumed the pattern of his comings and goings between Paris and the Pierres Sonnantes.

The winter, which came very early that year, was broken up by
such generous allowances of Christmas leave that Saint-Amand
and its vicinity were emptied of Allied troops as though from the
effects of a temporary demobilization. Edouard found himself
back with Maria-Barbara and the children around the Christmas
tree, to which the war seemed to give an added luster. The children of St. Brigitte's, formed into a choir and a company of actors, sang carols and mimed the wonderful story of the Three
Kings come from far Arabia to worship the Messiah. For the first
time in decades quite a thick layer of snow covered the countryside and coast of Brittany. From his first arrival, Edouard saw
his family, his house and the landscape with an unreal clarity,
which came perhaps from a kind of unwonted stillness, as
though things and people had been momentarily fixed, as in a
photograph. A photograph, yes, that was how the familiar world
looked to him, like an old photograph which is all that remains
after time has destroyed everything. And in its center tall Maria-
Barbara, ever serene amid that host of children, her own and the
innocents, mother and foster mother, protectress of all the inhabitants of the Pierres Sonnantes.

Edouard cut his stay short in order to be able to spend twenty-
four hours with Florence. He found her her usual self, not appearing to take either the war or Edouard in uniform, who personified
it in her eyes, very seriously. She sang him soldiers' songs in her
grave voice, accompanying herself on her guitar, "La Madelon,"
"Le Clairon," "Sambre-et-Meuse," a whole spirited and ingenuous
repertoire, and she gave the gay, swinging old march tunes such
a melancholy sweetness that they took on a mournful charm, like
an echo gathered from the lips of dying soldiers.

It was with relief that he returned to his winter quarters in
Saint-Amand and Angelica's big, fair, stalwart body, smelling of
hot bread. But once he had resumed the thread of his thermal
meditations, he found himself comparing the three women who
seemed to preside over his destiny. It had bothered him before
the war that his flesh and his heart were pulling different ways,

Maria-Barbara retaining all his affection while he no longer desired anyone but Florence. Surely this divorce between what he called his hunger and his thirst was as if love were decaying and already giving off a smell of death? The war had come to reconcile him to himself and had given him this Angi who was both desirable and touching, exciting and reassuring. But this gift had fallen out of a sky which had the faint, sad splendor of a wayside pulpit pervaded with dying scents. He was going to die and Angi was the farewell gift that life was giving him.

The photographic look the Pierres Sonnantes had seemed to wear during his Christmas leave and even more the sad march tunes Florence had sung had been proof that the grim, warlike skies of Saint-Amand were in the future to cover his whole life, since his three women—and also ultimately his children and his friends—were, each in their own way, giving him the same message. It was to Angelica, naturally, that the chief and primary role in this funeral pavane belonged.

She it was whom death struck first.

The spring of 1940 had burst with a fanfare of flowers. The fruit trees and cornfields promised magnificent harvests, as long as no sudden frost came to spoil the fine promise. A sudden frost or some other sudden attack . . .

On May 10 Edouard was at the thermal spa, in the hands of an energetic masseuse, when a distant rumbling followed by the sound of a number of small aircraft rushing over warned him that something was happening in the direction of the town.

He dressed hastily and hurried back there. The news was bad. The sleeping war had woken and the monster was storming northward. To be accurate, the German forces were pushing through the Netherlands, introducing a new kind of warfare in which tanks and planes worked closely together. A host of small aircraft, Stukas, designed for dive bombing, had appeared suddenly in the skies above Belgium and northern France. The effect was intended to be more psychological than physical and the handful of bombs allocated to Saint-Amand-les-Eaux had done only slight damage.

Now that Belgium was threatened and the French headquarters plan in that eventuality being to cross the frontier and advance to meet the enemy, the whole sector was in a ferment. They were expecting their marching orders hourly.

It was not until late in the afternoon that Edouard learned the news: one small high-explosive bomb had smashed into the bakery of the Golden Croissant, killing the baker's boy and seriously wounding Angelica. The owners, as it happened, were not at home. Edouard went to her immediately, but scarcely recognized her under her helmet of bandages. She died the next morning, while he was on his way to Tournai.

The surrender of the Netherlands on May 15, and then of Belgium on the 28th, following the capture of Arras by the Kleist Korps on the 23rd, Boulogne on the 24th, and Calais on the 25th, completed the chopping up of the Allied armies into several pieces which no efforts could serve to reunite. While 340,000 men were fighting on the beaches at Dunkirk, endeavoring to get away by sea to England, the 10th Infantry Regiment, together with the Fourth and Fifth Army Corps, was encircled at Lille.

During these tragic days, Edouard found himself curiously free of the presentiment of imminent death which had obsessed him since the outbreak of war. At first he put the change down to the urgency of the situation and the fighting in which he was taking part. Fear of death and the terror of dying are mutually exclusive. The terror drives out the fear as the north wind sweeps away the clouds of summer storms. The immediate threat quickens the blood and calls forth instant reactions. He needed other blows, other sorrows before he realized the truth that the threat of death which had been prowling around him for months had worn itself out by falling on Angelica, that fate had sacrificed her in his place and in his stead . . .

On May 18, the capture of Chéreng gave him the chance to give of his best. The French troops, thrown back on Tournai, had crossed the Belgian border at Baisieux to join the garrison at Lille. At that point the high command had been warned that an unknown force of the enemy was blocking the road ahead, firing having broken out on the outskirts of Chéreng, two kilometers further on. There was no air support to be looked for. No artillery could be got into position for several hours, and every minute counted. Edouard got permission to try to force a way through at the head of three platoons who were to converge on the center of the town. The men were all Bretons and it was in Breton that he explained to them what they were about to try to do. And it was in Breton also that he led them into the attack on the outlying houses, which had been turned into blockhouses by the enemy.

"War raok paotred Breiz! D'ar chomp evint! Kroget e barz dalh ta krog!"

What a flame those cries awakened in the eyes of the lads from Quimperlé, from Morgat and Plouha when their leader waved his arm and took them into the attack on the squat Flemish farmhouses, spitting fire from openings no wider than arrow slits! In less than an hour Chéreng was liberated and some fifty Germans taken prisoner. The next day, having been recommended for the Croix de Guerre, Edouard entered Lille, where the Fourth and Fifth Army Corps were dug in. They were surrounded but held out against the Wehrmacht's assaults until the end of May.

Taken prisoner at Lille on June 1, Edouard was sent, with hundreds of thousands of his comrades, to the camps at Aix-la-Chapelle, vast centers where the French, Belgian, Dutch and British prisoners were sorted out and distributed among the Stalags and Oflags of the Reich, as far away as the other end of East Prussia. The high spirits inspired in him by the fighting in May had evaporated during the grim days of siege in Lille. The disastrous news, his capture, the twenty days of waiting, marching and privations which brought him to Aix finally wore him out. At the first medical examination, his condition was reported serious. He was slipping slowly but surely into an insulin coma. Two months later he was in one of the very few batches of prisoners released for reasons of age or ill health.

CHAPTER XI

The Saint-Escobille Train

Alexandre

Paris is a lift and force pump. This strange function of the capital's is nowhere better illustrated than in the vast expanse of rubbish at Saint-Escobille. Paris has created a vacuum here—and now the only movement in this dead land, desert and steriliz•d, is a rare gust of wind that sends a flight of paper flapping into the air. As for the force part, that is provided by a railway line along which thirty-five wagonloads of refuse come from the capital to the center of the dump every morning. Miramas, with its silver hills, its sea gulls, its regiments of rats, its great mistral— that was a living, self-sufficient country having no obvious dependence on its links with Marseille. Saint-Escobille is actually nothing but the white shadow of Paris, its negative image, and while the Paris–Lyon–Marseille crossed Miramas without stopping, here the railway simultaneously plays the part of slave chain and umbilical cord.

White shadow, negative image, ought it not rather to be called *limbo?* It seems to me that vague, colorless, diaphanous word, with its mingled suggestions of the life before and the hereafter, suits this faceless, voiceless plain rather well. Am I still alive? Was the thing that I identified at Miramas as Dani's torn body not in truth my own corpse made unrecognizable by the moon's teeth and the sun's beaks? We are inveterate egotists and when we think we weep for another, our tears are really for ourselves. After my mother's death, what I was mourning for was her orphaned little boy, Alexandre, and on that terrible morning in September in the mistral, my kneeling soul offered up a last, agonizing tribute to my own remains. Then it came here, to these livid confines of the Great City and ever since it has been waiting, visited each morning by a funeral procession which approaches *in reverse.* For that is what the train running between Paris and Saint-Escobille does, three kilometers from here—just before the points that will send it to me—it shunts and proceeds backward up the single-line track to the refuse dump. So that the first thing I see coming through the early-morning twilight is the red light of the tail wagon, and the engine appears only as a distant puffing. I have never seen the driver of this ghost train and I should not be surprised to find he had a skull for a head.

This does not prevent me from taking trips into Paris and I must say that this period of "phony war" helps to add an air of unreality as well to the apparently unchanged life of the city. War has been declared. The armies are confronting one another across the borders. And everyone is waiting. For what? What signal? What dreadful awakening? The French seem to be doing their bit toward this postponement of the carnage with an incredible lightheartedness. The talk is all of mulled wine and entertainments for the troops. Christmas leaves were granted on such a massive scale that it began to look like a demobilization. And then a few days later my daily train was overflowing with beribboned Christmas trees and empty champagne bottles. When my men tipped all this gay rubbish out of the wagons, I was expecting to see dinner-jacketed men and women in evening dress tumble out, dead drunk amid the paper chains, glass baubles and angel's hair. Thus the capital sends me its news every morning by the ghost train, tons of news which it is for me to de-

cipher bit by bit so as to reconstruct the lives of each of its inhabitants down to the smallest detail.

But my comings and goings between Saint-Escobille and Paris
—between the unpeopled emptiness of my garbage dumps and
the populous emptiness of the big city—give me confirmation
every time that my solitude, temporarily shattered at Roanne,
has re-formed again around me. I fitted in down there, partly by
accident and partly from an affinity with a curious society which
was like myself, although its chances of survival were slight. As
we have seen. All I have left of it is Sam. For how long? I also
have sex, that eternal breaker up of isolation, and I daresay that
is what drives me to Paris—since it seems to me that now the pa-
renthesis of Roanne has been closed I am going to do my hunting elsewhere than on the wastelands. For Daniel's end has
shown me that the mysterious exogamy which always made me
seek my hunting grounds away from my familiar haunts is about
to come into force again, after a brief interruption.

Endogamy, exogamy. There is no end to the contemplation of
that twofold movement, those two contradictory commands.

Endogamy: stay with your own, do not depart from the norm.
Do not commit yourself with strangers. Do not look for happiness outside your own home. Woe to the young man who presents his parents with a betrothed of a different faith, of a social
standing inferior or superior to his own, who speaks another language, belongs to another nationality or even, the ultimate horror, to another race from his own!

Exogamy: go elsewhere to love. Go seek your wife elsewhere.
Respect your mother, your sister, your cousin, your brothers'
wives and so on. The family circle will permit only one person's
sexuality, your father's, and even then only strictly confined to
the needs of procreation. Your wife must bring new blood into
the line. Winning her will be an adventure which will take you
away from your own tribe to return to it matured and enriched
and bringing an additional member with you.

These two contradictory commandments coexist in heterosexual society and confine the area of the sexual quest to that between two concentric circles.

The small circle in the middle represents the family of the person concerned and comprises the people placed out of bounds by the ban on incest. On the outside, the large circle, C, is savage, unknown territory where the sexual quest is prohibited by the principle of endogamy. B—inside the large circle and outside the small one—is the privileged zone from which the young man is permitted to choose his mate. This zone may, of course, be of greater or smaller size. In some cases it may even be so constricted as to leave, in the end, only one possible woman for a particular man. I believe this situation arises in certain African tribes, but the problem of marrying royal princes under the Ancien Régime came very close to this limit.

These rules, drawn up by and for a heterosexual society, inevitably take on a new and piquant meaning in my own particular case.

Exogamy. I acknowledge that one of my most unfortunate natural inclinations would lead me to withdraw into myself, into a solitude made barren and exhausted from feeding on itself. My besetting sin is arrogance, *la morgue* it is called in French, an admirable word since it is used to describe the poison distilled within the soul by a particular kind of lofty and contemptuous pride, and also the place to which unclaimed corpses are taken.

Now against this *morgue,* my sexuality has been a powerful, irresistible sovereign remedy. Torn from my mother's skirts, driven from my room, cast out of myself by the centrifugal force of sex, I have found myself in the arms, between the thighs of—of any and every doorman, butcher's boy, van driver, chauffeur, acrobat and so on, young men whose charms acted all the more powerfully on me because they were of coarser origins and fibers and more remote from my familiar surroundings. I must add, also, that a quarry loses all his savor for me as soon as I have cause to suspect the purity of his heterosexuality. The brotherliness and even affection—a trifle abstract, to be sure—which I feel toward homosexuals cannot prevent this. Heterosexuals are my women. I want no others. That is my exogamic imperative.

Thus sex, for me, has always been a centrifugal force, hurling me outward into the distance, illumined by my own desires like a flare in the night. I have got rid of my arrogance on the cobbles of the most disreputable alleys in Rennes, on the gleaming, rain-soaked waterfront of the Vilaine, in the disinfectant-filled drains of every urinal in town. It would have been surprising if it had survived such treatment. The vilest, most degraded creature in the social scale was surrounded for me, from my earliest childhood, with a secret glory, as a potential object of desire, as the bearer of the trunked idol enshrined in his garments.

Endogamy. Nevertheless, this extreme exogamy possesses an invisible, secret and quite contrary aspect. For even as I adore it in my partners, this joyous, prancing virility is first and foremost the image of my own. At the root of homosexuality is narcissism; and if my hand is so expert in the art of grasping and caressing another's sexual organ it is because, from my earliest youth, it had been practiced in taming and cajoling my own.

Placed within the little circular plan, my loves succeed quite openly in flouting both heterosexual prohibitions at once. Because it is clear that I am always going to seek my quarry *too far off*, in C, the zone forbidden by endogamy. But the relationships I establish with these quarry of mine are fraternal, identical, narcissistic—which means that I bring them back to A and consummate them within the little circle forbidden by exogamy. All my originality, all my *visceral delinquency* stems fundamentally from my disinclination for the middle zone, B—neither near nor far—the very one to which the heterosexual confines his quest. It does not interest me. I leap over it in one bound, casting my line far out and then pulling in my little fishes to my familiar bank.

June 1940

Every morning, as soon as my thirty-five wagons have unloaded their picturesque contents on the side of the track and gone away again, I make my first tour of inspection. I am getting

the news. Not that my news is of the freshest, of course, no
fresher than the rotten things that carry it. The chrysanthemums
from All Hallows get to me about November 8 or 10 according to
the weather. On those days my wagons look like immense
hearses, catafalques overflowing with flowers, all the more ex-
pressive in their mourning because they are faded, wilted and
crushed. The leavings of the first of May come very much more
quickly and I do not have to wait until the third to find myself
snowed under with dead sprays of lily of the valley. Never mind,
I still prefer them to Good Friday's fish heads and guts!

But these large-scale and as it were ritual throwings away—all
in all not particularly informative—are fortunately the exception.
The rule is an apparently homogeneous flood, actually of a very
subtle composition, in which is written everything, absolutely everything about the life of Paris from the President of the Republic's first cigarette butt to the rubber from the last fuck of a
Montparnasse prostitute. For the time being, it is the newspapers
that I prefer to stab with Fleurette's point. Torn, stained, and
twenty-four hours old at the least, they still tell me quite enough
about the frightful thrashing the Germans are meting out to the
French army. Though the disaster may fall in with my predic-
tions and finalize a heterosexual quarrel which is no concern of
mine, yet I cannot help feeling a pang in my heart at this historic
catastrophe my country is suffering. Nor can I help thinking of
Edouard. He is quite capable of getting that great carcass of his
written off for honor's sake, which is to say for nothing. Which
proves that I am not as—as pure as I think. As bad as I look,
some might say.

Meanwhile, the roads of France are the scene of a vast southward exodus. The population is fleeing headlong from the bom-
bardments, massacres, famines, epidemics, and other wholly
imaginary scourges that are haunting their bird brains. I shall
not hold out for long against the temptation to go in the opposite
direction to this flood of refugees. I am too fond of going against
the grain with things and people not to try to swim against this
current, like a salmon fighting its way upstream. Besides, the
face of Paris, empty and abandoned on the verge of the apocalypse, is not something one will see again.

I have lost Sam. France may crumble—as indeed it is. My old "cynic" of a pal, who outclassed and edified me at the same time with his presence, has been swallowed up and digested by the great empty city. Now, after Daniel's death, the last survivor of my little world of Roanne has gone, and my former solitude is restored in all its proud severity. The dandy garbage man foolishly thought to escape his destiny. His skies cleared briefly and he secreted a friendly, even a loving environment about himself. Poor simpleton! Even a dog, the most hopeless mongrel, is much too good for you! But, Lord, a rat? Suppose I were to tame a rat—the trunked idol's rat—to fill my loneliness, would you permit me that? Probably not. How welcoming was Robinson Crusoe's island, how it swarmed with friendly presences compared to my desert of refuse!

Yet the day began very nicely. In order to cover the fifty kilometers from Saint-Escobille to the Porte de Châtillon by bicycle I set out at dawn on that Saturday, June 22. Sam was trotting gaily behind me. After Dourdan the road presented a strange and exciting spectacle. Not a sign of human life. Towns utterly deserted—shutters up, gratings drawn across windows, doors barred, and an ominous silence, like nighttime in broad daylight! But on the other hand the mess in the gutters and along the roadsides! A whole selection of every existing kind of vehicle, cars of every age and make, fiacres, buses, trailers, carts, motorcycles with and without sidecars, and even tricycles and baby carriages, and all accompanied, loaded and piled high with a vast confusion of furniture, crockery, mattresses, hardware, and provisions. This chaos, extending kilometer after kilometer under a blazing sun, had one obvious and striking implication: it was the refuse collector's triumph, a paradise of salvage, the dandy garbage man's apotheosis. That was certainly how I understood it, and as I pedaled merrily toward Paris my heart was dazzled like a little child's before the profusion of a Christmas tree, a profusion so great, so overwhelming that it deters one from touching it, from taking possession—as a whole landscape made of nougat, jam, angelica and pistachios deters the appetite—and I could not help but leave the proffered wonders where they were.

As we passed through Montrouge, however, we caught sight

of a delicatessen with its door broken down and gaping inward
on a promising darkness. Sam and I would have been glad to
share a knuckle of ham or a rabbit pâté after three hours on the
road. We made for its enticing smells, but before we were even
inside the doorway a fearsome mastiff sprang, foaming with
rage, out of the black hole and fell upon us. Naturally. The
strongest of the neighborhood's stray dogs, having conquered
this larder by main force, did not mean to share it with anyone.

That incident ought to have warned me of the danger Sam
was in. In fact, as we were going along I had noticed a striking
number of lean dogs prowling along by the walls of the empty
streets. I had to call Sam back a score of times when he showed
signs of parting company with me, lured by the scent of one or
other of these strays. The twenty-first time, just as we were entering the Place Saint-Michel, he vanished along the quays and I
have not seen him since. I hunted for him all day, haggard and
exhausted, losing my voice from calling him. I went down to the
edge of the Seine, I went back up the Quai d'Orsay, retracing
my footsteps tirelessly, hoping to find him every time I sighted a
pack in the distance, seeking his trail as though through prime-
val forests. When evening came I found myself, I don't quite
know how, in the Place du Trocadéro. I was dying of hunger
and as there was a pastry shop without a grating across it I
broke the window with a cobblestone. The bread was as hard as
sticks of wood and the cream cakes reeked mightily of cheese.
The biscuits, on the other hand, were intact and plentiful and I
also found two bottles of orgeat syrup in a cupboard. I stuffed
myself there and then until I felt sick. Then I stocked up with
cakes that were not too far gone and a bottle of syrup and left.

It was getting dark. I was staggering with fatigue. Wheeling
my bicycle, I walked up the esplanade of the Palais de Chaillot,
first between the two monumental blocks of the theater and the
museum, lined with a double row of elegant gilded statues, then
on as far as the balustrade overlooking the Champ de Mars. The
Pont d'Iéna, the Seine, the Ecole Militaire, the Eiffel Tower . . .
Paris was there, empty, unreal and fantastic in the sunset light.
Surely I was the last to observe the great city, emptied of its inhabitants because doomed to imminent annihilation? What was

to be the signal for the general destruction? Would the gilded dome of the Invalides burst asunder, or would Eiffel's formidable penis suddenly bend over and bow limply to the Seine? My sorrow and weariness, which these apocalyptic daydreams had momentarily overcome, fell back onto my shoulders, while the phosphorescent darkness of the June night deepened. Sleep. In a bed. Go into the first unlocked block of flats, break in the door of one of them and move in. After all, all Paris belonged to me, so why hesitate? With Sam, all things were possible. We would have taken over the best house in the Avenue Foch, we would have romped together over all the beds . . . But alone . . . You are getting old, Alexandre, if you are beginning to find pleasures unthinkable unless they are shared!

I came to a break in the parapet edging the terrace. There were six marble steps, a landing, and a doorway. Carrying my bicycle on my shoulder, I went down and pushed the door, which yielded. It was a garden shed. There were some empty sacks, tools and a standpipe for a big rubber hose which was rolled on a peg. It would do for one night. It was the Palais de Chaillot, after all, and spread out beyond my door was the loveliest urban landscape in the world. I shut my eyes. Let there be an end to this day of false sunshine, of black light, which had robbed me of Sam. Dani and Sam, Sam and Dani . . . I fell asleep to the lullaby of that mournful dirge.

I woke this morning to sounds of war. The clatter of boots quick-marching along the esplanade, harsh commands, the rattle of arms. The Germans! In the end I had forgotten all about them. Now I am going to see them for the first time. What shall I feel? I am striving to be neutral, indifferent, but an old chauvinistic core in me rebels. I look upon this dead city whose splendid corpse is stretched out at my feet as my own. These Saxons, Swabians and Pomeranians are coming between us.

A sudden silence up above. Then voices, footsteps. But civilian voices and unbooted feet. Someone laughs. I can make out only one word: "Photograph." If the object is simply to play tourists against the background of the Eiffel Tower, why the military escort? I am going to risk a glimpse. I slip outside, climb three steps. Then comes the encounter . . .

I knew him at once, with his flat cap with the monstrously high peak in front, his smooth face, flattened still further by the toothbrush moustache below the nose, and above all his pale, dead fish's eyes, eyes that saw nothing, that certainly did not see me, which was just as well for me. I knew him at once, the Great Heterosexual, Chancellor Adolf Heterosexual, the brown devil who has put to death in his horror camps as many of my brethren as fell into his hands. This meeting had to take place, and nowhere else but in the shadow of the Eiffel penis. The prince of refuse come from the ends of his rubbishy empire and the vulture of Berchtesgaden descended from his airy charnel house were bound to look one another in the eyes on Sunday, June 23, 1940, while the sunshine of the year's longest day burst in a fanfare of light.

For eight days now I have stood at the window of my asbestos cement shelter staring out at the great, white, motionless expanse of Saint-Escobille. Why did I come back here after that historic meeting at Chaillot? Probably because the middle of the finest refuse dump in the region of Paris is where I belong. It is a privileged observation post and waiting point on the edge of the dead capital, and the first signs of its return to life will reach me by the railway whose buffers are a stone's throw from my door and whose shining parallel rails meet on the skyline. But chiefly because I have not given up hope of Sam's return. After all, it's not so very far and the way is easy. I will even confess that as I cycled back here last week I was dreaming crazily that I would find him here to welcome me outside our hut. The truth is that I was trying to blot out the absurdly dangerous decision I made in taking him with me on my trip to Paris. I was playing a game of "let's pretend" that I had never taken him on the outing, which was childish and superstitious of me. And I cannot keep the two things I am waiting for—the return of the morning train from Paris and the return of Sam—from becoming mixed up in my mind, so that I find myself picturing Sam coming back to me, against all likelihood, perched on one of the wagons of the train, or even on the engine . . .

I was woken in the middle of the night by a very faint rustling sound and the lightest breath of wind, as if a bird were fluttering about the room. I lit a candle and saw that the little fan which used to make the hot summer hours pleasanter had come to life again and was purring merrily. So the electric current has been restored, the first sign that France is reviving. I am going to be able to have a normal light again and if I had a radio I could get the news.

Nevertheless, dawn breaks in a sky as brilliant and as empty as ever and except for the silky murmur of my fan I remain suspended in the void. That fan is more precious to me than I can say. The quiet, soothing rustle of the blades, blurred by their speed into a quivering, translucent circle, is a breath of spring, putting ideas in the mind of the lonely man bent over his writing table. It is a bird, hovering motionless a few inches from my face. I am reminded of Thomas Drycome's ruah. The Holy Ghost in the form of an electric household article is blowing a breath laden with words and ideas into my face. Little domestic Pentecost . . .

Nothing to be seen under the sun. Boustrophedon, boustrophedon . . . The extraordinary word floats on the surface of my memory and, since nothing will serve to sink it in oblivion once more, I have fished it out and probed it at length. It is a memory from my schooldays, from rhetoric in fact. Boustrophedon. The word's appearance, chubby-cheeked, paunchy and fleshy, has a good deal to do with its persistence. The thing it describes is, in any case, quite unrelated to its shape, but beautiful and strange enough to merit recollection. It is, I believe, a kind of ancient Greek script, snaking across the parchment in a single line from left to right and then from right to left. Etymologically it comes from the patient, continuous movements of plow oxen turning at the end of the field to retrace their furrow in the opposite direction from the one before.

This morning I leaped out of bed well before daybreak, spurred by a tiny, distant sound, no louder at first than the flight of a mosquito. But my ears could not deceive me. It was the train!

Previous experience told me I had ten minutes—but no more—
before it reached me and I took advantage of them to shave and
dress as carefully as possible in so short a time. The dandy garbage man owed it to himself to present an impeccable appearance when receiving the first message from humanity since the
fall of France.

The dawn was still gray when I went out, wearing my dark
hat and close-fitting embroidered waistcoat, with my cloak
wrapped around me and Fleurette in my hand. I was sure this
first delivery was going to be no ordinary one, for it was going to
bring me the essence of Paris in defeat, conquered, abject or, on
the contrary, stiff with dignity—I was going to find out very soon.

The engine's puffing became clearer, it drew closer, but this
time as usual the engine would remain unseen. The red dot of
the train's tail light winked in the distance, steadied and grew
larger. The brakes screeched. The driver knew his job and knew
precisely where to stop so that his last wagon did not hit the
buffers. I stretched up to try to get a glimpse of the load on the
nearest trucks but I could not make out the usual whitish mound
of refuse. I thought I could see limbs or some thin, bent sticks
projecting beyond the rails—twigs, possibly, or animals' feet? A
man came toward me. The driver, no doubt, and he whom I had
pictured wearing a death's-head turned out to be cheerful and
rubicund.

"All by yourself here, eh? Well, enjoy yourself, pal!"

His familiarity annoyed me. "I beg your pardon?" I said
coldly. It had no effect on him.

"Seen what I've brought you?"

He pushed up the handle on one of the side panels. It dropped
down at once and an avalanche of limp bodies bounced and
tumbled at our feet. Dogs! Hundreds of thousands of dead dogs!

"Talk about a gift! Thirty-five wagonloads of them! It was
inevitable! Before they left, the Parisians turned out all their
dogs into the streets. Well, after all! When the ship's sinking, it's
women and children first! So there were whole packs of them
running about all over the place. Dangerous, too! Inevitable!
Starving! People been attacked, they say. So the Boches agreed

with the council, had a roundup of dogs! Guns, pistols, bayonets, sticks, lassos, a real massacre! Inevitable!"

So saying, he loped off back to his engine, releasing the sides of the trucks as he went so that each spewed out its pack of corpses. I was half stunned and could only mutter after him: "Inevitable! Inevitable!" Of one thing at least I was certain as I saw the heaps of hundreds of dead dogs piling up. Sam was not among them. It was inevitable. But Sam would never come back. Never again! Because all those corpses "Inevitable" had dumped at my feet were so many avatars of Sam, they were the multiplied and debased expression of Sam, as a bag of pennies is at once the equivalent and the negation of a worn-out gold coin.

Inevitable was tireless. He promised me men and a wagonload of quicklime to cover the carcasses. If only it weren't the middle of summer! If only! In that I recognized the constant obsession of the little man with giving fate a shove. It is because he sees it as being like himself, something pathetic to be pushed about, and has no idea of the inflexible majesty of its progress.

The train went away, leaving me alone with a "cynical" charnel house running like a dike along beside the track, a heap of distended bellies, gaping jaws, frail paws and ears lying back across long skulls, long-haired and smooth-haired and of every color. Soon there will be the sun and the flies. I must hold on, hold on, clinging to the one certainty that, in the midst of the general disaster, the complete disruption of the entire country, I have the signal privilege—by virtue of my job and my sexual habits, both alike held in abhorrence by the mob—of remaining unshakably at my post, faithful to my function of clearsighted observer and liquidator of society.

Yesterday was a long day, a very long day. From the vast, dead pack lying like a frightful still life of trophies of the chase under the July sun, there rose a silent barking, one unanimous howl that drilled through my brain.

No train this morning, but a bulldozer arrived followed by a gang of six men. The dozer's trailer was loaded with bags of lime. They set to work at once.

Watching the bulldozer dig a neat trench into which the men

tumbled the dogs in batches, I was thinking that one of the para-
doxes of refuse is that even taken at its greatest depth it remains
essentially *superficial*. Three meters down, just as on the surface,
you find bottles, tubes, corrugated cardboard, newspaper and
oyster shells. Rubbish is like an onion, made up of superimposed
skins, all the way to the heart. The substance of things—the flesh
of fruit, meat, paste, cleaning materials, toiletries, etc.—has all
gone, used up, swallowed, absorbed into the city. The refuse—
the anti-city—piles up the skins. After the substance has melted
away, the form itself becomes substance. Hence the incomparable richness of this pseudo-substance which is nothing but an
accumulation of forms. After the pastes and liquids have gone,
all that is left is an inexhaustible profusion of membranes, outer
films, capsules, cans, kegs, baskets, flagons, bags, wallets and
haversacks, pots, demijohns, cages, crates and hampers, not to
mention rags, frames, canvases, tarpaulins and waste paper.

All this vast collection of junk has only one common factor, its
superficiality. This serves two purposes. The first is fulfilled in
the act of limiting, defining and encapsulating—thus ensuring
possession of the thing or substance, and that ultimate sign of
possession, transportation (to possess is to carry off). In this
sense, the garbage dump is a collection of signatures. The other
purpose is a *celebration*. For these signatures are loquacious,
even prolix, declamatory, exultant. They proclaim the brillian-
cies, the incomparable virtues, the peculiar merits of a thing or
substance—then go on to describe how it is used. And since the
thing, the substance is no longer there, this possessing encloses
emptiness, this declamation bursts upon the void, so becoming
absolute and absurd.

A collection of signatures and celebrations, emptiness, absurdity and absolute—in these characteristic elements of my natural
environment, I well recognize the constants of my mind and
heart.

P.S. But what was it Thomas Drycome was saying about the
Holy Ghost? Did he not define its two attributes as Sex and the
Word? And wind and breath as its only substance?

Objects, substances are not normally present on rubbish heaps, certainly. It seems that it may be otherwise on exceptional occasions, for they have just made a triumphal entry into Saint-Escobille.

This morning, I was alerted, like last week, by the puffing breath of Inevitable's engine in the gray dawn. Like last week, I stood by the buffers waiting for the train and saw Inevitable come trotting up, even ruddier and more cheerful than the last time.

"Well, well, old pal! Well, well! Wait till you see what I've brought you!"

What he'd brought me! With his enthusiastic air of mystery, he reminded me of Santa Claus, a Santa Claus with a gigantic, diabolical sack, full of great big horrible surprises.

"It was inevitable! People are coming back. Shopkeepers, too. So they're opening up the shops again. So all the food shops that were stuffed full a month ago, that's all rotten now. Inevitable. Rotten, rotten!"

As he spoke, he unfastened the side panel of first one truck and then another, letting a gargantuan larderful of very overripe food spew out onto the embankment. Each wagon contained the stock of one entire shop. Was it pastry you wanted? There were mountains of meringues with cream, chocolate éclairs and saint-honorés. Next door was the delicatessen counter, with coils of sausages, offal and hams. The butchers' shops were there as well, and the triperies, grocers' and greengrocers', but it was undoubtedly the dairies that gave off the sourest and most penetrating stench. I began to look back quite kindly on my dogs. With that great slaughtered pack, the horror reached a certain level and stayed there and the shock, when it came, struck at the heart. This time it was the stomach it attacked and this fearsome vomit, this puke that stinks to heaven, is a fair and terrible warning of the depths to which Paris and France will sink beneath the invader's heel.

The Breaking of the Stones

One cannot re-create nothingness. It is scarcely possible to conceive the state of mind of the French people in 1940, appalled, bewildered, despairing, with nothing to cling to but the last remnants of the prewar years. It took no less than a year for that void—into which, among other things, fell Charles de Gaulle's call of June 18—to become the crucible in which new concepts were born and took shape, ready to form the framework for new attitudes of mind: collaboration, Gaullism, Vichy, restrictions, black market, Jews, deportation, resistance (to begin with, it was called by the "official" name of "terrorism"), liberation, and so on. It was to be the same with the physical facts of life. It took at least a year, so that the first winter was harder than the rest and cold and hunger were added to the confusion of mind.

And yet life went on. It had simply fled elsewhere. Distances were increased because of transportation difficulties and so the provinces turned inward on themselves and the countryside was better able to withstand poverty than the towns. The rich provinces experienced a revival. In Provence, there was famine. But

if Normandy and Upper Brittany were short of grain, they were
rolling in meat and butter. Life at the Pierres Sonnantes took on
an intensity it had never known before. The restrictions had
swept away the factory's economic troubles. The weaving sheds
were working at full pitch and producing textiles that found a
ready market for exchange now that barter was the order of the
day. The children of St. Brigitte's were not the last to profit from
this comparative prosperity, and there had never been so many
of them, parents in those difficult times being particularly ready
to off-load their backward children. Maria-Barbara ruled tran-
quilly over a numberless household in which animals, innocents,
visitors and her own children mingled indiscriminately. A great
fire of fruitwood burned day and night in the huge hearth in the
living room. It was the only fire in the house, except of course for
the one in the old kitchen range which Méline loudly and incessantly abused. The room looked like a camp, they ate, slept and
worked there all the time, with games and arguments going on
all around. To the left of the fireplace, her back to a window,
Maria-Barbara sat in a plain, high-backed armchair, her tapestry
frame in front of her and a basket of multicolored wools within
easy reach, working with slow precise movements, a dog, a cat
and a rapturous innocent by her side.

Edouard had resumed his comings and goings between Brittany and Paris. The staggering contrast he beheld between the
warmth and plenty of his home and the physical and moral
wretchedness of Paris appealed to the provincial he still was and
inspired the comments he strewed about him. The black market
had been the first sign that urban life was becoming organized
again. Goods of every kind had vanished but early in 1941 things
started to appear again under the counter, at fantastic prices.
Edouard was outraged by the traffic at first but was obliged to
make concessions when he saw that even Florence—who was appearing in Pigalle at nightclubs stiff with Germans and black
marketeers—had, by force of circumstances, slipped into an underworld whose laws were not those of ordinary people. That
spring a ludicrous incident forced him to involve himself more
deeply. Alexandre, who was still running the depot at Saint-
Escobille, had been arrested for racketeering and infringing the

economy regulations. He, too, was obviously living slightly outside the law, although in a different fashion. All through the winter he had been operating a system for the "free" sale of coal. To
all appearances the term "black market" had never been more
appropriate, except that the goods delivered bore only the most
superficial resemblance to the coal which had been promised
and paid for with its weight in gold. In fact it was river pebbles
dipped in tar. The result looked good but produced nothing
when put on the fire beyond a little acrid smoke. Alexandre had
discovered early on the racketeer's golden rule: to make his victim an accomplice and so prevent him from bringing a com-
plaint. This was the fundamental principle of the black market.
It was probably the reason that the traffic in coal lasted the
whole winter. Edouard intervened to secure his brother's release,
on payment of a nominal fine. It was the occasion of a reunion
between the two which was far from cordial. With the passing of
the years, the difference in their ages became less obvious. Yet
what a difference between two men! Some fruits rot with age,
while others shrivel. Edouard, clearly, was beginning to blet,
whereas Alexandre seemed to be consumed by a dry flame which
left him nothing but skin and bone. They stared at one another in
surprise. Alexandre could scarcely believe that there was anyone
in the world prepared to intercede on his behalf. Edouard was
trying to see in this burnt-out bird of prey the delicate little
brother who was always hiding behind their mother's skirts. They
hovered for a second on the verge of an embrace, and settled in
the end for a handshake. Then they parted, convinced that
they would not meet again, for both of them had death on
their minds, Alexandre steeped in disgust and disillusionment,
Edouard contemplating a heroic end.

Not long after this meeting, an old friend of Edouard's, whom
he trusted absolutely, introduced him into a resistance network
which was being formed with help from London. The organization was still improvised and uncertain and the Germans
themselves had not had time to react to it. Nevertheless,
Edouard was immediately exhilarated at the prospect of hitting
back at last, of running risks and of making perhaps the supreme sacrifice. Above all, he congratulated himself on endan-

gering no one else. Florence performing for her unsavory audiences, and Maria-Barbara far away in the country, were both safe. So that when Florence failed to turn up one day to meet him and then could not be found in spite of all his efforts, his first thought was of some black-market business like that which had earned his brother some days in prison. This guess seemed to be confirmed when Florence's concierge finally admitted to him that she had seen the girl being taken away early in the morning by two men in plain clothes. But he could get no information from the French anti-fraud squad, where he was known since the business about the coal. It was his friends in the network who told him that they had begun rounding up the Jews in Paris and that Florence must have been one of the first victims.

Florence Jewish! Edouard must always have known it, only as time went on he had simply ceased to think of it. But how could he forgive himself for not having realized the Germans were eager for that kind of prey and that the girl was in real danger? He might easily have hidden her, sent her into the country, into the Unoccupied Zone, to Spain perhaps or simply to the Pierres Sonnantes, that unshakable island of peace. Anything would have been possible if he had only had a grain of sense. Back in his large flat on the Quai Bourbon, Edouard stared at himself wretchedly in the mirror and for the first time he hated himself. Then a torturing enlightenment came to him. First Angelica, his girl in the pastry shop in Saint-Amand . . . He huddled in a chair, his big body shaking with sobs. He fought off despair by devoting all his energies to the activities of his underground network.

But still La Cassine was a haven of peace, tucked away on the estuary of the Arguenon. The time he spent there was all too brief. He would gladly have stayed there now that Florence would no longer welcome him into her red lair, but the struggle against the occupation forces called him to Paris. And so, when he was at home, there was an air of festivity about the house. There was always a crowd in the big living room when he talked about Paris. He was the master, the father, he had behaved splendidly during the fighting in Flanders and now some mysterious business was keeping him in Paris. He talked and they listened, piously and with love.

Paul

Our childhood was long and happy, and it lasted until March 21, 1943. That day was the beginning of our adolescence . . .

That day, as usual, Edouard and Maria-Barbara were reigning happily over a tribe of children, innocents and household pets. Continual comings and goings between kitchen, cellar and woodshed ensured a constant supply of cakes, food, sweet cider and logs, and kept the room's three doors banging all the time. Maria-Barbara, sitting with her feet up on a cane sofa, a fringed plaid rug over her knees, was crocheting a vast mauve woolen shawl, watched ecstatically by a myxedematous dwarf with her little mouth wide open and a dribble of saliva trickling thoughtfully down her chin. Edouard was walking up and down in front of the fire, holding forth to his usual audience.

Encouraged by the warm atmosphere and his natural optimism, he had mounted one of his favorite hobbyhorses once again, and was comparing the peaceful contentment of the Pierres Sonnantes with the gloom, poverty and danger of the capital. We had only vague memories of Paris but we understood that without plowed fields, vegetable gardens, fruit trees and farm animals, the huge city was bound to starve. As for the black market, we pictured it like a fair held in the middle of the night, all in huge caverns, where every stallkeeper's head was covered by a hood with two holes pierced in it for his eyes. Edouard was describing the exploitation of poverty, the dishonest dealings, the shady characters one rubbed shoulders with in dubious surroundings.

"The people of Paris have sunk into such a state of apathy," he went on, "that it would be quite a relief if all this were inspired by greed and pleasure seeking. Because, you see, children, even greed and pleasure seeking are ways of loving life, debased but healthy. But it is not like that. Paris is sick of a disease, of fear, plain fear, a carrion fear. People are afraid. Afraid of bombs, of the occupation forces, of the constant threat of epidemics. But most of all there is the gnawing fear of want. They are afraid of going cold and hungry and of finding themselves helpless in a hostile world ravaged by war . . ."

He was walking up and down in front of the hearth as he spoke, this way and that, so that each time one side of his face was turned to the glow of the fire and the other to us, his hearers; and we, because this performance reminded us in some vague yet insistent way of one of our own private rituals, tried automatically to relate what he was saying to whichever side of his face was visible at the time, his right profile to sing the praises of the Pierres Sonnantes and the peaceful, fertile country life, his left profile to evoke Paris, with its dark streets, dubious shops and the shady characters who frequented them.

But it was also with his right profile that he asserted exultantly that not all Paris was abandoned to this dismal picture, that there were still, thank God, some generous spirits and eager hearts and that in that same underworld where the crooks of the black market flourished a secret army was forming, with no uniforms but practiced in all the skills of underground warfare. The peaceful countryside might work for the harvests which France would need in the hour of liberation. In the mean streets of Paris they were making ready to rise for liberty.

This was not the first time he had spoken of the Paris resistance in our presence. It was a subject he would enlarge upon at every opportunity with a kind of lyrical enjoyment from which he evidently derived great comfort, but if we had ever asked ourselves how much of what he had to say was real and how much imagination we would have been hard put to find an answer. He talked of secret networks, of stores of weapons, of radio links, of actions planned and carried out, of plans laid for joint undertakings in cooperation with London, of bombings and even landings on the French coast. And all these heroic deeds were woven in the same dank shadows as harbored the black market.

We would listen to him, but could not manage to share his enthusiasm. The armed struggle might possibly have held some attraction for us if its secrecy had not deprived it of the glamor in which warfare was dressed by banners and heavy armaments— guns, tanks, fighter planes and bombings. These people who fought by night, planting explosives or knifing a sentry and then stealing away in the shadows of the walls, found no way to our hearts.

But the thing that really put us off Edouard's tales was that they all took place in Paris. We felt relieved, certainly, but at the same time frustrated and vaguely ashamed when he contrasted the feverish miasmas of Paris and the calm contentment of the country—for needless to say the country to us meant nowhere but our own Guildo.

It was seventeen minutes past six on the twenty-first of March 1943, and Edouard's left profile was treating us to the adventures of an English airman who had landed by parachute on the roof of a block of flats, been taken in and cared for and smuggled home to Britain, when Méline burst into the room with a look on her face no one had ever seen before. The myxedematous dwarf must have been the first to see her because that dumb child, whom no one had ever known to utter a sound, gave vent to an animal howl that made our blood run cold. Méline's face was ashen, utterly gray, without a spot of color, the lifeless shade of an unpainted waxen mask. And in that mask her eyes were blazing, blazing with a brightness that could have been horror or joy but was certainly caused by some terrible, imminent disaster.

"Sir! Madam! The Boches! Soldiers! The whole German army is all around the house! Oh, my God! They are all over the place!"

Edouard stopped his pacing; he ceased to show us his side view but stood still, facing us, made suddenly taller and nobler by the calamity that was coming upon us, upon himself alone, as he believed.

"Children," he said, "this is it. I have been expecting it. I knew that sooner or later the enemy would make me pay the price of my work for the underground. I must say, I did not think they would come to get me at the Guildo, among you all. Here, at the Pierres Sonnantes, I thought myself unassailable, protected by the rampart of all my children, absolved by St. Brigitte's presence and safeguarded by Maria-Barbara's radiance. They are coming. They are going to arrest me, take me away. When shall we see one another again? Who can say? This is the moment of sacrifice. I have always longed for the ultimate sacrifice. Surely it is a supreme blessing to end like a hero, rather than as an invalid, a broken man, a wreck of humanity?"

He talked like that for some time, I do not know how long, amid an ominous silence. Even the fire had stopped crackling and roaring and had sunk to an incandescent glow in the hearth. Because he thought his end was near, Edouard, usually so reticent, so modest, was baring his heart to us. We were learning that this man whose temperament was so happy, so well attuned to life, so receptive to all the blessings and trials offered by ordinary human existence, was secretly tormented by the fear of death, the fear of making a bad end. Now, thanks to the war, this fear had found its remedy: the remedy was heroism, a heroic end, a useful and uplifting sacrifice. Such suicidal obsessions are less rare than one might think among men fundamentally in tune with life, all the more so in Edouard, in whom they went hand in hand with a very great and touching innocence.

He was interrupted when two German soldiers burst in, armed with automatic pistols and followed by an officer quite rigid with youth and zeal.

"Is this the house of Madame Maria-Barbara Surin?" he asked, glancing around him.

Edouard went forward to meet him.

"I am Edouard Surin," he said. "Maria-Barbara is my wife."

"I have an order for the arrest of—" He paused and rummaged in his briefcase.

"Let us waste no time on unnecessary formalities," Edouard said impatiently. "I am at your disposal."

But the officer was determined to do the thing properly and, having at last found what he was looking for in his briefcase, he recited: "An order for the immediate arrest of Madame Maria-Barbara Surin, née Marbo, at present living at the Pierres Sonnantes, Notre-Dame du Guildo. Charged with having contact with the enemy, making clandestine radio transmissions to London, sheltering enemy agents, supplying food to terrorists, concealing arms and ammunition . . ."

"This is a ridiculous misunderstanding," Edouard cried hotly. "My wife has nothing to do with it. I am the person you have come to arrest, do you hear, and I alone. In any case, whatever I may have been doing secretly in Paris . . ."

"We are not in Paris," the officer cut in. "We are in the Guildo, under the Kommandantur. of Dinan. I have no orders concerning you, Monsieur Surin. Our orders are to arrest Madame Surin, along with eleven workers from your factory and five members of the staff of St. Brigitte's Institution, all of whom are involved, as she is, in activities contrary to the conditions of your armistice. They are putting them in the trucks at this moment, in fact."

Maria-Barbara had finished off her work with a double knot of wool and was folding it in four, carefully, on the sofa. Then she went to Edouard.

"Now don't get so excited. You can see it's me they've come for," she told him, as though speaking to a child.

Edouard was stunned by what he saw, which was something like an understanding between his wife and the German officer over his head. For when the German mentioned a secret radio transmitter discovered in the abbey's loft, men brought in by submarine at high tide, men landed on the Ile des Hébihens and coming ashore at low water disguised as shellfish gatherers, boxes of high explosives found in a cave in the cliff by the Pierres Sonnantes and a maquis unit deep in the forest of La Hunaudaie whose lines of communication went through St. Brigitte's, it was clear that Maria-Barbara knew what he was talking about and, seeing that all was lost, was not troubling to feign ignorance; whereas he, Edouard, the proud organizer of the Paris underground, was being brought down with a bump and made to feel increasingly foolish for continuing to insist that he, and he alone, was responsible for everything and that Maria-Barbara's implication in the matter was the result of some misunderstanding.

In the end he was refused permission to go with Maria-Barbara to Dinan and the only concession was that Méline should go the next day to where she was being held with a suitcase of clothes for the prisoner.

She went without a word of farewell, without a backward look for the house of which she was the soul, for the host of children to whom she was the earth mother. Edouard went and shut himself in a room upstairs. He did not reappear until late the next day. We had last seen him the night before, a man enjoying a second youth. He came down to us wearily, an old man, with a ravaged face and the fixed stare of senility in his eyes.

If the arrest of Maria-Barbara and sixteen members of the staffs of the factory and the children's home was the beginning of old age for Edouard, for us it was the end of childhood and the start of adolescence.

The child, carried in its mother's womb, ascends after birth to the cradle of her folded arms and to her breasts by which it is fed. The day comes at last when it must leave, break with its native soil and itself become lover, husband, father, the head of a family.

At the risk of becoming a bore, I repeat that the geminate vision of things—richer, truer, more profound than the ordinary point of view—is a key which furnishes many revelations, the sphere of the twinless not excluded.

The fact is that the ordinary child, born without a twin, the single child, cannot get over his loneliness. He suffers from birth from an imbalance which will afflict him throughout his life but which in adolescence will direct him toward a solution, imperfect, lame, doomed to every kind of disaster but ultimately approved by society: marriage. Lacking a congenital balance, the single child leans on a mate as unstable as himself, and out of their twofold stumbling is born time, the family, human history, old age . . .

(Little girls play with dolls, little boys with teddy bears. It is instructive to contrast the twinless and geminate interpretations of these traditional games. It is generally agreed that a little girl playing with a doll is practicing in this way for her future career as a mother. And yet . . . Will anyone say as confidently that the small boy with his teddy bear is practicing for his role as a father-to-be? We would do better to remember that *real twins, of either sex, never play with dolls or with teddy bears.* Of course, this could be explained by the peculiarly geminate sexuality, the ovoid sexuality which does not lead to procreation. But instead of striving to interpret a geminate phenomenon in non-twin terms, there is always everything to be gained from doing the opposite. The truth is that the reason I never wanted a teddy bear was that I had one already and, what was more, a live one, in my twin brother. The bear and the doll for the single child are not foretastes of fatherhood or motherhood. The child does not care a jot about one day being a daddy or mommy. On the contrary, what it cannot get over is its solitary birth, and what it is projecting onto the teddy or the doll is the twin brother or twin sister it is missing.)

The single adolescent breaks out of the family circle and seeks a partner with whom to try to form the couple it dreams of. Maria-Barbara's departure pitched Jean-Paul abruptly out of childhood into adolescence, but it was a geminate adolescence, which is to a great extent the opposite of the non-twin's adolescence. Because while the single adolescent seeks fumblingly, far from home, right across the world for this imperfect partner, the twin finds him face to face from the start in the person of his twin brother. Even so, we can—we must—speak of a geminate adolescence which contrasts profoundly with the geminate childhood. For before that dreadful date, the twenty-first of March 1943, Maria-Barbara was the link between us. The essence of our childhood was that it was possible for us to take our minds off one another, to forget about each other for days at a time, since we were sure of being able at any moment to find a common anchorage in Maria-Barbara. She was the living spring at which each of us could slake his geminate thirst without worrying what his twin was doing. With Maria-Barbara gone, we were thrown back instinctively upon one another. Despair, fear and bewilderment in the face of the calamity which had befallen our world surrounded us as we clung together, bathed in tears and overshadowed by grief. But the devastation of the Pierres Sonnantes was only one aspect of a deeper truth, which was that Maria-Barbara's going had bestowed an *immediacy* on our fundamental relationship. We knew that from then on neither of us should look for our common denominator anywhere but in his twin. Now the geminate cell was rolling through space, free at last of the maternal plinth on which it had rested so far.

At the same time as our union was becoming momentarily closer, we could not conceal from ourselves that it was also becoming more fragile. This was what our adolescence, geminate adolescence, was: a brotherhood of which we were now the sole repositories and which depended on ourselves alone whether we broke it or brought it to fruition.

Thus it was that the slowing down of work in the factory, the return to their families of half the children of St. Brigitte's, Edouard's sudden aging and loss of interest in life—all these things which followed on the deportation of Maria-Barbara and sixteen familiar faces from the Pierres Sonnantes coincided with a wonderful completeness of the geminate cell. I have said that we had never played with dolls or teddy bears. At this period, although we were already quite grown-up, there was another thing which became a kind of fetish in our eyes, and it was Jean who introduced it into the game of Bep. This was a transparent celluloid ball, half filled with water. Two little mallard ducks floated and bobbed against each other on the surface. These two little ducks looked identical, but we learned to tell them apart by tiny signs, and each had his own. The Pierres Sonnantes were shattered and sinking but the geminate cell, with its Jean-duck and its Paul-duck, swam on, sealing itself off more firmly from the outside world as its surroundings grew more ominous.

Unhappily it was not long before Carder-Jean perverted the game of Bep and went on to betray our geminate solidarity . . .

Edouard had become no more than a shadow of himself. The factory was working at reduced speed under Le Plorec's direction, and Méline was in charge at La Cassine. We learned that our deportees had left France. The war was reaching a climax. The German cities were being pasted with bombs. The occupier's boot trod more heavily on the land. Of our missing ones there was no news at all, except for one unfamiliar German word, the unpronounceable name of a place where they were said to have been taken: *Buchenwald*. When Edouard was in Rennes, he went to see a man who had been a German teacher at the Lycée in Thabor, where he went to school. "We both hunted all over a map of Germany, a very detailed one, and even then we couldn't find the town," he told us on his return. "Apparently the name means *Beechwood.* That's rather reassuring, isn't it? Perhaps they are putting them to work as woodcutters? I can't see Maria-Barbara with an ax . . ."

It was the year after that that an event occurred which I have never been able to elucidate, for lack of evidence. One morning, Edouard got us all together in the big living room. He did not make a speech. He had lost his liking for them since that dreadful day. But he kissed us with evident emotion and we noticed, furthermore, that he had put on underneath his coat the tricolor sash he wore as mayor of our commune. He was going to Dinan. He came back in the evening, more dejected and defeated than ever. Once again, I can only guess at the purpose of that mysterious and solemn journey. But I do know for sure that two days later a group of nine "terrorists"—as they called the resistance members then—who had been caught red-handed, were shot in Dinan. Posters were put up everywhere with their names and photographs and the wording of the sentence signed by the colonel in charge of the region. The youngest of them—he was eighteen—came from a village near our own and it is possible that Edouard may have known his family. Naïve though he was, I do not think he would have gone to Dinan to plead for mercy for the boy. According to some stories—borne out by his farewells to us that morning—he went to ask a different favor of the colonel at the Kommandantur in Dinan, which was to take the young resistance fighter's place before the firing squad. They laughed in his face, of course. If they had granted him the magnificent death he craved, at whose expense would it have been, if not of the occupation forces and their reputation? They showed him the door and he never spoke of the business to a living soul. Poor Edouard! He was fated to see the young and well-beloved fall around him and himself go on to die, a sick and broken man, in his bed.

His worst ordeals came with the Liberation, which occurred in our region by July 1944 and into the following year. Of the sixteen deportees from the Pierres Sonnantes, ten came back, one by one, from the hospitals or rehabilitation centers where some attempt had been made to restore them to health. Even so, three of these died before the autumn. But no one could, or perhaps would, give any news of Maria-Barbara. Edouard strove with a passion that broke him to learn something of what had become of her. He had pasted two pictures of Maria-Barbara on a sandwich board, along with her name and the date of her arrest, and he patrolled all the camps for displaced persons in Germany, Switzerland, Sweden and France with these grim panels hung about his neck. That agony continued for six months and was quite fruitless.

In November 1947 he made another journey, to Casablanca, to see to the sale of some property which had belonged to Gustave, the eldest of the Surin brothers. We were allowed to go with him on the trip, which coincided with the death of our uncle Alexandre, who was murdered in the docks of that great Moroccan port.

Edouard himself died, nearly blind, in May 1948.

CHAPTER XIII

Death of a Hunter

Alexandre

Casablanca. In Africa I can breathe more easily. I recite to myself the Arabic proverb: women for a family, boys for pleasure,
melons for ecstasy. Heterosexuality here lacks the quality of op-
pression and constraint which its monopoly gives it in Christian
countries. The Moslem knows that there are women and boys
and that one must ask of each what each is fitted to provide.
Whereas the Christian, immured in heterosexuality from childhood by intensive training, is thereby reduced to asking everything of woman and treating her as a substitute boy.

I can breathe more easily. Is it really because I am in an Arab
country? If I tell myself so, it may be self-deception to give myself the illusion. Why pretend otherwise? I am at the end of my
tether. These sordid years of trafficking and black marketeering,
coming on top of Dani's death and the loss of Sam, have drained
me. The life force in me had to suffer a terrifying fall in order
that I might learn to estimate it. I know now how to take my

temperature by how much I can still fancy boys. For me, to love
life is to love boys. But over the last two years there is no denying I have not loved them as much. I have no need to ask my
friends or to look at myself in a mirror to know that the flame
which set me apart from heterosexuals is flickering, guttering,
and I am in danger of becoming before long as gray, dismal, and
dead as they are.

At the same time, I am also losing interest in garbage. In my
childhood and in my youth I was always drifting, I wandered in
exile wherever I went. I was, as the police say, of no fixed abode.
Providentially succeeding my brother Gustave gave me a kingdom, the white plains of Saint-Escobille, the silver hills of
Miramas, the gray matter of Roanne, the black mound of Ain-
Diab and some other territories, all abhorrent to respectable folk,
all superficial, right down to their deepest depths, made up of an
accumulation of enveloping, prehensile forms.

Well, these special places no longer attract me! I shall go, of
course, tomorrow—or the day after—and inspect Ain-Diab. I shall
do so without feeling, without excitement.

And yet yesterday, when I felt the gangway of the old *Sirocco*
which brought me from Marseille swaying under my feet, when
I saw the swarming djellabas on the mole and breathed in the
treacherous smell of kef from the alleys of the old medina, I
trembled for joy and a wave of life surged through my body.
Was it the warmth of contact with this land of love? Or is it not
rather that notorious remission, the kind of beatitude which her-
alds one's last hour and which those about the dying person
sometimes mistake for the promise of recovery, but which he
knows well enough is the surest of all sentences? After all, what
does it matter? Perhaps I shall be lucky enough to die beautifully, at my best, fit, alert, supple, and light, with Fleurette in
my hand? I ask no more.

Anal hygiene of the Arabs. Islamo-anal civilization. An Arab
going to shit does not take with him a handful of paper, but a
little water in an old jam jar. He professes himself properly
shocked at the coarseness and inefficiency of Western toilet
paper. The superiority of an *oral* over a *written* civilization. The

Occidental is so besotted about paper that he even stuffs it up his ass.

Pouring water over the anus after shitting. One of the very real comforts of living. A flower with crumpled petals, sensitive as a sea anemone, the grateful, euphoric little organ dilates and contracts jubilantly beneath the caressing waves its mucous corolla lined with a fine lace veined with violet.

Afterward, on wings of happiness, I walk along the beach where the sun roars and the ocean shines. Hail, deities of rose and salt! This detachment, this affectionate delight in everything, this gentle, friendly melancholy . . . perhaps they are favors death has sent to me, and they will lead me dancing toward it. I have always had a suspicion that while birth is a nasty, brutal shock, so death should be the opposite, a most melodious, Mozartian embarkation for Cythera.

Just now I passed a strange, disturbing little procession. Two enormous policemen, large-bellied and moustached and hung about with belts, holsters and revolvers, each with a truncheon of penis-like rigidity and hardness at his waist, were escorting a group of pallid louts, lanky youths of a wild beauty. In order to control them, the police had put handcuffs on them. But the handcuffs were imaginary, invisible, and the boys were simply clasping their hands, some over their crotch and some behind. Among the latter, I noticed one in particular, taller than the rest, with a wolfish eye which was, I saw, observing me through the lock of hair that fell over his bony face. Moreover, his hands sketched an obscene gesture which could only have been meant for me. By now the police are probably inflicting all sorts of torments on them while their imaginary handcuffs prevent them from escaping.

His close-cropped head looked black, hardening his features and giving his eyes a disturbingly fixed stare. A man's shirt, much too big for him, with the sleeves rolled up, hung on his thin torso and, with the short, tight trousers that reached down below his rounded knees, gave him a look of Murillo's beggar boy with the grapes. He was homerically dirty and patches of thigh, buttocks and back were visible through numerous holes. He slid among the passers-by on the Boulevard de Paris, under the arcades where the smart shops are, like a wild animal among a flock of sheep.

He overtook me. I observed his sauntering, loose-limbed gait, the swing of his whole body which sprang evidently from his bare feet. Instantly I was invaded by that delicious intoxication called desire, and the hunt was on. A special kind of hunt in which the aim is, simply and paradoxically, the metamorphosis of the hunter into the hunted—and vice versa. He stopped in front of a shopwindow. I passed him. I stopped before a window. I watched him coming. He passed me but he had seen me. The cast had been made from me to him, for he stopped again. I passed him. I stopped in my turn, watched him coming. To check the strength of the line, I let him pass me, then dawdled slightly. The exquisite uncertainty set my heart thudding. He might go on, disappear. That would be his way of declining to play. No! He had stopped. A glance at me. The intoxication deepened, grew into a numbness, a happy drowsiness that made my prick hard and my knees weak. The metamorphosis had happened. From now on, I was the quarry, a fat prize which he was going to do his best to lure gently into his net. He went on. Stopped. Glanced around to make sure I was following meekly, but no longer letting himself be overtaken. Now it was he who was calling the tune. He turned right, down a side street, and crossed over so as to keep an eye on me more easily. I amused myself by worrying him, stopping and looking at my watch ostentatiously. The action gave rise to the thought. Turn back? Impossible! The invisible line was drawing me irresistibly into darker and darker, narrower and narrower alleys. I let myself slide happily after him into the depths of the Arab town. I gathered that we were making for the docks. A sense of danger added its tiny tinkle to the deep booming of desire that was throbbing through my arteries.

A headlight clove the darkness suddenly and a small motor-bike came popping up. Riding it was a hungry-looking youth with a much younger boy riding pillion behind him. It jerked to a halt in front of Murillo. A brief exchange of words. It swung around, popping. Now the youth was by me and I recognized the lean wolf of the other day. They hadn't held him very long, but he had a bruise on one cheek.

"You want him?"

Did he mean Murillo or the child he had up behind him? I answered roughly.

"No, bugger off!"

The bike leaped back to Murillo and once again its headlights swept the leprous housefronts. Another brief exchange. The motorbike vanished with a roar of its engine.

I didn't move. Danger was one thing, but suicide? I caught sight of a faint glimmer of light in an adjoining alley. A kind of grocer's shop. I went in. While they weighed me out a kilo of muscat grapes, I got a glimpse of Murillo's black head through the window. I went out again. For the first time, we were *together*. Our personal areas of space had interlocked. Our bodies were touching. Desire was roaring thunderously in my head. I offered him a bunch of grapes and he snatched it quickly, like a monkey. I watched him nibble at it. Heavenly magic! I had conjured a boy out of a picture in the Munich Pinakotek and he was there, warm and ragged, beside me. He looked at me, still eating, stepped back, moved away, and the race toward the docks was on again.

The docks. The black mass of the containers. Coils of rope. Dark passages between the stacks of crates where I could barely pick out Murillo's light shirt. The hardness, the pitiless harshness of this country. What a long way from the soft whiteness of the garbage dumps! It crossed my mind that I had plenty of money on me, but that I had left Fleurette at the hotel. As if to give a shape to my fears, a man loomed up suddenly in front of me.

"What you are doing is extremely dangerous!"

He was small, very dark, and in ordinary clothes. What was he doing himself in this place at this hour? Was he a plainclothes policeman?

"Come with me."

I thought fast. One, Murillo had run off and I would not find him again after this. Two, I no longer had the slightest idea where I was. Three, desire had faded abruptly and I was dead

tired. The stranger led me to a crossroads lit by hanging lamps
swinging gently in the breeze. There was a small car there and
we got into it.

"I'm taking you back to the town center."

Then, after a long silence, just as we were drawing up in the
Place des Nations Unies: "Don't go down to the docks at night.
Or if you do go, take some money. Not too much, but enough.
No flashy jewelry, and above all no weapons. If it came to a
fight, you wouldn't have a chance, do you understand me? Not a
chance!"

The thought of Murillo haunts me and I curse that priest or policeman, that priest-policeman in plain clothes who spoiled my
hunting, for his interference. Boy hunting is the great game that
has given color, warmth, and savor to my life. I might have
added pain also, for I have got more than one scar from it. I
have lost fur and feathers in it. Three times I have even come
close to disaster. Yet if I had to frame a single regret, it would be
that I have too often sinned through excessive caution, have not
seized the prey that came within my reach more boldly. Most
men become less daring with age. They become cowards, exag-
gerating the risks to be run, and yield to conformity. It seems to
me that I am being more logical in developing the other way. In
fact, a venturesome old man presents less of a target than a
young one. He has built his life, it stands firm and largely unassailable because it is behind him. If one must be injured, crip-
pled, imprisoned, or killed, surely it is more troublesome at
eighteen than at sixty?

A strange thing has happened to me, yes, more than that, fantastic. This morning, as I was coming back from the depot of Ain-
Diab, I stopped at the lighthouse whose white tower soars above
the corniche road. The weather was glorious, I had inspected the
great garbage dump called the black mound for the sake of appearances, and I wanted for a moment to enjoy the magnificent
view of the coast, most of which, unfortunately, is both dangerous and inaccessible. After that, I went back to my car and
joined the colorful crowd in the old medina. I had not walked

far when I noticed a boy looking through the copper ware outside a shop. He was blond, very slight and rather delicate-look-
ing, but bright and alert. How old would he have been? At first
sight about twelve. Looking more closely, almost certainly more,
fifteen perhaps, because he seemed naturally slender. In any
case, he was not for me. I'm a homosexual, yes, but not a ped-
erast. Already, with Dani, I feel that I have been cruelly
punished for falling for someone much too young. So that I
should certainly have paid no attention to him if I had not been
absolutely certain that I had last seen him a few minutes before
at the lighthouse on the corniche. Now not only had I come from
the corniche to the medina by the most direct route, but the
blond boy looked as though he had been in the shop for some
time, because when I got there he had already set aside a chased
tray and a little nargileh. Must I credit him with the faculty of
flying through the air?

I was sufficiently curious to keep an eye on him. He idled
about the souks for another half hour, then he took a taxi—I followed it as best I could in my car—and was set down at the
Hotel Marhaba, on the Avenue de l'Armée-Royale, a very short
journey which would have taken him ten minutes on foot.

A few minutes ago, I caught sight of the lean wolf on the motor-
bike steering a diabolical slalom through the cars on the Boulevard de Paris. He had Murillo's grape-eating boy up behind him.
A pang of desire, but a dull pang, a muffled pang. My heart was
no longer in it. Or at least, not so much. I am preoccupied with
that ubiquitous child.

One thought leading to another, I stopped off at the Hotel
Marhaba, which was close by. I walked into the foyer. To the
porter's greeting and inquiry I responded with the truth, that I
was looking for someone. Eternal truth, the profoundest of all
truths for me, the mainspring of my existence. Then I looked in
the ground-floor rooms. I very nearly missed him: he was curled
up in the depths of an enormous leather armchair, his bare legs
tucked under him. He was reading. His features were extraordinarily sharp and fine-drawn, as though carved with a razor.
Reading—and even more perhaps deciphering, decoding—would

seem to come naturally to that face with its habitual expression
of calm, studious concentration. If it had not been for his size
and his schoolboy clothes, I would have thought him much older
this time than in the medina. Sixteen perhaps. Can this boy, who
seems not to be bound by space, exist equally outside time?

I am watching a peacock and his peahen (is that the word?)
who adorn the little interior garden of the hotel. Because of the
way he displays himself in his pride, the peacock has a reputation for vanity. That is wrong on two counts. The peacock is not
proud. He is not vain, he is an exhibitionist. For what does his
pride amount to but baring his bottom and showing his ass? And
so that there may be no possible doubt about it, once he has
kilted up his skirt of feathers he pivots daintily on the spot so
that no one can miss the display of his cloaca framed in its
corolla of mauve down. The movement is posterior, not anterior
in its nature. Once again I notice the way so-called common
sense strives to interpret things back to front, in accordance with
a priori opinions and principles. I suppose it is my "good sense"
which gets me labeled an invert.

The ubiquitous one has been displaying his powers again, in the
most spectacular fashion. The heat and my cynegetic passion
drove me to the splendid municipal swimming pool which, with
its size and luxury, endeavors to take one's mind off the inaccessible beach and the sea's murderous breakers. As soon as I was
in the water I recognized him, hauling himself up and twisting
around in one lithe, easy movement to sit on the edge. It was the
first time I had seen him relatively undressed. Small and spare as
he is, he is undoubtedly perfectly proportioned, but he left me
cold. No doubt it was partly on account of his bathing trunks.
There can be nothing more unflattering than that garment, with
its horizontal line breaking the vertical lines of the body in the
middle and spoiling the line. Bathing trunks are neither nakedness nor the original and sometimes disturbing language of
clothes. They are simply nakedness denied, ruined, smothered
under a gag.

    An hour later, after leaving the pool, I was crossing the Boule-

vard Sidi-Mohammed-Ben-Abd-Allah to have a look at the famous aquarium. There he was, in front of the iguana pit, dressed
in white with his hair dry. It was then that, as people say vul-
garly, I fell madly in love. I felt irresistibly drawn to this boy,
more than that, fated to live with him and for him, henceforth
and forever, or else the sun would be darkened and a rain of
ashes fall on my life. It was a very long time since such a thing
had happened to me. So long, indeed, that I could not remember
anything like it. The "I am looking for someone" I uttered in the
hotel foyer the other day has turned into "I have found someone." In short, I am in love, and for the first time. Thank God I
know that he is staying at the Hotel Marhaba and so I have a
hope of finding him fairly easily. I even consider the idea of
moving and taking a room at the same hotel.

I am struck by one thing. I was able to look at him quite
coolly at the swimming pool. Why this blaze when I found him
again a little while later in the aquarium? There is only one possible answer, but how mysterious it is: ubiquity! Yes, it is always
the *second* encounter that strikes me and inflames me, because
only that one gives proof of the phenomenon of ubiquity. It is
this ubiquity I am in love with!

In the restaurant. At the table next to mine is an American family. Two boys—five and eight, probably—both equally athletic,
blond, pink and blue. The younger, a real little tough with an
impish snub nose, is attacking his brother, who laughs and lets
him. He is pinching, twisting, choking, rumpling, boxing, licking,
and biting him. What a wonderful toy he has, another self,
bigger and stronger and totally passive and consenting! A slap
from the mother interrupts this friendly sparring—for thirty seconds.

Watching this little scene, I felt an idea creep into my mind. It
has been prowling around for three days now but I have been
rejecting it with all my might. What if my ubiquitous boy were
two? Suppose they were two identical twins, quite indistinguishable but yet sufficiently independent from one another to
prefer to do different things and go to different places?

Ubiquity, geminateness. I bring the two words together, set

them side by side and one on top of the other. At first sight they
are unrelated. And yet, if there are twin brothers, then ubiquity
has been the guise in which their geminateness has appeared to
me these past few days. The apparent ubiquity was nothing but
a concealed geminateness, and a geminateness temporarily broken, also, since in order for there to be apparent ubiquity the
twins must appear separately, one after the other. Whence I
could explain quite plausibly the attraction I felt for the child
caught in flagrant ubiquity. Because the apparently ubiquitous
one was in actual fact a *dispaired* twin. Which is to say that
there was beside him an empty place, a powerful *call to being,*
the space left by his absent brother, toward which I am irresistibly drawn.

All of which is all very well, but surely it is all in the mind?

I have paid my bill. I have fastened my suitcase and left a note
in a prominent place asking for it to be sent to the Hotel Marhaba for Monsieur Edouard Surin.

Not only has the die been cast, but the number has come up:
black, odd and *manque*. As though to prove to me that the wheel
has come full circle, just now, when I came in, I found the
Murillo on guard outside my hotel. He was waiting for me. He is
waiting for me still. Not much longer now.

This morning, fate took me along the road to Fedala, along a
beach of dunes dotted with gorse and juniper, one of the rare
spots on the coast where the sea is tame and accessible. No
doubt that was why a great many Arab youths were swimming
and playing there, but I had no heart for browsing. For the first
time in my life I had a long and complicated plan to carry out
together with the knowledge that the energy at my disposal was
no longer boundless, so the time for idling was past. I stretched
out on the sand. Sand is generally supposed to make a bed as
soft and yielding as a mattress. Nothing of the kind. It is as hard
as concrete, the hardest thing there is. Play with it idly in your
hand and sand is feathery enough, but to the body lying solidly
upon it it reveals its true quality of stone. Even so, the body can
still hollow out a mold to fit itself and this I did, with little wriggling movements. A sarcophagus of sand. A story came into my

mind which I had heard once from an ex-spahi and which had impressed me greatly. The man had been patrolling with a mounted company in the Tassili Mountains when one of his men died of peritonitis. When the information was conveyed to Algiers by radio from the nearest fort, back came the fearful order to bring the body back in order that it might be handed over to the man's family. This meant weeks on the back of a camel and then on a truck, an apparently lunatic undertaking in that climate. All the same, they were determined to try. The body was put into a box which was nailed down and loaded onto a camel. Now the wonder was that not only did no smell penetrate the planks but the box grew lighter every day. Until in the end the men began to wonder if the body was still there. They prized up a plank to make sure. The body was there all right, but desiccated, mummified, as hard and stiff as a dummy made of leather. What a wonderful climate, so sterile that bodies are immune from putrefaction in it! That is where I should go to die, away in the far south, in a deep hollow molded to every curve of my body, like the one that I was lying in now . . .

I closed my eyes against the brilliance of the sky. I heard clear voices, laughter and the slap of bare feet. No, I was not going to open my eyes again to watch them go by, charming as they no doubt were. I would not open my eyes, but I recalled a detail from the education of Athenian children mentioned by Aristophanes in *The Clouds*. When they had finished their exercises on the beach, they were made to wipe out the imprints of their private parts in the sand, so as not to disturb the warriors who would come to exercise after them . . .

More bare feet, but only one person this time, a quiet one. I opened one eye. Yes, it was the one that I was waiting for, the ubiquitous boy. He walked with a firm, confident step, a step that matched his slim, perfectly balanced body, his sharp, watchful features, going to a place he knew, somewhere special and urgent. And I got up and followed him, sensing that the miracle of ubiquity was going to happen again and that suddenly, beside this boy who was not my type—whose puny fairness and something lucid and questioning about him rather repel and chill me

—a space, a gap, an empty place was going to appear like an overpowering summons to me.

I followed him. We went around the huts where they sold french fries and soft drinks. He headed for the dunes and disappeared into the belt of mimosa that separated them from the shore. I lost him. There were several ways he might have gone. I had to climb a dune and look down into a dip, a valley of sand, and more dunes. He could not be far because he would have had to climb another dune himself for that and I should have seen him. I hunted and hunted, and I found him.

The pariah and the pair. There they are, the two of them, utterly indistinguishable, entwined together in a hollow in the sand. I stood on the edge of the hollow, as I did outside Roanne, watching the quarry and the quarry's quarry, as I did at Miramas, finding Dani's body under a swarm of rats. They were curled up in a fetal posture, a perfect egg, in which all that was visible was a tangle of limbs and hair. This time the ubiquitary miracle failed to occur. On the contrary, ubiquity had dropped its mask and become geminateness. The summons which vindicated me, which transfused me with joy, never sounded. Geminateness, on the contrary, rejected me because it is completeness, absolute sufficiency, a cell enclosed upon itself. I am outside. I do not belong. These children have no need of me. They have no need of anyone.

I came back to Casa. I still had a hunch to check up on. At the Hotel Marhaba they said yes, a Monsieur Edouard Surin was staying there, with his two sons, Jean and Paul. The twins are my nephews. As for my brother, I have no wish to see him. What should I have to say to him? If fate grants me a reprieve, then I will reconsider the matter.

I dress myself. My embroidered waistcoat is adorned with five medallions from Europe and one from the black mound of Ain-Diab. What was the stranger's advice about the docks? No jewels, no weapons and some ready money? Then I shall not take a sou. Fleurette shall be on my arm and in my ears shall shine the Philippine pearls.

Here I am, little Murillo. I am going to buy you a bunch of

grapes, like the other evening, and together we shall explore the darkness of the docks.

Paul

The day before yesterday we read in the papers that three bodies, covered with blood, had been found among the peanut warehouses at the docks. Two Arabs, killed by a single sword thrust through the heart, and one European, with seventeen knife wounds in him, at least four of them fatal. The European, who had no money on him, must have turned on his attackers with a sword stick which was found beside him.

Edouard did not tell us anything at first. Later on we learned that it was his brother Alexandre, our shocking uncle. His presence in Casablanca was explained by his job as director of the garbage dump, the black mound at Ain-Diab. So it was Uncle Gustave's ghost that had brought us all together in Casablanca.

It is the tragedy of the generation gap. I have often regretted that, Edouard being my father, a gulf of thirty years and more divided us irremediably. He was not much of a father, but what a wonderful friend he could have been! A friend rather easily influenced, of course, to be guided by me toward a more satisfying, more fulfilled and more successful destiny. I should have brought to his life the clarity and purpose which he lacked and which would have given it that *constructive* element without which no solid happiness is possible. Edouard's life went steadily downhill, in spite of his real goodness and his many gifts. But he did not know how to build on the riches he had been given. He trusted fortune right up to the end, but fortune gets tired of eternal beneficiaries who are incapable of responding to her favors.

Edouard would have understood me, followed and obeyed me. He was the father-twin I should have had. Whereas Jean . . .

It was the same generation gap which made me miss my appointed meeting with Alexandre. I was too young—too fresh and desirable—when ill luck put me in his way for the first time. Through no will of my own, I struck him to the heart and killed him outright.

And yet I should have had much to say to him, and much to learn from him.

Geminate communion has us head to tail in the same ovoid position as the double fetus. This position expresses our determination not to become involved in the dialectic of life and time. Twinless loving, on the other hand—whatever the position adopted—places the partners in the unbalanced, asymmetrical attitude of a walker taking his first step.

Halfway between these two extremes, the homosexual couple strives to form a geminate cell, but with non-twin elements, making it counterfeit. Because the homosexual is twinless, there is no gainsaying that, and as such his vocation is dialectic. Only he rejects it. He rejects procreation, growth, fertility, time and weather and their vicissitudes. He goes wailing in search of the twin brother with whom to enclose himself in an endless embrace. He is usurping a condition which does not belong to him. The homosexual is like the Bourgeois Gentilhomme. Intended by his plebeian birth for useful work and a family, he clamors wildly for the free and uninhibited life of a gentleman.

The homosexual is a playactor. He is a non-twin who has escaped from the stereotyped path laid down to cater to the need to propagate the species, and is playing at twins. He plays and he loses, but not without some lucky breaks. Because once he has succeeded at least in the negative stage of his undertaking—the rejection of the functional course—he improvises freely—along the same lines as the geminate couple, certainly, but with unexpected innovations. The homosexual is an artist, an inventor, a creator. In his struggle against unavoidable misfortune, he sometimes produces masterpieces in every sphere. The geminate couple is the complete opposite of this mobile and creative freedom. Its destiny is fixed once and for all on lines of eternity and immobility. Welded together, the couple cannot shift, suffer or create. Except by the stroke of an ax . . .

CHAPTER XIV

Misadventure

Paul

Jean brought her to La Cassine one evening, never having mentioned her before—or not in front of me, at least. She would have had no trouble fitting into the Pierres Sonnantes in the great days when La Cassine was filled with the huge family of Surins, centered on Edouard and Maria-Barbara and people from the factory, and always among them a sprinkling of innocents escaped from St. Brigitte's. It was a Noah's Ark, noisy, welcoming and hospitable, with Méline, forever grumbling and scolding, as the element of sense and moderation. Family, friends and neighbors mingled unceremoniously in this hubbub of every age and sex; while above it, like a cork, like a sealed bottle, floated the cell which was Jean-Paul. Looking back, there must have been a special atmosphere about La Cassine, secreted by the inhabitants of the Pierres Sonnantes and not easily breathed by strangers. That is what I deduce from the way that little society, fairly ill-assorted all in all, hung together, and most of all from

the way, whenever Peter married, he would disappear, never to
return, as though each time the particular spouse had made it a
condition of the marriage that he should break completely with
the tribe.

Things were very different by the time Sophie came here. The
factory, which had been dying ever since the arrests of March
21, 1943, closed altogether after Edouard's death. Two years
later St. Brigitte's was moved to "functional," specially designed
premises at Vitré. We, Méline and Jean-Paul, were left alone,
and even Jean was shuttling to and fro between the Pierres Sonnantes and Paris, just as Edouard used to do, on the excuse of his
law studies. Had she been stupid, Sophie might have pictured
herself fitting easily into this big, empty house, lived in by two
brothers and one old servant immured in her deafness and her
own little obsessions. But I trust her. From the first moment she
sensed that the three of us together formed a structure of formidable strength, and also that the sum of our personal spaces
filled the house from cellar to attics. There is, I believe, a law of
physics according to which a volume of gas, however small,
sealed in a balloon, expands to fill the space available. Every
human being has a greater or lesser capacity for expanding his
personal space. This capacity is finite, so that being placed all by
himself in an enormous house he leaves a greater or smaller portion of it vacant and unoccupied. I make no claims, but it would
not surprise me if the geminate cell, not bound by the same
rules, should reveal itself to be like the gases, infinitely expand-
able.

Unless my memories are mistaken, Sophie was not particularly
pretty but she had an attractively serious, unassuming air about
her which seemed to indicate a great willingness to understand,
so as to do the right thing. She had certainly sized up the problem of our twinship and was not underestimating the difficulties.
Indeed, that in the end was why their marriage did not take
place. Only an idiot would have rushed into it blindly. Any
thought must have been death to the plan.

I suppose Jean put off the moment for introducing Sophie to
me for as long as possible. He must have been afraid of my reac-

tion, knowing how much I hated anything that was likely to come between us. But the ordeal finally had to be faced.

I shall never forget that first meeting. All day long a gale and its aftermath had washed and combed the coast. It was nearly evening before it was possible to go out. The moist air was cool and the sun, already slipping down into the luminous gap between the horizon and the ceiling of cloud, bathed us in a light that had an illusory warmth. The tide was out and added the shimmering desert of the beach to the ravaged sky.

We walked to meet each other along the rough path that follows the cliff, he coming up with Sophie from the west, I going down toward the beach. We stopped without a word, but even years later I still start and tremble when I recall the terrible solemnity of that confrontation. Sophie gazed at me for a long while and I felt for the first time the spear thrust of *alienation,* the wound which has never since healed but has bled, month after month, on and on, at once the reward and the punishment of my quest for my twin brother. For what was in her eyes was more than the harmless incredulity and amazement of all newcomers, startled by our resemblance. Beneath that ever-present astonishment, I divined something else, an unbearable expression which to myself I call the *alienating light,* and still I have not plumbed the depths of its bitterness. For with her intimate knowledge of Jean, she knew all about me also—though I knew nothing of her. I had been known, penetrated, inventoried—with none of that reciprocity which makes for an equilibrium and an elementary justice between two people. A woman violated by a stranger while she slept, or in a faint, might feel a similar sense of dispossession on meeting the man again. Of course, such knowledge as she had of Jean-Paul was all of a non-twin's sort. Its strictly utilitarian character—its subjugation to the propagation of the species—set limits to its light and heat. Obviously non-twin partners can only attain halting embraces, adulterated joys, and cannot hide from themselves that the solitude in which each is immured can never be broken. Even that was too much for me. I read in her eyes that she had held me naked in her arms, that she knew the taste of me, that she knew something—even if only at second hand—of our ritual preliminaries and com-

munion. And I was looking at a stranger! Did Jean think it was
jealousy that set me against Sophie? I can hardly believe that he
had moved so far from our geminate intimacy and had so far
adopted the twinless point of view as to be unaware that what
was at stake was not him personally but that it was Jean-Paul
and the integrity of the cell that I was fighting for through him.

A young man introduces his fiancée to his brother. The girl
and her future brother-in-law exchange some trivial remarks,
conventionally friendly on the surface, inwardly chilled by the
barriers raised between them by the artificial kinship in which
they are to be joined. Jean and Sophie worked so convincingly
and so infectiously to maintain this fragile edifice above the
geminate abyss that I could not help but play their game. Of the
three of us, it was Jean who seemed the least self-conscious,
probably because—helped in the beginning by the odious Malacanthe—he had been schooling himself for years to behave like a
non-twin. Alone with Sophie, he must have played the part
rather well. It all became more difficult when I was there, but he
still seemed able to cope with the situation. For Sophie, on the
other hand, my appearance had been a shock which neither a
girl's natural nervousness nor the trifling astonishment which our
resemblance ordinarily aroused was quite enough to explain.
There was something else—more serious, more wounding—which
I divined because I was badly hurt myself and which made anything possible.

Sophie

I was a coward. I ran away. I may regret it all my life, while at
the same time wondering whether I did not draw back just in
time on the edge of an abyss. How can I tell? I was too young, as
well. Today it would all be different.

I thought Jean rather insignificant the first few times I saw
him. It was only just after the war. We were all trying to con-
vince ourselves that we were well and truly out of the woods
and we were having a lot of fun. Those were the days of "surprise parties." Why surprise? Nothing, on the contrary, could
have been less unexpected than the little parties which were

held in turn at the home of each member of our little gang. To begin with, I hardly noticed the rather small, blond young man with the gentle face that seemed to be immune from aging. Everyone liked him because he seemed to have more team spirit, to be more attached to the group than any other member of it. I ought to have suspected that that community spirit, that eagerness to "belong" sprang precisely from the fear of "not belonging." At twenty-five, Jean was a beginner at communal living. I think he remained one, never managing to achieve integration into any group.

He did not begin to interest me until the day I saw his personality and destiny taking shape, which ought rather to have put me off, since what they signified was danger, matrimonial prospects nil. The obstacle I sensed excited me at first, because I had no idea of its dimensions.

The "party" that day was at his flat. I was impressed at first sight by the huge, somber apartment on the Ile Saint-Louis. Indeed, there was a moment's general silence in the face of those high-ceilinged rooms, inlaid parquet floors and long windows giving glimpses of a view of stone, leaves and water. Jean exerted himself at once to dispel this atmosphere of constraint, and he succeeded by letting loose a flood of hot jazz and setting us all to work pushing the furniture back against the walls to make room. Later, he explained that it was the bachelor flat his father had used when he wanted some distraction from the boredom of life in Brittany. That was the first time he had mentioned his family in my presence. We had danced and drunk and laughed a lot. It was very late when I wanted my bag, which was in the bedroom that was doing duty as a cloakroom. Was it chance that took Jean there just at that moment? He joined me as I was trying to tidy myself up. We were both a little drunk and so I was not particularly surprised when he put his arms around me and kissed me. There was a moment's silence.

"There," I said rather idiotically at last, holding up my bag which I still had in my hand. "I've found what I came for."

"And so have I," he said, laughing, and kissed me again.

On the mantelpiece there was a photo in a frame made of two

sheets of glass, showing a nice but slightly superior-looking man with a little boy who could only have been Jean.

"Is that you with your father?" I asked.

"It is my father, yes," he told me. "He died quite young, some years ago now. The kid, no, that's my brother Paul. He was Papa's favorite."

"He's so like you!"

"Yes, everyone makes the same mistake, even us. We are real twins, you see. When we were tiny, they put bracelets on our wrists with our names on them. Of course we swapped them for fun. Several times. So that now not even we know which is Paul and which Jean. You will never know yourself."

"What difference does it make?" I said, stupidly. "It's only a convention, isn't it? So we'll agree as from this evening that you are Jean and your brother— But where is he actually?"

"He's at our place in Brittany, the Pierres Sonnantes. Or at least he should be. Because how do you know he's not here, talking to you now?"

"Oh Lord! I've drunk too much to work it out!"

"It's often quite hard, you know, even if you are completely sober."

Those last words did put me on my guard, in fact, and through the mists of tiredness and alcohol I suspected for the first time that I was up against a slightly sinister mystery, that it might be prudent to beat a retreat at once, but on the contrary my curiosity and a certain leaning toward the romantic urged me to go on into this forest of Broceliande. Besides it was as yet only a vague presentiment to which the night alone gave some consistency.

Jean led me into another room, smaller and more private than the temporary cloakroom where someone might come in at any moment, and it was there that I became his mistress—since that unsuitable, old-fashioned word is still the one used to describe a man's sexual partner. (*Lover*, which in theory would be simpler and more accurate, is, if possible, still more absurd.)

At that time he was studying law in Paris in a casual way and I never managed to get him to be at all clear about the way he saw his future. This was not because he was unwilling. It came

from something deeper, a fundamental inability to picture himself in any stable and concrete setting. The closing of his father's
factory had left him with a little capital but that, clearly, was not
going to last long. His lack of concern ought to have worried me,
since it jeopardized any marriage plans from the outset. On the
contrary, it was infectious and the only plans we made concerned the traveling we would do together. Marriage in his mind
seemed in fact to have only one side to it, which was the honeymoon, a wedding trip that would go on indefinitely, whereas it
seems to me that it sets the seal on a particular kind of settling
down. Another trick of his imagination was always to link travel
with the seasons, as if every country corresponded to one period
of the year and every town to certain days within that period.
There is something in it, of course, and there is an example in a
popular song which the radio was dinning into our ears at the
time, called "April in Portugal." But, as was so often the case
with Jean, the most worn-out clichés, the most hackneyed popular crazes seemed to be revivified and raised to a much more
brilliant and distinguished level when he took them up.

While everyone in the street was humming "April in Portugal," he acquired his first long-playing record, Vivaldi's *Four
Seasons;* and it was as if the popular song was reinforced, proved
and vindicated by the masterpiece of the little red-haired Venetian priest—you could almost imagine it had grown out of it, like
a trivial version of the same thing.

He had drawn up a kind of calendar—his "concrete year" as
he called it—based not on regular astronomical data but on the
changing weather conditions in each month. For instance, he
would fold the two halves of the year over one another, so bringing the opposite months together and discovering symmetries,
affinities between them: January–July (midwinter–midsummer),
February–August (very cold–very hot), March–September
(end of winter–end of summer), April–October (leaves bud-
ding–leaves falling), May–November (flowers of the living–flowers of the dead), June–December (light–dark). He
would point out that these pairs were opposed not only in content but also in vitality, and that the two factors varied in inverse
proportion to one another. Thus September–March and Oc-

tober–April had obviously related contents (temperature, condition of vegetation), whereas their vitality (veering toward winter–veering toward summer) was moving in the opposite direction. While the opposition of January–July and December–June rested entirely on their static contents, the vitality of those months was rather feeble. In this way he was endeavoring —for reasons I still cannot fathom—to reject the abstract framework of the calendar and live instead in contact with what was most colorful and concrete in the seasons.

"There it is then," he would say dreamily, "on our honeymoon we'll go to Venice, the city of the four seasons. From there, with proper preparations, we'll go in turn to those countries where the particular season at the time is at its best. For instance, well, winter at the North Pole, no, in Canada. We'll have to decide between Quebec and Montreal. We'll choose whichever city is coldest . . ."

"Then it will be Quebec, I think."

". . . and buried deepest, and most wintry."

"Then it will be Montreal."

He would talk about Iceland also, the big volcanic island inhabited by more sheep than men, whose eccentric situation, in the far north, on the edge of the Arctic Circle like a kind of longitudinal Wild West, would set him dreaming. But most of all it was the white nights of the summer solstice that attracted him, the midnight sun shining brightly down on silent, slumbering towns. After that he would picture us under the blaze of the same sun, but now gone raving mad, in the far south, across the Sahara, in the Hoggar, or better still the Tassili Mountains, which were said to be even more spectacular.

I marveled at his powers of invention, which expressed themselves in endless monologues, like a kind of verbal purring of a childish sort, very soft and soothing and melancholy, which, as I understood later, derived—like his premarital lovemaking—from the famous Aeolian, the secret language he spoke with his brother. For Jean, who knew only Paris and the Côtes-du-Nord, would describe every country as though he had lived there for a long time. He obviously had his head stuffed with the accounts of the navigators and tales of exploration, and could quote Bou-

gainville, Kerguélen, La Pérouse, Cook, Dampier, Darwin and
Dumont d'Urville at the drop of a hat. But he had his own private key to this imaginary geography and that key, as I soon realized, was a meteorological one. He told me more than once
that what interested him in the seasons was not so much the regular recurrence of the astral configurations as the fringe of cloud,
rain and fair weather which surrounded them.

"I know each country from books," he explained. "I am not
expecting our wedding trip to do away with my prejudices about
Italy, England and Japan. Quite the reverse. It will only confirm,
enrich and deepen them. But what I want this journey to do is to
give to the countries I have imagined that concrete touch which
is unimaginable, the something or other which is like the inimitable stamp of reality. And that touch, that something or other I
see first and foremost as the light, a color in the sky, an atmosphere, the meteors."

He insisted on the necessity for restoring its proper meaning to
the word "meteor," which is not as is commonly believed a stone
fallen from the sky—that is called a meteorite—but any atmospheric phenomenon, hail, fog, snow, the aurora borealis, the science of which is meteorology. The book of his childhood, the
book of his whole life, was Jules Verne's *Around the World in
Eighty Days* and it was from this that he had drawn his philosophy of travel.

"Phileas Fogg has never traveled," he explained to me. "He is
the typical sedentary man, a stay-at-home and even something of
a crank. All the same, he has a knowledge of the whole world,
but of a special kind: from yearbooks, timetables and almanacs
from all over the world, which he knows by heart. His knowledge is a priori. He concludes from it that it would be possible to
girdle the earth in eighty days. Phileas Fogg is not a man, he is a
living clock. Punctuality is his religion. His servant, Passepartout,
on the other hand, is an inveterate nomad who has done everything, including being an acrobat. Phileas Fogg's phlegmatic
coldness is continually contrasted with Passepartout's mimicry
and excitability. Phileas Fogg's bet will be jeopardized by two
sources of delay: Passepartout's scrapes and the caprices of the
weather. In fact, both obstacles are one and the same: Passepar-

tout is meteorological man and as such the opposite of his master who is chronological man. This chronology precludes equally being fast as well as slow, and Phileas Fogg's journey must not be confused with a race around the world. This is shown in the episode of the Hindu widow whom they save from the pyre on which she should have shared the fate of her husband's body. Phileas Fogg uses her to fill in time when he is inadvertently ahead of his timetable. There is to be no question of going around the world in seventy-nine days!

"'Save that woman, Mr. Fogg!' the brigadier general cried.

"'I still have twelve hours in hand. I can devote them to it.'

"'By Jove! You are a man with a heart!' said Sir Francis Cromarty.

"'Sometimes,' Phileas Fogg replied simply. 'When I have the time.'

"The truth is that Phileas Fogg's journey is an attempt by chronology to get the better of meteorology. The timetable must be kept to in spite of *wind and tide*. Phileas Fogg makes his journey around the world purely to proclaim himself the master of Passepartout."

I used to listen to his theories with mixed enthusiasm. I must say that even in my most foolish moments I never ceased to feel —very remotely sometimes, I admit—a presentiment, a vague awareness, disquieting but exciting at the same time, that there was *something else,* a hidden but fundamental reality behind the Jean I saw and could believe I knew. I was warned by the way that, starting from something as apparently childish as *Around the World in Eighty Days,* he had gone on with absolute, unshakable seriousness to develop ideas so abstract that they bordered on the metaphysical, and later on I understood why: everything with Jean stemmed from a very distant reality, going back to his early childhood, to his relationship with his brother Paul, to be precise. In this contrast between Phileas Fogg and Passepartout, for example, I could see that it was with the sympathetic Frenchman Passepartout that he was identifying. But this identification, apparently very much the same as that of most children reading the novel, took on a graver significance with Jean, because there was obviously a Phileas Fogg in his life and it was not hard to put a name to him. (Incidentally, I notice what an affinity so many childish things have with abstract thought. Then what is it they have in common? Is it a basic simplicity and impartiality? As though a kind of silence, antedating adult language, were to meet the serene contemplation of the heights.)

I could give more examples of the *something else* affecting Jean's behavior. His loathing of mirrors, which had nothing to do with the contempt for their personal appearance men consider it virile to display. His anxiety to be part of the group, to "belong," which betrayed a belonging lost and mourned for in secret. The strange words, catchwords and turns of phrase he now and then let fall—and always in our moments of greatest intimacy—and which I learned were snatches of Aeolian. And since I have brought up the subject of intimacy, I may as well admit that for a man of over twenty-five he made love like a small child, with an awkward, fumbling enthusiasm, lacking not so much the means as the conviction—like an explorer doing his best to conform to the habits, customs and cooking of the exotic tribe among whom he has decided to effect a return to nature. Afterward he would go to sleep in my arms but always in his sleep he would gradually move around until we were head to tail, so that I was obliged to imitate his position, curled up with his head buried between my thighs and both hands flat on my behind. I should have had to be very stupid not to understand that in so doing he was making me take the place of someone else.

When he took me to the Pierres Sonnantes for the first time, he had told me so much about the house and about his family that I might have thought myself safe from any surprises. I knew that I should not meet his mother—arrested by the Germans in 1943, deported and disappeared—or his father—died in 1948—or Peter, which was his funny name for all the rest of his brothers and sisters, who were all scattered far from their birthplace; but I knew them all from hearing him talk about them, and at the Pierres Sonnantes I found their traces, their ghosts, like familiar things from my own past. I have always been surprised to find how easily we can incorporate other people's memories into our own. Stories told me many times over by my father or mother have become inseparable from my own past life, even though they happened long before I was born. As soon as I got to the Guildo I "recognized" it all, the country, the coastline, the houses, all of which I was seeing for the first time, even the air—with its mixture of seaweed, mud and meadow—whose smell was the smell of the twins' childhood. I recognized it all because I had foreseen it all, except the most important thing, the *something else* which hit me like a thunderbolt in spite of the innumerable warning signs it had been sending me ever since my first meeting with Jean.

It had been raining all day but the evening was turning out fine. We were climbing up, Jean and I, from the beach by a steep little path to the clifftop. Then we saw someone coming down to meet us. Someone? Why not be precise? I knew at a glance—when he was still only a distant outline—*who* was coming. I might have put the slight giddiness I felt at that moment down to the cliff we were climbing, which was growing steeper as we climbed. Perhaps the thought may even have crossed my mind. Not for long, because I had only a few seconds left in which I could, for one last time, disguise with a twinless interpretation the *something else* I had been striving for so long not to see. I was stunned by the appearance of that terrifying person: *a stranger who was Jean*. My eyes drank in that extraordinary presence, with its devastating effect, postponing the reckoning of the damage that was being done inside me, around me—and the precautions I should take to try to contain it.

Introductions and a conversation bordering on the ridiculous threw out bridges between us. Jean, of course, seemed to be the one least embarrassed by this misadventure. He was acting as go-between to his brother and his fiancée. Paul came with us to the house, where we found old Méline—the last witness of the time, not so long past, when these walls had been overflowing with busy life. Jean had assured me she was senile, but that was not the impression she gave me. Certainly she was always gazing into space and muttering things that one could barely understand, since she never addressed herself to anyone in particular. But the little I did catch never seemed to me to lack sense, quite the opposite, and I have a feeling that what made her unin-

telligible was that too much was meant and implied. It was like
the things that she was always scribbling, even though she was—
by what everyone said—completely illiterate. I should have liked
some expert archaeologist or philologist—which was it exactly
that Champollion specialized in?—to have had a look at those
school exercise books covered with a close writing wholly illegi-
ble to us.

"She is illiterate," Jean would say, "but she doesn't know it.
Haven't you ever heard a baby babbling in its cradle? In his own
way, he is copying the speech of the grown-ups he hears around
him. He may even think he is talking like them. Méline is copying other people's writing, even though she doesn't know how to
write. I got hold of one of her books one day. I said to her, 'Are
you writing, Méline? Well, however much I look, I can't make
anything of it.' 'Of course not,' was what she said to me. 'I'm not
writing to you.' That made me think of Aeolian, which is a
made-up language intended for one person alone."

It is no good letting oneself be carried away by a liking for
wonders, even in a place as charged with sorcery as the Pierres
Sonnantes. But really, if there is still any meaning in the word
"witch" it is because of creatures like Méline. She was a good example of the mixture of shrewd but limited intelligence and obscure, vaguely supernatural maleficence which is covered by the
word "malignity." She was supposed to be deaf and would not
answer questions, any more than she obeyed orders. But I have
observed more than once that she heard the slightest sound and
understood very well what was said around her. Dressed always
in black, except for the white goffered headdress which covered
her from forehead to neck, she was not wearing mourning, she
was the personification of it. She stood on intimate, long-stand-
ing, almost familiar terms with death. I think I gathered that her
husband, Justin Méline, was a quarryman and died about the
same time as Edouard Surin, having had eleven children by her,
not one of whom survived. The deaths of these infants had accompanied the successive births in the Surin family like a coun-
terpoint, so that it was almost as if a Méline had to go in order
that a Surin might appear. Then the deaths of the two fathers
finally bound them together, as though Justin Méline had never

been anything but Edouard Surin's shadow. Only Méline seemed
indestructible—ageless and everlasting as death itself.

Her familiarity with evil expressed itself in a most odd way.
She had, in fact, a gift for softening and domesticating it, taking
the sting out of anger and disgust, horror and despair with language of alarming moderation. In anyone else, it would have
been called a genius for euphemism. When it came to Méline, so
rough and unpolished, one trembled to hear her describe as a
"bad lot" a young man who was reported in the papers as having
killed his mother and father with an ax, or, referring to the innumerable losses she had suffered in her life, remark that she had
had "plenty of trouble," or merely stigmatizing a housebreaker
who had robbed a nearby farmhouse and beaten up the owners
as "impudent." Although she described the war as a "nuisance," I
suspect that she had not lost by it—if only because Maria-Barbara's deportation had made her the mistress of the house. I cannot deny that I am prejudiced against the woman because I hold
her chiefly responsible for my departure from the Pierres Sonnantes. Was she afraid of no longer being the only woman in the
house, or did it go deeper; was she, like Paul, protecting the integrity of the geminate cell? From the first day that crazy
gloomy old Breton woman frightened me, and I knew that she
was going to be the worst enemy to my happiness with Jean.
The situation was all the more disturbing in that, far from ignoring me and keeping me at a distance, on the contrary, she drew
me into her orbit—with the approval of the twins, to whom it
was natural for the newcomer to be taken in charge and as it
were initiated by the oldest inhabitant. As a result, I had to endure the monologue that flowed from her lips like a sulphurous
spring all the time she was going about her work and doing her
shopping. I don't think I was mistaken in discerning a mixture of
aversion and fear in the local people's attitude toward her and
she treated them with stern contempt. Was she even able to
count? Apparently not, but nothing was certain with that
woman. The fact remains that she had only one way of making a
purchase. She would hold out a coin or a note to the shopkeeper
and say, "Give me some butter, bread and sausage meat for
this . . ." This involved various calculations. Often the amount

was not enough and the quantity of goods would be very small. Then the tradesman was punished with a tight-lipped, heavily reproachful look, as though he had been guilty of cheating her.

I was never able to think of more than one explanation for the natives' evident dislike of Méline. Only fifteen years before, the old abbey and its surrounding buildings had been overflowing with noise and life. There had been the textile and carding works, St. Brigitte's home and its children, and above all the innumerable Surin family with Maria-Barbara in its midst. In addition there had been this woman heavy with mourning whose power spread far and wide. Now all was deserted. The factory was closed, the children's home moved away and the Surin family scattered and decimated by death. Who was left? Méline, grimmer and more bad-tempered than ever. Had she really played no part in the disaster? I believe witches were burned for less in the Middle Ages. And it seems to me that today she broods jealously over the Pierres Sonnantes, silent now, and is ever ready to smother any seeds of new life that may settle in this ravaged soil. Like my love for Jean, for instance.

Paul

Did I take advantage of Jean and Sophie's coming to the Pierres Sonnantes to break off their engagement by seducing the bride-to-be? In a sense, yes, but a trivial, two-dimensional, twinless sense. The truth becomes something different as soon as the third dimension is given back to it. The first time I met Sophie, the *alienating light* blinded, dazed, and rooted me to the spot. It took me some time to get used to it, time to recover and let my head clear again; but when I was ready to fight back I realized that I held an undeniable fascination for her. Under any other circumstances that would sound unforgivably complacent. In fact, it is said with the utmost humility because it was obvious that what Sophie found attractive in me was my twinship and that alone. She was discovering suddenly that a thousand and one aspects of Jean's personality were nothing but bright, fractured gleams from that great hidden sun in whose secret she henceforth had a share. And surely it was natural—even right and proper—that I should possess a greater share of that charm than Jean, since I had always been the guardian of the cell, the keeper of the geminate seals, while he is continually denying his origins and prostituting their virtues?

Sophie

At first I blamed those sea-green shores, that opaline sea, the landscape with its baleful aquamarine transparency, and the house also, full of ghosts jealously guarded by old Méline, the empty workrooms and the disused abbey haunted by memories of a host of innocents and monsters. But if the surroundings mattered, they were only the flesh around the nut. At first it seemed to me that, steeped once more in his old environment, Jean put on a warmer, brighter gloss, swelled with a happy energy and a return to boyhood. What is more natural? I thought of the legend of Antaeus, whose strength was renewed whenever he touched the earth, so that Hercules was only able to throttle him by lifting him clear of the ground. One night he held me in his arms with a tenderness, a passion, an efficiency—why shrink from this rather cynical word?—to which our fumbling embraces had not accustomed me. The next day it was as though a veil of misery had fallen on him, a gray veil beneath which he huddled wretchedly, casting hunted glances at me. I was at a loss to understand. I thought I did understand, more's the pity, when I saw Paul come up and watched them together, and then it was my turn to feel wretched, horribly lonely and bewildered in the face of both brothers. Because for one thing I saw in Paul all the masterful assurance of my lover of the night before, and for another I saw Jean approach him and once within the field of his brilliance take color and warmth from it. Paul was unquestionably the master of the Pierres Sonnantes, but which of the two was my lover and which the man I was engaged to? I would never bring myself to ask Jean the hideous questions which might have enlightened me.

More hideous still were those I should have had to ask him a few days later to relieve myself of a fresh suspicion. Much to Méline's wrath, we were occupying the middle bedroom, which had been Edouard and Maria-Barbara's. It was furnished rather oddly with two double beds, which offered the agreeable alternative of physical separation or sleeping together in one or other of the beds. We would regularly begin the night, one in each bed, then visit one another for varying lengths of time, always with the possibility open to each of us of retreating to the empty bed to go to sleep on our own. In spite of this freedom, I very soon noticed that Jean would leave the room nearly every night on escapades which might take him away for hours. He had explained to me that in this he was reverting to an old childhood habit. The group of buildings and courtyards which made up La Cassine, the abbey and the adjacent factory provided an inexhaustible field for nocturnal wanderings, supposing one were fond of shadows and mysteries. To begin with, I accepted the explanation as just one more of the novel peculiarities of this strange house and its strange inhabitants. Then something seemed to cast light on the mystery, in one respect at least, but the light was a sinister one. After his nocturnal rambles, it was Jean's habit to get into the other bed and we would finish the night apart, very often coming together again with the first light of dawn. On this particular night, however, whether on whim or out of absentmindedness, I felt him slide in beside me. It was unwise of him because as soon as he was in my arms I was surprised not to notice the unmistakable chilliness and fresh smell of one who has been out at night. On the contrary, he was slightly sweaty, as though he had that moment come from bed, and even from sleep, and there was a smell on his skin that was not unknown to me, it was the smell of my splendid love of a few days earlier. It was obvious that he had come straight from Paul's room.

Jean

Sophie, you were not strong enough, you were too weak, on at least three occasions.

You suffered your first defeat at the hands of the formidable alliance ranged against you by the Pierres Sonnantes, Méline, Paul and even, alas, myself! You felt lonely, isolated, betrayed.

Betrayed by me, who ought to have been your unswerving ally
in this place. But how could you fail to understand that part of
me was still faithful to you, why didn't you hear it calling to you
for help? Why didn't you confide your fears, your suspicions,
your unhappiness to me? I could not speak to you myself—I tried
to more than once when I saw how lost you were—because for
Jean-Paul these things are too closely bound up with the secret,
silent dialogue of Aeolian. That was one of the very ways I
needed you, when you should have taken the initiative boldly,
even brutally, so as to unlock my tongue, so that I might learn to
speak the language of the heart and of sex, like everyone else.

The third time you failed was in that sudden flight, with no
explanation, as though I had hurt you so cruelly that I no longer
deserved any consideration. What did I do? What did I do to
you? I know I let Paul dominate me again. There were nights,
yes, when I reverted to the ritual of our childhood—exorcism,
ovoid position, seminal communion—but wasn't it for you of all
people to release me from it? You interpreted my weakness as a
betrayal—and drew the conclusion that there was no longer anything to bind you to me.

Sophie

I had already decided to go, only I did not know how to break
the news to Jean, especially as in my mind it amounted to the
end of our engagement. Yet it would never have occurred to me
simply to cut and run if Méline had not thought of it for me.

I was going with her to Matignon, where she had some shopping to do. A neighbor had lent her his horse and trap and she
drove as vigorously as a man. She went straight through the town
and did not stop until she reached the station.

"Your train leaves in fifteen minutes!"

It was the first thing she had said since we left the house. I
was dumbfounded.

"My train?"

"Your train to Paris, for goodness' sake!"

"But—what about my case?"

The whip handle was jerked toward the back of the trap.

"In there. All packed. I'll get it out for you."

She had never been so communicative—or so obliging. It crossed my mind that this could be Paul's doing—perhaps with Jean's connivance, who could say? Afterward the twofold suggestion seemed to me altogether improbable, but it showed how upset I was and helped to make me give in. After all, if I had to go why not get it over with at once? I got down and joined my suitcase on the pavement. The horse, whipped up viciously, set off noisily with the trap and as I watched it trotting away I breathed a sigh of relief.

Paul

When Méline told me the young lady had taken the first train to Paris, I suspected that she had something to do with that abrupt departure. But I knew well enough that if I were to question her she would withdraw into her deafness and that would be that. I daresay it was bound to happen. I had certainly got Jean back again and Sophie, part consenting, part deceived (the disingenuous female mind is at home in ambiguous situations), had become my mistress. From a non-twin point of view it was the classic threesome of wife + husband + lover. Geminateness gave, it is true, an additional dimension to the Jean-Paul-Sophie threesome. Could it have worked? The geminate structure is undoubtedly an absolutely rigid one. Its small rituals leave no room for any play, no flexibility in adapting to a new situation. A dialectical piece could not be added to the identical couple. It would reject it at once. Yet the memory of Maria-Barbara suggests to me that Sophie might perhaps have been able to fit in with us even so. When we were little boys, our mother was the common base in which our twinship was rooted. Could Sophie have taken over that role? Her sudden departure shows that she could not find in herself a sufficient appetite for novelty, or pleasure in experimenting, or power of invention to lend herself wholeheartedly to that kind of game. Although not equal to the inflexibility of twinship, the ways of women run as true to form as the building of a bird's nest or the construction of a beehive. These two inflexible systems, the geminate and the feminine, had no hope of adjusting to each other. If you want flexibility, novelty, and an inquiring mind, then you must look for them in a certain type of non-twin man. Our father, Edouard, for instance, might have been willing to experiment—and after all what is adultery but a kind of receptivity?—but only within certain rather cautious limits. But I was thinking more of his brother Alexandre, our shocking uncle, whose whole life was nothing but one quest for love which ended magnificently on the docks at Casablanca. He is one person I shall never stop being sorry I did not meet and have for a friend—because he was a remarkable man and also because he stood at the ideal distance from non-twins and from twins to see and be seen, hear and be heard. His homosexuality—the facsimile of twinship among non-twins— might have given us valuable insights, been an irreplaceable aid to penetrating the mysteries of twinship and twinlessness alike.

Jean

Each of us has played our part in this affair, in which all have been losers, and all the more innocently because each has remained true to his or her inmost self. So that Paul and Méline also were equally blameless. Besides, what did Paul do? He did no more than the flame which by its very existence attracts and burns the moths. Sophie and I were burned by his radiance, and we were false to the course we had laid down for ourselves. I think that Sophie, with her woman's instinct, will soon find the way that is right for her again. When her unhappiness has faded, her scratches healed, when she has become a wife and mother, she will look back on her excursion into the realm of twinship as a youthful folly, perilous, incomprehensible and sweet. It may be the only remarkable thing that will ever have happened to her. The memory of it may be worth a few bruises, perhaps? As for me . . .

If Paul thinks that everything is going to go on again just as before now that Sophie has gone, then his obsession with twinship must have affected his brain! I had been counting on Sophie to keep him at a distance. With Sophie gone, the only way that distance can be created and maintained is by traveling. In other words, now that the *sedentary* dialectic which would have been my life here if I had had a wife and children has not worked out, there is nothing left for me but the cruder and altogether superficial dialectic of travel. What has failed in time shall be translated more easily into space.

I am going away, then. Where to? We were planning to get married very quickly and go on a proper honeymoon to Venice. I made the suggestion to Sophie in a spirit of conformity, out of respect for the conventions. Having elected to do the commonplace thing, I should have gone to Venice, *like everyone else.*

I can see now that that comfortable label covered goods of a rather different order, and they appear to me now in all their tantalizing nakedness. Once upon a time, on Ascension Day, the Doge of Venice would go alone aboard the *Bucentaur* and out into the Adriatic, surrounded by a procession of magnificently decorated vessels. When he reached the Lido channel, he would throw a wedding ring into the sea, with the words: "Sea, we wed thee, in sign of real and perpetual sovereignty." That solitary wedding trip, the ring thrown into the sea, the marriage ceremony in which one party was an impersonal element, the sea, the whole stern, splendid mythology satisfied some taste in me for breaking away, for solitude, for departures aimed at no known goal and yet attended by magnificent ceremony, and told me that, beneath the picture postcard of mandolins and gondolas, Venice is inhabited by a corrupt and vagabond spirit.

I was to have gone to Venice with Sophie. I shall go to Venice without her.

Paul

Jean has gone. Three days after Sophie. My beloved "geminate intuition," which reveals to me so many truths invisible to non-twins, has these occasional lapses, blanks, blind spots which appear unforgivable after the event. While I was congratulating myself that that absurd marriage plan had come to nothing, Jean was fastening his suitcase.

I had realized that he was not really cut out for marriage. One step further and I should have foreseen that once his engagement was broken off, there would be nothing for him but to go away. Simply because the same centrifugal motion which was making him break up the geminate cell by marriage, and then break up the conjugal cell by a reversion to Bep, was ultimately bound to take him away from this place strewn with debris and carry him goodness knows where! To gain his freedom, he used Sophie against me and me against Sophie at the same time. Poor consolation! I am wondering if I ought not to have come to some arrangement with Sophie so as to tie the inveterate nomad down. What a lesson!

Now what am I to do? My first thought was to shut myself up in the Pierres Sonnantes with Méline and let my renegade brother go to the devil, and so I did to begin with. While Méline barricaded herself in her kitchen, writing one of her interminable scribbles in which she relates to an imaginary correspondent —or thinks she does—everything of interest that happens at the Pierres Sonnantes, I spent long hours on the Guildo beach. I watched the high spring tides, which are always impressive in these parts, coming in toward me. The thing that fascinated me about the spring equinox was the contrast between the immense height of the waves, which this year was quite extraordinary, and the calmness of the weather. *A quiet storm.* I turn this incredible paradox over and over in my mind, although I must have come across it a number of times over the years, but oddly enough Jean's going seems to make me more aware of it. Could it be that there is a *dispaired vision*—belonging to one twin on his own—which is to some extent a *mutilated version* of the geminate vision?

The pure, pale sky, the April sun, more bright than hot, the warm, caressing southwesterly breeze, all nature withdrawn into apparent meditation after the ax blow that has severed the geminate cell, and in that still, silent landscape the sea rearing its green spine—a sea calm in itself and smooth as a baby's cheek— the resistless swelling of the flood pouring this year over roads and fields, noiselessly and without violence. A peaceful cataclysm.

I can bear it no longer. At the Pierres Sonnantes my situation as a dispaired twin is untenable. The twinless would construe that to mean: everything here reminds him of his missing brother and helps to overwhelm him with sadness. That cliché-ridden sentence conceals a reality far deeper and more subtle.

If, more's the pity, I am compelled to learn how to live a twinless life, the Pierres Sonnantes is the last place I have a hope of performing that dismal business with any success. The truth is that the whole place has been dedicated to twinship since time immemorial. Everywhere, absolutely everywhere—in our own room, of course, but also in the living room at La Cassine, in the old factory, in every cell of St. Brigitte's, in the garden, on the beach, on the Ile des Hébihens—I am calling Jean, speaking to him, conjuring up his ghost, and toppling into emptiness when I try to lean on him. There is nothing like this sudden amputation to make one grasp the nature of the geminate vision and at the same time measure the poverty of life without a twin.

Every man needs his like in order to perceive the outside world in its totality. Other people show him the scale of things a long way off and warn him that there is a side to everything which he cannot see from where he stands, but which exists because it is visible to others standing further off. This goes for the very existence of the outside world, which is only vouched for by the confirmation of our neighbors. What makes my dreams' pretensions to reality null and void is that I am the only witness to them. Take a man entirely on his own—Robinson Crusoe on his island, for example—and his vision of the world would be unimaginably impoverished and insubstantial. Such a man would not live his life, he would dream it, all he would have of it would be a frayed, intangible, evanescent dream.

Jean's going reduced me to a comparable state as regards my thoughts, ideas, feelings, emotions, everything, in short, which is usually called our "inner" world. The normal state of individuals with regard to their "inner" world was now brought home to me in all its frightening poverty: a frayed, intangible, evanescent dream that was the ordinary spiritual landscape. In exchange for Jean-Paul's!

You playing, Bep? It did not need the magic words for my

twin to echo my moods and in so doing lend them solidity and substance. Simply by virtue of our bipolarity, we inhabited a space stretched tight between us, woven with emotions, embroidered with ideas, as warm and colorful as an oriental carpet. A *spirit unfurled*, yes, that was Jean-Paul's—not cramped like the spirits of non-twins.

You playing, Bep? The imperative, ritual formula would set us on the oriental carpet, face to face, identical and yet apart, differing merely in the position that we occupied in space, like two acrobats eyeing one another, legs astride, gathering themselves, eyes meeting and hands joining, while on a single note a quick, frenzied roll of drums announces that the act is about to begin, and the two identical bodies come together violently to perform, one by one, the five obligatory figures of the great geminate game.

That game had only one object, which was to wrest us from the attraction of the non-twin earth, wash us clean from the stains of the dialectical sphere in which we had bathed despite ourselves ever since our fall into time, and restore us to the eternal, unmoving, unchanging identity which was our original state.

Bep has played the dialectical game. Assailed by the corrosion of the non-twin world, he has allowed himself to be carried away on the tide of procreation. Our youth was by rights eternal, unchanging, stainless, its brightness immune from spot or scratch. Bep has so far forgotten that basic truth as to wish to become a husband, father, grandfather . . .

But he failed to achieve his metamorphosis. Having embarked on the dialectical process, he got no further than the first stage, the engagement and the honeymoon journey, the nomadic, wandering stage, corresponding to the exogamic imperative. But if that trip were a nuptial flight, the female would settle once she was fertilized. . . . Now that he has lost his fiancée, Jean will never know the settled happiness of his own fireside, the monotonous joys of fidelity, the noisy pleasures of fatherhood. Betrothed without a betrothed, he is doomed to a perpetual wedding trip. Little Jean, I know where you are! If I wanted you back, I should not look for you in Sophie's petticoats. You decided, you and Sophie, very properly, to do the traditional thing

and honeymoon in Venice. It was your idea, and Sophie raised
no objection to its triteness, because she knew the conventional
path she was meekly treading. While I am writing this, you are
getting out of the train at the Stazione Santa Lucia. Like the true
vagabond you are, you have no luggage. And so you are the first
to step onto the moving planks of the *motoscafo* that will take
you to the other end of the Grand Canal. You watch the dramatic façades of the palaces moving past, each with its private
landing stage and the posts painted in spirals of many colors to
which the gondolas are tied like restive horses, but your eyes
keep dropping to the uneasy, oily waters, churned up by oars
and propellers, like black milk.

CHAPTER XV

Venetian Mirrors

Paul

When I landed at Marco Polo Airport this morning, it was pouring rain. I refused to shelter in the cabin of the *vaporetto*, which was packed with a crowd of all nationalities. I stayed on deck and all through the forty-five-minute journey I watched the passing posts, each capped with a sulky sea gull, that lined the channel. To know Venice, there is no need to have been there, it is so much a part of the mental landscape of every European. At most, one goes there in order to *recognize* it. That lane of piles driven into the mud of the Lagoon is the trail of white pebbles dropped by Tom Thumb to find his way home. For any moderately educated Westerner, there can be no city with more preconceived ideas about it than Venice.

As we drew nearer, each one of us was stepping into a private dream and greeting the familiar details that proclaimed the approach of the mother city with a joyful excitement. The first was a compact flight of pigeons that wheeled about the boat's funnel

and then sped off again like the dove from Noah's Ark. Then a
gondola broke through the curtain of rain—our first gondola—
eleven meters long and one and a half wide, of shiny black wood
with a small bunch of artificial flowers stuck on the foredeck, like
a banderillo in the collar of a bull, and with the steel *ferro* with
its six teeth standing for the six quarters of Venice at the prow.
At last the rain stopped. A ray of sunshine pierced like a sword
through the wet mist in which we had been moving and struck
the white dome of the Church of Santa Maria della Salute with
its encircling ring of statues. The boat stopped and it was only
then I turned and "recognized" the Campanile in St. Mark's
Square, the two columns in the Piazzetta, the arcade of the
Doges' Palace . . .

I let the crowd stream ashore. A terror held me back, for I
knew what was going to happen. I had "recognized" Venice.
That was only the first beat of the rhythm to which I was going
to be living now. In the second, I was going to be "recognized"
by Venice.

I stepped out hesitantly along the gangway. It did not take
long. A porter in a red waistcoat came up to me and picked up
my case with a smile.

"I knew you would come back, Signor Surin. People always
come back to Venice."

I felt a pang. His face was illumined by the *alienating light*
that had hurt me for the first time in Sophie's face. He knew
Jean. He took me for my brother. Whether I liked it or not, he
was identifying me with Jean.

At the Hotel Bonvecchiati they welcomed me like the prodigal
son, and promised me my old room—light and quiet.

"She has been waiting for you faithfully, Signor Surin," the
receptionist said jokingly.

And it was true, room 47 was light, its window looking out
over the rooftops of the Calle Goldoni, narrow as a mountain
crevasse, but wasn't what illumined it still the alienating light? I
looked at the double bed—a bit too narrow, though, to be really
matrimoniale, just about twin-sized—the twisted glass luster,
pink and white like a set piece in icing sugar, the tiny bathroom,
the fragile desk, but what held my gaze was a plan of Venice on

the wall. I had just made out two interlocking hands, the right above the left—separated by the blue snake of the Grand Canal. The station was at the base of the right index finger, the Salute at the tip of the left thumb, St. Mark's Square just above the right wrist. . . . If I had had the slightest doubt about the mission I had come to Venice to fulfill, I should have had to yield to the evidence: the geminate key to the city had been handed to me, as though on a velvet cushion, as soon as I arrived.

What else is one to do in Venice but see Venice? Looked at in non-twin terms, my mission of "recognition" comes down to a sightseeing trip. Sitting on the terrace of an *osteria*, slowly sipping a cappuccino, I watch herds of visitors crowding after a guide, who holds aloft a flag, an open umbrella, an enormous artificial flower, or a feather duster as a rallying point. This crowd has a certain originality. It is not a bit like the one that winds through the lanes of Mont-St.-Michel every summer—which is the only comparison I possess—nor, I suppose, like the ones at the pyramids of Giza, at Niagara Falls or the temples of Angkor Wat. To define the character of the Venetian tourist. Point number one: Venice is not profaned by this crowd. The thing is that the high spots for tourism are, unfortunately, very often places originally dedicated to solitude, to prayer or meditation. They stand at the junction of a spectacular or desert landscape and a vertical spiritual line. Hence the frivolous, cosmopolitan crowds nullify the very thing that has brought them there. There is nothing like that here. Venice is fulfilling her eternal role in welcoming the gay, colorful—and what is more, rich!—flood of foreigners on holiday. The tide of tourists ebbs and flows in a twelve-hourly cycle, too fast for the liking of the hotel and restaurant owners, who complain when they see the morning's visitors go away in the evening with no profit to the trade, since they manage to bring their own packed lunches with them. But this crowd does not mar a city dedicated through the ages to carnivals, voyages and commerce. It is an integral part of the immemorial spectacle, and the two little red marble lions outside the basilica bear witness to it, their backs worn away by fifty generations of children, come from the four corners of the

world to ride on them. In its funny way, it is like a childish version of St. Peter's foot, worn away by the kisses of a thousand
years of pilgrims.

When the tourists have had enough of wandering about the
narrow streets, the churches and museums, they sit down at a
café terrace and look—at other tourists. One of the tourist's principal occupations in Venice is to watch himself in a thousand international avatars, the game consisting in guessing the nationality of the passers-by. This proves that Venice is not merely a
spectacular, but also a *specular* city. Specular—from the Latin
speculum, a mirror—Venice is in more ways than one. She is so
because she is mirrored in her waters and her houses are built on
nothing but their own reflections. She is so, too, because of her
fundamentally *theatrical* nature, by virtue of which Venice and
Venice's image are always presented simultaneously, inseparably. Truly, there is enough there to discourage any painter.
How can one paint Venice when it is a painting already? There
was Canaletto, of course, but he was not the foremost of Italian
painters, far from it! On the other hand, there can be no other
place in the world on which so much photographic film has been
used up. Because the tourist is not creative, he is a born con-
sumer. The images are given him here at every step and he copies them right and left. Moreover, the subject of his snapshots is
always himself, in front of the Bridge of Sighs, on the steps of
San Stefano, in a gondola. The tourists' "souvenirs" of Venice are
all so many self-portraits.

You take the Calle Larga San Marco which brings you to the
Rio di Palazzo, which is crossed downstream by the Bridge of
Sighs. The bridge in front of you leads directly to the workshops
of Old Murano. This is the kingdom of glass. Downstairs, before
glowing ovens, the glassworkers turn the lumps of milky dough
on the ends of their long rods, huge, multicolored blobs that
droop earthward as soon as they stop revolving. The rod is hollow. It is a sort of pipe and by blowing into it the craftsman
swells the blob and turns it into a bulb, a bubble, a balloon. The
sight is disconcerting to the imagination because it contradicts
its own physical logic. The ovens, the dough, the cooking, the
kneading, yes, the first thing it reminds you of is a bakery. But at

the same time you *know* that the dough is glass—and in any case the fumes it gives off and its very consistency have something noxious and decidedly inedible about them. Besides, you are watching, step by step, the birth of a flask, a bottle, or a cup, by means of such paradoxical operations as pressing out the base with a pontil, modeling the spout with pincers, strengthening the edge with a rim and applying a thin sausage to make patterns, twists, plaits and handles.

After the torture and humiliation of the fire, the rods and the pincers below, the glass is only restored to its essential, sovereign self on the upper floor. For glass is cold, hard, breakable and brilliant. Those are its basic attributes. To make it soft, malleable and smoking hot, it must be subjected to frightful torments. In the exhibition rooms it displays itself in all its icy, mannered pride.

The first thing is the ceiling, which is covered with a thick efflorescence of lusters, lamps and hanging lights. They are in every color—marble, jasper, lacework, angelica green, sapphire blue, salmon pink—but all in the same acid, sugary tones and carved from the same hard, translucent caramel. It is as if a vast forest of crystal jellyfish were stabbing down at us with crystallized spines, with their vitreous intestines and sheaves of glossy tentacles, vitrified flounces, floating around them in a cloud of frosted lace.

But the mysterious impressiveness of these huge rooms comes even more from the profusion of mirrors, multiplying them, breaking them up and putting them together again, sending their proportions crazy, wrenching planes awry and creating endless perspectives. The majority are tinted—greenish, blue, or yellow—making them look more than ever like the surface of some frozen fluid. One in particular held my attention, not so much for itself as for its frame. For the frame was composed of tiny mirrors angled in different directions and was disproportionately large, so that the oval mirror it contained seemed the smaller. I lingered in front of the little image of myself, lost in its shimmering depths, troubled by the throng of images that beset it.

"Monsieur Surin, you have not gone away yet, I see, and are getting the better of these mirrors you disliked so much."

He was a little, bald, smiling man with a moustache. His strong Italian accent emphasized the admirable fluency of his French.

"Yes, I put off going on account of the weather," I told him cautiously. "It's not wonderful here. What must it be like in other places!"

"I can tell you that, for any country you care to name, Monsieur Surin. In London, there is fog. It is raining in Berlin, drizzling in Paris and snowing in Moscow. In Reykjavik, darkness is falling. So you do well to linger in Venice. But if you want to stay, I advise you not to look in that mirror for too long."

"Why? Is it a magic mirror?"

"It is probably the most Venetian of all the mirrors in this room, Monsieur Surin. And I think that is why it does not inspire you with the horror which you have told me you feel in the presence of such things."

"What is there about this one that makes it more Venetian than the rest?"

"Its frame, Monsieur Surin. That huge, disproportionate frame, which almost makes you overlook the actual mirror lost in the midst of it. Now the fact is that that frame is made up of a lot of little mirrors facing in all directions. So that you are not allowed to be complacent. Your eye no sooner comes to rest on the reflection of your own face in the center than it is distracted right and left, above and below, by the minor mirrors each reflecting a different view. This is a distracting, a *diverting* mirror, a centrifugal mirror that throws everything that approaches its center outward to the edge. This one is, undoubtedly, particularly revealing. But all Venetian mirrors, even the simplest and most open, share in this centrifugal nature. The mirrors of Venice are never straight, they never give back his own image to one who looks in them. They are angled mirrors, which force you to look elsewhere. There is certainly an element of slyness, of spying in them, but they save you from the perils of a barren, moody contemplation of yourself. With a Venetian mirror, Narcissus would have been saved. Instead of remaining glued to his own reflection, he would have got up, tightened his belt and gone out into the world. It would make a different myth: Narcissus become Ulysses, the Wandering Jew, Marco Polo, Phileas Fogg . . ."

"A change from the settled to the nomadic life."

"The nomadic life! Exactly so, Monsieur Surin. And that metamorphosis is the whole magic of Venice. Venice attracts but she repels immediately. Everyone comes to Venice; no one stays here. Unless they come to die. Venice is a very good place to die in. The air of Venice sucks up, I might almost say *greedily*, the breath of those who come here to breathe their last. Cimarosa, Wagner, Diaghilev all answered that strange call. It was a French poet, was it not, who said that absence is a little death? He should have added that dying is a long absence. We know that in Venice . . ."

We were outside now, and my companion seemed to know which was my hotel because, as far as I could judge from the alleys we went by, he was taking us in that direction. As he walked, he continued to hold forth eloquently on the fundamental nature of Venice.

"This city of ours has no proper balance, Monsieur Surin. Or rather, she once had such a balance and lost it. One knows nothing of Venice unless one knows the twin city which balanced it at the other end of the Mediterranean. Because Venice, originally, was no more than a bridgehead for Constantinople, to which she owed the essence of her spiritual and material life. In relation to the rest of Italy, to Siena, Genoa and above all to Rome, she was insistently Byzantine, proclaiming her affinity with the Eastern Empire, and Western visitors disembarking at the Riva degli Schiavoni, and seeing the crowds in their flowing, embroidered clothes with caps and bonnets on their heads, the octagonal architecture with its domes, its latticed grilles and its mosaics, such visitors might have thought themselves transported to the East. And then Constantinople disappeared, swamped beneath the onrush of the Turkish barbarians, and you know, Monsieur Surin, the most appalling thing about that historic tragedy was the attitude of Venice. Incredible as it may seem, the Venetians did not receive the news of the disaster of 1453 with any very convincing show of horror. It was almost as if they experienced a secret satisfaction at the demise of their sister city—

richer, holier and more venerable, certainly, yet without which
they would never have existed. From then on, Venice's fate was
sealed for, deprived of the counterpoise of Byzantium, she gave
free rein to her mercantile, roving and adventurous inclinations
and, however much she grew in wealth, prosperity and power,
without a soul her body was doomed to ineluctable decay. When
your angry little Corsican delivered the final blow to the Serenis-
sima by handing her over to Austria in 1797, she was already
nothing but a corpse to which only habit gave some semblance
of life. That, Monsieur Surin, is all that is to be read in the mirrors of Venice."

We had reached the entrance to the broad arbor of foliage beneath which was the hotel restaurant. My companion handed me
his card.

"Goodbye, Monsieur Surin. If you should ever need my humble experience, do not hesitate to come and see me."

He tripped away briskly, and when he had gone I looked at
his card:

Guiseppe Colombo
Ingegnere
Stazione Meteorologica di Venezia

I woke in the middle of the night. The Italians never sleep.
When the streets are not echoing to the shouting and singing of
nocturnal revelers, it is the bells of a hundred churches chiming
to the dawn-pale sky. Last night, I brought up a book which was
lying in the lounge for the use of hotel guests. It was a volume of
the *Memoirs* of Casanova: *My Escape from the Leads of Venice.*
Another "centrifugal" Venetian whose whole life was a succession of seductions and partings. Yet Casanova was no Don Juan.
There is something of the hunter and even of the murderer in
Don Juan. That Spanish puritan hates women and the flesh in
which he is imprisoned. He despises the frail, wanton creatures,
though he cannot do without them, for he is soiled and damned
by them all. And when he leaves them, it is with sneers of scorn,
while his valet enters one more name in the ledger where he
keeps the list of his master's hunting trophies.

Whereas Casanova . . . He adores women, deeply and sin-

cerely, all women, and is never happy himself until he has succeeded in pleasuring his partner of the moment to the full. We
must not, of course, ask too much of him. For faithfulness, for
marriage and a family, he is no use at all. He is attracted to a
pretty creature, drawn to her (why call him a seducer when he
is the first to be seduced?), he hurries to her, envelops her in
every tenderness calculated to bring down her defenses, disarm
her, and have her at his mercy, then he rewards her for her brief
enslavement with an hour's bliss and instantly flits away again
forever, but smiling and blowing kisses, more and more wistful
as they fade into the distance. And afterward, he will recall the
memory of her with nothing but heartfelt respect and tenderness . . .

But the Venetian cannot escape loneliness and even imprisonment, any more than the Sevillan. This is because the non-twin
society to which he wholeheartedly belongs, in spite of his incurable levity, cannot readily tolerate so much freedom. At daybreak on July 26, 1755, Messer Grande, the chief of police, comes
to arrest Casanova at his lodging, as a "disturber of the peace."
He is handed over to the jailers of the "Leads," he is cast into a
lightless cell. This is the ordeal of solitary confinement, to which
new prisoners are traditionally subjected at the start. Casanova
has only one contact with the outside world: the sound of a
clock striking the hours. He falls asleep . . . "The chimes of midnight woke me. How frightful the awakening that makes one
long again for the oblivion or illusions of sleep. I could not believe that I had passed three hours unconscious of my troubles.
Unmoving, lying as I was upon my handkerchief, which my recollection assured me I had placed there . . . I was groping with
my hand when . . . Lord! What a shock when I felt another
hand, as cold as ice! I was electrified with fright from head to
foot and all my hair stood on end. Never in all my life had I
been seized with such terror, nor should I have believed myself
capable of it. I certainly lay for three or four minutes not merely
motionless but powerless even to think. As I gradually recovered
my senses, I mercifully concluded that the hand I had thought I
touched was no more than a figment of my imagination, and firm
in this belief I stretched out my arm again in the same place,

and found to my horror I was gripping the selfsame hand. Utter-
ing a piercing shriek, I released it and drew back my arm. I was
trembling but when I was once more in command of myself I
decided that a corpse had been placed beside me while I slept,
for I was sure that there had been nothing on the floor when I
lay down. At first I pictured to myself the body of some innocent
person—and chiefly of my friend—whom they had strangled and
placed beside me like this so that I should see before me on waking an example of the fate I might expect. This thought enraged
me. I reached my arm out to the hand for the third time, I
grasped it and at the same time endeavored to raise myself to
draw the body toward me and so ascertain the full atrocity of
the deed. But when I came to rest my weight on my left elbow,
the cold hand I was holding fast in mine came to life and withdrew itself, and in that moment I realized to my astonishment
that what I was holding with my right was none other than my
own left hand, which had lost all movement, warmth and feeling
and become stiff and benumbed as a result of the soft, yielding
and reposeful couch on which my poor person had been lying.

"This incident, comical though it was, did nothing to cheer
me. On the contrary, it gave me food for the gloomiest reflections. I perceived that I was in a place where, if the false appeared true, the truth would surely appear a dream, and where
the understanding must lose half its privileges."

Thus the libertine, foe to husbands and fathers, disrupter of the
family circle and disturber of the peace, is subjected to the ordeal
of solitude. Then what happens? Under the dominion of darkness
and numbness, his right hand thinks it recognizes in his left the
hand of his best friend—dead. There is a faint reference to twinship there, and specifically to twinship dispaired. It is as though,
under the effect of darkness and imprisonment, this inveterate
non-twin—this wordly intriguer and rake—were creating a fan-
tasy of twinship for himself, going from his own hand to a dead
friend, whereas a twin brother would normally stand halfway
between the two.

This adds to the mystery of Venice, and I wonder whether it
helps to clarify or deepen it. How can one help connecting Casanova's manual hallucination with the image of the two hands,

interlinked and yet divided by the Grand Canal, which is to be seen in the plan of the city? Other themes superimpose themselves upon these two. The lost twin city, the Byzantium that fell in 1453, leaving Venice dispaired, mutilated, but drunk with freedom. The oblique mirrors in which the gaze is deflected and rests on someone else indirectly and, as it were, by the way. The centrifugal force of this city of seamen and merchants . . . Here one is continually coming across the dream of twinship broken, a blurred, fleeting image as elusive as it is persistent.

Venice as a city is like a perpetual cipher. She is always promising us the answer just around the corner if only we are a little wise, but she never keeps her promise.

I got up this morning before daybreak and dawdled about St. Mark's Square, where huge puddles of water made isthmuses, peninsulas and islands on the paving, all packed with pigeons, their feathers fluffy with sleep. The folded chairs and tables of the three cafés in the square—Florian on the right, the Quadri and Lavena on the left—stood in tight, regimented rows, waiting for the sun and the customers it always brings with it. It was a strange, hybrid scene, like the country in its silence and the absence of all motorized traffic, and citylike in its exclusively monumental setting, with not a tree or blade of grass or a spring of fresh water.

I rounded the Campanile, crossed the Piazzetta, and made for the porphyry steps of St. Mark's quay, six steps clothed in waving green weed going down into the choppy water. The tide covers and uncovers three of them in its ebb and flow—an average variation of some seventy centimeters altogether—but at this time of the year there is a danger of much greater differences.

I walked for a long time along the Riva degli Schiavoni, crossing the little stepped bridges that span the outlets of the *rii*. The boats moored to the bollards get larger and shabbier the further you go from the center. The fragile gondolas give way to *motoscafi* and to *vaporetti*, then you find yachts and small ferryboats and finally cargo vessels, their steep, rusty sides looming above the quays. At last I found a café which was open and I am sitting outside, just opposite a landing stage. The weather is very

mild but all the more ominous for that. The rising sun sets fire to
the thick, ragged clouds and then blazes down the length of the
quay and up the axis of the Grand Canal. This deserted waterfront, gleaming from the rain and cluttered with jetties, moor-
ing posts, ropes, bollards and gangways, the empty boats and the
hollow slap of the waves along their sides—although there is no
wind a yacht's halyard is taken with a sudden frenzy and starts
to rattle furiously against the mast—the streaks of red light fading into the distant, misty huddle of domes, towers and palatial
façades . . . Where am I? Perhaps one of these vessels, come
from the lands of men, has just set me down in the city of the
dead where all the clocks have stopped? What was it Colombo
said? He said that Venice was not a city to linger in, except to
die, and that the air here greedily sucked up the breath of the
dying. But am I really alive? What does one know of a dispaired
twin indeed, especially when the fate of his lost brother remains
a mystery? I am an absolute sedentary. A motionless equilibrium
is the natural state of the geminate cell. It is Jean's going that
has set me on the move. I must find him. To tell him of the wonderful discovery I have made since he left—should I say *because*
he left? To stop the crazy process which, through Sophie's fault,
condemns him to perpetual wandering. To take up again with
him the circular thread of our eternal youth, broken for a while
but reconnected and even enriched by the break. Thanks to the
alienating light, I have incontrovertible proof that he has been
here. Everything I hear convinces me that he has gone. First, because those who knew him think that I have *returned,* or else
that I decided not to go. But mostly because Venice—this city
which is the very image of him—was bound to drive him away,
and send him rushing off again, like a ball bouncing back hard
off a stone wall.

But I? What am I doing here? If Jean is following his nature
by traveling the world—and starting with Venice—then what am
I doing in this galley? (Truly a marvelous galley, weighed down
with velvet and gold, and fashioned like *Bucentaur!*)

A fat man has just seated himself heavily on my left. He is
covering the fake marble tabletop with a whole array of tourist's
writing materials, postcards, envelopes, various pencils and, most

important, a thick, much-worn notebook which must contain addresses. He grunts and snuffles as he fills in his cards earnestly. He curses when the waiter doesn't come, when a fly keeps settling on his nose, when a pigeon pesters him for food. Until in the end I am convinced that all he is sending to his family and friends are *abusive postcards*, and he is going to dispatch them in a little while with vindictive sneers. I too may sneer, for the fact remains that I am never going to send a postcard to anyone, from Venice or anywhere else. Méline? I can see her already, sniffing suspiciously and disapprovingly at the rectangle of card covered with an indecipherable scrawl, its gaudy colors depicting an unimaginable country. Méline has nothing but horror and contempt for anything she does not know. And I have no one else! I have only Jean—and him I have just lost. It is one of the pinpricks of the *alienating light*, the way I instinctively reject any welcoming overtures coming from a non-twin. I can see that Jean is making friends wherever he goes, flinging himself into the arms of all and sundry simply in order to escape from the geminate cell, Sophie having failed in her mission of emancipating him. And in spite of myself, I am reaping the benefit of this friendliness—this amiability—which he is scattering broadcast, and which must be nipped in the bud because my mission is the direct opposite of this madness of his.

Loneliness. There are some bachelors, to all appearance doomed to solitude, who have the gift of creating little, mobile societies wherever they go, changeable but alive and revived continually with new recruits—or else of insinuating themselves painlessly into already existing groups. Whereas if men who form one of a pair and are apparently armored against any danger of loneliness should happen to lose their partner, they fall into a hopeless dereliction. Jean is obviously trying to move out of that category into the first, but as far as I am concerned, any such transformation is out of the question, for I can see no hope of success.

The quay is getting busier every minute. A succession of *vaporetti* are coming up to the landing stage and lots of little folk are trotting off them. They are the inhabitants of the working-class suburb of Mestre who come in to work in Venice during

the day. Little folk, quite literally. It is a fact that they seem
to me to be below average height. Is it only an illusion fos-
tered by their obviously humble circumstances? I don't think so.
I am quite prepared to admit that wealth and power and social
standing are reflected in a man by extraordinary height, weight
and bulk. And I think of myself immediately, of my five feet six
inches and my hundred and twenty pounds, and I have to admit
that I'd be no great shakes even among these people. That is a
thought that would not have occurred to me a mere two months
ago, before Jean's betrayal. Because although it is true that Jean
and I are both on the puny side, that has only been apparent
since our separation. Both of us are certainly skinny and under-
sized but together—as we were meant to be—we are a formidable
giant. And it is that giant I am mourning and searching for. But
what is the good of going over it unendingly?

The mainland sends these boatloads of little people out to
Venice. The sea laps us in a warm, humid breeze. This is the
"bora," the Greek wind from the northeast. The whole city of
Venice is a bone of contention, squabbled over incessantly by
land and sea. The water flowing in the *rii*, with its ever-changing
levels, is a brine whose degree of salinity goes up and down several times a day. I note that I am becoming increasingly preoccupied with meteorological phenomena. It is true that at the
Pierres Sonnantes we have always lived in close contact with
winds, clouds and rain. And, of course, with the tides which follow their own private rhythm undisturbed, as independent of the
changes of the weather as they are of the succession of day and
night. But this independence of the tides is something I was not
fully aware of until three months ago, shortly after Jean's departure, and I have observed that the discovery of the "quiet
storm" seemed to be the outcome of a dispaired geminate vision.
My meeting with Giuseppe Colombo here came just at the right
moment. (But then, wasn't it Jean who sent him to me, or rather
who sent me to him by luring me to Venice? That is a leading
question. It sets me wondering whether by following in my de-
fecting brother's footsteps—conforming to his flight in all its details and especially in the encounters along the way—I am not
fulfilling my own particular destiny as a dispaired twin, a destiny

quite contrary, yet complementary to his own. What destiny? The only answer to that question will lie in the continuation of my journey, its continuation and its end.) For yesterday I did what Colombo had suggested. Having phoned to say that I was coming, I got a *motoscafo* to take me out to a small islet in the Lagoon, the Isolotto Bartolomeo, with a single small house on it, one of the Stazione Meteorologica of Venice.

A feeling born of the first sight of the station and confirmed by the visit is that the place we are in is *universal*. There is nothing here to remind one of Venice, of the Lagoon, or even of Italy, Europe or anywhere. This little house, the masts, pylons, stays and equipment, the setting, at once scientific and romantic—this unpretentious, simple, ramshackle little world in direct contact with the heavens and meteors—would be exactly the same whether it were in California, Cape Town or the Bering Strait. Or so, at least, everything here seems to say, since it is not, of course, a field in which I have any direct experience.

Colombo, eager and eloquent, showed me around.

The station works around the clock, staffed by three teams of two men each who relieve each other in eight-hour shifts, at 8 A.M., 4 P.M. and midnight. Basically, their job consists of compiling and transmitting in Morse—whether manually or by punched tape—reports of wind velocity, temperature, atmospheric pressure, type and altitude of cloud and tide height. During the day they measure the height of the cloud base by sending up a small red helium balloon—and Colombo gave me a demonstration. The balloon rises at a known rate and they measure the time it takes to disappear into the cloud. At night, measurements are made by means of a beam of light reflected off the cloud base onto a sensor fifty meters away from the projector. The angle of reflection is measured automatically. But it was the anemometer which gave me the keenest satisfaction. Outside, there is a little windmill made up of four red cups which turns continually with an infectious, childish gaiety. It is connected in some mysterious way to a board which lights up so as to show the speed and direction of the wind. The eight points of the compass (N, S, E, W, NE, SE, SW, NW) are represented on the board by eight visual indicators, one of which is constantly illu-

minated. A red winking light in the center of the board shows
the velocity of the wind while another underneath it—green this
time and with a much slower pattern—acts as a control. Colombo
explained to me that the wind speed in knots is obtained by
counting the number of red flashes in between two green ones
and then multiplying by two. He waxed lyrical as he went on to
show me the seven points on the horizon from which the prevailing winds in these parts come, *la sizza, lo sirocco, il libeccio, il
maestrale, la bora, il grecale* and *il ponentino.*

Outside, it was not so much the screen containing thermom-
eters, hygrometer, and rain gauge that attracted me as a thing
like an outsize garden rake with the teeth pointing vertically skyward and a handle that swiveled so as to draw a needle across a
disk with the compass points inscribed on it. This was the *nepho-
scope,* which enabled them to fix the direction and angular speed
of cloud movement. It is actually a rake for the clouds. It rakes
the sky and scratches the underbellies of the soft, gray monsters
that graze there.

This doll's house packed with delicate and preposterous instruments, perched on its tiny island bristling with childish toys—the
red balloons, propellers, revolving drums, wind socks, and above
all that great rake fixed on its wooden base—gives off a peculiar
aura of happiness and I am still trying to find the secret of it.
There is something undeniably funny about it, which comes in
part from the way events are continually giving the lie to the
meteorologists' forecasts—a subject for endless jokes—but it goes
very much further than that. Is that childish paraphernalia set
out on an island no bigger than a man's hand really all that
human genius has to set against the tremendous movements of
the atmosphere on which, nonetheless, man's life and survival to
a large extent depend? It is all, and even that may be too much
when we consider man's total helplessness in the face of the meteors. The terrible power of machines, the creative and destructive force of chemicals, the unprecedented boldness of surgery,
the whole industrial and scientific inferno in short, may destroy
the earth's surface and darken the hearts of men but it stops
short of the fires and waters of the air and leaves them to a
handful of cranks and their paltry instruments. It is probably this

contrast that is so startling and entertaining. That rain, wind and sun should be the sphere of these few, so poor in spirit and equipment, scattered throughout the world but brothers in their simplicity and in constant communication with one another day and night over the air—what a happy and refreshing paradox that is.

Then, as he was accompanying me back to the jetty where my motorboat was waiting for me, Colombo drew my attention to a post, an ordinary post driven into the muddy bottom and protected from the waves and currents by a semicircle of concrete with the open side facing us. The post was marked out in meters and decimeters and was for measuring the range of the tides. Colombo explained to me that the very existence of Venice depended on a discrepancy—on which a continual watch was kept —between the fluctuations of the tide and the periodical high winds. Between, in fact, the "quiet storm" and the meteorological storm. If the two events should ever coincide, Venice— where St. Mark's Square was only seventy centimeters above the mean sea level—would be submerged as surely as the town of Ys.

Thanks to this visit, I have moved one step further into the nameless, virgin territory which seems to be the especial domain of the dispaired geminate intuition.

A quiet storm. Those two words, whose juxtaposition gave me such a shock a few weeks since at the Pierres Sonnantes, express perfectly the existence of two skies, two superimposed and antithetical celestial levels. Colombo reminded me that the earth is surrounded by three spherical layers, like three concentric envelopes. Up to twelve thousand meters is the *troposphere*—the sphere of disturbances. All the weather we experience occurs in the first four thousand meters of this sphere. This is the great circus of the caracoling winds, where the cyclones erupt, where the herds of cloudy elephants amble past, where aerial threads twist and untie themselves, and where the vast, subtle combinations which result in squalls and fine spells are woven.

Above that—from four thousand to twelve thousand meters— stretches the vast, radiant pathway that belongs to the trade winds and the countertrades alone.

Higher still—beyond twelve thousand meters—is the absolute void, the great calm of the *stratosphere*.

Finally, at above a hundred and forty thousand meters, you enter the unreality of the *ionosphere*, composed of helium, hydrogen and ozone, which is also called the *logosphere* because it is the invisible, intangible vault which bounces back the soft, massive twittering of the thousands upon thousands of voices and musical notes of all the world's radio sets.

The tropospheric layer, the field of disturbances, a warm, windy chaos, an unpredictable confusion of interacting weather changes, is ruled by a serene Olympus whose revolutions are as regular as a sundial, an eternal astral sphere, an unchanging world of stars. Out of this Olympus come peremptory commands, perfectly predictable, known and constructed, which pass through the troposphere like steel arrows and affect the earth and the seas. The tides are the most obvious effect of this *astral authority*, since they depend on the major heavenly bodies, on the combined or opposing presences of the sun and moon. The "quiet storm" displays the sovereign power of the great luminaries over their subjects, the tumultuous and effervescent waves. In contrast to the orders from the troposphere—which are contradictory, unsystematic and unpredictable—the heavenly bodies impose upon the ocean a regular oscillation, like the swing of a pendulum.

I do not think I am giving way to my abiding obsession in noting the analogy between this opposition of the two spheres and that between the turmoil of the non-twin masses—with their untidy, fecund loving, mingling their seed with mud and blood—and the pure, sterile geminate couple. The analogy is surely unavoidable. And it fits my theory. For if the heavenly bodies impose their own serene, mathematical order—the "quiet storm"—upon the earth and the seas, should not the geminate cell, in all fairness, bend its members—if not the rest of mankind—to its private order?

Find Jean. Bring him back to Bep. But in framing this design I see another, incomparably vaster and more ambitious, taking shape behind it. That is to acquire a hold over the troposphere itself, to command meteorology and make myself master of rain and shine, no less! Jean has fled, swept away on the currents of the atmosphere. I can fetch him home, yes. But what I am trying to do will go beyond that really quite modest goal, and in the process I may become myself the shepherd of winds and clouds.

Were the three orchestras playing in unison to begin with? I am not really sure. It is enough of a miracle that Florian, the Quadri and the Lavena are all playing Vivaldi, and *The Four Seasons* in particular, at the same time. It would be too much to ask of them that they should coincide among themselves as well, so as to form a single orchestra divided into three in different parts of St. Mark's Square. At the moment, the Quadri is coming to the end of "Winter"—and that is what I can hear best since it is outside that café I am sitting. But if I strain my ears past the pianissimos and pauses of that black and gold music I can make out that the Lavena is attacking "Autumn." As for Florian, on the other side of the square, my orchestra would have to fall silent for me to hear, but as far as I can guess, they must be in the middle of "Summer." Since the daily repertoire of these small orchestras never exceeds four or five pieces, I am not surprised, when Quadri's have finished "Winter," to hear them begin again, after the briefest of pauses, with "Spring." Besides, isn't that how it is in real life? The round of the seasons continues without interruption, never-ending.

It seems to me remarkable that the best-known work of the most famous Venetian composer should depict the four seasons. For there can be few places in the world where the seasons are less marked than in Venice. The climate here never reaches extremes of heat or cold but, more than that, the absence of vegetation and animal life leaves us without any natural points of reference. There are no primroses here, no cuckoos, no ripe corn or falling leaves. But perhaps it was precisely to compensate for the lack of real seasons in this city that Vivaldi gave it musical ones, like arranging artificial flowers in a vase or simulating the view of a long, noble avenue of trees on the backdrop of a theater?

"I'm glad to find you in Venice again, but I have some very sad news for you."

After one *alienating* look—the shock startles me less and less, although I can hardly claim to be getting used to it—a young woman (is she really young? The truth is, she is ageless) has seated herself confidently at my table. She is rather beautiful, in spite of making no obvious effort to attract, and perhaps this studied plainness is only apparent, is in fact the height of studied elegance, because I cannot think of any style more suited to that clear-cut face, so stark as to be almost provocative, its few planes making up a regular, perfectly balanced whole. Her velvet eyes and full mouth offset the severity of the too regular features and scraped-back black hair.

"Deborah is dying. I am not even sure whether she is still alive. And Ralph, too, is just finding out that his wife has been carrying him completely all through the forty years they have been together."

She speaks quickly, with a kind of fierce energy, taking a pack of cigarettes and a lighter out of her bag. She lights a cigarette and smokes in silence, while I hear, through Florian's springlike trills, the wintry snarling of the Lavena.

"I thought you were there with them. You should have gone. You ought to be with them. You wouldn't be in the way, I am afraid."

I nod, like a man considering and about to come to a decision. The thing that strikes me most is that she has called me *tu*. I am amazed, shattered by that. Of course it was bound to happen sometime, now that Jean is not here. But all the same, it comes as a considerable shock. *Because it is the first time anyone has ever called me that.* All through our childhood, Jean-Paul never heard anything but *vous*, because the fusion of the twins never reached the point of people regarding them as a single individual. No, what did happen was rather the reverse—I mean that even when we were apart each one of us would be called *vous*, since whatever was said to one would concern the temporarily absent brother just as much. With the result that I came quite naturally to regard *tu* as a crude expression, a trifling, contemptuous familiarity invariably reserved for non-twin children, whereas we twins, even when apart, were entitled to a polite (I nearly wrote "royal") *vous*. However much I tell myself that to interpret it in this way is a childish delusion, still that *tu* hurts

me because—trifling or not—it establishes me further in my condition as a non-twin, and I kick against it with all my might.
And then again, why allow the misunderstanding to continue? I
have no cause to deceive this woman and she may be better able
to help me when she knows the facts. Florian's spring is coming
to the end in a flowery climax, Lavena's winter is still moaning
away and Quadri's are putting rosin on their bows, as I say:
"You are mistaken. I am not Jean Surin. I am his twin brother,
Paul."

She stares at me in amazement, amazement and incredulity,
with a suggestion of hostility in it. This is the first time since
Jean's going that I have cleared up the misunderstanding. I can
guess what she is thinking. She doesn't believe me at first. But
then, what is one to think of a man who suddenly tries to wipe
himself out, to disappear by passing himself off as a twin
brother? It is an objectionable trick to play, crude and unforgivable. But that is what she is going to think if Jean has never told
her about me, and especially if he has some motive for disap-
pearing.

Her face is stony. She is going to open her bag again and start
redoing her makeup, keeping her eyes fixed on the mirror in her
compact. At least, that is what any other woman would do in the
circumstances, to justify that blank look and give herself time.
But not this one. She has decided to put her cards on the table.

"Jean never said anything to me about a twin brother," she
says. "It's true he never told me anything about his past, or his
family. Not from any love of secrecy, I'm sure, but because, for
the time being at least, we were not on those terms. All the same,
what you are telling me is a bit much!"

She is studying me. It's no use, pretty lady. If you can find the
slightest difference between the Paul you have in front of you
now and the Jean you know, then it will be only in your imagination. We are the same, remorselessly the same!

"Very well then. Let us suppose that it is true and you are not
Jean, you are his twin brother."

She puffs at her cigarette thoughtfully. Florian is tiptoeing beneath summer's heavy foliage. The Lavena is beginning on
spring, just as Quadri is finishing it. The seasons . . . It suddenly

occurs to me that in them the two skies, the mathematical sky of the heavenly bodies and the other, the muddled, meteoric sky, overlap. Because, of course, the seasons mean the showers of spring, the dog days of summer, the violins of autumn and the snows of winter. All of them in a succession of approximations and near-misses which cause women to observe that the weather is unseasonable. That is because the meterological skies are by nature capricious and intransigent. They do not readily obey the other sky, the sidereal one, which is as regular as a great clock. For that sky, the seasons are according to the position of the earth in relation to the sun. The June solstice indicates the beginning of summer. The September equinox marks its end. The December solstice concludes the autumn, the March equinox is also the first day of spring. And these dates are fixed to the nearest second, and can be predicted several centuries in advance. Now it is not enough to say that the meteors fit only rather remotely into these four divisions. Not satisfied with upsetting the calendar by jumping about and not doing what they are supposed to, they also permit themselves a regular, constant variation, an almost predictable discrepancy in relation to the astronomical dates of between fifteen days and three weeks in most cases. But the final blow is that this discrepancy is not a delay, it is not a case of the muddled meteoric sky obeying the commands of the mathematical sky reluctantly, lackadaisically, like a naughty child dragging its feet. No, *it is an advance!* There is no gainsaying this shocking paradox, that the muddled sky of the meteors runs an average of twenty days ahead of the mathematical. Winter and its frosts do not wait until the twenty-first of December to declare themselves. They have come by December 1. Yet the date of December 21 is not an arbitrary one, it is laid down by simple, quite infallible astronomical calculations. The solstices are fixed by the farthest distance between the earth and the sun and the greatest difference in the lengths of day and night. The equinoxes correspond inversely to the shortest possible distance between the earth and the sun and day and night being of equal length. These are cast-iron astronomical facts. One might accept that rain and shine could be slow to respond to them, because of a degree of viscosity in them. But they get there first!

"Do you know why I am going to accept for the time being that you are not Jean? Because we are in Venice. Yes, there is something about this city which makes it easy to believe in tales of twins—which actually suggests the idea of twinship. Though I'd be hard put to say what!"

These observations were too much in tune with my own reflections about Venice for me to let them pass.

"You're quite right. Venice expresses herself in customs, stories and attributes relating to broken twinship. The twins you meet in Venice are always dispaired. Like the mirrors—"

"Let's not talk about Venice, if you don't mind. If you are not Jean, then let me tell you my name is Hamida and I come from El Kantara, on the island of Djerba in Tunisia. My friends call me Hami."

"Hami, where is Jean?"

For the first time, she smiles. And the Lavena is bringing its spring to an exquisitely graceful conclusion.

"Where is Jean? You are forgetting that I have not entirely discounted the theory that *you are Jean*. So that what I can hear, like a distant echo behind your question, is: where am I?" She laughs.

"You see, Hami, ever since we were children Jean and I have played on our twinship. It has been like a musical theme with our bodies as the instruments, and the theme is truly inexhaustible. Between ourselves we call it the game of Bep. Now since Jean has left me, the game of Bep has not stopped, I am only playing it on my own—with the help of this city, admittedly, and that is no small thing. And then you pop up all of a sudden and take a hand in the game. And you are complicating it enormously because you come under the same law as all the rest of mankind—all mankind except for Jean-Paul—which makes it impossible to tell Jean from Paul. So that when I say to you: where is Jean?, it really might mean: where am I? In other words, all my problems—such as where Jean is hiding, for example—are doubled, or even squared for you. Did Jean tell you he was engaged, and that he was in Venice on his honeymoon?"

"He told me that, yes."

"Did he tell you why Sophie broke it off?"

"No."

"Like you, Sophie came up against the game of Bep. And she ran away, because she realized that she was going to lose herself in a gallery of mirrors. So be sensible. Follow the guide. And tell me, where is Jean?"

"Honestly, I don't know."

The mathematical sky is always three weeks behind the meteoric sky. Does that mean that Jean, having chosen the side of rain and shine, will always be irreducibly ahead of me? Does it mean that unless I too take the side of the meteors, I shall never find my brother? I have arrived at that conclusion by a strange, but nonetheless compulsive route and I recognize the form of the dispaired intuition in it.

"I don't know, but that is really Bep's fault. Before I met you here, I believed Jean was at El Kantara. When I took you for him, I concluded at once that he had not gone. If you are not Jean, well, it is back to El Kantara again!"

"Very well then, El Kantara it is. Go on. Tell me about El Kantara. You mentioned a name, too. Deborah."

"Jean was here only three weeks ago. He met a couple, the man, Ralph, an American, the wife, Deborah, English. They live at El Kantara. They were cruising in the Adriatic on their yacht. They are not young. He is in his seventies. She is a bit older. When Deborah was taken ill suddenly, Ralph took her ashore at the nearest port. Which was Venice. Deborah was taken to the Ospedale San Stefano. That was when Ralph met Jean. Whenever Ralph was not with Deborah, he was going the rounds of the bars, hanging on to Jean's arm. He used to call him his prop. Every time he met someone he knew, he would stop and point to your brother with his free hand and say: 'This is Jean. I like him.' And then he would go on. When Deborah insisted on going home to Djerba, Jean went on board with them. At least, that was what I thought until I met you—and it is what I am beginning to think again. Ralph always had a passion for mascots. It's an impossibly bad time of year but they had a miraculously good

crossing. That is all I have heard, in a cable from Djerba. Is
Deborah still alive? Is Jean with them? I have no idea."

"The best thing is to go and see."

"Go on, then. But I'd be surprised if you found your brother.
Something tells me Jean-Paul is dead, finally dead."

"You don't know. You know nothing about it. There is a morbid atmosphere about this city, and it makes you say anything at
all, so long as it reeks of death!"

"Death is on this city. Surely you can feel the terrible threat
hanging over it?"

I could feel it and I told her so. As the rain persists, you sense
the ever-increasing fear of flood growing in this city standing at
water level. Perhaps the fearful, long-heralded coincidence between the quiet storm controlled by the astronomical sky and the
meterological storm is really about to happen? I picture Colombo's post getting hourly deeper in the dark waters, the level
rising above the red line of danger point. Venice drowned by the
Adriatic tide swollen by the sirocco.

"I was living here during the great floods of 1959," Hamida
says. "I woke with a start that night and, to my indescribable
horror, saw a slimy black tongue creeping under my door and
oozing forward, an inch at a time, thrusting out fingers, peninsulas, and tentacles in all directions, and slowly covering the
whole of my bedroom floor. I hurried to get dressed, paddling
about in the liquid mud, and I was in the middle of it when the
electric light went out. I shot out of the room as if I was in danger of drowning in there. Outside I found nothing but a gulf of
lapping darkness, with only the lights and torches flickering on
some boats in the distance to show how deep it was. People
shouting and crying, and the fire department's sirens breaking
through the silence left it just as dense. We had to wait until the
evening of the next day for the water to flow back out of the lagoon into the sea through the three channels—the *bocche di
porto* of the Lido, Malamocco and Chioggia. Then in the dusk,
made still darker by a ceiling of leaden clouds, we saw all the
streets and squares, and the ground floors of all the houses covered equally in a thick layer of oil and rotting seaweed and
decomposing bodies."

She fell silent, her eyes fixed on the flashing movements of a brightly painted yo-yo which a street vendor was running up and down on his finger.

"Jean at El Kantara, where Deborah is dying, and you here in Venice, which goes in fear of death by drowning," she went on. "There is something ominous about these separated twins, running after one another. It is as if your two paths are doomed to be strewn with deaths and disasters. Why?"

"I don't know, really I don't. But perhaps I shall know one day, because I can sense some things that are still vague but may become clearer. To start with, Jean and I formed an autonomous cell, didn't we, and that cell was undoubtedly dropped into a world which we call twinless because it is full of people born in isolation, without twins. But that geminate cell was enclosed, like a sealed bulb, and all the emissions, emanations and ejaculations of each were completely absorbed by the other. The non-twin world was protected from us, as we were from it. The only thing that had a solvent effect upon that cell was the atmosphere of singularity. A day came when it got the better of its tightness. The sealed bulb broke. From then on the twins were divided and acted, not on one another any more, but on other people and things. Is that action pernicious? The fact that either of us is present at the point where some disastrous accident occurs does not necessarily prove that we are responsible. Perhaps the word 'affinity' will do. It may be that when dispaired twins are launched upon the world, among cities and individual people, they do not actually cause things to break up, come apart or explode, but simply have a—a magnetic attraction for such phenomena."

"Yes, but how can you tell whether that attraction isn't reciprocal? The twins being attracted to a certain place because a disaster *may* happen there could hasten its occurrence simply by being there . . ."

"The twins? Of the two, I was the conservative one, the one who wanted to keep things as they were. Jean, on the other hand, always had a leaning toward separating and breaking off. My father ran a factory which used to do weaving and carding. Jean was only happy with the girls who did the carding, whereas

I liked being with the warpers. After that, I am tempted to believe that Carder-Jean spreads ruin and discord wherever he
goes simply because it is in his nature to do so. That is one more
reason why I should try to find him and bring him back to Bep."

"If I still had any doubts about who you are, you would have
removed them for me. You blame your brother. You are making
him into a bird of ill omen. But all I saw in him was a nice,
friendly, likable boy who was miserably lonely."

"To escape from Bep, Jean is throwing himself into the arms
of anyone he meets. I'm not surprised he should have got himself
adopted by Ralph and Deborah. When we were children, the
fact of being twins left us very little time for filial feelings. Having broken with twinship, Jean is looking for a father. But I
know him better than he knows himself. It can come to no good.
Besides, surely you told me yourself that there was bad news?"

The wheel has come full circle. By what miracle did the three
orchestras manage to come together at that precise moment? All
at once they are playing in concert, and it is summer, the beautiful, fecund baroque summer, laughing and overflowing like a
horn of plenty borne aloft in triumph by a procession of cherubs
and sileni. Truly in concert? Well, not quite, perhaps, for then I
was only hearing the nearest, Florian's, and there is no denying
that I can make out the Lavena and the Quadri also, so that
there must be a slight time lag, just enough to produce the effect
of a very subtle echo which gives depth and density to the work.
And thanks to this very special kind of stereophonic effect, the
music seems to emanate from the whole of St. Mark's Square itself, from the paving, from the arcades, from the tall windows,
from the clock tower, from the absurdly masculine campanile
and from the fivefold feminine curves of the basilica.

I ponder on the geminate vision which enables us to see things
simultaneously from within and from without.

CHAPTER XVI

The Island of the Lotus Eaters

Jean

The first time I met Ralph was in Harry's Bar. The first thing I saw was his strength, his majesty, his inebriation and his loneliness. I felt that I was in the presence of a godlike Silenus, fallen from Olympus, abandoned by his roistering companions and doomed to nameless debaucheries. He had just been visiting his wife, who was in the hospital with something very bad which, from what I could gather, must have been lung cancer. He was recruiting his strength before going back on board his yacht, which was moored in one of the canals of the Giudecca, and was cursing the sailor who had been with him and had disappeared into the city.

We left arm in arm. We had adopted one another, instantly and mutually, and I could not say what occurred in his mind and heart. But I discovered something in myself that I had never been before, a son. Ralph suddenly cured an old fatherhood frustration. Edouard? I loved him dearly and I am still mourning his unhappy death. But in all honesty, he was not really cut out for a father's role. Friend, lover, even brother in a pinch—although he did little enough, as far as I know, to keep on close terms with Uncle Alexandre—but father . . . Unless it was that I was no good at being a son, for the very reason everything was distorted by my being a twin. Perhaps with his authority, his dominance over me, the function of guardian of the cell which he thought it necessary to assume, Paul usurped the paternal role and at the same time deprived Edouard of it. I have played the game of Bep enough to know that the geminate cell aspires to time-lessness, and so to be uncreated as well as eternal, and that it rejects with all its power any parental claims that may be made upon it. It acknowledges only a putative paternity. The fact is that I was no sooner free from Paul's obsessive presence than I found a father.

His name is Ralph. He was born in Natchez in Mississippi. He landed in Paris in 1917 in the uniform of the U.S. Navy. The war over, he came under the spell of the wild postwar years. He never went back to America.

Paris, Montparnasse, Dada, surrealism, Picasso . . . Man Ray, staggered by the young American's startling, extraordinary, al-most inhuman beauty, took him as his model. Then Italy, Venice, Naples, Capri, Anacapri. For Ralph, Tiberius' island was the scene of three decisive meetings which were to change his life.

The first was with Dr. Axel Munthe, whose whole life was bound up in a house, petrified in a villa bowered in flowers and suspended above the Bay of Naples. To identify with a dwelling, build one's whole life into a house conceived *ex nihilo,* then built up stone by stone and enriched daily, personalized to the ulti-mate degree, like the shell that the snail secretes about its soft, naked body, but a shell being secreted, complicated and per-fected to the last gasp because it remains a living, moving thing, in close symbiosis with the creature that inhabits it.

The next encounter was with Deborah, an English divorcée a little older than himself, highly strung, sharp as a needle and devoured by a feverish intelligence, the ferment of restless activ-ity that was lacking in the man of Natchez.

Lastly there was the mouth of the oracle, speaking through the lips of a ninety-one-year-old retired Englishman living in Capri who, after seeing Ralph and Deborah, gave them to understand that they were not yet where they belonged, that they should leave and go further south, to the Near East, to the coast of Africa, and pitch their tent on the island of Djerba.

They did as he told them. That was in 1920. At El Kantara they found a fortified casbah, battered by the waves, a vast, delapidated Second Empire mansion, and nothing else but an immensity of golden sand dotted with palm and olive groves sheltering behind earthworks bristling with cactus. Ralph and Deborah were the first. Adam and Eve, in fact. But the Garden of Eden was still to be created.

For a handful of dollars, they bought an acre of desert by the sea. Then they dug for water. Thereafter, a wind pump revolved improbably, like a gigantic child's toy, above the treetops and fresh water was first collected in a cistern and then distributed throughout the gardens by a system of watercourses, opened and shut by small sluices. Then they began to plant and build.

The creation had started. Since then it has never stopped for, unlike the unchanging and eternal desert that surrounds them, this house and garden keep, in their fashion, a record of time, preserving traces of everything that comes and goes, of all that they have experienced of growth, resorption, change, decay and rebirth.

Man—opaque and subtle—when he builds himself a house, finds himself clarified by it, explained and extended in space and light. His house is his elucidation, and his affirmation also, because at the same time as structure and transparency it means possession of a patch of earth—carved out by the cellar and foundations—and of a volume of space, defined by the roof and walls. It is as though Ralph had been inspired by Axel Munthe's example only to run counter to it. Instead of the belvedere of San Michele, gazing proudly out to sea, he chose a low house, bowered in greenery and built not so much on street level as on garden level. Axel Munthe wanted to see, and equally to be seen. Ralph cared nothing for external views and what he sought was privacy. San Michele is the house of a solitary, an adventurer, a conqueror, the eagle's nest of a wanderer between jour-

neys. Ralph and Deborah's house is a lover's bower. They were
in love with one another but also with the country, with the soil,
and were determined to remain in contact with it. There is no
view from the windows and the light that enters them is filtered
several times through screens of leaves. It is a terrestrial, a telluric house, provided with the vegetable extensions it demands,
the product of a long, visceral growth.

Once the worsening of Deborah's condition had shown itself
by a sudden, deceptive remission, the sick woman insisted on
leaving at once for Tunisia and the south. It seemed a matter of
course that I should go with them, especially as one of the two
seamen had got himself a job at the Danieli and had decided to
remain in Venice. How many days did the crossing take? Ten,
twenty? But for the brief calls we made at Ancona, Bari, Syra-
cuse, Sousse and Sfax it would have been utterly timeless. It was
only when we landed that we were back with the calendar, with
trouble and old age. I am quite willing to admit it, everything in
me that—in spite of myself—shares Paul's obsession with stillness,
eternity and incorruptibility emerged in those days from its long
sleep and had a brief moment of glory. The clear, sunlit sky,
stirred by a slight breeze from the northwest, lapped us in a
happy oblivion. Deborah's deck chair could be put up on the af-
terdeck, sheltered by a rush mat. The tall sailing ship bending
gracefully to the lapis lazuli sea, the emaciated shadow of a
woman—all forehead and eyes—wrapped in camel-hair tweeds,
the ripple of the water along the sides of the hull and the froth-
ing wake astern that marked our passage, where were we? In
what slightly primitive, idealized print of a seascape? Ralph was
a different being, transformed into the captain, the responsible
master of the ship and of the lives she carried. If he was still
drinking, he was never drunk. We obeyed instantly every one of
his few, unequivocal orders. Each day stretched before us so
empty, so like the foregoing that we seemed to be reliving the
same one over and over. We were moving, no doubt, but surely
our progress was like the stylized movement of the discus
thrower, fixed in stone for all eternity? And if my happiness was
complete, so too was Deborah's condition static. For me, that
was the quintessential voyage, raised to an unsurpassable pitch

of perfection. It was surely what I was born for, because I cannot remember ever having experienced such fulfillment. Why did we have to arrive? We had barely sighted Houmt Souk when the sky filled with clouds and Deborah was seized by a terrifying fit of breathlessness. By the time we got her ashore at El Kantara in a sandstorm, she was dying. At that moment, she emerged from her silence.

Feverish and obsessive though it was, what she said remained sensible, coherent, almost practical. *She talked of nothing but her garden.* She was frightened because it could not do without her. It was more than her work, her child, it was an extension of herself. I have seen for myself the miracle of that riot of vegetation in the midst of the desert, on an arid soil producing nothing but alfalfa, prickly pear and aloes. The miracle of a forty-year struggle in which every day had seen the arrival at the harbor of Houmt Souk of packets of seeds, bundles of bulbs, sacking-shrouded shrubs and, above all, bags of chemical fertilizer and humus. But it was a sympathetic miracle also, the wonder of a woman whose green fingers seemed to have the power to make anything grow anywhere. Seeing Deborah and her garden it was clear that this was a *continuous* process of creation, by which I mean one that was renewed every day and every hour, just as God, having created the world, did not sit back but continues to keep it going, to breathe life into it, without which all would return to nothingness in an instant.

Gone was the radiant sunshine that had so triumphantly escorted us on our voyage. A rampart of leaden clouds was building up hourly on the horizon. Meanwhile, Deborah was moaning and wringing her hands, blaming herself for having deserted her garden for so long, as though she had committed a crime. She was afraid for her oleanders because their next flowering season would suffer if no one had deadheaded them. She worried about whether the azaleas had been pruned, whether the lily and amaryllis bulbs had been lifted and divided, whether the pools had been cleared of the duckweed and frog spawn that infested them. These pools caused her the greatest anxiety because on their waters floated the blue water lilies, the nenuphars of the Nile, the azure hyacinths, from them rose the papyrus plants, their long stems ending in fragile umbels, and above all the fat white flowers of the lotus which flowered only for a day but left behind a curious seed head pierced with holes like a pepper shaker within which rattled the seeds of forgetfulness. Djerba, incidentally, is generally held to be the island of the Lotophagi where the companions of Odysseus forgot their homeland, but it seems that Deborah alone was responsible for restoring the plant to its ancient habitat, for no lotuses are to be found there anywhere but in her garden.

The storm burst at last one night in a great clamor over our heads. As the lightning flashes showed us for a fraction of a second what torments the garden was suffering, Deborah's agitation rose to fever pitch. Deaf to our entreaties, she was determined at all costs to go out and protect her darlings and, weak as she was, two men had to be constantly at her bedside to restrain her. Dawn broke on a vision of devastation. The wind had dropped but rain was falling, heavy and persistent, on the leaves that strewed the ground. It was then Ralph sobered up enough to decide to give in to Deborah's wish and ordered us to help him carry her outside. There were four of us to carry the stretcher, so that it should have felt light enough, but we were weighed down by Deborah's suffering and the answering desolation of the ravaged garden. We had feared the shock that the sight of her obliterated work would be to her. But as we squelched across the sodden ground, trying to avoid the fallen trees, she was smiling, in a complete hallucination. She was seeing her garden as it had been at the height of its beauty and her face, dripping with rain and plastered with wisps of hair, was radiant with an invisible sunlight. We had to go right down to the sandy edge of the beach where, in her delirium, she saw a bank of Portuguese acanthus lifting their flowering spikes six feet in the air. As we went, she called on us to admire the imaginary pink fruits, like long-tailed parrots, on the silkweed, and chimerical mirabilis jalapa of Peru, sometimes called "pretty-by-night" because they open only at twilight. She stretched out her arms to grasp the tubular red and white pendent blossoms of the daturas and the blue panicles of the jacarandas. We had to stop under a bamboo arbor wrecked by the wind because that was where the Egyptian dolichos had twined its rampant purple-flowered shoots in its day. Our erratic progress through that tropical downpour would have been merely tragic but for Ralph who was as drunk as Deborah was delirious and turned the thing into a kind of wild adventure. I think he was only trying to humor the dying woman but he entered into the pretense with terrifying thoroughness. He slipped in the mud, tripped over fallen branches, stumbled into the irrigation channels and more than once nearly overturned the stretcher. We waited endlessly in a little storm-battered orchard while he made a pretense of harvesting lemons, oranges, mandarins and kumquats, laying them in a rush basket he had found in a puddle and giving the whole into Deborah's hands. Then, when she worried about the damage done to the water plants by the terrapins which infested the pools, Ralph plunged his arms into the mud in an attempt to capture one of the creatures. He showed it to Deborah, wriggling with the frantic, jerky movements of a clockwork toy, then set it down on a stone and tried to kick it to death. In vain. Its shell was too hard. He had to find another stone and hurl it viciously at the terrapin, reducing it to a mass of palpitating entrails.

That hellish expedition might well have gone on much longer if I had not become aware that Deborah's wide-open eyes had ceased to blink although the rain was falling harder than ever. I stopped the procession and before Ralph had time to lose control I had closed the dead woman's eyes. As we neared the house, we saw that a branch had fallen from a baobab and smashed through the glass roof of the aviary. Two birds of paradise had been killed by flying glass; the rest of the birds had flown.

Paul

I had to go to Rome to get a flight to Tunis. A ceiling of gray, ragged cloud, curled and teased, tattered by the storm. The aircraft heaved itself out of this dirty weather, full of turbulence and air pockets, and instantly there was blue sky and sunshine and the peace of the high tops. Although we never went above twenty thousand feet, the contrast provided a striking illustration of the existence of a mathematical sky, ordered by the heavenly bodies, above a muddled sky that was subject to all the caprices of the meteors.

At Carthage I got into a tiny airplane bound for Djerba. The weather was still appalling and the two-hour flight to the airfield of Mellita something of an ordeal, for this time we did not ascend to the heights of Olympus but swam underneath the cloud ceiling while it discharged all its flatulence and precipitations upon us.

There is nothing more dismal than these sunny countries when they are deprived of the blue and gold of fine weather. The airport's midget runway was swept by watery gusts and away beyond was a heartrending vision of palm trees taking an undignified battering from the gale.

When I asked a taxi driver to take me to El Kantara, he inquired which of the two El Kantaras I meant. I blamed my own haste because one glance at the map would actually have told me that there are two villages by that name, one on the island of Djerba, the other on the mainland, on either side of the entrance to the bay of Bou Grara. Moreover, they are linked by a Roman causeway about six kilometers long. So I told him about Ralph and Deborah and their garden—wonderful, according to Hami—and the fact that Deborah had died some days previously. He recalled having heard tell of a funeral held recently, at the height of the storm, in the cemetery of the mainland El Kantara, and decided to take me there.

Hami had always seemed oddly reluctant to talk to me about Ralph and Deborah, their life, their garden and their house. She came from a family of small craftsmen in Aghir and had been quick to take advantage of her contacts with the tourists of all nationalities—but chiefly Germans and Americans—who began to invade the little island after the war. Sociologists will analyze the astonishing upheavals created among the peoples of poor but sunny countries by the influx of visitors from the north. Although some of the natives may hold off from shyness or suspicion, the majority seek to make what profit they can out of the rich foreigners by hiring out their sun, their sea, their labor or their bodies. Hami was one of the first to assimilate the newcomers' language and habits, with the aim of making herself one with them. I think she made a business of selling the products of the local craftsmen, at first on the spot and later on for export. Later still, she became a decorator in Naples, Rome and finally Venice, where I met her. The palaces of Othello's city lent themselves to interior decoration in the Moorish style and Hami had been clever enough not to forget her Djerban origin. For several years she had been profiting from the efforts being made to restore some of the fine Venetian houses.

The six kilometers of Roman road linking the twin villages were not without their dangers because, in addition to the gusts of wind that shook the car, the waves had covered the causeway with shingle and shells and, worse still, with patches of sand and mud.

The *djebbana* of El Kantara was in its way a cemetery on the shore, for the slope on which the plain Arab tombstones were set —one stone for a man, two for a woman—faced the sea, but being in the bay it had its back to the main expanse of the Mediterranean. As a result, we were comparatively sheltered as we walked about the paved alleys, accompanied by a child who did duty as the keeper of the place. He remembered the funeral procession which had accompanied the coffin a fortnight earlier but, although I looked hard at him, I could discern no trace of the alienating light in his face. So Jean had not been present at the ceremony. The child did tell us, however, that the violence of the storm had made the causeway crossing very dramatic. The men had said that they had almost given up after the sea had twice broken over the roadway and threatened to sweep them away with the coffin. That meant that Ralph's property was at the island El Kantara. We did not linger by the rectangle of newly turned earth to which the child had led us, but made our way back along the causeway to the island.

At the island El Kantara I had no difficulty in locating Ralph's property for the seemingly impenetrable mass of greenery was visible from a long way off, like an oasis in the desert. I paid off my taxi and set out alone through the trees. What a short while before must have been a vast and magnificent tropical garden was now no more than a litter of fallen tree trunks, smashed

palms and drifted leaves, with creepers swarming and twining in
coils over them, their ends dangling in space. I made my way
with great difficulty toward the center of the tangle where the
house ought logically to be. The first sign of human habitation I
found was an overturned wind pump, its wooden flyer and vanes
smashed and splintered and its metal legs in the air. One did not
have to have a horticultural degree to realize that in this desert
climate it was the heart of the garden's vegetable life that was
lying at my feet. I was deep in contemplation of the fairly simple
mechanism of the big, broken toy when I was startled by a peculiar sound that seemed to come out of the sky. It was a rapid,
gentle whirring, interspersed with an occasional squeak. If you
shut your eyes, you could imagine a windmill—a little windmill
turning lightly and briskly, and a chain—a drive chain, perhaps.
You could imagine . . . a wind pump turning merrily in a stiff
breeze, and the pump laboring partly underground to bring up
the water. That was the first time I experienced in the grounds
of El Kantara the feeling of being a prisoner in a magical place,
saturated with hallucinations and invisible presences. The wind
pump I was hearing, alive and performing its life-giving task,
was there, broken, dead and stilled forever. Suddenly the busy,
friendly little sound was interrupted by a squawk of abusive,
hysterical laughter. There was a noisy clatter of wings in a small
almond tree close by and I made out a big red, blue, green and
yellow macaw shaking itself delightedly. That certainly gave me
a positive, rational explanation for what I had taken for a hallucination. But that explanation was too strange in itself—with
something evil and maleficent about it—to give me much comfort
and it was with a heavy, uneasy heart that I walked on through
the devastated gardens.

The house was so hidden in a jungle of hibiscus, laurels and
castor-oil plants that I did not see it until I almost bumped into
it. I had to walk all the way around to find the way in, five shallow steps leading up to a classical porch over which a huge
bougainvillea writhed in a fretwork of interwoven branches. The
cedarwood doors stood wide open and I entered without hesitation, as though drawn by a strange sense of familiarity. It was not
exactly that I seemed to recognize the patio with its central pool

adorned with a small bubbling fountain. It was something else. It was almost as if the place itself knew me and was welcoming me as a familiar figure, deceived of course by my resemblance to Jean. For the first time, in fact, the *alienating light* which I had looked with fearful curiosity to see reflected in every human face for two months past was showing itself in the very objects—in the cool, dark air of this patio. I could not doubt that Jean had been here long enough to fit into this house, to belong in it, like one who had always lived here, like a son. Whereas I walked in a fearful intoxication, not unlike the flashes of paramnesia one gets sometimes, which give one an absolute conviction of having lived through a particular brief incident in our lives before, down to the smallest detail. O Jean, my twin, when will you stop placing quicksands beneath my feet and building mirages before my eyes?

I perceived a passage on my right and at the end of it a huge, vaulted drawing room with a great bay window over the hearth and a low table made out of a piece of marble set on the capital of a broken column. But the room's proportions and luxurious style of decoration only made its ruined state the more tragic, for the bay window had broken inward, strewing daggerlike splinters of glass and mounds of decaying vegetable matter over the furniture and carpets. I had no wish to see any more. I went outside again and round the corner of the house. Past a small thicket of paulownias and prickly pear, I came upon a mutilated stone kouros, clothed in aristolochia. It stood in the middle of a semicircle marked out within a border of stone and divided into six beds each containing a different variety of rose. It was there I saw Ralph for the first time. He was cutting the few flowers which the storm had spared. He must have seen me, because he mumbled in explanation: "They are for Deborah's grave. The most beautiful grave in all the world . . ."

Then he turned away and plodded over to a small rectangular mound of freshly turned earth. I wondered if I had understood him rightly. But if Deborah were buried here, then what was the meaning of the grave in the *djebbana* of the mainland El Kantara? Ralph had flung his armful of roses down among the white campanulas, some mauve bracts and orange clusters of African marigolds which, with some sprays of asparagus fern, were strewn in a fragile, quivering mass upon the grave.

"There will be a stone erected here, shaped like half a circle. It's a sundial I brought back from Carthage. They are engraving it for me at Houmt Souk. Just the one name, Deborah. And two dates. The year of her death here, yes, but not her date of birth. No. The year we came to El Kantara, 1920."

He looked up at me, his blue eyes blurred with old age and drink. With his close-cropped white hair, bull-like neck, coppery complexion and heavy, regular features, he looked like some old Roman emperor, overthrown, exiled and desperate, yet so inherently noble that no disgrace could wholly degrade him. He advanced three steps and laid his hand on my arm.

"Come. Let us go in. Tani shall give us some mint tea."

He turned back stiffly to the garden and embraced it with a vague wave of his hand.

"It was Deborah's garden. Now, it is Deborah."

He peered up at me.

"You understand, don't you? She is not just in that hole over there. She is everywhere, in the trees and in the flowers."

We resumed our silent, plodding walk. Then he stopped once more.

"I have understood it all now. We came here forty years ago. It was all sand. Deborah didn't make this garden then, no. The garden grew naturally out of her green fingers. Her feet became roots, her hair leaves and her body a trunk. And like a fool, I didn't even notice. I thought Deborah was gardening! Deborah was turning into a garden, the most beautiful garden in the world. And when the garden was finished, Deborah disappeared into the earth."

I objected. I was seeing again the fallen trees, the leaves stripped off and above all the wind pump that was the heart of the garden thrown down and broken.

"All right, Ralph. But what about the storm?"

"The storm? What storm?"

He was staring at me with a bewildered air. The truth was obvious. He was refusing to accept the destruction of the garden by the wind and rain. He was rejecting the reality and seeing only what he wanted to see. This was clearer than ever when we entered the house and started a panic-stricken exodus of chickens, guinea fowl and peacocks. There had been a poultry yard somewhere which had been damaged, and the birds were everywhere. But Ralph did not seem to see them flapping clumsily about among the ornaments and leaving their droppings on the carpets. They did not fit into his imaginary world. I realized in the same way that I had no hope of clearing up the confusion relating to myself. Out of a sense of duty, but knowing what the result would be, I declared: "I am not Jean. I am his twin brother, Paul."

Ralph gave no sign. He had not heard. His attention was resolutely turned away from the words which brought a new and incomprehensible confusion into his life. He had enough to cope with—for a long time to come—in Deborah's metamorphosis into the garden. What business had I to bother him? I saw again Hamida's incredulous and suddenly hostile expression, the effort it had cost her to assimilate the immense paradox of a Jean who was not Jean. I could not inflict that now on this old man already withdrawn into a world of his own. I was beginning to realize how serious and far-reaching was the vertigo which had seized me on entering the house a little while before, which I had thought then was simply a variation—atmospheric, by and large— of the alienating light. For as long as I remained on the island of the Lotus Eaters I would be a prisoner of that garden, of that house and of the man who utterly refused to let me be myself. Here the misunderstanding had the force of law. It was not in my power to assail it. Who could say if in the end I might not even come to believe that I was Jean?

Ralph dropped onto a sofa, sending a hen pheasant clattering off. An old Chinese—or possibly Vietnamese—in a dirty white suit brought in a tray with two tall, steaming glasses containing a decoction of mint leaves. Ralph laced his with Bourbon. He drank in silence, his eyes fixed on a patch on the wall where the rain had run down it. He was not seeing it, he was blind to the smashed windows, the fallen ceilings, the prevailing damp and the invading livestock, to the fact that the house and the luxuriant oasis that surrounded it were clearly doomed. With Deborah

gone, house and oasis were vanishing from the face of the island
with an amazing, a terrifying, an almost magical swiftness. Before very long this earth would be smooth sand again and visitors treading it would wonder where Ralph and Deborah's house
had stood, or if it had ever been.

As though he had divined something of what I was thinking,
he remarked: "We had the yacht for holidays. But even here we
lived as if we were on a boat, Deborah and I. Because the desert
around us is like the sea. A boat we built together over forty
years. You see, this is the earthly paradise and Noah's Ark rolled
into one."

And he put out his hand toward a golden pheasant which fluttered out of reach.

Caught by my own imposture, I found myself faced last night
with an unexpected problem. Which was Jean's room, *my* room?
I could not ask Ralph, or Tanizaki, or Farid, or little Ali who
goes to the market in the village every day on his bicycle to buy
food. I thought I had found a way of doing it after dinner, and I
asked Farid to put another blanket on my bed, with the excuse
that the weather was cooler. But the fellow eluded my vigilance
and surprised me a quarter of an hour later by telling me it had
been done. So I was reduced to inspecting all the bedrooms one
by one to try to find out which bed Farid had put the blanket on,
and carrying an oil lamp at that, as the electricity had been cut
off ever since the storm. My choice was made easier, in fact, by
the state of dirt and dilapidation in which I found all the rooms.
Cats and birds were roosting companionably on the rain-soaked
beds and carpets and had no intention of allowing anyone to dis-
possess them. In the end I took refuge in the library, a small octagonal room with a domed roof and shelves lining the walls. I
collected enough from three of the beds to make myself reasona-
bly comfortable on a sofa. I was woken in the morning by a
greenish light filtering uncertainly through two small windows
overgrown with foliage. Later on, a ray of pale sunshine touched
the floor with its black and white marble tiles laid in the shape
of an eight-pointed star and in the center a fragment of broken
statuary, a severed head of Neptune, blind-eyed. I explored the

shelves. There was everything there. Old volumes of the classics —Homer, Plato, Shakespeare—and great modern authors—Kipling, Shaw, Stein, Spengler, Keyserling—while the quantity of postwar French writing—Camus, Sartre, Ionesco—showed that Deborah, in her desert, had kept abreast of everything, read everything, understood everything.

Although this room was probably the one that had suffered least from the ruin which had overtaken the house, it was also the most steeped in melancholy. The old bindings and yellowed pages exhaled a delicate aroma of mildew and long-dead wit. It was a necropolis of genius and intellect, the ashes of two thousand years of ideas, poetry, and drama after some atomic apocalypse.

There is, of course, a moral in all that desolation. Which is that a pair of non-twins, framed for a dialectical existence, cannot, without cheating, encapsulate themselves in defiance of time and society. Like our shocking Uncle Alexandre—although in radically different ways—Ralph and Deborah usurped a condition which is the privilege of identical twins.

Like many old men who are not really so very old but diminished by alcohol, Ralph has moments of perfect lucidity followed by terrible patches of total blankness. But whether his mind is clear or clouded it always revolves around Deborah.

This morning he was so bemused that he forgot she was dead and was looking for her, calling her all through the garden with frantic persistence. We got him indoors by dint of promising to find her for him. He consented to take a sedative and lie down. Two hours later he was awake, as fresh as a daisy, and lecturing me about the Bible.

"If you'd read your Bible, you'd have noticed something. God first created Adam. Then he created the Garden. Then he put Adam into the Garden. Well, Adam was mighty surprised, being in that Garden. It didn't come natural to him, see? With Eve now, it was different. She was created after Adam. She was created *in* the Garden. She belonged in that Garden. So that when the two of them were driven out of the Garden, it wasn't quite the same for Eve as it was for Adam. Adam was going back where he'd begun. He was going home. But Eve now, she was being exiled from her birthplace. If you forget that, you don't know a thing about women. Women are exiles from paradise. All of them. That was why Deborah made her garden. She was creating her own paradise. Wonderfully. I was just looking on. And marveling."

He paused. He was crying. Then he shook himself and went on.

"This is disgusting. I'm an old fool. I'm a disgusting old fool."

"If you really were an old fool, you wouldn't say that."

He considered the objection interestedly. Then he found an answer.

"But I don't always say it!"

He poured himself a shot of Bourbon. But just as he put the glass to his lips he was interrupted by a female voice, hissing viciously: *"Ralph, you are a soak!"*

He turned awkwardly toward the sideboard whence the remark had come. The macaw was perched on top of it, showing first his green tail, then his black beak as he revolved on the spot.

"True enough," Ralph acknowledged. "She often used to say that."

"Ralph, you are a soak!"

At that, he resignedly put down his glass.

I am still close enough to Jean to understand why, having attached himself to this couple, he should have run away—and not because of their collapse, but in spite of it. At first Jean had a vision of Ralph and Deborah not as they were when he knew them in Venice—Ralph sodden with drink and Deborah mortally ill—but as they had lived the best part of their lives, supremely intelligent and fiercely independent, without ties, without children, absolutely free. That, at least, was how he pictured them; and bitterly he mourned the magnificent life he had never been able to share because he came too late, was probably even born too late.

Yet the image he made for himself of this couple was never more than partly true. It was as they were on their travels, on their holidays at sea, when they left El Kantara and were to some extent taken out of themselves. Jean must have experienced some kind of happiness with them on board their yacht. But what a leaden yoke must have descended on his shoulders when he entered this garden and this house! For the spell of this place can be measured almost arithmetically in its strength and kind. Indeed, this islet had recorded day by day and hour by hour the forty years that have gone to its making. Those fifteen thousand days, three hundred and sixty thousand hours are here, visible, like the concentric rings that tell the age of a felled tree trunk. Under this roof, Jean was lost amid a fabulous collection of stones, carvings, drawings, shells, feathers, gems, woodwork, ivory, prints, flowers, birds, sketches—and each one of these things telling him about its day, its hour, when it had been brought here, admitted, incorporated gloriously into Ralph and Deborah's island. He felt himself drawn into the formidable mass of that long span, as though into the vertiginous blue depths of a glacier.

He ran away, because he could not fail to recognize the affinity of what had been created at El Kantara with the geminate cell. Differing in sex, age, and nationality, Ralph and Deborah did not want a normal, temporal, dialectical union which would have found its complete fulfillment in a family, in children and grandchildren. The phantom twinship which haunts every pair of non-twins to a greater or lesser extent drove these two to unusual extremes. It sterilized them and sent them into the desert. There, in a preordained spot, it made them build an enclosed, artificial domain, in the image of the earthly paradise, but a paradise the man and woman would secrete about themselves together, in their own image, like the shell of their twofold organism. It is an actual, physical cell, with a geographical location, which *is* its own long history because every one of its ups and downs and furrows is the result of some past event, and it weighs incomparably heavier than the invisible web of ritual that twins weave between them.

I have been here only a very little while. I have a deep love of hidden, sheltered, inward-looking places. Is it, then, because I am being compelled to be Jean that I am stifling, painfully, in

this forty-year-old shell created by an organism not my own? I
know only too well what made Jean take off again so soon.

Idly exploring the house, I caught sight of a small snapshot,
pressed between two pieces of glass. It must have been about
thirty years old. I recognized Ralph and Deborah easily. He was
looking straight at the camera, as handsome as a Greek god, cool
and powerful, with a smile of such calm assurance that it would
have been almost complacent, but for the considerable *backing*—
I use the word intentionally, as though of a check—of his obvious
and impressive force of character. The years are so cruel to the
exceptionally privileged! Deborah looked like a 1920s flapper
with her short hair plastered close to her face, her tip-tilted nose
and long cigarette holder. (It was the tobacco that killed her,
they told me here.) She was not particularly pretty, but had such
a look of intelligence and determination. Just then, that look was
directed downward, with a watchful, protective air, at a little
girl, a lean dusky-skinned creature, her thin face half hidden
under a mass of tightly curling hair. The little girl, for her part,
was looking at Ralph. She was gazing up at him with an expression of concentrated sadness in her glowing, passionate eyes.
There was a whole small tragedy in those three faces, the godlike male's, preoccupied with his own magnificence, and those
of the two women, one in the full flower of her beauty and
confidence—but for how much longer?—and the other with the
future in her hands; she might triumph over her rival but she
was not wholly aware of it as yet, she was entirely absorbed in
the frustrations of the present. I had a sudden thought which
gradually became a certainty. The little girl was Hamida. She
must have been about twelve years old at the time and as emotionally precocious as she was physically underdeveloped, a not
uncommon condition in these parts and one that makes an ideal
breeding ground for misery.

Hamida

The foreign tourists broke over our enclosed, fierce, fevered Arab
life in an intermittent, colorful tide. They brought money, lei-

sure and shamelessness into our medinas hedged about with the traditions of a thousand years. Such a painful shock it was! Like the stroke of the surgeon's knife letting air and light into the inmost secrets of the body! The shock was doubly violent for a girl. I once heard this scrap of conversation between two Europeans in one of the alleys of Houmt Souk which was used by a gang of children as a playground.

"What a lot of children! What a lot of children there are in these Arab towns!"

"Yes, and these are not all! You only see half of them. Maybe even the smaller half!"

"How do you mean, the smaller half?"

"Well, look at them! Only the boys are out in the streets. The girls stay shut up indoors."

Shut up, indeed, and in those days we could not go out without a veil. My adolescence was a frenzied struggle for the right to have my face uncovered, for the right to light and air. Our bitterest opponents were the *adjouzas,* the old women who were the guardians of tradition and who never went outside except swathed in their muslin veils, holding them in place between their teeth. On some evenings, the frogs in Ralph's pool make a dry, croaking noise, like a person clicking his tongue. I have never been able to hear it without shivering, because it sounds exactly like the rude, familiar noise the youths used to make after unveiled girls in the streets.

I must have been about seven when I first entered Ralph and Deborah's house. I fell under their spell instantly, for as a couple they seemed the personification of all the best in intelligence, freedom, and happiness that the West had to offer me, something which in comparison with the common run of tourists was like a heap of copper coins to the equivalent in gold. They adopted me. From them I learned to dress—and likewise to undress—to eat pork, smoke, drink alcohol and speak English. And I read all the books in the library.

But inevitably the balance between the three of us altered with the years. Deborah was slightly older than Ralph. The difference, which for a long time was scarcely perceptible, became suddenly noticeable around the age of fifty. Ralph was still resplendent, in the prime of life, when Deborah—growing thin and lined—crossed the inevitable line beyond which affection—kindness even—takes over from desire in mankind's physical relationships. She was sufficiently brave and clearsighted to face up to the consequences sensibly. I was eighteen then. Did Ralph tell her I had become his mistress? Probably. To deceive her for long was unthinkable, and in any case it made no difference to my relations with her. Ralph was a monogamous type. There would never be any woman in his life but Deborah. We all three knew that, and it preserved our threesome from all tempests. But for me, that calm was another name for despair. The truth was that the couple who seemed to have adopted me were enclosed together in an egg of marble. I might have broken my nails on its surface. I did not try.

So deep was the union between them that Ralph's decline followed hard upon Deborah's aging, although it took a different form and even a quite different direction. Ralph had always been a drinker, but at home and never disgustingly. One day, he went out to see his lawyer in Houmt Souk and did not come back. Deborah knew the island's meager resources well enough, she had enough friends, contacts and servants to follow Ralph's progress from brothel to brothel and bar to bar. Three days later, some boys brought him home unconscious on the back of a mule. They had found him asleep in a ditch. We nursed him together. That was when she laid a command on me which was like a shower of roses, but roses with venomous thorns.

"Try and be kind to him more often," she told me.

After that, I was in hell. Every time Ralph went on the spree, I could feel deserved reproaches heaped on my head for my failure in the role of mistress and nurse. Deborah never said anything, but I was made miserable by my own unworthiness.

Only their travels on the yacht gave me some respite. I took advantage of one such absence to go away to Italy to live.

Paul

Where is Jean? And above all how could he have gone away so suddenly? Whatever the power of geminate logic, I cannot see how he can have run away before Deborah's funeral, leaving this despairing old man who treated him like an adopted son. There must be some other explanation of his behavior. But what?

Macabre and maleficent ideas haunt me like ghosts and my mind is overcast. The fact is that my brother's prolonged absence —the first time I have had to face up to it for so long—has a profoundly disturbing effect on me. There are times when I feel as though I am teetering on the edge of hallucination, and how far is it from hallucination to madness? I have very often asked myself why I run after my brother, why I am making such efforts to find him and to bring him home again. To such answers as I have been able to offer to those questions, must I add another: to save myself from going mad?

The first of my hallucinations was suggested to me by Ralph himself. Jean has not vanished *because I am Jean*. While at the same time, of course, not ceasing to be Paul. Two twins, in fact, in a single man, Janus Bifrons. Jean told me that one day when he was standing in front of a mirror and was sure that the person he saw there was me, he was appalled by the substitution. I can see in that, all too clearly, alas, his hostility to twinship. For me, on the other hand, those three words *I am Jean* are soothing and reassuring, almost they persuade me to give it all up and go home. But for that kind of recovery by duplication to be success-ful it would be essential that Jean should not actually be pursu-ing his vocation as a carder by spreading trouble in Herzegovina or Baluchistan. In short, I should have to dare to set it down in black and white that as soon as I feel growing within myself the possibility of my assuming the whole personality of Jean-Paul, Jean's death becomes an acceptable eventuality, almost a so-lution.

Could Jean be dead? There is another idea that haunts me, scarcely even an idea, more a rather blurred picture. I see the car carrying Deborah's coffin over the causeway at the height of the storm. Waves are breaking over the road, spray is beating on the windshield and patches of mud and drifts of sand imperil the vehicle's progress. Jean is not one of those accompanying the coffin. Yet Jean is there, *inside the coffin*. Because I got from Farid an explanation of those two graves, those two funerals, one at the island El Kantara, the other on the mainland. Ralph had asked the mayor of the village for permission to bury Deborah in her garden, but permission was refused. He made up his mind to go ahead without it, while still making a show of complying. So Deborah was buried in her garden while another coffin, an empty one, was interred for form's sake in the *djebbana* of the mainland El Kantara. They must have put something in it as a makeweight. Something, or someone?

I have furthered my aquaintance with Tanizaki, Ralph's yellow manservant—who may well prove to be the key figure in my stay at Djerba. Because although he gave me no direct answer to the question I was asking myself the other day, what he said undoubtedly has a bearing on it.

Tanizaki is not Chinese or Vietnamese, as I had thought, but Japanese. He comes from Nara, which is south of Kyoto, and the only thing I know about it is what he told me, that Nara is full of sacred deer. Every traveler is met on the station platform by a deer which never leaves him throughout his stay. In fact, the whole town is one huge garden, skillfully laid out and sanctified by many temples. Now that I have come here, to Deborah's garden, I can see that I shall only leave it to go on to another garden, to other gardens. That must mean something. The future will show what. Because although Tanizaki's duties here include practically everything *except gardening,* that is not for want of interest or ability, far from it. He has not concealed from me, by means of veiled hints and allusions, his disapproval of Deborah's work. That work was crude and barbaric and the collapse that we were seeing was inherent in its very beginnings. He would say no more, however much I questioned him. There were times when that Asiatic reminded me of Méline in the way he insisted on speaking in halftones and never giving a straight answer to a question. I said to him: "Deborah worked hard to make a fairy-tale garden grow in the middle of the desert. Of course it was doing violence to the land. What's more, the land is avenging itself with staggering speed, now that the woman with the green fingers is no longer here to protect her work. Is it the violence you object to?"

He smiled in a superior fashion, as though he despaired of

making me understand a truth too subtle for me. He was beginning to irritate me and he must have sensed it, because he did relent enough to tell me something. "The answer is at Nara" was what he said. Is he trying to send me all the way around the world simply in order to find out why Deborah's garden was doomed? Struggle as I may, I have a nasty feeling I am not going to be able to avoid going to Nara. Because I have noticed that while everything and everyone else here reflects the same alienating light, Tanizaki's face alone remains smooth and cold. But what I might at first have taken for the famous Oriental impassiveness was something deeper, the absence of the alienating light. Only Tanizaki has not "recognized" me here, because he alone knows that I am not Jean.

I was sitting on the veranda yesterday when he put a tall glass, misted with coolness, down beside me.

"Some lemonade for you, Mr. Paul," he murmured softly, as though it were a secret. And it came so naturally that I did not register at first. Mr. Paul? I leaped up and grabbed him by the lapels of his white barman's jacket.

"Tani, where is my brother Jean?"

He smiled gently.

"Who is it that is buried in the *djebbana* at El Kantara on the mainland?"

"Why, Mrs. Deborah," he said at last, as if it were the most obvious thing in the world.

"And here? Who is buried here?"

"Why, Mrs. Deborah," he said again. And he added, as though it explained everything, "Mrs. Deborah is everywhere."

Never mind the ubiquitous Mrs. Deborah! After all, what did it matter to me? I was not here to inquire into Deborah's death.

"Now tell me, Tani, where is my brother?"

"Mr. Jean saw that he must go to Nara."

That was all I needed to know.

Icelandic Pentecost

Paul

We took off from Fiumicino at 1430 hours into a uniformly gray sky. The plane headed north, flying a course which would take it, by way of Paris, London and Reykjavik, up to the North Pole and then down again to Anchorage and Tokyo. There is a way of counting, of thinking, even of living there which it was the business of this journey to teach me. I knew, for instance, that at the latitude of the equator day and night are of equal length at all times of the year, but that the seasonal differences increase the further you go from the equator toward either pole. I knew . . . but did I really know? Possibly one of my brain cells had been storing up the information ever since it had been put there in the course of some lessons in geography or astronomy. The journey made me experience it intensely. Because as soon as we broke through the gray ceiling and the sun was established once more in splendor, ruling by divine right over a nation of ragged clouds, I observed its height above the horizon and I knew, and

checked minute by minute, that it would not budge from that
position throughout the duration of our northward flight. The
journey which at first looked like a movement in space was, in a
deeper sense, concerned with time. Time by the clock and meteoric time. The weather changes that accompany the journey—
which may divert or impede its progress—are only the decorative
additions or dramatic accompaniment to a hidden, unfailing
mechanism. My left hand was resting on the rim of the oval window through which I could see the western horizon where the
sun hung suspended. My wristwatch, the white cloud cavalry,
the unmoving sun . . . They were all gathered together in a picture as primitive in its way as those illustrations in elementary
geography books where cars, trains, boats and airplanes are
shown racing one another through a single landscape. Only here
the four symbols of travel through space were changed into
three symbols of travel in time. We were to land at Reykjavik at
midnight. I knew that the sun would not have moved. Then what
of the clouds? And my watch? Surely that, too, ought to have
stopped? But how could it? It is a self-winding one that keeps
going automatically as long as I wear it on my wrist, day and
night. (Of course, one has to be a comparatively restless sleeper.
To begin with, I used to amuse myself pretending to the gullible
that I drank coffee every night for that very purpose. Then I got
tired of the yarn.) A mechanism simple enough in principle enables it to tap and store a tiny part of the energy I waste every
time I move my left arm. What would become of that energy if
my watch did not make use of it? Does it make me infini-
tesimally more tired? I suppose there comes a time when my
watch has had enough. After that it does no good to agitate it, as
when the basin of a fountain is full, the amount of water that
pours out over the edge is precisely the same as that being
pumped into the center. The watch accumulates enough energy
to keep it going for a dozen or more hours—somewhere between
fifteen and eighteen—but after that it stops and no amount of
movement can set it going again. Then you have to use a winder,
just as for an ordinary watch. It doesn't matter. To that refine-
ment, I should prefer one that would adjust my watch automatically to the local time. I am going to have to be continually tor-

menting it to make it perform its rightful function of telling the correct time—not in the place I have come from, wherever that may be, but in the place where I am.

I slept a little after the brief stop at Orly which involved a certain amount of passenger movement, some alighting at Orly and others boarding for the remainder of the flight. On my right I now have a diminutive blonde with delicate, regular, clear-skinned features. She apologized for sitting next to me and we exchanged a swift glance. Did the "light" shine in hers? I am not sure. I can even assert that it did not. Yet there was *something like that* in her eyes, but what it was exactly I could not say.

We come down again, in London this time. There is more coming and going. It is like being in the old bone-shaker that used to run between Plancoët and Matignon, stopping at every hamlet—except that the sun never stayed in its course for that, which actually does make quite a difference! My neighbor has stayed put. Is she going with me all the way to Tokyo, or will she leave me at Reykjavik? I should miss her because her fresh, dainty presence does me good. I try to get a glimpse of the label on the bag she has placed at our feet and, having plenty of time, I finally manage to make it out: *Selma Gunnarsdottir Akureyri IC.* That's it, then. I am going to lose her at the next stop. As though she has guessed the direction of my thoughts, she smiles at me suddenly—with a glint of the "pseudo-light"—and says to me innocently out of the blue, "It's funny, you look like someone I don't know!"

It is a weird, contradictory remark but it fits in so well with the pseudo-light that it does not surprise me. She laughs at the absurdity of the situation, although not, clearly, as much as she was prepared to, because my attitude expresses moderate, polite interest but nothing more. Do you know, little Selma, that Bep does not treat such matters lightly? To cover her embarrassment, she leans over to the window on the other side of me. Rents in the white carpet of cloud reveal a rocky archipelago pitted with volcanoes.

"The Faeroes," she observes, then adds, a trifle apologetically, "I work as a guide, you see."

She laughs and suddenly wins back all the points she has lost by these gratuitous confidences by continuing: "Just after we touched down in London you spent a quarter of an hour trying to read my name and where I come from on my luggage label. I know your name, it is Surin."

Definitely not. I am not going to get involved in this dubious banter. I press the button that releases my reclining seat and lean back, my eyes fixed on the ceiling as though preparing to go to sleep. She follows suit and says no more, so that all of a sudden we look like a pair of carved figures on a tomb. It is 2230 hours by my watch and the sun is still in the same place, suspended above a sea gleaming like a plate of finely hammered copper. The clouds have gone. We are entering the hyperborean zone whose timeless dignity shows in the cessation of bad weather as well as in the sun's standing still.

"I know your name is Surin because the man I am engaged to wrote to me about you. He even sent me a snapshot of the two of you together. I thought you were still in Iceland."

Silence is decidedly not her greatest gift, but I am grateful to her for letting me into the secret of the "pseudo-light." She has put up the back of her seat again to talk to me and, as I am still lying down, her small, willful face is bending over me.

"My fiancé is French. We met at Arles, which is where he was born. I was at the University of Montpellier, learning your language. I brought him back to Iceland. Girls in our country are supposed to introduce their future husband to their parents. We also have a tradition of having an engagement trip, rather like your honeymoon only before, you see, as a kind of trial. Sometimes it is a great help. Only Iceland is a magic country, you understand. Olivier has never gone back to France. It is nearly eleven years now."

For several minutes the plane has been coming in to land. Tongues of black, broken ground crisscross the blue field of my window. A disappointment. Iceland is not the isle of immaculate ice, adorned with eternal snows, that I have dreamed of. This is more like a slag heap, a succession of narrow valleys cut into a heap of carbonaceous spoil. We are getting near. The bright spots of houses stand out against the sooty ground. Their roofs

are green, red, pink, blue, orange and indigo. Their roofs and
their walls, but roofs and walls invariably in different and clash-
ing colors.

By the time we touch down at Reykjavik, my mind is made
up. I am breaking my journey to Tokyo with a stop in Iceland.

The rooms in the Gardur Hotel are all alike: a narrow, unyield-
ing bed, a table whose sole purpose seems to be to support a Bible—in Icelandic—which lies upon it, two chairs, and above all a
huge window unprovided with either curtains or shutters. Lastly,
and not to be forgotten, a radiator which keeps the room as hot
as an oven. I spoke to the chambermaid about it. She replied
with a helpless gesture: it is impossible to turn it down, much
less to switch off the heat. The radiators are run straight from
hot springs which take no account of the time of day or year.
One simply has to get used to the volcanic heat, just as one does
to the perpetual daylight. Besides, no one, obviously, comes to
Iceland in June to sleep. That much I am learning from the pale
blue sky and the sun shining there, more bright than warm, this
merciless window, this inhospitable bed, the quiet murmur of
slow, rural life that never stops . . . and my watch, which says
one o'clock in the morning. In any case, I am not sleepy. So I
shall go out . . .

Silent men are laying carpets of lawn on the black earth of
gardens. I imagine them being rolled up carefully in September
and put away for the nine months of winter. Do I have to say in
so many words that it is real turf, fresh and living? Others are
painting their houses. Roofs and walls of corrugated iron, armored houses in a way, but armored gaily and lightheartedly because the people obviously like the most explosive colors, and
keep them shining bright. Everywhere there is life, men, women,
children, dogs, cats, birds going about their business, but all
without making a sound, as though this sunlit night imposed its
own obligations to silence, a general acceptance that talking,
shouting and making any noise is simply not done. In addition,
the men are as fair, the women as transparent and the children
as merry as Hyperboreans who have learned to read from the
stories of Hans Andersen. Yet I am met at every street corner by

the same bird's call, a silvery tinkling, at once plaintive and gay,
and so regular that it seems to be following me, flitting from
rooftop to rooftop so that I can hear it all the time. But I try in
vain to catch a glimpse of it. I even wonder whether by some
magic I am the only person who can hear it, because every time
I ask someone, even at the very moment when the silvery note is
sounding, "Did you hear that? That bird, what is it?" the person
inquired of only listens and raises his eyebrows in surprise. "A
bird? What bird? No, I didn't notice."

Olivier is a long, thin, gloomy person, his gangling height emphasized by long hair and a drooping moustache. He makes one
think of a young Don Quixote or, at the other end of the scale,
an aging, cynical d'Artagnan. He came to see me the day after
my arrival and began talking to me at once as if I were Jean. I
lacked the strength to disabuse him, just as I had with Ralph.
Among the ironies of being a dispaired twin is that the non-twins
one meets will often ignore the truth, or even reject it outright.
They assimilate the dispaired one quite naturally as one of themselves, holding his small stature, his earnestness, his poor performance against him, and treat his claims to twinship with skepticism, trying not to listen—as though he were speaking out of
turn.

Nor did Olivier seem to feel the slightest desire to clarify the
circumstances of Jean's leaving and my arrival here—always supposing Jean has gone on his way to Tokyo. All this is far beyond
such faint attention as he is willing to bestow on the affairs of
other people.

What am I doing myself sitting in the back of this bus next to
a sullen and grumbling Olivier and separated from Selma, our
guide, by a batch of English tourists? *I am doing what Jean did.*
Because that is the unwritten law of my journey, that I may not
skip a stage—not even to be more certain of catching up with
him—but am constrained to go at the same pace because I must
tread exactly in his footsteps. For my journey is not like the
flight of a stone hurled from a sling and stroked by the air as it
passes through it. It is more like a snowball rolling downhill and
adding to itself at every turn, so that in a sense it carries with it

the tale of its journey. I have to find in Iceland whatever it was that Jean came here to find, the thing he must have found, in fact, if he has really resumed his flight to Tokyo, for he would not have gone away empty-handed.

The bus is traveling through a valley whose grassy sides and patches of snow do not make one forget the uniformly black earth of this basalt island. A black, white and green country. We drive for hours without seeing the smallest sign of human habitation, and then suddenly a farm building looms up with a little church alongside it—both of them prefabricated, obviously delivered by the same firm at the same time. Presumably the farmer turns himself into a pastor from time to time and his family into his flock. A few ponies are grazing in a paddock but the mandatory vehicle is the Land-Rover, surmounted by the long, supple antennas of a small radio transmitter. Each one of these details—and plenty more, like the huge barns where they must be able to store enough provisions for a year—speaks of the unimaginable loneliness of the people who live on this land, especially in winter when unrelieved night comes down on them. I'd be interested to know the suicide figures for Iceland. Perhaps it is distinctly lower than in Mediterranean countries? Man is such a curious animal.

Talking of animals, it is the feathered kind which seems to predominate here. One does, of course, see little groups of sheep —often no more than a ewe and a couple of lambs—on the stony pastures. They run off trailing long skeins of dirty wool and leaving lumps of it clinging to rocks and bushes. The creatures appear to be so wild that anyone who wants mutton to eat probably has to bring them down with a gun. But apart from the ponies, those are the only mammals. These big farms don't even seem to have dogs. Winged species, on the other hand, reign supreme. I have just seen a splendid sight: a big black swan with outstretched wings and threatening beak driving away a little flock of sheep who were grazing along the shore of a small lake and must have got too close to its nest. The sheep scattered in panic, pursued by the bird which ran along on tiptoe, its wings flapping about it like a great black cape.

I point out the scene to Olivier who raises an eyelid as heavy and creased as the hood of a stagecoach and gazes without the slightest interest. Meanwhile the diminutive Selma is crouched over her microphone next to the driver, conscientiously retailing the part of her commentary that goes with the scene unrolling itself outside. "Farming was at one time the Icelanders' principal occupation, but it has declined in importance since the growth of the fishing and allied industries. Even so, agriculture is the second-largest source of employment. Sheep rearing is the main activity. There are about eight hundred thousand sheep in Iceland, or four per head of the population. In the summer, they roam freely on the mountains and pastures. They are brought in to the farms in September and this is the occasion for all kinds of popular celebrations . . ."

Olivier slides a lackluster glance at me. "Just like the people. The whole country works by day and sleeps and enjoys itself by night. You'll note that I say day and night. Others call it summer and winter. For us, it comes to the same thing, but we only talk about summer and winter so that foreigners can understand. Six months daylight, six months darkness. Believe me, it's a long time!"

He pauses, as though to allow the length of that day and night to sink in. Selma, meanwhile, is continuing conscientiously: "The Icelandic tongue which is spoken today has changed very little from the language originally brought by the Vikings in the ninth and tenth centuries. Because our island has been largely cut off from outside influences, our language is purer than in neighboring countries. To some extent, it is the fossil language out of which Danish, Norwegian and even English have developed. Suppose there were an island in the Mediterranean which had remained cut off for two thousand years and where they still spoke classical Latin. That is a bit what Iceland is like in relation to the Scandinavian countries."

"I came here for a month. One month, thirty days, or thirty-one as the case may be," Olivier continues. "Of course, I hadn't realized that a day lasted six months and a night another six. As soon as I set foot on this island I found my thirty days beginning to turn into thirty years. Oh, the change didn't come about just like that. If it hadn't been for Selma I think it might not even have happened at all. You, for instance, and all these nice English people, you are hardly aware of anything. Only that you have stopped sleeping and you're not sleepy. That's remarkable enough and it will give you some idea of what has happened to me. The fact is that Selma has *Icelandicized* me, if you see what I mean. It's pure matriarchy, do you see? She came and found me at Arles, where I was doing no harm to anyone, and she brought me home with her. And then she Icelandicized me. That means that I live through a French summer now, for example, like a day in Iceland, and the French winter like an Icelandic night. According to the French calendar I have been here nearly eleven years. Well, I don't believe it! I have no memory of those eleven years. To me it seems that if I were to go back to Arles tomorrow, say, my friends would say to me, 'Why, Olivier! You went away for a month and here you are back again after eleven days! Didn't you like it in Iceland?'"

NAMASKARD

A livid landscape, pallid and greenish, with mucous streaks like warm pus, a glaucous suppuration, toxic fumes and witches' cauldrons of boiling mud. Within them are visions of a mess of molten sulphur, saltpeter and basalt. The fearful presence of that unnameable, that utterly unnatural thing, liquefied stone . . . Sulphur springs emitting jets of poisonous vapor, slow coils of steam. The intense, improbable blue at the geyser's bottom. The tiny lake empties at a gulp, as though by some powerful suction from within, then in an instant the liquid flows back and leaps up to the sky, scattering in spray and falling back, pattering onto the rocks. The contrast between this wholly mineral landscape and the living, intestinal activity that appears in it. These stones spit, blow, belch, smoke, fart and shit and finally erupt in an incandescent diarrhea. This is the fury of the subterranean hell against the surface, against the sky. The subterranean world is pouring out its hatred, spewing in the face of heaven all its vilest, most scatological abuse.

I remember Djerba and the incandescent heavens ravaging the earth—and there it was the waters sucked up by the wind pumps from underground which flowed out, bringing their blessed milk up to the parched earth and allowing the oasis to flourish . . .

"And that is not all," Olivier goes on. "I have been doing this circuit once a week each summer for eleven years, and yet it isn't really a circuit at all! I don't know, but I have a feeling that if we could go all the way around the island clockwise in the bus, everything would be quite different. But there it is! The road that goes around the island comes up, in its southeasterly corner, against the great glacier of Vatnajökull. At Fagurhólsmyri, a plane brings us a batch of tourists from Reykjavik and takes back those we have just put down at the foot of the glacier. And off we go on the same trip in the other direction! Well, you know, there's something very depressing about going backward and forward like that. I always feel as though I'm undoing something I've just done. It's become almost an obsession with me, to go full circle. To complete the ring that is broken by the giant glacier. Then the spell would be broken. Selma and I would be able to get married at last and go back to Arles." And he adds with a shade of embarrassment, "Perhaps I must seem to you a little mad?"

Poor Olivier! Fiancé with a broken ring, everlastingly hopeful but brought up short every week by the moraine of the formidable Vatnajökull and retracing his steps in the perpetual daylight of the Icelandic summer, only to be back again in another seven days, and turn, and come again . . . no one is better equipped than I am to comprehend your fate in which the meteors, the elements and your heart and your body are so inextricably mixed!

"In the winter, it is different. The tourists who flock here in the summer in their thousands know nothing about Iceland. Iceland is not the midnight sun, it is the midday moon. In January we can see a little lightening of the sky at about one o'clock in the afternoon. That is bad, but it does not last. Soon kindly night falls again on our slumbers. For we hibernate like dormice, like marmots, like brown bears. It's rather lovely. You hardly eat and don't go out at all, except as little as you need to to forgather in low rooms for immense drinking bouts after which you lie down anywhere. The first time, you think you're going to be fright-

ened, you think you'll cry for the light, cry for the sun like a
scared child. But the opposite is true. The prospect of the return
of summer comes to seem a nightmare, an assault, an injury. Iceland is a magical country, believe me! Are you quite sure you
can escape?"

I am quite sure I can escape, because I have found what I
came to look for. At Hveragerdhi there is the biggest collection
of greenhouses in Iceland. The temperature in these vast conser-
vatories, crammed with flowers and foliage, is maintained at a
constant 30° C. by volcanic springs. The countryside all around
steams like a laundry but it is a benign water vapor with no mal-
ice in it. We are a long way from the savage, toxic eructations of
Namaskard. I was in a kind of daze as I moved through the
moist, fragrant atmosphere—to be greeted on entering by the
gravelly shriek of a cockatoo—because at a distance of three
thousand miles I found myself transported back to Deborah's
garden. They were all there, the amaryllis, the daturas, the mirabilis and asclepias, the banks of acanthus and jacaranda, the little lemon- and mandarin-bearing trees, even the bananas and
date palms, all the tropical flora, just as at El Kantara, but
within a few miles of the Arctic Circle and, of course, simply by
virtue of the fires within the earth. In warm water tanks there
were even the water lilies, the hyacinths, and the lotus, the
flower with the gift of forgetfulness in its seeds.

I have still not exhausted the possibilities of the comparison of
these two gardens, the oasis at El Kantara and the greenhouses
of Hveragerdhi, and I have a premonition that Japan will shed
more light on the subject for me. What is it they have in common? The fact that in both cases the conditions are wholly unsuitable for the cultivation of tender, succulent plants, at Djerba
because it is too dry, in Iceland because of the cold. But what
the ground withholds, the underground supplies—water drawn
from the phreatic layer by wind pumps at Djerba, heat exhaled
by the thermal springs in Iceland. These two gardens are the expression of the blooming, precarious victory of the earth's depths
over its surface. And how extraordinary it is that the inferno of
rage and hatred I saw unleased at Namaskard should here be

tamed and industrious, laboring to bring forth flowers, as though the devil himself had suddenly put on a straw hat, picked up a watering can and taken to gardening.

Was it another sign? Yesterday evening I strayed as far as the shores of Lake Myvatn—smooth and still as a sheet of mercury now that the dredger which by day extracted the diatomaceous mud from it had stopped work. I had noticed some large brown birds with fawn bellies standing on the ground here and there, so still as to be almost invisible. I had been told that they were skuas—or jaegers—which have the characteristic of not hunting or fishing for themselves, preferring to capture their prey from other birds. I had been warned that they could be aggressive if I went too near their nests. It was not a skua that went for me but a little gull with a forked tail—a tern, to be precise—as quick and streamlined as a swallow. I saw it flying in ever-decreasing circles over me, then making little dives at my head. At last it remained stationary a few inches above my hair, hovering on the spot with its tail tucked forward and keeping up a stream of indignant chatter. *Go away, go away, go away!* Was that really all that the white swallow of Lake Myvatn had to say to me that sunny June night? It came to me not long afterward that it was the eve of Pentecost, and I thought of the Holy Ghost descending on the heads of the Apostles in the form of a bird to loosen their tongues before sending them out to the four corners of the world to preach . . .

P.S. I know only too well that dispaired twinship is the driving force behind this voyage around the world, a kind of false ubiquity—and I cannot tell where or when my journey will end.

But what about *dispaired cryptophasia?* When the cryptophone has lost his twin, is he reduced to the alternatives of absolute silence or the defective language of non-twins? The truth is that I am sustained by a hope which is unverifiable, yet if it were ever to be disappointed I should collapse. This hope is that the false ubiquity to which Jean's flight has condemned me will lead ultimately—if my twin absolutely refuses to be found—to something unprecedented, inconceivable, something which can only be called a *true ubiquity*. In the same way perhaps the cryptophasia, rendered useless by the loss of the one person I could speak to, may merge into a universal language, similar to the one the Apostles were gifted with at Pentecost.

CHAPTER XVIII

Japanese Gardens

Paul

We cross the Arctic Circle and the sun, which swung like a lamp depending from a flex in the Icelandic sky, is motionless once more.

The polar lands—Greenland, four times the size of France, and then Alaska, three times the size of France—have all the things that go to make a proper country: plains, plateaus, rivers, cliffs, lakes, seas . . . At times one could be flying over the valley of the Seine, at others over the Pointe du Raz or the bare shoulders of the Puy de Dôme. But everything here is pure, uninhabited, uninhabitable, frozen, carved in ice. A country left in cold storage until the time comes for it to live and to bear life. A country held in reserve, preserved in ice for the future use of mankind. When the new man is born, then the protective covering of snow over this land will be withdrawn and it will be bestowed on him, brand-new and virginal, preserved for him from the beginning of time . . .

ANCHORAGE

An hour's stop, and the sun takes advantage to slide a degree
closer to the horizon. The aircraft decants its passengers through
a mobile tube into a hall of glass. We are not going to get a sniff
of the air of Anchorage. I am reminded of the greenhouses of
Hveragerdhi. But here the glass shelters only human beings. The
leap—from vegetable to man—must undoubtedly be made, but
not as crudely, as abruptly as this.

Another eight hours' flying and then there is Japan, proclaiming itself in the huge, graceful outline of Mount Fuji, draped
in its ermine cloak. Only then is the sun permitted to go to bed.

Shonin

Why carve with a hammer, a chisel or a saw? Why torment the
stone and make its soul despair? The artist is a beholder. The
artist carves with his eyes . . .

In the sixteenth century according to your calendar, General
Hideyoshi, going one day to pay a visit to a vassal who lived six
hundred miles to the north, noticed a wonderful stone in his garden. Its name was Fujito. He accepted it from his vassal as a
gift. Out of regard for its soul, he wrapped it in a sumptuous
piece of silk. Then it was placed in a magnificently decorated
wagon, drawn by twelve white oxen, and throughout the journey, which lasted for a hundred days, a band of musicians
played to it with sweetest melodies to calm its fears, stones being
by nature sedentary. Hideyoshi set Fujito in the garden of his
castle of Nijo, and later of his house at Jurakudai. Today it is
the principal stone—*o ishi*—of the Sambo-in, where it is still be
be seen.

The sculptor who is also a poet is not a breaker of stones. He
is a collector of stones. The shores of the 1,042 Nipponese islands
and the sides of our 783,224 mountains are strewn with an
infinite number of pebbles and fragments of rock. The beauty is
there, to be sure, but just as much buried and concealed as that
of the statue which your sculptor draws with taps of his mallet

out of the block of marble. To create this beauty, one has only to
know how to look. You will see in tenth-century gardens stones
selected at that period by collectors of genius. The style of those
stones is incomparable, inimitable. Of course, the Nipponese
beaches and mountains have not changed in nine centuries. The
same fragments of rock and the same pebbles are still strewn on
them. But the tool for collecting them has been lost forever: the
collector's eye. Stones like those will never be found again. And
the same is true of every inspired garden. The stones with which
it is filled are the work of an eye which, while leaving behind
the evidence of its genius, has carried away the secret of it forever.

Paul

Something which had been worrying me ever since the idea of
my going to Japan first arose fortunately solved itself the moment I set foot in the main hall of Tokyo airport. I had been
afraid that my Western eye, seeing no further than those features common to all yellow races, might lump all Japanese together in one seething, undifferentiated mass. It is a weakness
that appears in more than one Western traveler—"they all look
alike"—but for me it would have mattered vastly more. To be
honest, I was afraid of finding myself immersed in a society fea-
turing the unheard-of and alarming phenomenon of a *universal
twinship*. Surely no worse mockery could be imagined for a dispaired twin, going about the world grieving in search of his lost
brother, than to find himself suddenly the only non-twin amid a
countless host of identical twins? Fate could not have held a
crueler trick in store for me.

Well, it is not like that at all! The individual characters of the
Japanese are in no way obliterated by their racial characteristics.
There are no two people here I could not tell apart. What is
more, I find them physically attractive. I like their lithe, muscular bodies, their catlike gait—a stocky figure and short legs give
obvious advantages in the way of balance and relation—and I
like their eyes, so perfectly outlined that they seem always to be
wearing makeup, their hair, incomparable in its quality and

quantity, like a solid, black, shining helmet, and their children, strongly molded in smooth, rounded golden flesh. Moreover, the racial characteristics are clearer in the old people and the children so that they are nearly always more beautiful than the adults whom Westernization has made commonplace. But none of these general characteristics prevents me from distinguishing between *all* the people I encounter beyond any possible error. No, if this country has anything to teach me, it will not be in the crude guise of an entire race of twins. I must look rather to its gardens, its stones, sand and flowers.

Shonin

Garden, house, and man are a living organism which it is wrong to break up. The man must be there. The plants will only grow well under his loving eye. If the man quits his home for any reason at all, the garden withers and the house falls into ruin.

The house and garden should mingle closely with one another. Western gardens do not obey this law. The Western house is simply dumped down in the middle of a garden with which it has no sympathy or understanding. And this mutual ignorance gives rise to hostility and dislike. The wise man's house surrounds his garden with a series of light structures mounted on wooden piles which themselves rest on flat stones. Sliding panels, some translucent, some opaque, enclose a mobile area within which renders doors and windows unnecessary. House and garden breathe the same air, bask in the same light. In the traditional Japanese house there are no drafts, there is only the wind. A network of bridges and alleyways makes the house appear to melt into the garden. In fact, one cannot tell which of the two invades and absorbs the other. It is more than a happy marriage, it is a single entity.

The stones should never be simply laid on the ground. They must always be partly buried. For a stone has a head, a tail, and a back, and its belly needs the warm darkness of the earth. A stone is neither dead nor mute. It hears the crash of the waves, the ripple of the lake, the roaring of the torrent and it laments if it is unhappy, and that lament rends the heart of a poet.

There are two sorts of stones, standing stones and inclining stones. It is a grave error to incline a standing stone. As it is also —although less grave—to make an inclining stone stand erect. The tallest standing stone should never be higher than the floor of the house. A standing stone under a waterfall, with a hard, clear arm of the fall bursting in a myriad of droplets on its head, stands for the carp, an age-old fish. The standing stone captures the *kami* and filters out bad spirits. Inclining stones transmit energy along their horizontal axis toward their head. That is why that axis should never be turned to face the house. Generally speaking, the house is so oriented that its axes do not coincide with the axes of the stones. The geometrical strictness of the house contrasts with the curves and angles of the garden which are intended to neutralize the spirits emerging from the stones. The Western world has copied the systematic lack of alignment of the Japanese garden without understanding what it is for. A gully filled with pebbles below the overhang of the roof collects the rainwater. The pebbles are dull and gray when the sun is shining, but in the rain they become black and shining.

The stones in a garden are classed in three degrees of importance: the principal stones, the additional stones and the *Oku* stone. The additional stones escort the principal stone. They form a line behind the reclining stone, they are grouped about the base of the standing stone, they gather like a support below the inclined stone. The *Oku* stone is not visible. The final, intimate, secret touch which animates the whole composition, it can fulfill its mission while remaining unperceived, like the soul of the violin.

Paul

Driven out into the street at daybreak by the capriciousness of sleep, not having yet got over the change in time, I watch the city waking up. The perfect courtesy of passers-by in seeming not to notice the unaccustomed sight of a Westerner abroad in the streets at this early hour. Outside every restaurant is a metal bucket in which bundles of chopsticks used by last night's customers are being burned. This is their way of doing the washing

up. Watching the refuse trucks on their rounds, I am reminded
of Uncle Alexandre. He would have loved everything about the
garbage men and their equipment, baggy trousers stuffed into
extraordinary pliable black rubber boots which reach up to their
knees and have a thumb for the big toe—mittens for the feet, in
fact—with thick white gloves and a square of muslin to go over
the nose and mouth, kept in place by elastic around the ears. It
is like coming across a completely different species of man, designed by certain anatomical features—such as the divided, black
feet—to do the city's coarsest jobs. Equally coarse are the only
birds which inhabit the city, so far as I can see. These are crows
and I wonder if my ears are deceiving me because it seems to me
that the call of the Japanese crow is noticeably simpler than that
of its Western counterpart. However hard I listen, all I can hear
is *Ah! Ah! Ah!* uttered not like a merry laugh but on a note of
gloomy acquiescence. I'd give a lot to listen once again—just
once—to the soothing, melancholy silver chime of that mysterious
bird of the Icelandic night which I was apparently the only one
to hear. Some of the rooftops have poles on them with a gilded
windmill on the top and great carp made of multicolored cloth
with a tiny wicker basket for the gaping mouth flying from them.
This is because the fifth of May is the day they celebrate the
feast of young boys and each carp stands for a male child in the
household. Something else that would have delighted my shocking uncle . . . Nothing could be gayer than the huge rosettes
made of pleated paper that I see being carried in procession. Unfortunately that is a crude, barbarian misunderstanding: the procession is a funeral and the rosettes are the equivalent of our
wreaths. The sacred deer of Nara turn up faithfully but I must
confess that I am disappointed in them; worse, I even find them
slightly revolting. They are so tame and well-fed and have such
cadging ways that they are like fat, wheedling mendicant friars,
right down to their brown and cream habits. The cats and dogs
have better manners. No, I expect these graceful animals to be
proud, timid, slender and to keep their distance. There is ultimately something flabby and repulsive about the traditional picture of the earthly paradise in which all creatures live peaceably

with one another and with man in a simple, idyllic promiscuity, probably because it is entirely against nature.

Shonin

The stones stand for certain mystical animals which share with them a superhuman longevity. They are the phoenix, the elephant, the toad, the deer with a child on its back. One rock is a dragon's head holding a pearl in its mouth; two small shrubs serve it for horns. But the fundamental rock animals of the Japanese garden are the crane and the tortoise. The tortoise is often represented with a long tail made of a bunch of seaweed at the end of his shell, like a wise man's beard. The crane is the transcendental bird that speaks with the spirits of the sun. The tortoise and the crane symbolize the body and the spirit, the *Yin* and the *Yang*.

These two principles divide the garden equally between them and they should be in equilibrium. If the visitor to the house turns his gaze to the south and looks at the waterfall on the other side of the lake, then the western side of the fall is on his right. In the *Ghinden* dwelling, that is the women's side, the dowager's, the private, domestic, and impure part, belonging to the earth, the domain dedicated to autumn, to the harvest and to nourishment, to the shadow, in short to the Yin. The eastern half is on the left. That is the prince's domain, given over to men, to ceremony and entertainment, the public zone, associated with the sun, the spring, the martial arts, in short to the Yang.

There are two kinds of waterfall. Leaping waterfalls and creeping waterfalls. Both ought to issue from a dark, hidden place. The water should seem to well up out of the stones, like a spring. The experts who built one of the waterfalls of the Sambo-in at Kyoto in the sixteenth century worked for more than twenty years to complete it. But today it is considered to have succeeded perfectly, in particular because of its incomparable music. Bad spirits move in a straight course from northeast to southwest and therefore running water ought to take account of this direction, because its task is to take charge of the bad spirits and, after it has gone around the house, to assist in their evacuation.

Paul

At four twenty-five this morning there was a slight seismic tremor. A few minutes afterward came a violent hailstorm. What connection was there between the two events? None, probably. But that does not prevent the mind, terrified by hostile manifestations it cannot understand, from making them still more fearful by putting them together. Can there be a link of cause and effect between the two disasters? Yes, answers my teacher, Shonin. Because the typhoon comes from the movement of a very small zone of intense depression which, instead of being filled by the atmosphere, generates an eddy of wind on its periphery from the influence of the earth's rotation. Now, assuming that in certain parts of the earth's surface, where the telluric pressure is weak, the balance is maintained by atmospheric pressure, it is reasonable to suppose that a sudden, steep drop in atmospheric pressure over a small area would produce a disturbance of the balance and trigger off an earthquake.

Typhoons, earthquakes . . . I cannot help seeing a relationship between these convulsions of earth and sky and the art of gardening which unites those very elements according to subtle and meticulous rules. Is it not said that when the sages and poets turned aside from the major elements in order to devote themselves to minute areas of space, the sky and the earth, left to their own devices, returned to the tremendous primitive games they had indulged in before man came on the scene, or at least before his history began? These cataclysms might even be seen as the rage and grief of monstrous children angered by the indifference of men, who have turned away from them, intent on their own tiny creations.

Shonin replied that there was some truth in my opinions, although they were far too subjective. The art of gardens, situated at the point of union between earth and sky, actually went beyond the simple desire to create a perfect balance between human and cosmic space. Nor was the West entirely ignorant of this function of human art, for the house offered its services in contriving the nonviolent transfer of the fires of heaven down to the center of the earth by means of the lightning conductor. But the ambitions of the Japanese landscape artist were loftier, his knowledge wiser, and the risks he ran consequently much greater. Djerba and Hveragerdhi had already given me instances of daringly paradoxical creations constantly threatened with annihilation—and even as I write I can confirm that the desert dunes have already closed over Deborah's fairy-tale garden. The balance which the Japanese had created between human and cosmic space, these gardens situated at their point of contact, constituted a wiser, more ordered undertaking in which failures were fewer—theoretically even impossible—but when the impossible did take place, earth and sky seemed seized with a mad frenzy.

This balance—which is called serenity when it wears a human face—seems to me, in fact, to be the fundamental value of Eastern religion and philosophy. It is extraordinary that this idea of serenity should have so small a place in the Christian world. The story of Jesus is full of crying, weeping and sudden dramas. The religions that have sprung from it have wrapped themselves in a dramatic atmosphere which makes serenity look lukewarm, like indifference or even stupidity. The failure and discrediting of Madame Guyon's quietism in the seventeenth century provides a good illustration of Western contempt for all values that do not relate to action, energy and emotional tension.

These thoughts came to me when I visited the gigantic Buddha of Kamakura. What a far cry from the Christian crucifix! The forty-five-foot-high bronze figure, standing in the open air in the middle of a wonderful park, radiates gentleness, protective power and lucid intelligence. The top half is bending a little forward in an attitude of attentive and benevolent welcome. The huge ears, their lobes ritually distended, have heard everything, understood everything, remembered everything. But the heavy lids droop over eyes which decline to judge or to punish. The robe is open at the front, revealing a plump, soft chest which seems to have something of both sexes. The hands resting in the lap are as idle and useless as the legs folded in the lotus position, like a plinth. Children laugh and play in the Founder's shadow. Whole families have themselves photographed in front of him.

Who would ever think of having his picture taken in front of
Christ crucified?

Shonin

The gardens we have been talking about so far were tea gardens,
made for strolling with friends, for spiritual argument, for making love.

There are other gardens in which no one ever sets foot, where
only the eye is allowed to wander, where only ideas meet and
embrace. These are the austere Zen gardens, intended to be
viewed from one predetermined point, usually the veranda of
the house.

A Zen garden is to be read like a poem of which only a few
half lines are written and it is up to the sagacity of the reader to
fill in the blanks. The author of a Zen garden knows that the
poet's function is not to feel inspiration on his own account but
to arouse it in the soul of the reader. That is why contradictions
sometimes seem to run riot among its admirers. The samurai
praises its fiery, brutal simplicity. The philosopher its exquisite
subtlety. The lover shows what intoxicating consolation it
affords. But the most striking paradox of the Zen garden lies in
the contrast between wet and dry. Nothing is apparently drier
than that expanse of white sand with one, two or three rocks arranged upon it. Yet in reality, nothing is wetter. Because the
skillful undulations imprinted in the sand by the monk's fifteen-
toothed steel rake are none other than the waves, wavelets and
ripples of the infinite sea. The stones that strew the narrow alley
leading to the garden do not suggest the dry bed of a mountain
stream but on the contrary the boisterous eddies of the water.
Even the very bank set with slabs of stone is really a dry waterfall, petrified and immobilized in an instant. The sandy lake, the
stone stream, the dry waterfall, a gaunt, clipped shrub, two rocks
heaving up their twisted backs, these niggardly materials, dis-
posed in a carefully prearranged pattern, are merely the canvas
upon which the beholder can embroider his own private landscape and give it his own style, are merely a mold into which to
pour his mood of the moment and make it serene. In its apparent

bareness, the Zen garden contains potentially all the seasons of the year, all the countries of the world and all states of the soul.

Sometimes the Zen garden looks out over a natural landscape, sometimes it is enclosed upon itself with walls or panels, sometimes, again, there are windows cut in the walls or panels to allow occasional glimpses of some carefully selected piece of nature. The interrelationship between the Zen garden and the natural environment cannot be too precisely calculated. The classic solution consists of a low, terra-cotta-colored wall topped with a ridge of tiles erected on the opposite side from the viewing gallery, which defines the garden without enclosing it and allows the eye to roam over the foliage of the trees but not to lose itself amid the irregularities of the rough ground.

Just as an actor in the Kabuki plays the part of a woman with more itensity than any actress, so the imaginary elements in a garden produce a *fuzei* more subtle in essence than the real elements would do.

Paul

I came out of the temple of Sanjusangendo, where I had been walking in the covered gallery among the thousand life-sized statues of the merciful goddess Kannon. That regiment of identical goddesses with their twelve arms forming a breast-high corona like an echo of the sunburst halo blossoming behind their heads, that gilded wooden host, that thousand times reiterated litany, that vertiginous repetition . . . there, yes, but only there, did I experience again the fear of an infinitely multiplied twinship which I had when I first landed in Japan. Shonin, my teacher, soon disabused me of that illusion, however. These idols are identical only to the crude eye of the profane Westerner who can only add up and compare accidental attributes. In reality the statues are perfectly distinguishable from one another, if only by the position they occupy in space, which is peculiar to each. Because that is the fundamental mistake of Western thought: space is considered as a homogeneous environment, having no intimate relationship to the essence of things, and consequently they can be moved about, arranged and rearranged with impunity. Per-

haps the terrible *efficiency* of the West springs from this rejection of space as a complex, living organism, but it is also the
source of all its troubles. The idea that one can do and place
anything anywhere, a fearful prejudice, may be both the secret
of our power and our curse . . .

That encounter with the thousand twin statues of Sanjusangendo was an excellent preparation for another that touched me
far more closely. After leaving the temple, I strolled about a little in the pedestrian precinct that surrounds it, among the
doughnut stalls, the barbers, bathhouses and secondhand shops.
Until I came upon a canvas displayed among a jumble of other
furniture and ornaments and stood rooted in fascinated surprise.
The canvas was in a wholly Western style, although with some
slight, superficial Japanese touches, *and it was a perfect likeness
of Jean.*

In Venice, in Djerba and in Iceland, as I have said, I came
upon my twin's trail in an exclusively geminate fashion through
the appearance in a more or less pure and vivid form of that
alienating light which was both wounding and reassuring to me
at once. Now that phenomenon had already failed to occur in
Djerba, with Tanizaki alone—although all the conditions were
right for it. And since I have been in Japan I have not once
caught a flash of the light I am searching for so feverishly, despite the pain it gives me. I know now that Japan—the Japanese
—are absolutely proof against the phenomenon, and thanks to
the thousand goddesses of Sanjusangendo I am beginning to understand why.

I went into the antique shop. The girl in the kimono, her hair
drawn into the traditional chignon, toward whom I was making
did not move as I approached, and I saw a little man in a black
silk shirt pop out from behind a curtain and bow several times.
My likeness to the portrait on display was so obvious that I was
expecting some reaction of surprise or amusement, something at
any rate corresponding to the "light" and more distantly related
to what Jean and I used to call the "circus." But there was nothing of the kind, not even when I led the shopkeeper up to the
picture and inquired about the author of it. He preserved an
enigmatic smile, lifted his bony little palms to the ceiling and

shook his head with an expression of regretful helplessness. In short, he knew nothing about the artist whose signature was confined to the two initials U.K. At last I could not resist asking the question that was burning on the tip of my tongue.

"Don't you think the person in the picture looks like me?"

He appeared surprised, intrigued and amused. He studied me, then looked at the portrait, then at me again and at the portrait. Considering the glaring likeness between the two faces—mine and the painted one—there was something almost lunatic in his behavior. Then, becoming suddenly serious, he shook his head.

"No, really, I cannot see it. Oh, there is a faint similarity no doubt . . . but then all Westerners look alike."

It was infuriating. I left hurriedly. My eye was caught by a garish, neon-lit Pashinko hall, full of noisy bells and the chink of metal. I got rid of the handful of tokens I bought as I went in in record time. Perhaps after all it was not the desire for a moment's pleasurable enjoyment that kept all those young men glued so tensely and feverishly to their glass-fronted machines with a revolving colored disk or a set of trundling steel balls inside, but the wish to get a dreary chore over and done with as fast as possible? Out into the street again. What now? Back to the hotel? But the antique market drew me irresistibly. I went back. The portrait was no longer on display. Decidedly, I still had a great deal to learn if I was going to live peacefully and serenely in this strange land! I was on the point of moving off when I noticed a girl in a gray raincoat who seemed to be waiting for me. It took me a moment to recognize the Japanese girl in traditional costume whom I had seen earlier inside the shop. She came up to me and said, her eyes on the ground, "I have to talk to you. Please, may we walk together?"

Her name is Kumiko Sakamoto. She had been the girlfriend of a German painter called Urs Kraus. A month ago my brother was living with them at Kumiko's father's junk shop.

Shonin

A collector of pebbles at Lo-Yang possessed a *k'ouai* stone, set on white sand in a pool of clear water three feet long and seven

inches deep. Ordinarily, stones only manifest their inner life dis-
creetly and to the eyes of the wise alone. But this stone had so
much spirit dwelling in it that it seeped out despite itself at
every pore. It was riddled with it, ravined, pitted and grooved,
it had valleys, gorges, gulfs, peaks and canyons. It listened and
marked through a thousand ears, blinked and wept with a thousand eyes, laughed and sang with a thousand mouths. What was
to happen, happened. The seed of a pine tree, drawn by such a
hospitable nature, came and settled on it. It settled on the *k'ouai*
stone and instantly slipped inside it. Like a mole into its tunnel,
like an embryo into the womb, like the sperm into the vagina.
And the pine cone germinated. And the seed, whose power is colossal because all the strength of the tree is concentrated in it,
split the stone. And out of the crack wriggled a young pine,
bending and writhing like a dragon dancing. The stone and the
pine share the same essence, which is eternity, the stone indestructible and the pine evergreen. The stone surrounded and embraced the pine like a mother her child. After that there was a
continual exchange between them. The sturdy pine cracked and
split the stone to nourish itself. But after three thousand years its
roots became rock and fused into the stone from which they
were born.

Paul

Kumiko met Urs in Munich. He was a mechanical draftsman and
copied working drawings of rods, gears and screws onto graph
paper in plan, section and elevation. She was a secretary in an
import-export business. By day, that is. Because at night he
painted portraits, nudes and still lifes, and she devoted herself to
Zen philosophy. When she returned to her father in Nara, he
went with her.

I have seen a score or so of the pictures he painted during the
two years he spent in Japan. They reflect the slow, laborious
penetration of the lesson of the East into the dual world of the
mechanical draftsman and Sunday painter. The East, which appears initially in the form of folklore—or even tourism—gradually
creeps into these naïve, meticulous paintings, losing all its pictur-

esqueness until it ceases to be anything but a particularly penetrating vision of people and things.

One of his pictures—painted in bright, hyper-realistic detail—depicts a building site with busy little men in blue overalls and yellow helmets. Concrete mixers tip back their revolving drums and gape skyward, open-mouthed, sheaves of piping run into silver cisterns, tongues of flame stream out from blazing torches and cranes, derricks and blast furnaces are silhouetted on the skyline. And what is the product of all this frenzied industry? Quite simply, Fujiyama. An engineer holds a plan showing the famous volcano complete with its collar of snow. Laborers are carrying plates that are clearly portions of the thing under construction and its unfinished shape is just discernible behind the scaffolding.

Another canvas features the same marriage between tradition and the industrial age, only the other way around. We are in a vast modern city bristling with high-rise apartments, girdled with hover-trains and ringed about with highways. There are even flights of helicopters and little airplanes in the sky. But it is peopled weirdly by a crowd that seems to have escaped out of the prints of Hokusai. There are old men with bald sugar-loaf domes and long, thin, straggling, snaky beards, babies with hair tied in bunches pushing against each other and waving their bare bottoms in the air, a team of oxen driven by a monkey, a tiger lying on the roof of a truck, and a bonze holding a peach while a child tries to take it from him.

This medley, pure and simple, of the old Japan and the youthful West is expressed with more depth in a series of small landscapes, each one of which is an exciting poetical enigma. The hills, woods and riverbanks are bare of buildings or of human life so that theoretically there is no reason why they should be set in Japan any more than in Swabia, Sussex or the Limousin, either in the species of trees, in the configuration of the landscape or in the color or movement of the water. And yet from the first glance there is no doubting for a moment that this is Japan. Why and by what test? It is impossible to tell, and yet the certainty is there, instant, unshakable, and with no justification at all: it is Japan.

"Urs had made a great deal of progress when he finished that series," Kumiko observed.

Indeed he had! He had managed to catch an essence, a cipher in everything, relating it directly to the cosmos, something simpler and more profound than all the attributes, colors, qualities and other properties that follow from this relationship, which we normally go by. In these canvases, the Japanese landscape was no longer cherry trees in blossom, Mount Fuji and the pagoda or the little humpbacked bridge. Going beyond those movable, interchangeable, imitable symbols, here was the cosmic formula of Japan, the outcome of a vertiginous but by no means infinite number of coordinates, made sensible and obvious but at the same time explicit and inexplicable. In every picture one was vaguely aware of the hidden presence of that formula. Its effect was emotional but not informative. It was spilling over with promises but did not really fulfill any of them. The phrase that comes to my pen is the spirit of the place. But perhaps the image that conjures up is one of a little sunshine filtering through a thick mist?

It was in the portraits that this somewhat metaphysical insight was at its most remarkable. Portraits of children, of old men, of young women, but most of all portraits of Kumiko. In the girl's case, the face I saw on the canvases was undoubtedly that of the youthful twenty-year-old I knew. But when you looked more closely it was bathed in a light that was timeless, ageless, eternal perhaps, yet still alive. Yes, that twenty-year-old face was ageless, or rather it was all ages and you could see in it the inexhaustible tolerance of the grandmother who in a long life has seen and suffered and forgiven all, as well as the radiant delight of the child just waking to the world, and the piercing clarity of the adolescent who has cut her teeth. How could Urs Kraus have united such contradictory expressions, except by going out and gathering the spark of life at its very source, at the point where all the implications are still combined in the potential state—and it is up to the spectator to pursue whichever soul has an affinity with his own.

Shonin

One morning the people in the marketplace of Hamamatsu noticed that their provost, Fei Chang-fang, who used to oversee the market from a raised platform, was not in his usual place. They never saw him again and no one ever knew what had become of him. It was not until another week had passed that they noticed someone else had also disappeared, an old man, a seller of simples and a stranger to the town, who would sit without moving under the gourds of all sizes that hung from the roof of his stall. For you must know that to us the gourd is like a horn of plenty and since medicines, also, are kept either in small gourds or else in gourd-shaped flasks it is also the emblem of healing. It would have taken a very wise man to have connected these two disappearances and penetrated the secret of them. For this is what had happened.

High on his platform, Fei Chang-fang had seen the herb seller, in the evening after the market was closed, make himself suddenly as small as small could be and creep into the smallest of his gourds. He was so much amazed that the very next day he went to him and bowed three times and presented him with meat and wine. Then, knowing that all deceit would be in vain, he confessed that he had chanced to observe the strange metamorphosis which enabled him to vanish every evening into his smallest gourd.

"You did well to come tonight," the old man told him. "For tomorrow I shall no longer be here. I am a genie. I did wrong in the eyes of my fellows and they condemned me, for one season, to put on the guise of an herb seller by day. By night, I am permitted a repose more fitting to my nature. But today is the last of my exile. Do you wish to come with me?"

Fei Chang-fang accepted. The genie touched him on the shoulder and at once he felt himself become the size of a gnat, and his companion with him. That done, they went into the gourd.

Within there grew a garden of jade. Silver cranes disported themselves in a lake of lapis lazuli surrounded by coral trees. Up in the sky there was a pearl for a moon, diamonds for the sun and gold dust for the stars. At the center of the garden was a cave made of mother-of-pearl. Milky stalactites hung from its roof and from them a quintessential ichor was dripping. The genie invited Fei Chang-fang to take suck from the cavern for, said he, you are only a very little child in comparison with the antiquity of the garden, and this milk will give you a long life.

But the most precious teaching that he gave him is contained in this precept: *Possession of the world begins with the concentration of the subject and ends with that of the object.*

That is why the Zen garden leads logically to the miniature garden.

Paul

Urs has left eleven portraits of Jean here. Kumiko's father, frightened by my visit and my inquisitorial manner, had hidden the revealing collection behind a screen. Kumiko arranged them in a semicircle around me in the shop. I am beginning to understand what happened. I asked Kumiko where Urs was. She answered me with the little smothered laugh that the Japanese use to apologize for alluding to a painful and intimate subject.

"Urs? Gone!"

"Gone? With Jean?"

"After Jean."

"Where to?"

She made an evasive gesture. "Over there. To the West. To America, perhaps. To Germany."

Although he had met her in Munich, Urs was born in Berlin. I thought I had found a clue in a picture which, from its crude, naïve idiom, seemed to belong to Kraus's earliest Japanese manner. It was an expanse of water plowed in all directions by a variety of ships. To right and left, upon either shore, two children stood facing one another with legs astride. Their faces were hidden by the binoculars which they were directing at each other. I shivered, because of the episode in our childhood when we made an advertising film for a brand of binoculars.

"Kumiko, who are those children?"

A helpless gesture. "But the water is the Pacific Ocean," she added. "So the shore to the left, with the docks and things, must be Yokohama, and the shore on the right, with the trees on it, Vancouver."

"Vancouver or San Francisco?"

"Vancouver, because of Stanley Park. It's famous. The big maples come right down to the water. To the Japanese, Vancouver is the gateway to the West."

That is true. While the drift of all human migrations used to be from east to west—following the direction of the sun—in the past twenty-five years the Japanese have been migrating in the opposite direction. Abandoning their incursions into Korea, China, and Russia, they have turned to the Pacific and the New World, first as armed conquerors and then as businessmen. That was something that would suit my carder-brother! Jean in Vancouver? Why not? That famous city which nobody knows would be just like him! But why had Urs Kraus gone after him?

I search the eleven portraits which must hold the answers to these questions. Rarely has the initial spark that is the wellspring of every human being been so brutally laid bare. And as I learn from them to understand my brother—getting to know him better and better through those eleven stages—so I recognize myself there less and less. I am gradually coming around to the Japanese point of view which is inimical to the alienating light and claims to perceive no resemblance between these portraits and myself. If that is what Jean really looks like now, then it must be admitted that his morbid instability and his burning passion for new horizons have altered his appearance profoundly in a very short while. All I see in that face is a frantic wanderlust that turns to panic whenever a stay anywhere threatens to become too prolonged. It is a ship's prow worn by the waves, a figurehead eroded by the spray, the profile of an eternal migrant sharpened by the winds. There is something of the arrow and the greyhound in it, and it reflects nothing but a fury to be gone, an itch for speed and for a mad flight to some unknown destination. Wind, wind and more wind is all that is left in that brow, those eyes and that mouth. It has ceased to be a face and become a compass. Is it possible that Sophie's going and this long journey have so simplified my brother? It is as though he were breaking up and would disintegrate altogether in the end, like those meteorites that dissolve in a blaze of fire upon contact with the atmosphere, to vanish entirely before they reach the earth. The sense of a continual enrichment which, on the contrary, I feel that I am gaining with every stage, throws more light on this fate of my brother's. Our pursuit takes on a terrifying logic and significance: I am growing fat on the substance he is losing, I am incorporating my fleeing brother into myself . . .

Shonin

After conversation and contemplation comes communion. Miniature gardens correspond to a third stage in the interiorization of the earth. Whereas the Western house is in the garden and the Zen garden in the house, the miniature garden may be held in the hand of the master of the house.

It is not enough for the tree to be small, it must also appear very old. Therefore you choose the most stunted seed from the weakest plants. You sever the main roots and put the plants to grow in a tight pot. Then you twist the stem and branches gradually so that they become knotted. Thereafter, prune, pinch out, twist and cut back the branches regularly. Bending the branches with the aid of wires and weights will give them a sinuous shape. You make holes in the trunk and insert croton into them, which will have the effect of making them supple, flexible and easy to manipulate. To give the branches a jagged line, you make a cut in the bark and introduce a drop of *golden juice*. (Cut a bamboo tube so as to keep two joints in it and leave it for a year in a cesspool. The liquid it contains then is *golden juice*.)

The contortions of the dwarf trees, acquired with such pains, are synonymous with great age. In the same way the Taoist engages in arduous exercises of his limbs simply in order to lengthen the progress of the breath of life through his body and so achieve longevity. The twistings of the dwarf trees suggest similar choreographic figures. The Taoist bends over backward—hollowing his back—so that he is looking at the sky. Dancers, sorcerers, dwarfs and magicians are all recognizable by the deformations and deformities which make them look up at the sky. The crane by stretching up its neck, the tortoise by extending it refine their breath, increase their range and gain in longevity. It is for this reason—and no other—that the old man's gnarled stick is a sign of great age.

Dwarf trees may be cypress, catalpa, juniper, chestnut, peach, plum, willow, fig, banyan, pine . . . On a grave, a willow or poplar is planted for a peasant, an acacia for a scholar, a cypress for a feudal lord, a pine for a Son of Heaven. The grave is a house, a mountain, an island, the whole universe.

The dwarf garden, the smaller it is, the greater the part of the world it embraces. Thus, for example, with the porcelain figure, the clay animal, the terra-cotta pagoda that inhabit the miniature garden, the smaller they are, the greater is their magical power to transform the pebbles and hollows around them into rocky mountains, dizzy pinacles, lakes and precipices. So the scholar in his humble home, the poet at his desk and the hermit in his cave can possess the whole universe at will. They have only to concentrate enough to disappear into the miniature garden, like the apothecary-genie into his gourd. Furthermore, by dwarfing the landscape, one acquires an increasing magical power. Evil is banished from it and its dwarf foliage breathes an eternal youth. Which is why the most eminent sages may be supposed to possess gardens so small that no one can suspect their existence. So small that they can stand on a fingernail, so small that they can be enclosed in a medallion. From time to time, the sage takes a medallion from his pocket. He lifts the lid. A tiny garden is revealed where baobabs and banyans grow around immense lakes joined by humpbacked bridges. And the sage, become all at once the size of a poppy seed, strolls delightedly in a space as vast as the heavens and the earth.

(Some gardens are set in pools and represent an island. Often they consist of a porous stone—or a piece of coral—into which the root hairs of the dwarf tree grow, creating the most intimate fusion of water, stone and plant.

Because Japan is made up of a thousand and forty-two islands, the garden in a pool is the most Japanese of all miniature gardens.)

CHAPTER XIX

The Vancouver Seal

Paul

I watch the handful of scattered islands, big and small, which is called Japan grow smaller and merge into the deep blue of the Pacific. Japan Airlines flight 012 links Tokyo and Vancouver in ten hours and thirty-five minutes' flying time on Mondays, Wednesdays, and Fridays. The time change is six hours and twenty minutes.

Vacuum and plenum. Instructed by Shonin, my soul oscillates between these two extremes. The Japanese are haunted by the fear of suffocation. Too many men, too many things, too many signs, not enough room. A Japanese is first and foremost an over-crowded man. (There are the often-quoted "shovers" on the underground railway, whose job is to stuff travelers into the coaches by main force, since otherwise they would prevent the doors from closing. If that were the whole of their task, it would be an infernal one, contributing to the process of suffocation. But the shovers in are also pullers out. For when a train stops, the doors are able to open, but the travelers, wedged in a compact mass, are incapable of getting out by themselves. It takes the vigorous efforts of those assigned to the job to pluck them out of the lump of humanity and restore a certain ease of movement.)

To remedy this dread, there is only the garden and it is a fact that the Japanese garden is the one place in Japan where one can live and stretch oneself. But this is only true in the highest degree in the tea garden. With the Zen garden, an abstract void is created in which the thoughts can range, aided by occasional landmarks. As for the miniature garden, it brings cosmic infinity into the house.

Through all these hours of flying over the Pacific, one image has haunted me continually. It is an *empty* room with a surface area calculated to be covered by an exact number of tatamis—which invariably measure three feet by six, which is what a Japanese needs to lie on. And the dull gold color of the mats—kept clean and new—reflects more light than the dark wooden ceiling. The light, quivering, translucent screens—like a living skin—are, of course, completely bare. Not a picture, not an ornament, only a single piece of furniture, a small red lacquered table on which stands the miniature garden. All is in readiness for the sage squatting on his mat to give himself up to unseen orgies of willpower.

Yet the dominant impression of my stay in Japan is an uncomfortable one and the lessons to be drawn from it are enigmatic. It is the memory of the tortures inflicted in a variety of subtle ways upon the trees in order to miniaturize them and reduce them forcibly to the scale of the potted gardens.

VANCOUVER

First sight of the suburbs of Vancouver is through the narrow window of the monstrous metal bus, built like a tank, which brought us from the airport. A livelier, more colorful and heterogeneous city than Tokyo. Sex films, shady bars, furtive figures, sodden refuse on the pavements, all that residue of people and things which is the greatest charm of travel in some people's eyes. And, lest you should forget the nearness of the sea, here and there a gull, motionless upon a post, bollard or rooftop.

The uniform yellow of Japan is diversified here into at least four varieties, although it probably takes a little experience to distinguish them at a glance. The largest group consists of the population of Chinatown, who rarely venture beyond their own districts. Then there are the Japanese—mostly in transit and recognizable by an indefinably foreign and temporary air. You can tell the Indians, like wizened young mummies in clothes that are too big and floating on them and with little bright black eyes gleaming from below their broad-brimmed hats. But most easily recognizable are the Eskimos, with their characteristic long heads, coarse hair growing low on their foreheads and especially their broad, plump cheeks. Obesity is widespread in this country, but the fat of the Eskimos is different from the whites'. The latter is made of pastries and ice cream. The Eskimo's has an aroma of fish and smoked meat.

A salmon thrusting powerfully upstream, leaping dams and breasting rapids . . . That was how I saw myself landing in Vancouver. Because I have never felt so distinctly the sense of approaching a country back to front. Vancouver is the natural terminus of the long east-west migration that starts from Europe and crosses the Atlantic Ocean and the North American continent. It is a city not of beginnings but of endings. Paris, London, New York are all cities of beginnings. The newcomer to them is given a kind of baptism and is prepared for a new life, full of strange discoveries. The same may be true of Vancouver as far as the Japanese arriving in a Western country are concerned. That point of view is wholly alien to me. The movement of the sun from east to west drew the barbarian adventurers out of Poland, England and France and ever onward, across Quebec, Ontario, Manitoba, Saskatchewan, Alberta and British Columbia. When they reached this shore with its stagnant waters shaded by pines and maples, the long westward march was over. There was nothing more for them to do but sit down and admire the sunset. For the sea at Vancouver is shut in. These shores extend no invitation to take ship and sail out to explore the Pacific. The view is

Gemini

blocked by Vancouver Island, as though by a stopper. No revivi-
fying breath from the high seas is ever going to come to fill their
lungs and swell their sails. There is no going on. But I, no, I am
arriving . . .

"This is my kind of city!" Urs Kraus sighs, stopping to gaze up at
the sky.
  It rained all night and then at dawn the curtain of black
clouds began to break up. Now they are splitting into ragged
piles with cracks of blue opening between them where the sun is
bursting through. The tall wet trees in Stanley Park are shaking
themselves in the wind, like dogs after a swim, and their woody
smell which already has autumn in it clashes with the reek of
mud and seaweed rising from the beach. Nowhere else have I encountered this strange marriage of sea and forest.
  "Just look at it," he says, waving his arm. "You'd have to be
mad to leave that. Yet I'm going away! I'm always going away!"
  Walking along the beach strewn with old tree stumps polished
like pebbles, we are halted by a little group of strollers pointing
field glasses and telephoto lenses out to sea. On a rock about two
hundred yards away, a seal stares back at us.
  "There!" Kraus exclaims. "That seal is just like me. He is fascinated by Vancouver. Yesterday's high tide washed him up onto
that rock. And ever since he has been goggling out of his little
beady eyes at this city which is quick and dead at once, at these
suspicious-looking people in the distance, this place which is
journey's end for Westerners and a jumping-off point for the
Japanese . . . Apparently a seal in Vancouver is rather rare. His
picture was on the front page of all the local newspapers this
morning. He'll have to go away sometime, won't he? But you see
the tide is out now. His rock is quite a long way out of the water.
He could jump in. But then he couldn't get up again. So he is
waiting for the tide to come in. When the water comes up and
tickles his tummy, he'll do a bit of fishing for his dinner. Then
he'll go back to his lookout post before it goes down again. That
could go on for a long time. But not forever. He'll tear himself
away and go. And so will I."
  We have resumed our walk between the woods and the sea.

The sky is all one luminous devastation now, vapory castles top-pling and snow-white squadrons charging furiously. Against this dramatic backdrop, families are sitting down to picnic, baby carriages bouncing on their high wheels, and bicycles are silhou-etted as they pass.

"Have you noticed the endless variety of Canadian bicycles? Handlebars, saddles, wheels, frames, every part is capable of infinite variations. I'm still a draftsman at heart and I find it enchanting. Canadian bicycles are bought to order. You go to the dealer and build up your own machine by choosing its com-ponents from the wonderful collection in the shop. I have always been interested in bicycles because there is no other machine so accurately designed to fit the anatomy of the human body and the way it is powered. The bicycle is the ideal marriage between man and machine. Unfortunately in Europe—and particularly in France—cycling as a sport has made a stereotype of the bike and killed off all creativity in this remarkable field."

We sit down in the shelter of a tree trunk as big as a house. Is it part of a sequoia, or a monkey puzzle or a baobab? It must have been here for a long time because it is deeply embedded in the sand and there are great cracks gouged in it. Urs reverts to his pet subject.

"It changed my life the day I realized that where a thing, or a person, was positioned in space was not simply an accident but, on the contrary, affected its very nature. In short, that *there can be no transference without change.* That contradicts geometry, physics and mechanics, all of which first and foremost presup-pose an empty, undifferentiated space within which any move-ment, shift and permutation is possible without producing any significant alteration in the objects so moved. You had the same revelation, you told me, among the thousand gold statues of San-jusangendo. And immediately afterward you happened to come across one of the portraits I painted of your brother, and like it or not you finally admitted that, in spite of its strict accuracy, the portrait was not like you. You explained the paradox to yourself by deciding that what the portrait showed was essentially the inner nature of Carder-Jean, dedicated to a perpetual schism. That was not bad. A simpler and so more elegant explanation would have been to have admitted that it portrayed, along with your brother, the infinite complexity of the position he occupied in space. Because you'll admit that that position is strictly personal: however alike two twins may be, they are distinguished by their position in space—short of superimposing one upon the other exactly. And since Jean left you and fled around the world, a basic dissimilarity, aggravated by every mile, would be in danger of turning you into strangers if you did not set yourself not merely to travel the same journey but actually to follow in his very footsteps. That is true, isn't it? The reason you are chasing Jean is certainly to find him, but in a more subtle and exacting sense than is usually given to the word. It would not satisfy you at all to be told that Jean was going to come back to you after he had been around the world. Because if he were to come back to you at the end of an immense journey you had not made yourself, you would not only not be sure of 'finding' him, you know that you would have lost him forever. Everything he gains, everything he experiences on his journey, it is vital to you that you should have it after him. That's it, isn't it?"

I put a finger to my lips and, raising my hand, point silently to a fissure in the trunk above us. Urs looks, takes off his glasses, wipes them and puts them back on his nose. It is certainly enough to make one doubt one's eyes. There is someone there! A man, a young man is fast asleep above our heads. His body is curled snugly into a long groove in the trunk, nearly invisible because of the way its wooden couch is folded around it, the way it merges with the ligneous form, is cradled by the great maternal stem.

Urs remarks softly, "In some old German tales there are those woodland creatures with branches for hair and roots for toes. This is like a variation on the Babes in the Wood. The boy in the wood. That's Vancouver all over!"

I found him without much difficulty in this city, which is not unduly large and every quarter of it has its own special character. I knew from Kumiko that he had brought a number of canvases with him in the hope of making a living selling them on the way. I went the rounds of the few galleries in Gastown which might have been interested in his work. I recognized one of his pictures at once, at the back of the third one, by the flatness of its style—without depth or relief—and its crude, flat colors, reminiscent of strip cartoons. He had left the address of a modest hotel in the Robsonstrasse. I went there directly.

Urs Kraus is a gentle giant with red hair and a milky complexion who seems doomed by his very size to be a butt, a victim, a tame bear used from infancy to being led by the nose. What a strange couple he and the diminutive Kumiko must have made! His pictures, nonetheless, are the work of a real painter, and almost certainly he owes it to her. But this painter is unlike any other I have known, if only because of the one peculiarity that he is a painter who talks. Urs holds forth passionately and unendingly; it must answer some need for self-expression, self-defense, and his remarkable gift for languages is an extension of it, because this German speaks English fluently, had made, according to Kumiko, a brilliant start on Japanese, and conversed with me entirely in French.

"As a painter," he explains to me, "I am *involved*, fundamentally involved. It is my whole strength and my whole weakness. I told you how it all started. When I was a draftsman, space was a purely negative concept to me. It was *distance*, that is to say it was the way that things were kept *apart* from one another. Across this gap the coordinate axes threw threadlike bridges.

"With Zen, everything changed. Space became a solid, complete substance, rich in qualities and attributes. And things were islets cut out of the substance, made *of* it, movable, certainly, but only on condition that the movement was accompanied and recorded by all the relations between their substance and the substance outside themselves. Suppose that you were able to isolate a liter of sea water and move it from Vancouver to Yokohama without taking it out of the sea or putting it into anything other than a completely permeable envelope. That is what it is like when a thing moves or a man travels.

"Only, you see, I, the person who is putting all this into my painting, am myself made of the same substance and my envelope is one hundred percent as permeable. That is why I am involved, unreservedly, in each one of my pictures. So that when I started painting under Kumiko's influence, I had to learn Japanese, had to go to Japan and live at Nara. And I was slipping in to the most unshakable Nippon sedentariness when that devil Jean dropped out of the blue with that compass rose he has instead of a head, as you so rightly said. He routed me out. He shook my whole edifice and made me suddenly take off east."

"Urs, I find your ideas very exciting, but tell me, where is Jean?"

He gestured vaguely toward the horizon.

"We arrived here together. And we fell out at once. Jean sniffed the wind. He invented what he called 'the Canadian method.' If I understood it rightly, the method consisted of *walking*. Yes, walking! Eastward, if you see what I mean. Crossing the American continent, in short, from one side to the other. But I had fallen in love with Vancouver instantly, this city where it rains all day long and then produces the most sublime sunsets. It's impossible to paint here! The intoxication of impotence! The canvas stays blank while you feast your eyes! It was a drug and I wanted to test its powers to the full before moving on. We parted. He set off for the Rocky Mountains, hippie style, without a bean, determined not to stop at the foot of the glaciers, or in the vast prairies, or even on the edge of the Atlantic. Oh, we shall meet again! We have a date at my home in Berlin on the thirteenth of August. And from what I know of him, he'll be there, although I wonder what he'll invent to create chaos on the banks of the Spree! Walter Ulbricht and Willy Brandt had better look out!"

"We're not there yet. What am I to do? You know that if Jean has gone off on foot, I can't take the plane to Montreal. I must follow in his footsteps."

"Walk, then! Vancouver to Montreal is only about three thousand miles."

"You must be joking."

"There is a middle way. The train! It leaves every day from Vancouver and winds its way through the Rocky Mountains and the lakes in the middle and the east like a great big, rather lazy red dragon. It stops everywhere. Perhaps when Jean has worn his shoes out he'll get into your carriage somewhere or other. I'm staying here. A little more Vancouver, Sir Twins, I beseech you! If you feel like it, meet us on the thirteenth of August at 28 Bernauerstrasse, in Berlin. My old mother will give us all a bed . . ."

And so the great journey is about to start again. At least I shan't have the same agonizing feeling of turning my back on France as I did when leaving Tokyo, going east. From now on, every step is taking me nearer to the Pierres Sonnantes. I hug the comforting thought to myself as I wander alone along the waterfront of Coal Harbour, newly polished by a fierce downpour. The Royal Vancouver Yacht Club and its next-door neighbor, the Burrard Yacht Club—scarcely less smart—are a brilliant shopwindow of dainty yachts, of every possible design and rig, all streaming with lights. But as you draw nearer the docks the lights grow sparser and the boats more workmanlike, until at last the black, tormented shapes of the old trawlers, still rotting away here after they have fished their last, loom up in a sinister halflight. Nothing could be more desolate than those slimy decks, littered with ends of rope, sagging ladders and warped tiller bars, those rusted plates, choked winches and lengths of broken chain. They are so many floating deathtraps, each one surmounted by a torture chamber open to the winds. One is surprised not to see dislocated and dismembered bodies there, contorted in agony. Some black-and-white birds—something between crows and gulls —seem to be expecting them too. Nor is it pure imagination, for the horror of these boats reminds one of the wretched fate of the men, the fishermen who spent their lives in them.

I retreat into a seaman's bar and drink a large cup of coffee, watching the rain which has begun to fall again. The coffee is the light, plentiful kind of the New World, fragrant and thirst-quenching, bearing no relation to the nasty, thick, greasy, tarry-tasting syrup they distill for you a drip at a time in France and Italy and which poisons your palate for the rest of the day. This time tomorrow I shall be in the big, lazy red dragon Kraus has told me of.

As always on the eve of a journey, I am seized with alarm, inveterate sedentary that I am, and searching for a saint to commend myself to. In the end, the person I appeal to for protection is Phileas Fogg. Yes, it's not St. Christopher, patron saint of wanderers and migrants, I turn to in my traveler's terrors but Jules Verne's rich Englishman, inured to all the malignity of fate and armed with an exemplary patience and courage in rising above the vagaries of the railway, the inadequacies of the stagecoach, and the steamer's failings. He it is who is truly the greatest patron of travelers, possessing as he does on a heroic scale that highly specialized knowledge, that craft so long to learn, that rarest of virtues: travel.

CHAPTER XX

The Prairie Surveyors

Paul

Tuesday 1815 hours. So here I am on the famous Canadian Pacific Railway, the great red dragon with the shrieking voice and topped with Plexiglas domes that meanders through the Rocky Mountains and across the great prairie from one ocean to the other. It was not for nothing that I recalled Phileas Fogg. In my minute "single," in which it is hardly possible to move at all once the bed has been let down, I am back again in the old-fashioned luxury of the Orient Express in Grandma's day, a mixture of plush, mahogany, and crystal. Snug in this padded shell, I feel all my fears melt away and indulge in a bout of childish glee at the idea that I shall be here for more than three whole days and nights, since we do not get to Montreal until 2005 hours on Friday. Our timetable can be summed up in three sets of figures: 69 stations spread over 2,879.7 miles to be covered in 74 hours and 35 minutes. We start at 1830 hours.

Tuesday 1902 hours. Milepost 2,862.6 COQUITLAM. I note: (1)

That it is too bumpy to write while the train is in motion. I shall have to make do with the stations. (2) The distance is recorded on mileposts, only starting from Montreal. We set out from 2,879.7 and are going toward 0. I rather like the idea. After all, on this journey I am going *back*.

Tuesday 1940 hours. Milepost 2,838 MISSION CITY. The forest already, the real northern forest, which is to say not the neat, thinly planted woodland of Stanley Park, where every tree is a landmark in itself, but an impenetrable tangle of small trees all growing into one another, a real paradise for game of all kinds, furred and feathered. Conclusion: the beauty of woods is man-made.

Tuesday 2020 hours. Milepost 2,809.6 AGASSIZ. The sliding door of my compartment opened suddenly and a black steward slammed a prepacked meal down on my tabletop. One glance assures me that the restaurant car is not working. So it is total seclusion then, until tomorrow morning at least. I shall make the best of it in my tiny cell, the outside wall of which is a clear window letting in the dense, black, close-set pine forest with the rays of the setting sun breaking through it mysteriously from time to time.

Tuesday 2215 hours. Milepost 2,750.7 NORTH BEND. A lengthy halt. Shouts and people running on the platform. I get the impression that this is the last station of any importance before the long night's haul. I have time to ask myself the old question which is bound to occur to a sedentary like myself on any journey: why not stop here? There are men, women, and children who look on these passing places as home. They were born here. Probably some of them can't even picture any other land over the horizon. So why not me? What right have I to come here and go away again knowing nothing at all about North Bend, its streets, its houses, and its people? Isn't there something in my nocturnal passing which is worse than contempt, a denial of this country's very existence, an implied consigning of North Bend to oblivion? The same depressing question often comes into my mind when I am dashing through some village, town or stretch of countryside and I catch a lightning glimpse of young men laughing in a square, an old man watering his horses, a woman hanging out her washing with a small child clinging round her legs. Life is there, simple and peaceful, and I am flouting it, slapping it in the face with my idiotic rush . . .

But this time, also, I am going on. The red train heads wailing into the night and the mountains and the platform slips by, taking with it two girls deep in earnest conversation, and I shall never know anything about them, or about North Bend . . .

Wednesday 0042 hours. Milepost 2,676.5 ASHCROFT. The heat is stifling and I am lying naked on my bunk. Since this is placed directly under the window—feet foremost—I can see, or guess, or feel the great sleeping country gliding past against my legs, my side, my cheek, the depth and silence of its dark silhouettes, its patches of bright moonlight and signals, red, green and orange, the tracery of a coppice caught in a car's headlights, the thunder of a metal bridge, its X-shaped struts slashing across the window frame, and suddenly a moment's total, impenetrable, bottomless blackness, absolute night.

Wednesday 0205 hours. Milepost 2,629.2 KAMLOOPS. I am cold now, in spite of the blankets I have piled on top of myself. By day, the dispaired twin can put on a good face if he must. But at night . . . at two o'clock in the morning . . . Oh, twin, why aren't you here? After the cruel glare of the station, the merciful darkness covers my eyes again and they bathe in their own tears like two wounded fishes on the bottom of a brackish sea.

Wednesday 0555 hours. Milepost 2,500 REVELSTOKE. I have had to let two or three stations go by in a kind of doze. I was too tired and too miserable to write. My window is frosted right over.

Wednesday 0905 hours. Milepost 2,410.2 GOLDEN. Aptly named! We are winding our way, at speeds of up to eighty, among precipitous gorges with a boiling green torrent below and larchwoods rising in tiers up the sides. The sky is blue, the snow is white, the train is red. We are trapped in a Technicolor photo out of the *National Geographic* magazine.

Wednesday 1030 hours. Milepost 2,375.2 FIELD. While the Rocky Mountains unroll their grandiloquent scenery above our heads, we are guzzling enthusiastically beneath the Plexiglas domes of the coaches. The staff being unequal to the task, we serve ourselves from the kitchens and then take our trays up the little staircase leading to the view. I am beginning to realize the part that food plays in Canadian life—surely greater than in any other country I know. Even in Vancouver, I noticed the extravagant number of food advertisements on the television screens. The Canadian is first and foremost an eating man and putting on weight is his besetting sin, even as a child, in fact especially then.

Wednesday 1235 hours. Milepost 2,355.2 LAKE LOUISE. It is all over. The grandiose scenery has been packed away to wait for the next train. In its place is a countryside that still owes some unevenness to the foothills of the Rockies. But everything proclaims the plains. Two white pigeons are kissing on the black shingle roof of a house. Next door to them, two blue rock thrushes are billing on the red corrugated-iron roof of another.

Wednesday 1320 hours. Milepost 2,320 BANFF. We are following the course of the Bow River, which goes through Calgary, the capital of Alberta. Some horses are galloping away in a staggered bunch, as though swept aside by the wind of the train.

Wednesday 1610 hours. Milepost 2,238.6 CALGARY. A thirty-five-minute halt enables me to take a quick walk through this onetime Mounted Police post, now a city with a population of 180,000. A scorching, dust-laden wind blows through the streets, which are numbered and laid out on a grid system. The center of this concrete desert is the thirty-six-story International Hotel building, looming over a landscape as flat as your hand.

It has been claimed that skyscrapers are justified because of the shortage of space in American cities, as on the island of Manhattan. This is typical of the kind of limited, utilitarian explanation which dodges the real issue. What it should be saying is the opposite: that skyscrapers are a natural reaction to too much space, to the terror of being surrounded by wide-open spaces, like chasms in a horizontal plane. A tower dominates and commands the plain around it. It is a rallying point, to call men from afar. It is centrifugal for the person who dwells in it and centripetal for the one who sees it from a distance.

Wednesday 1910 hours. Milepost 2,062.8 MEDICINE HAT. The guzzling is in full swing again all along the train. It is nothing but massive portions of ice cream, giant sandwiches, hot dogs, and plates of goulash in every coach. And to go with it we are passing through the vast grain-growing region, with agricultural machines like huge diplodocuses rolling across it and nothing on the horizon but the tall shapes of concrete silos. This is the granary of the whole world, the cornucopia out of which cereals flow to Latin America, China, Russia, the Indies, Africa, to all of starving mankind.

Wednesday 2030 hours. Milepost 1,950.3 GULL LAKE. The little envelopes of granulated sugar have the arms of the Canadian provinces on them, Newfoundland, Ontario, British Columbia, and so on, along with the motto: "Explore a part of Canada and you'll discover a part of yourself." It is, of course, aimed at persuading Canadians to get out of their home province and discover their own country in a spirit of national unity, which it seems they are not much inclined to do. But what far-reaching implications that sentence has for me! In which of Canada's provinces am I going to discover that part of myself?

Wednesday 2212 hours. Milepost 1,915.4 SWIFT CURRENT. Another night. Perhaps because I did my share of guzzling this afternoon I refused the black steward's prepacked dinner, which seemed to upset him considerably. Now that it is dark again, the window no longer exhibits the same grotesque shadows that it did last night. The plains have made it a wide, gray screen, a shore of silence on which nothing happens, except that now and then there is a highway with a stream of cars moving along it, each one pushing its own little sheet of light ahead of it.

Thursday 0028 hours. Milepost 1,805 MOOSE JAW. Worry keeps me awake. I make up my mind to take a sleeping pill. Today a pill, tomorrow alcohol, and after that tobacco and then drugs, and ending in suicide, perhaps? All the weaknesses of non-twins, sick of their own terrible loneliness, who am I now that I should be immune from them?

Who am I? There is one question, the only one that will matter to me on the day I give up trying to find Jean: *what basic difference is there between a dispaired twin and a non-twin?* Or, in other words, once Jean's disappearance must be accepted as

Gemini

an accomplished fact, how am I to go on living as a twin? How can I wear my geminate heritage in an active and living way?

It is here that Alexandre's ghost haunts my mind persistently. Once again our shocking uncle emerges as the ideal mediator between twins and non-twins. What basic difference is there between Paul crossing the prairie in his red train and the dandy garbage man sitting in his stationary railway carriage among the white hills of Miramas? Both are dispaired twins. Alexandre suffered his disparity from birth, it was *congenital;* mine is *acquired.* Alexandre never experienced geminate contact. He did not learn twinship by growing up in it. He was like one of those kittens who are taken from their mothers too early and never learn to lap, like the baby rats taken from their mothers too early who when they grow up and meet a female run around her in a panic with no idea where to begin. Cast, alone and suffering, on this earth, Alexandre spent his whole life walking into the unknown, into the black night, seeking a geminate paradise he could not find anywhere, since he had nothing behind him to give him a viaticum, a start, a direction, some intimation of the goal he wanted to reach. Whereas I, still impregnated through and through with happy twinship, what I find in my childhood is more than a solemn promise, it is a foreshaping of the end I am called to.

Thursday 0815 hours. Milepost 1,461.5 PORTAGE LA PRAIRIE. Under the influence of the sleeping pill, I slept like a log, the true, brutish sleep of the twinless, cutting all connection, I mean, breaking contact absolutely, a gloomy insistence on solitude almost amounting to annihilation—whereas geminate sleep is a continuing dialogue, silent but all the more intimate, pursued in the matrical warmth.

I must have the courage to face it: ever since Jean left I have been deteriorating inexorably. Has the process been hastened or retarded by this journey? Both at once, perhaps. Hastened because the journey—like oxygen puffed on a blaze—hastens everything, growth and disease alike, and every day's experiences and encounters are thrusting me forward. But where would I be today if I had stayed at the Pierres Sonnantes, all alone with Méline, waiting passively, eating my heart out in the unlikely

hope of Jean's return? Here at least I am searching, searching, I
am doing something, I am doing something . . .

Thursday 0920 hours. Milepost 1,405.9 WINNIPEG. We stop for
half an hour. I would have time to have a look at the city, but
my experience at Calgary has put me off the idea of leaving my
mobile den. *Winnipeg. Capital of Manitoba and Canada's great
corn market,* the guide tells us. *Population 270,000. Built on the
site of the fort erected by La Vérendrye in 1738 at the junction
of the Red River and the Assiniboine.* Very well. We'll leave it at
that. Go to Winnipeg and stay cooped up in one's compartment
reading the page about Winnipeg in the Blue Guide . . .

Thursday 1043 hours. Milepost 1,352.3 WHITEMOUTH. I have
lost the use of my arms and legs . . . Just as the train was stopping, I saw the heads of some travelers moving past my window
and I recognized Jean among them . . . There could be no mistake. Non-twins, whose identifications are founded on similari-
ties and approximations may be fallible, may recognize without
cause or be blind to their dearest friend or nearest kin. Identical
twins know one another instantly, with an infallible instinct, because each can—so to speak—put his finger on the essence of the
other. That is the very thing that worries me. Because if I recognized Jean immediately and without a doubt, he, if he saw me,
would have no more doubt than I, and surely then he would
have run away?

He was wearing a thick red woolly hat and was dressed in
brown corduroy, more like a woodsman than one of those hip-
pies, young bourgeois intellectuals, dropouts from good families,
that Urs Kraus described. Moreover, that elusive expression of
the Tokyo portraits no longer canceled out the thing we had in
common, far from it; it was truly my twin whom I saw just now
for a brief instant on the Whitemouth platform.

Thursday 1215 hours. Milepost 1,280.2 KENORA. I think I would
lock myself in my compartment if I could. I am afraid. When the
ticket collector came banging in just now, I nearly died of fright.
What am I afraid of? That Jean will come in! Have I gone mad?
If Jean did get on at Whitemouth and were to burst into my
compartment, I'm not the one who should be called mad. Let us

not reverse the roles, brother, if you please, sir! It is I who am seeking you, not the other way around.

Reversing the brothers . . . We played that game often enough when we were children! It was the very essence of Bep. By tearing myself away from the Pierres Sonnantes and traveling the world in Jean's wake, have I not made the proper sacrifices for us to be metamorphosed into each other?

Thursday 1930 hours. Milepost 986.8 THUNDER BAY. I undertook a search of the whole train, coach by coach, compartment by compartment. Counting the stops at Dryden and Ignace, when I was obliged to get out onto the platform to observe the travelers leaving the train, I may say it has taken me all afternoon. An interesting and instructive excursion. This journey right across the continent is so long and monotonous that the train becomes a kind of caravan with a multitude of cells, all quite separate from one another. There are nursery cells with little hammocks slung between the luggage racks, between the lines of drying diapers. Musical cells with banjos, woodwinds, brass, percussion and even pianos. Ethnic cells, with families of Mexicans, igloos of Eskimos, tribes of Africans and a Jewish ghetto. Kitchen cells with people frying and stewing things on stoves, having presumably considered the meals served under the domes inadequate. Cells religious, erotic, studious, alcoholic, psychedelic, professional . . .

It was among the latter I came nearest to finding what I was looking for, although there was nothing to establish it for certain. There were three of them, three youngish men in country clothes —something between campers and sportsmen—bearded like tramps and bespectacled like students. The equipment piled all around them told me what they were: articulated chains, rods, prismatic squares, ropes, pantometers and so forth. What I was looking at was a survey party and *they were all wearing the same red woolly hats.* I remembered the fluorescent orange jackets of the men working on the highways, and I think those hats served them as signals, and as points of reference when they were taking measurements. Jean was not with them. I watched them without them noticing me, which was not difficult because they were making a terrific racket, drinking and laughing uproariously.

There. I have come back to my solitary hole with a new awareness of what a variegated society we are on board this train. But the thing I remember most from my voyage of discovery is how isolated all these groups are, how mutually exclusive, and the way the compartmentalization of society is echoed in the compartments of the train. As for Jean, I am beginning to wonder whether I did not mistake one of the three surveyors for him.

Thursday 2110 hours. Milepost 917.2 NIPIGON. This is the last stop tonight, the one where travelers intending to sleep on firm ground must get off. Leaning out of the window, I saw the surveyors passing their equipment out through the door and stacking it on the platform. Just as the train was starting, the black steward passed along the corridor. He gave me a broad grin in which for the first time in weeks I caught a gleam of the alienating light, and said, "Not going with your surveyor friends, sir?" I dashed to the window. In the middle of the crowd jostling toward the way out I glimpsed the backs of the red hats. I had just time to count. *There were four of them.*

Friday 0155 hours. Milepost 735.6 WHITE RIVER. This is the unforgiving hour. The pill I took to make me sleep seems to have worn off, leaving me a mental and emotional wreck on the verge of sleep, like a shipwrecked sailor washed up half dead on the sands. Of all kinds of loneliness I have learned to know since Jean went away, this of the middle of the night is the worst. If Jean really got out with the surveyors at Nipigon, then every turn of the wheels is taking me further away from him. I feel like jumping off the train. Is it to go to him, or to kill myself?

Friday 1015 hours. Milepost 435.3 SUDBURY. A halt of three quarters of an hour. Huge crowds on the move. A lot of the cells are departing, bag and baggage. This is because one branch of the Canadian Pacific Railway turns south for Toronto and the U.S.A. We are going on to Ottawa and Montreal.

It is nearly twenty-four hours since Jean got on this train. Jean came to join me on the train and I let him go . . .

Friday 1447 hours. Milepost 239 CHALK RIVER. Surveyor Jean . . . Oh, my twin, you are traveling on, obedient only to the mo-

ment and your own vagabond mood. And here am I running
after you, notebook in hand, interpreting your journey, theoriz-
ing about your circuit of the world, calculating the equation of
your trajectory. Kraus, with his conversion to "rich space" by
Japan, provided me with some valuable starting points. It ought
to be possible to read Canada, also, in terms of space.

Friday 1740 hours. Milepost 109 OTTAWA. I have been on this
train for more than seventy hours. My feelings are muddled and
contradictory. I can't take any more. I am suffocating with boredom and impatience between these narrow walls which I know
in every detail until I am sick of them. And at the same time, I
am scared of arriving. The way out, the shock of the unknown
seem like terrifying prospects to me. A prisoner seeing the end of
his sentence approaching must feel the same twofold anguish.

Friday 1841 hours. Milepost 57.5 VANKLEEK HILL. Since Ottawa, we have been running along the right bank of the Ottawa
River. Amazing number of aboveground electrical installations.
Enormous pylons loaded down with cables, gigantic floodlit
masts and stays, gantries, transformers, circuit breakers . . . This
aerial forest of metal has replaced the other and must herald the
approaches of the great city. We shall be in Montreal this evening, at 2005 precisely.

MONTREAL

This is the very image of Canada as I have seen it gradually taking shape ever since Vancouver. For the emptiness of the prairie
is still present in these broad streets, in these groups of smoked-
glass buildings, this mighty river, these parking lots and shops
and restaurants. It has simply taken on a different form, become
urbanized. Human warmth, animal contact and the sense of all
sorts of people, of many different races, is quite missing from this
huge city. Yet life there is, vibrant, explosive and dazzling. Montreal, or the electric city.

The revelation came to me almost before the hotel porter
closed the door of my room on me. Outside the big glass bay I
could see only the myriad windows of a skyscraper whose top
was out of sight. Offices, offices and more offices. At this hour all

of them deserted and all as bright as day, so that each one could be seen to contain the same metal desk, the same swivel chair, with the secretary's typewriter under a yellow cover to one side and the metal filing cabinet behind.

A few hours' restless sleep. My body, used to the movement of the train, is completely disrupted by the stillness of this bed. The offices are no longer deserted. Charwomen in gray overalls with white caps on their heads are sweeping, dusting, emptying waste-paper baskets.

The lessons I learned in Japan before I crossed Canada have not been wasted on me. In fact, the two countries throw light on one another, and I am usefully applying the Japanese graph to the Canadian chart.

Like the Japanese, the Canadian suffers from a space problem. But while the first is cramped into a tiny, scattered archipelago, the second is reeling with vertigo in the midst of his vast plains. This contrast, which makes Canada an anti-Japan, is responsible for more than one characteristic feature. The Japanese is not afraid of wind or cold. In his paper house, quite unsuitable to any form of heating, the wind comes and goes as it likes. Here, on the other hand, even in summer, one is constantly reminded that the winters are formidable. The roofs of the houses have no gutters because slides of snow and ice would rip them off. Shops, garages and shopping centers are built underground, suggesting that for eight months of the year the citizens lead molelike lives, going from homes to cars, to shops and places of work without ever putting their noses out of doors. To get into the houses one passes through hall-cloakrooms with four doors, airlocks for the prolonged dressing up before going out and the patient undressing before coming in. And even the morbid hunger which has the Canadian stuffing himself at all hours of the day and night, even that is only a defense mechanism against the surrounding vastness and the icy winds howling across it.

To counter the terrors of the besieged, the Japanese invented the garden, the miniature garden and also *ikebana*, the art of flower arrangement. All are ways of making openings in over-crowded spaces, openings inhabited by structures which are light, witty and detached.

To counter the horizontal abyss, the Canadians dreamed up the Canadian Pacific Railway. What else could they do, indeed, but try to *innervate* their vast territory, to cover it with a network of nerves, at first very loosely woven but drawing tighter and tighter, closer and closer together?

That is why Jean's reaction to this country is perfectly rational, logical and understandable. He has responded to the space of Canada in Canadian fashion. By doing his utmost to *cover* the territory. "Cover" is a splendidly ambiguous word, with its simultaneous meanings of traverse (on foot), protect (with a cloak), be prepared for (an eventuality), defend (with troops), roof over, hide, disguise, excuse, justify, compensate, impregnate and so on. Here, Carder-Jean has turned into Surveyor-Jean. To survey a country is *to clothe it intelligently* with the help of chains, rods, drop arrows and graphometer. Once it has been surveyed, a country ceases to be literally *immense*—that is, measureless. It has been measured and so, contours, gradients and such inaccessible areas as marshes and dense undergrowth notwithstanding, assimilated by the intellect and ready for demarcation and land registration.

The little gray women in the offices have been succeeded by a different species of humanity. This kind includes both sexes. The men are in shirt sleeves, the women in blouses—shirts and blouses alike of an immaculate whiteness. The day's work has started. There are jokes, smiles and chatter. I can see the same little scenes going on in the thousand little pigeonholes piled one on top of another, as close as the cells in a beehive. I am reminded of one of those entomologist's observation hives, where one wall has been replaced by a window. Only my vantage point has its limitations: I can't hear.

What is a living being? A little piece of heredity moving in a particular environment. And nothing more: everything in a living being that does not derive from heredity comes from the environment. And vice versa. Nevertheless, in the case of twins, to these two elements is added a third—the identical brother—who is both heredity and environment, with something else as well.

For twinship embeds a bit of the environment in the midst of what was homogeneous heredity, and this not only is a mutilation but also lets light, air and noise into the inmost privacy of a being. Real twins are a single being with the monstrous faculty of occupying two different positions in space. But the space which divides them is of a special kind. So rich and vital is it that the space in which the twinless wander is a barren desert by comparison. This intergeminate space—the extended soul—is infinitely extensible. It can shrink to almost nothing when the twins are asleep, entwined together in an ovoid posture. But should one of them flee to a great distance, it grows thin and stretched—but never tears—until it is big enough to embrace earth and sky. Then the geminate cipher covers the whole world and its cities, forests, seas and mountains take on a new meaning.

Which leaves one final question which has been plaguing me ever since Jean went: what of the extended soul if one of the twins should disappear forever?

The fact is our whole story would have been nothing but one long, adventurous meditation upon the idea of *space*.

A walk about the city. Daylight does not suit the electric city.

The offices, shopwindows and stores are still lit up, of course, but the advertisements, the revolving signs, the wan magic of the neon lights are washed out by the sun. Like those nocturnal predators who wait for dusk before spreading their white wings, the electric city suffers the sun's tyranny in silence, patiently dreaming of the coming night.

Is it an illusion? Touching the wall of a building, I felt a kind of prickle in my fingers. Can it be that this city is so saturated with electricity that it seeps out of the houses, like damp or saltpeter rot in other places? I recall the forests of pylons loaded with cables and catenaries—like stylized Christmas trees festooned with paper chains—planted on the banks of the Ottawa and St. Lawrence rivers. And most of all I remember that not so many miles away the thunderous roaring of Niagara Falls is feeding the largest hydroelectric scheme on the whole North

American continent with an installed capacity of 2,190,000 kilowatts.

There is innervation on the same scale as this outsize country! What the surveyors are endeavoring to achieve patiently with their childish paraphernalia—and still more by what they survey —Niagara Falls, extending into billions of wires endlessly divided and ramified, achieves in an instant and with sovereign force.

Body and spirit. The formidable mass of water tumbling down with a noise like the crack of doom into a gorge a hundred and fifty feet deep, the steady erosion of the underlying rock which can be measured by the rate at which the face of the falls is moving gradually upstream, the cloud of spray that rises into the sky and dims the brightness of the sun, all this is matter, brute force and physical substance. But out of that convulsed and shrieking body comes a kind of spirit, in the shape of those 2,190,000 kilowatts, the fabulous, unseen energy which spreads on silent wings throughout the country at the speed of light and makes such a firework display in the electric city that every stone fizzes at a touch, it is so overflowing with wasted energy.

The surveyor's thick, studded boots raise a white dust along the road and sink into the newly turned black earth of the prairie. He stops, sticks in his poles, peers through his sights, kneels down to grasp the handle of his measuring chain and waves to his companion in the red hat standing fifty yards off holding the other end of the chain, who goes down on one knee also. But as he rises, he sees in the sky the gigantic yet delicate structure of the pylons, immense steel candelabra holding from the tips of their white porcelain-ringed insulators bundles of high-tension wires dotted with red balls. They too are linked by chains and they survey the great prairies with giant strides, crossing lakes, bestriding forests, leaping over valleys, and jumping from hill to hill to vanish at last as minute dots on the infinite horizon. The surveyor, who has always longed to lie down on this earth and cover the whole country by extending his arms and legs indefinitely so as to innervate it with his own body, feels a bond of friendship with the great wire-carrying chandeliers striding away, skeletal and enormous, into the darkness, the wind and the snow.

CHAPTER XXI

Behind the Berlin Wall

"Perhaps one day I will introduce you to my friend Heinz. He was badly wounded in the war. He stepped on an antipersonnel mine in the Ukraine. The explosion tore off the whole of his left side: leg, side, arm and part of his face. His right profile is wonderfully regular and healthy, smooth and glossy pink in a rather unearthly way, as though all the strength and vitality from his left side had gone into his right. But the left side is all one huge wound, hideously mangled.

"You French people, you see only the healthy side of Germany, and it impresses you with its miraculous growth rate, a currency that is worth its weight in gold, a balance of trade perpetually erring on the side of large profit margins and a better-paid, more disciplined and more productive work force than any other country in Europe.

"But there is the other side. The Oder-Neisse line that cuts off half of West Prussia and the whole of East Prussia from the body of the nation, East Germany, gray and embittered, and Berlin, that pseudo-capital like a running sore in the middle of

Europe. German prosperity is like the parable of the cripple with the mighty arms."

"Very well, but what of the left side? If you think it looks so bad, if you dislike it so much, isn't it because you are looking at it the wrong way around? Perhaps East Germany wasn't designed to be seen from the West? Do you know how it looks from Poland, Czechoslovakia or Russia?"

"I don't much care. I can see how it looks to the East Germans. Since 1949, when East Germany was created, 2,900,000 of its people—including 23,000 members of the armed forces—have come over to the West. And the numbers are increasing: 30,444 in July, 1,322 on the first of August, 1,100 on the third, 1,283 on the fifth, 1,741 on the eighth, 1,926 on the ninth, 1,709 on the tenth, 1,532 on the eleventh, 2,400 on the twelfth . . . And it is not just the numbers we have to consider. Most of these refugees are young, at the age when they are most useful to a nation. East Germany is being drained of her lifeblood."

"That's a development that ought to alarm any German, even one from the West. A quarter of the territory of the former Reich has been annexed by the U.S.S.R. and Poland. Another quarter—East Germany—is losing its German population. What is this migration leading to? To a desert, which the eastern countries are bound to be tempted to colonize, while seventy million Germans will be squashed into the narrow boundaries of the Federal Republic. West Germany has nothing to gain by having as a neighbor a bloodless East Germany on the verge of collapse because it is being sapped of its vital forces. On the contrary, what it ought to want is a prosperous sister state that bears it no grudges, with whom it is possible to negotiate and reach an understanding."

"It is entirely up to the East German leaders to make their country a paradise of freedom and well-being where even the West Germans dream of going to live . . ."

Sunday, August 13, 1961. A little after midnight, units of the People's Police (Volkspolizei) and of the National People's Army (Nationale Volksarmee) drove in columns to the border between the eastern and western sectors of Berlin and closed it with coils of barbed wire and chevaux-de-frise. The few people who were moving from one part of Berlin to another at this late hour were driven back. Tanks and armored cars took up positions at the main vehicle crossing points between the sectors, such as the Brandenburg Gate, the Potsdamerplatz, the Friedrichstrasse and the Warsaw Bridge. In other places, engineers of the Volksarmee were tearing up paving stones and breaking up the surface of the roadways to erect barricades. Watchtowers and machine-gun posts were set up at vantage points. Traffic by S-Bahn (urban railway) and U-Bahn (underground) between the sectors was halted.

First thing in the morning, East Berlin radio broadcast details of the step taken by the East German Council of Ministers on August 12, 1961, after consultation with the Warsaw Pact countries.

> In order to put an end to the injurious activities of the militarist and revanchist forces of West Germany and West Berlin, controls such as normally exist at the frontiers of all sovereign states are henceforth to be set up at the borders of the German Democratic Republic—including that with the western sectors of Greater Berlin. There is a real need for effective surveillance and control along the border with West Berlin for the purpose of dealing with provocation from without. Citizens of the German Democratic Republic may no longer pass these borders except with special permission. Until such time as West Berlin becomes a free city, neutral and demilitarized, citizens of the German Democratic Republic must obtain special passes to cross the border into West Berlin.

> It has been decreed by the Council of Ministers of the Democratic Republic that citizens of Democratic Berlin may no longer work in West Berlin. Citizens of Democratic Berlin who have been going to West Berlin daily to work are requested by the President to present themselves either at their last place of work within Democratic Berlin in order to resume their employment, or at their local employment offices, where new work will be assigned to them.

The wall which divides Berlin along a line from north to south is ten miles long, up to a yard wide, and between seven and fourteen feet high and has a total volume of 335,000 cubic feet. It is built of reinforced concrete covered for the most part with cement facing or sheets of colored plastic material. It is reinforced and extended by some eighty miles of barbed wire, principally along the rooftops of all the houses on the border. Sixty-five wooden hoardings block the view at all points where the inhabitants of the two Berlins might be able to see and communicate with one another by signs. But there are also 189 watchtowers, equipped with floodlights, to enable the Vopos to maintain a day-and-night watch on the border. There are 185 forbidden zones patrolled by Alsatian dogs on chains running on horizontal wires. Mantraps bristling with barbed wire have been sunk in the waters of the Spree and the Teltow Canal wherever they coincide with the border.

Meanwhile, a curious dialogue is carried on between the two Berlins. The East has chosen the spoken, the West the written word. The voice of socialism preaches, with the help of forty-three loudspeakers, to the crowds from the West that gather up against the newest border. It says that in the future the capitalists' continual provocations will be foiled by the "rampart of peace." It says that, thanks to the wall, the third world war which the Nazi revanchists wish to start has been nipped in the bud. It says that the traffickers in human flesh who have been luring the workers of the German Democratic Republic over to the West with fallacious inducements will have to cease their shameful trade.

In the West, meanwhile, at the corner of the Potsdamerstrasse and the Potsdamerplatz, an illuminated news sheet catapults its message from a gantry of steel girders. *Die freie Berliner Presse meldet* . . . For the expenditure of one Deutschmark one may also purchase a newspaper printed in giant type, legible through binoculars at a distance of a hundred and fifty yards or more, which one holds out at arm's length toward the watchtowers. But the people of the East do not gather at the foot of the wall, like those of the West. So these messages are directed mainly at the eastern policemen along the border. The Volkspolizei and the Nationale Volksarmee, who bear the brunt of this psychological offensive, stand up to it well. Billboards urge the West Berliners to be nice to them, reminding them that 23,000 Vopos have deserted to the West since 1949. "It is the most unreliable army ever. The number of victims of the border guards would be ten times higher if the order to open fire immediately in the event of any attempt at an illegal crossing were carried out to the letter. Do not abuse them! See the man behind the uniform. Make contact with a friendly wave. Try. Your attitude will do more to breach the wall than the most powerful charge of explosives."

In any case, what is called on one side "the wall of shame" and on the other "the rampart of peace" is, to begin with, in many sectors no more than a coil of barbed wire down the middle of the street. Crowds gather on both sides. Signals, messages, parcels and sometimes even small children are handed across it. That is when the Vopos are put to their severest test. Out of the 14,000 border guards—some 11,000 men from the first, second, and fourth brigades of four different regiments reinforced in each case by a training battalion of 1,000 men—most are young recruits, ill prepared for special duties of this kind. Nevertheless, their orders are detailed and specific. The guards are to take their eight-hour spells of duty in pairs, judiciously selected so as to have as little as possible in common. So a bachelor will be paired with a married man with a family, a Saxon with a Mecklenburger, a raw recruit with a veteran. Ideally, they should not know one another before they go on duty together and should not meet again afterward. But the rules require that during their hours on duty they shall never be more than twenty-five yards apart. In fact, if one should desert it is the duty of the other to shoot him down.

Orders to be carried out in the event of a violation of the border. After the fugitive has crossed the first obstacle—a chevaux-de-frise, perhaps—the guard is to call out: "Halt! Sentry! Put your hands up!" If the person so addressed fails to comply, the guard is to fire a warning shot. If, in spite of this warning, he continues his escape, the guard is to fire at him, regardless of the number of obstacles that remain for him to clear. If the fugitive is so close to the border that a simple warning would permit him a chance of success, the guard is to shoot him down forthwith. Should he be either on the last barbed-wire entanglement or on top of the wall, there is no need to fear that he will fall into

West Berlin territory since a man who has been hit invariably
falls toward the side whence the shot has come. It is necessary to
avoid injuring civilians, policemen or Allied soldiers in the West.
Therefore the guards will fire parallel to the border, or in such a
way that the shots shall spend themselves in the ground or in the
air. Should members of the Red Cross of West Berlin endeavor
to cut the wire in order to go to the aid of a fugitive they are to
be fired on, but not in the case of Allied troops.

The classic question which is put to the border guards in training is: "What would you do if the person escaping were your
own brother?" The correct reply is: "A defector ceases to be a
brother and becomes an enemy of the people, a traitor to society
who must be neutralized by any means."

The experienced eyes of the crowd in the Potsdamerplatz have
noticed a degree of vacillation in the behavior of one of the
Vopos on duty in the Leipzigerstrasse, in front of the ministry
building. People stop to look. Why is he on his own? Why is he
glancing to right and left? The face beneath the shadow of his
helmet seems to be a very young one, reflecting his emotions
guilelessly. The atmosphere is unusually tense and strained.
Something is about to happen, but the situation is becoming increasingly dangerous. There is sudden encouragement from the
crowd. "Come on! Come on now!" The Vopo casts one last
glance behind him, in the direction from which death can come.
Then he makes up his mind. He drops his gun, springs forward,
crosses one roll of barbed wire, then a second, then scales a
fence. West Berlin police surround him and lead him away.
They question him. No, he is not married. Yes, he has left someone in the East, his mother. And an elder brother also. But he is
not afraid of reprisals against them because his brother is a
police official. He will take care of their mother. And they won't
do anything to him. At worst, the incident will slow down his
promotion, and that will be no bad thing. It doesn't do for policemen to get on too quickly, especially in the East. So there you
are! Now there is one brother on one side of the wall and one on
the other.

He laughs nervously. But the passers-by are calling for him.

He comes out of the police station again, bareheaded, and smiles in a dazed way. This evening there will be the radio and television. A deep gulf has opened up in his life. The crowd disperses. One more . . .

For three days Paul has been the guest of Frau Sabine Kraus in her old-fashioned flat at number 28 Bernauerstrasse. As soon as he arrived, he felt that the address augured well. The Bernauerstrasse formed the boundary between the districts of Wedding in the French sector and Mitte in the Soviet sector. The pavements, the roadway and the buildings on the north side of the street belonged to West Germany. Number 28, like all the houses on the south side, belonged to East Berlin. But you only had to step outside to be in the French sector. Warper-Paul was satisfied with this half-and-half situation.

But on the morning of August 13 the building rang with shouts and cries and running feet and the sound of furniture being moved and hammering. Paul was at the window when Frau Kraus's wailing voice reached his room.

"But what is happening? What is happening? And Urs hasn't come, although he promised me!"

The street and the pavement opposite—in the French sector— were littered with furniture, mattresses, bundles and trunks, making islands around which whole families were encamped.

"Everyone is moving out, Frau Kraus," Paul explained, "and I am wondering whether we're not too late to do the same!"

Frau Kraus, in a dressing gown with a scarf around her head, came in and joined him at the window.

"There are the Schultheisses, our neighbors from downstairs! What are they doing with their suitcases out on the pavement? Hullo! Hullo! I'm waving at them but they can't see me."

"Look. There are workmen, with a guard of Vopos, nailing up the doors of the flats. Now the people are getting out of the ground-floor windows."

He hung halfway out so as to get a better view of the street.

"Frau Kraus, you won't be going to mass in the Versöhnungskirche this morning. They've just finished bricking up the doorway."

"Poor Father Seelos! What will he do without his church? He is my confessor, you know."

"There is still time. People are still getting out of the windows on the ground floor. Frau Kraus, shouldn't we try to get out into the French sector? It's only a few yards away."

But the old lady shook her head in a worried way and reiterated: "No, my son must find us here. But wherever can he be?"

In the afternoon, the police broke into the flats on the ground floor and began blocking up the windows. People went on moving out faster than ever by way of the windows on the next floor.

Paul missed none of the activity that went on beneath his window. Why was it that he had to be here to witness this sealing of the border (*Abriegelung*), this tearing apart of the very substance of Germany, this hacking apart of the two Berlins, like the two halves of an earthworm? He remembered a conversation with a woman, a stranger, in St. Mark's Square in Venice. "Twins may not cause disasters, but there is no denying that the imminence of a disaster attracts them to the place where it is going to happen," she had said. Or was it he who had put forward that idea? What did it matter? To be shut up in a flat with an old Prussian lady when one had flown over Greenland, Alaska and the Pacific and crossed the Rocky Mountains and the great prairie in a train, after drinking in so much space to be reduced to so little room, what meaning could there be in such a fantastic reversal? To what Japanese garden—the more painfully miniaturized, the more charged, secretly, with infinity—was this brutal contraction leading?

When the masons from the East began walling up the upper windows of the thirty-nine apartment buildings facing the Bernauerstrasse, firemen from the West stationed themselves in the street to assist the exodus which was still going on from the windows of the upper stories. The use of firemen's ladders would have constituted a violation of the border and risked provoking clashes with the Vopos. But there was nothing to prevent them from stretching safety sheets to catch the fugitives.

There was something simultaneously tragic and ridiculous in the spectacle of those terrified men and women compelled to hurl themselves into space because they had left it too late before deciding to change sectors. One thought kept haunting Paul's mind all the time: We are not at war. There is no earthquake, no fire, and yet . . . Surely it is very sinisterly typical of our times that what is, after all, a purely *administrative* crisis should lead to such scenes? This is not a matter of guns and tanks, but only of passports, visas and rubber stamps.

For a while, the attention of the whole street was focused on the troubles of one old lady who hung back when the moment came to jump into the sheet from two floors up. When no amount of urging would serve to bring her to the point, they set about lowering her, as in romantic novels, with the aid of sheets knotted into a rope. She was already swinging in space when the Vopos burst into her flat and appeared in the window, trying to pull her back again by hauling in the sheets. There was a growl of anger from the street and a Western policeman drew his revolver and threatened to fire on the Vopos if they did not go away. They conferred together and withdrew, but not before one of them had tossed a smoke bomb into the firemen's sheet.

The best drop was when a four-year-old child was thrown by its father from the fifth floor and caught gently by the firemen in their canvas sheet. Others were not so lucky. Rolf Urban (born 6.6.1914), jumping from the second floor; Olga Segler (born 7.31.1881), jumping from the third floor; Ida Siekmann (born 8.23.1902), jumping from the fourth floor; and Bernd Lünser (born 3.11.1939), jumping from the roof of the building—all missed the firemen's sheet and were killed.

Not one of these incidents, whether tragic or funny, altered Sabine Kraus's determination to stay where she was until her son's return. But they did work a transformation in her which astonished Paul. As the situation deteriorated, so the old lady emerged from her depression and took on a new lease of life, as though benefiting from the electricity charging the atmosphere. The dressing gown, slippers and headscarf gave way to black overalls, rubber running shoes and an amazing kind of turban that descended over her forehead and kept her plentiful gray hair in place. A plump, agile, sexless figure, she flitted about the doomed apartment, running from window to window and concocting startling banquets from the ample store of provisions in her cupboards.

"This reminds me of 'forty-five, the Battle of Berlin, the blanket bombing, the soldiers of the Red Army breaking in and raping everybody," she kept saying, flushed with pleasure. "I feel fifteen years younger! If only the Allies would blow up the wall! Then there'd be another war!"

She paused in the middle of rolling the pastry for a tart, her mild blue eyes lost in dreams of slaughter.

"You see, Paul, I wasn't made for quiet times. Urs wanted me to go and live near him in Munich. But I never would. Here, with these four sectors, so wonderfully absurd, I could smell the powder. Berlin is a tragic city. Its climate is a tonic I need. I am lymphatic. I need to be whipped up, whipped up, whipped up," she repeated fiercely, digging her plump fingers into the dough.

Then she harked back to her childhood and early adolescence.

"I was a big, gentle, blond girl, very quiet and easygoing. Everyone used to say how good I was. The truth was, I was bored. Bored to death! I only really came to life in 1914. I was thrilled by all the rumors, from Potsdam—where the Kaiser lived—from the Wilhelmstrasse—the ministries—and most of all from the front, and they gave me the energy I needed. The darker and more careworn my father's face became, the more my heart sang. War was threatening and my fear was that it might not break out. It did break out. I was afraid it would only be a flash in the pan, as I heard people around me prophesying. There, again, I was not disappointed. I was in love with Rudolph Kraus. Doesn't the name Rudolph Kraus mean anything to you?"

Paul shrugged his shoulders.

"These young people don't know anything! He was one of our most famous Luftwaffe aces. Downed nineteen enemy planes, officially confirmed, and eight more probables." Then, remembering that Paul was French: "Oh, I'm sorry, Herr Surin! But there must have been some English, Belgians, and Americans among them, you know!"

She giggled, holding her hand in front of her mouth like a little girl caught out in mischief.

"We were married as soon as the war ended. Rudi was a regular officer and he was out on the streets. I didn't worry. Such a strong man, so brave and so brilliant!" Her mobile face fell. "What a disappointment! His lovely air officer's uniform was no sooner put away in mothballs than Rudi turned into a retired man in carpet slippers and a middle-aged spread. No more ambition, no pride, no anything! All he ever thought of was complaining about the wretched pension he got from the Weimar Republic. That's what peace does to a man!"

Paul was gazing in amused fascination at the delightful, grandmotherly old lady, with her snub nose, twinkling eyes and baby face, who seemed to have such a bellicose turn of mind.

"And yet Berlin was such an exciting city! The theater of Max Reinhardt, *The Threepenny Opera*, expressionism. And as if that were not enough, there were politics, unemployment, inflation, all the consequences of losing the war and the Kaiser's abdication. I spent my whole time shaking Rudi, trying to dig him out of his armchair. I told him his place was out there in the street, shoulder to shoulder with his old comrades from the front. In the end I went myself and enrolled him in the Stahlhelm, because I had a brother in that."

She heaved a deep sigh and rammed her small fist into the ball of golden dough.

"He was killed almost at once. Run over by a truck in a scuffle with Karl Liebknecht's men."

Three days after this, at four o'clock in the morning, the men blocking up the windows knocked on Frau Kraus's door. Alarms of this kind had become so commonplace that people had stopped getting undressed to go to bed and the old lady let in the men from the East dressed in her assault kit of track suit, running shoes and headband.

"We've come to make sure you don't have any trouble with nasty weather or too much sunshine coming from the West," the NCO in charge said jokingly.

"I can't go on living in this house with no windows!" Frau Kraus burst out indignantly.

"I don't suppose you'll have to go on living here for long," the

NCO said sardonically.* "But until the order comes to evacuate
the houses along the border you'll be issued with oil lamps and
the necessary fuel."

"But what about the electricity?"

"It was cut off an hour ago. See for yourself."

And Paul watched with horror as the rectangle of sky outside
the windows shrank and shrank until it became a square, and
then a rectangle again, the other way up, and then vanished altogether, as the daylight shrinks and vanishes in a man's head
when he shuts his eyes.

There began for them then a strange, timeless existence, by
the pallid, flickering light of two oil lamps—one per person—
which they carried from room to room. Now the rare sounds
from the dead street no longer reached them except muffled by
the thickness of the bricks and mortar blocking the windows.

Paul said little. Often he would stay shut up in the dark in
Urs's room, where he was sleeping, or else he would follow Frau
Kraus, lamp in hand, as she moved about the flat, listening to her
tireless chatter.

And so, after the reflections of Venice, the fires of Djerba and
the perpetual sunshine of Iceland, he was plunged, even at the
height of summer, into a darkness all the more oppressive because it was the darkness of a prison, brought about by the will
of men. On the following Friday he was to find himself descending some degrees deeper yet.

"My brethren. It would be exceedingly presumptuous of us to
imagine that the fate which has befallen us is remarkable, unprecedented or unique. Remarkable, unprecedented, unique?
Why, who are we? How are we so very different from others like
ourselves, past and present, that we should suffer extraordinary
trials? No, my brethren, let us beware of that proud and gloomy
complacency which would have us muttering that such great
tribulations could only happen to ourselves. Let us rather say
with the Preacher that there is no new thing under the sun and if

* The buildings on the south side of the Bernauerstrasse were evacuated
between September 24 and 27, 1961 and demolished in October 1962.

there is a thing of which it is said, 'Lo, this has never been seen,' it is because things which are old are not remembered.

"When we have convinced ourselves that the disasters that have fallen on us have struck twenty, a hundred, a thousand generations before us, when we acknowledge that misfortune is always unimaginative, our pride will suffer, to be sure, but our hearts will be uplifted by a feeling of profound, of massive warmth and solidarity with our brethren in the blackness of time.

"And so we are gathered together here on this Friday evening in the crypt of our beloved church of the Redemption. Why on a Friday? Because the forces of evil are more vigilant on Sunday, certainly, and by coming together here on the Lord's day we should be exposing ourselves to their retribution. But do you not see that, few as we are, this Friday communion of ours recalls another Friday, a day of blood and of mourning—but prepared for secretly at the great Paschal feast? In the crypt, I said. Why in the crypt? Crypt comes from a Greek word meaning *hidden*. Crypt also means a cave, an underground place, a catacomb. And so we are reminded of the time of the first Christians, who had to pray in secret because the secular power persecuted them with fire and the sword.

"As for the event which is in all our minds, this sword stroke which has severed so many ties, dividing mother from son, husband from wife and brother from brother, do you think then, to recall the words of Ecclesiastes, that this is a new thing under the sun? We have seen a German raise his gun and fire upon a German before this, and we shall see it again, alas. But fratricide occurs in every age, in every generation. 'And Cain talked with Abel his brother: and it came to pass when they were in the field, that Cain rose up against Abel his brother, and slew him. And the Lord said unto Cain, Where is Abel thy brother? And he said, I know not: am I my brother's keeper? And he said, What hast thou done? The voice of thy brother's blood crieth unto me from the ground.'

"And it is as though that first fratricide had served as a model throughout the legends and the history of mankind. Of the twin brothers, Jacob and Esau, the Bible tells us that they struggled together in the womb of their mother Rebecca even before they were born. And then there were Romulus and Remus, Amphion and Zethos, Eteocles and Polynices, and brothers and enemies, all fratricides . . ."

Father Seelos paused for a moment and all that could be seen in the dim, flickering lamplight was the whiteness of his bowed head and clasped hands.

"I am thinking of our dear, martyred city," he resumed, "and I realize that these old tales, these legends I have been talking of all bring me back to it, for you see they all mysteriously have one thing in common. That thing is a city. A symbolic city which seems every time to demand the fratricidal sacrifice. After killing Abel, Cain fled from the face of God and founded a city, the first city in human history, and called it after the name of his son, Enoch. Romulus killed Remus, then marked out the walls of Rome. Amphion crushed his twin, Zethos, beneath blocks of stone in building the walls of Thebes, and it was below the walls of that same Thebes that the twins Eteocles and Polynices slew one another. We must take the long view and not let our eyes be clouded by everyday things.

"I am speaking to you about East Berlin. But not so many days since Father Otto Debelius, driven out of his diocese of Berlin-Brandenburg, was preaching only a few yards from here, in the Gedächtnisskirche in West Berlin. Father Debelius is a Calvinist and I am a Catholic but I doubt if what we had to say was very different. And the border guards always go in twos, they are Germans and they wear the same uniform, but if one jumps over the wall it is the other's duty to shoot him in the back.

"This whole history is obscure and full of echoes from far back in the immemorial past. That is why we must pray with humility, my brethren, and not take it on ourselves either to interpret it, or to judge or to condemn. Amen."

Paul could not believe his eyes. The surprise Sabine Kraus had promised him—and she had kept him shut in his room while she was getting everything ready—was a Christmas tree. It glittered in all its frosty whiteness, with its little candles, its gilded garlands and glass balls colored opal, azure and ruby red.

She clapped her hands as she welcomed him in.

"Yes, Paul, a Christmas tree! I found it at the back of a cupboard with a whole box full of decorations. But we must make the most of what we have, you know! We are nearly out of oil, so we'll light the room with the Christmas tree! The last time it was used was in—in 1955, I think. Real trees were scarce, expensive and very ugly. I bought this one, which is made of plastic, with the idea that it could be used again. I was right, you see."

She bustled around the table, talking all the while, arranging gilt sprays on the white cloth.

"I said to myself, let's have a Christmas celebration while we're about it! And I opened a tin of foie gras and got out a pudding. What extraordinary times we do live in! That mass down in the crypt on Friday evening . . . Only a handful of us. And all through the service I kept on asking myself which one was Judas, who was it would go that very evening and report that underground mass to the police. And now Christmas! I believe in it, you know. I'm quite sure that any moment there'll be a knock on the door. You'll go and open it, Paul. And it will be Santa Claus with his sack of presents."

Paul hardly listened to the old lady's chatter. Even before this, in Iceland—and likewise throughout the whole of the flight from Rome to Tokyo—he had been aware of the curious way time was infected by space, the transmutation whereby any considerable movement in space produced an upheaval of the times of day and of the seasons. And now here was the Berlin wall carrying that space-time confusion to its height by creating a perpetual darkness and out of it a sham Good Friday followed by a sham Christmas. He saw that the setting for this dislocation of the year had to be somewhere enclosed, mineral, a stone vault— like a kind of sealed crucible—and he sensed that he had to go further yet, that *depth*—as prefigured by the crypt of the Church of the Redemption—was an indispensable element in the fulfillment of his voyage of initiation.

"I think there is someone knocking at the door," he said quietly.

Frau Kraus stopped what she was doing and listened. Another very faint tap made itself heard.

"What did I tell you? Santa Claus! Well, Paul, go and open it!"

It was a little girl, her hooded cape and rubber boots streaming with rain.

"It's Anna, our neighbors' daughter," Frau Kraus told him. "Well now, Anna! It seems it's raining in Berlin? We can't see anything in here, you know."

"It hasn't stopped for three days," the little girl answered. "I've brought you this."

She pulled a letter out from under her cape. Then her eyes widened at the Christmas tree and the decorations on the table.

"Is it Christmas here? Downstairs, in our house, we're having Grandma's birthday party three months early. We've got out all the things from the storage cupboard." And since no one seemed to be paying any attention, she added softly, as though to herself, "We're going too. Only Grandma's staying behind."

The letter, addressed to Paul, was in Urs's handwriting.

"My dear Paul, I am here with Jean. No hope of reaching you. Thank you for taking care of Mother. I am entrusting her to you. You will have earned all my gratitude, and for a very long time to come. See that you are both ready night and day. We will come for you. Follow blindly the man who introduces himself by a reference that only you can understand."

"I come from the Vancouver seal."

The man did not smile at the oddity of the introduction. He was dressed as though for skiing or mountaineering.

"Are you ready?"

"What can we take with us?" asked Frau Kraus, who had been making up bundles of all sizes for three days past. The answer was categorical.

"Nothing." A pause, and then: "With all this rain you'll have enough trouble taking yourselves."

Paul felt no surprise when the man took them down to the ground floor and then into the cellars of the block. It was logical that the long night in which he had been incarcerated for longer than he could remember—literally since time *immemorial* —should be the prelude to an excursion underground, logical that it should culminate in a descent into the underworld.

Some of the cellars in the Bernauerstrasse were intercommunicating. It was possible to go from one building to the next amid a smell of mildew and sudden bursts of light from flashlights. There was water running down the walls and the ground was sodden underfoot. How many were gathered there in that last and deepest dungeon of all? A dozen, a score? It was hard to count the shadows fidgeting in the dark around a freshly dug hole gaping in the ground. The muttering stopped when one of the men got up on a chair to give the final instructions. Someone pointed a flashlight at him, making him look grotesquely distorted.

"The tunnel we are going through comes out in a cellar in the Ruppinerstrasse, in the French sector. It is about fifty meters long."

He paused, aware of something like a sigh of relief from the little group of refugees.

"Don't be too quick to rejoice. Every one of those meters is very long indeed. Fifteen meters from the end there has been a collapse, caused by the continual rain of the past few days. We've shored it up as best we can, but the earth isn't holding. At least, it is holding—just. What we needed were proper jacks. We've made do with the jacks of cars and trucks. You have to crawl through the mud just there. It's no joke, but it can be done, and then you're into the last lap. We've worked out that it takes ten minutes to get to the Ruppinerstrasse. You needn't smile. It's a very long ten minutes. We'll go at the rate of one person every fifteen minutes."

There were helmets for all the fugitives, each with a small light fixed to the front. In addition, the guides distributed pocket flashlights for emergencies to those who had not brought them. German thoroughness, Paul thought with a smile. Perhaps Frau Kraus had guessed his thoughts? She was looking at him, her face radiant. She looked young, eager, unrecognizable in her athlete's training gear. Poor Sabine! If all went well there was a serious risk that in three days' time she was going to find herself

safe in the depressing peace of her son's flat in Munich. This
muddy tunnel was her beloved, tragic city of Berlin's parting gift
to her lymphatic soul with its thirst for universal excitements.
Consequently, she was in no hurry. Her age entitled her to be
among the first to go, but she would not.

Ten minutes. Eternity. Fifty meters. Like crossing a desert.
This passage was a funnel. A short person could cover the first
twenty meters standing upright. After that the roof descended
inexorably lower and the ground grew more and more slippery.

Paul went forward steadfastly. He was one of the last. Frau
Kraus had gone ahead of him so that he could help her if need
be. In a little while he could be in the Ruppinerstrasse, in the
French sector, and Urs Kraus would probably be there with his
mother. As for Jean . . . Did Paul still believe that he was going
to find him at the end of his long journey? Perhaps, but he no
longer pictured him in the shape of a brother of flesh and blood,
one to be greeted with backslapping and shouts of laughter.
There might still be a reunion, but not in any such simple fashion. In what fashion, then? He could not have said, but he did
not doubt that every stage of the journey—from the Venetian
mirrors to the prairie surveying party—would have played its
part in the restoration of geminate cell in whatever form. He
could not conceal from himself that, insensibly, the meaning of
his dash around the world had altered. It had begun as a
straightforward pursuit, such as two non-twins might have embarked on, but for a few specifically geminate aspects, such as
the alienating light. But little by little it had become apparent
that the superficial object of the exercise—to catch up with the
fleeing brother and take him home—was merely a cover, growing
ever more tattered, threadbare and transparent. To begin with,
Paul's feeling that it was incumbent on him to follow the course
taken by Jean without deviating from it a fraction—sacrificing
the advantage he might have obtained by cutting corners—might
have looked like an exaggerated version of the usual dependence
of pursuer on pursued. In reality it was the beginning of Paul's
own autonomy, showing that it was more important to him to get
all that was to be gained from every stage than to catch up with

Jean by the quickest way. After that the crossing of the American continent had been the first time that their two courses diverged and, paradoxically, it was Jean, in the end, who came to join Paul on board the red train. And now this molelike progress through the subsoil of Berlin was an original ordeal for himself alone in which Jean had no part. Paul had undoubtedly crossed a decisive threshold and was moving toward radical transformations. A new life, a changed life, or perhaps quite simply death?

He was sinking up to his ankles in mud now and already the tunnel was forcing him to walk doubled up. The walls were pressing inward so suddenly that he could not help fearing that the tunnel was giving way under the rain much more quickly than anyone had foreseen.

He was tripping over timbers and jacks half buried underfoot. So the falls had been too much for the guides' improvised shoring up and he must fear the worst. Turn back? That might be the sensible course because from that point on a cave-in could occur behind him and cut off his retreat. He went on, nevertheless, on all fours now, struggling to scramble over the barriers of wood and metal formed by the collapsed stays. After that, there could be no more going back because he was crawling forward and it was no longer possible to turn back. Fifty meters. Ten minutes . . . The guide had not lied, it was a very long way indeed. He banged his helmet on a piece of timber. The knock was not a hard one but it broke the lamp above his forehead. Paul got his emergency flashlight out of his pocket. After several attempts he decided to grip it between his teeth.

This was death beyond a doubt. For now the tunnel ended in a wall of red clay advancing slowly toward him. With the strength of despair, he tore a jack, an iron bar, a wooden beam out of the mud. Hurry, shore it up again before the red mass buried him. He braced himself, gathering a pathetic assortment of material around him, and as the soft, slithering jaws closed slowly over his crucified body he felt the hard edges grinding into it like teeth of steel.

The Extended Soul

Paul

There was black night. Then flashes of pain, rockets, clusters, sprays, showers, suns of pain shot through the blackness. After that I became a witch and a cauldron.

The cauldron was my body, the witch my soul. My body was coming to the boil and my soul bending over the fevered stirrings of the black brew, eagerly observing the phenomenon. There comes a time when it would be possible to have music, books, visitors. The soul rejects these untimely distractions. It has other things to do. It does not wish to be distracted for an instant from its theater of sickness. The fever of the body absorbs the soul, keeps it from boredom, from dreams, from escape. These are the fantasies of convalescence. It is as though the body, exalted by fever, penetrated by fever as though by a kind of spirit, is growing closer to the soul, which is itself weighed down and as it were materialized by suffering. And they stand face to face, fascinated by the strange kinship they are discovering.

(Perhaps it is a step toward the life of animals. Animals never show signs of boredom, of the need to fill the vacant hours with some invented pastime, the need to be amused, for amusement is a deliberate divorce of soul and body. It is a property of mankind to separate body and soul—and this is diminished by illness.)

This time the reversal has begun. The witch draws back and looks up from her cauldron. But only for an instant, because now the seething brew is threatening to overwhelm her. It is turning red and rearing up into the air. It is the gaping jaws of a shark, bristling with teeth. No, I know it now, it is the living wall of the Berlin tunnel advancing on me. Panic! I brace myself against the pain, this slithering red mass that is coming at me. As long as I have strength to hold on, I shall survive, but I can feel my strength running out. Panic! Now I am all one screaming pain . . .

"*Give him injections of Novocain intravenously, ten cc.'s at one percent. But not more than four in twenty-four hours.*"

Who am I? Where am I? The little fairy Novocain, in snatching me away from pain, has stripped me of all personality, all existence within time and space. I am an absolute I, timeless and placeless. *I am* and that is all. Am I dead? If the soul outlives the body, surely it is in such an extremely simplified form as this? I think, I see, I hear. That ought to be: it thinks, it sees, it hears, as we say that it is raining or that it is fine.

"*If it hadn't been for those timbers, bars, and jacks he would have got away with nothing worse than slight asphyxia. But all that iron and steel, that metal stuff carried along by the collapsed soil . . . Knives, scissors, saws! And then after that, the danger of gangrene in the arm and that crushed leg. We had no choice but to amputate.*"

Who are they talking about? My right side certainly feels heavy and inert, lying in these sweaty sheets. But in my left leg and my left arm I am alive, I can feel and stretch.

I stretch myself. My bed is merely the focal point, the purely geometrical center of a sphere of sensitivity whose volume is variable. I am in a bubble—which expands and contracts. I am that bubble. Sometimes its outer membrane collapses flaccidly and clings to my body, fitting my own skin, at others it swells out, enveloping the bed and invading the room. At such times it is painful if anyone enters the room. Yesterday the bubble was filling the whole room when Méline came in to bring me tea. She barged in roughly with her wheeled trolley and I screamed out silently—unless it was that she had grown deaf, she and the doctor and all the rest of them, because for a long time now my words and my screams have ceased to reach those around me.

Pain is no longer that red wall in the Berlin tunnel against which I braced myself with all my strength. Now it is like an invisible beast that is tearing at me and I am striving to master it, tame it and bend it to my will. But at any moment it will rear up again and bite me.

Just now, I was watching the sun sinking into the horizon in a great welter of purple clouds. Was it that the light was too bright for my hypersensitive eyes? Or were those incandescent caverns all too eloquently illustrative of the fires raging in my two stumps? The blazing sky became my own wound. I gazed in fascination at those vast, flaming subsidences of which I was the tortured consciousness. My suffering body covered the whole sky and filled the horizon.

This feeling was not so illusory that it stopped me from falling peacefully asleep as soon as the last ray of the setting sun was extinguished.

I must escape from the alternatives of pain or anesthesia. I must dismiss the little fairy Novocain. Make my fingers let go of this life buoy which keeps me from plummeting into pain. Face the onslaught of pain naked and alone, without the shield of anesthesia. Learn to keep afloat in pain.

I have known this for some while. Ever since pain ceased to be as massive and all-enveloping as night's blackness and began to thin and vary in texture. It is no longer a deafening, voiceless

roar that batters the mind. It is not yet a language. It is a gamut
of shrieks and squeals, of resounding bangs, clicks and whispers.
It is time to release these myriad voices of pain from the gag of
anesthetics. Time they learned to speak.

*"He won't take the Novocain any more? If he is in too much
pain, we might consider surgical intervention, periarterial sym-
pathectomy or arteriectomy, commissural myelotomy, prefrontal
leucotomy . . ."*

Pain is a capital which must not be dissipated. It is the raw
material which must be worked, transformed and used to best
advantage. Let no one try to take this pain away from me, for it
is all I have. It strips me of everything, but I know that in it I
must find everything again, the countries I shall no longer travel,
the men and women I shall no longer meet, the loving that is denied me, all these will be re-created out of the stabbings,
wrenchings, tensions, cramps, barbs, burnings and hammerings
that occupy my poor body like a frantic zoo. There is no other
way. My injuries are the narrow scene within whose confines I
must rebuild the universe. My wounds are two Japanese gardens
and from this tumid red earth, crusted with blackened scabs,
cracked with pools of matter whence the severed bone emerges
like a rock, in that scoured, churned-up, leprous terrain it is for
me to make a minuscule replica of heaven and earth . . . which
will deliver up to me the keys of heaven and earth.

Three o'clock this morning was a moment that was special,
blessed and superhuman. In a crystalline silence of divine serenity I heard three o'clock strike from the Guildo church. And also
from Sainte-Brigitte, Trégon, Saint-Jacut, Créhen and even from
Matignon and Saint-Cast. From ten kilometers around those
three strokes rang out on a hundred different notes and in a hundred different rhythms, and I heard and identified them all beyond the possibility of a mistake. For the space of a few seconds,
I glimpsed that state of hyperawareness to which the terrible
and painful metamorphosis on which I am embarked may ultimately lead.

I have paid dearly since for that sublime instant. Until sunrise,
I hung gasping on a cross, my breath cut short by the cord of a

garrot, my hands and feet crushed into wooden vises, my heart
bleeding from repeated stabs.

But nothing will ever make me forget those hundred chimes
telling the three hours of the morning into the limpid dark.

*"Given the condition of his stumps, it's too early to be think-
ing of prosthesis. Meanwhile, we can't let his muscles atrophy
completely. He needs to move about, sit up, and let his body do
a bit of work."*

Work. Yes, I remember. Travail. From the Low Latin *tripal-
ium*, a frame made of three posts used to master restive horses
and for women in childbirth. I am a restive horse, snorting and
foaming in the trave. I am a woman in travail, shrieking and
straining. I am the newborn child: the world bears down on him
with the weight of a great pain, but he must assimilate that pain
and become its architect, its demiurge. Out of that opaque, oppressive mass, he must make the world, as the great Jacquard of
the Pierres Sonnantes made a fine-woven, translucent fabric out
of a solid, tight skein.

An organism which allowed itself to be destroyed by attack
from outside without fighting back, in a total passivity, would
not suffer. Pain expresses the body's immediate reaction to injury, as it begins to parry, to repair and rebuild what has been
destroyed—even if that reaction is often vain and ridiculous.

Neither vain nor ridiculous in my case, I know that.

I am looking for a word to describe the state I am moving toward now, and the one that comes to mind is *porosity.*

"It's soaking," Méline said as she came into my room this
morning. She was referring to the heavy, warm rain that had
been pattering down all night onto the fallow leaves and overripe fruit of autumn.

I knew. Or at least I might have known, by asking my body
and contemplating the warm, sodden shroud that enveloped it.
There is sickness still, yes, and great pain. Yet hope swells my
heart as I realize that I am in direct contact, plugged in to the
skies and to the pattern of the weather. I begin to perceive the
birth of a barometric body, a pluviometric, anemometric, hygro-
metric body. A porous body through which all the winds of

heaven may breathe. No longer the useless organism rotting on a mattress but the living, breathing witness of the meteors.

It is only a hope as yet, but a crack is appearing in the Berlin tunnel and through it the sun and rain are entering.

This is something I shall not dare to confide to anyone, not so much for fear that they would think me mad—for what does that matter to me after all?—but for fear of hearing it scoffed at, mocked, treated as absurd, when what it is is a thrilling miracle. When I woke up the day before yesterday I felt, quite distinctly, something moving inside my two lots of bandages. A large insect in the bandages on my arm, a little mouse in the ones on my leg. Then Méline came in, the day wore on and I forgot both the insect and the mouse.

Every evening, when the cares and rituals of the day are about to be cast off for the great crossing of the night, I suddenly find myself back in the environment and state of mind of the early morning, and it is then I recall the ideas, dreams, and sensations left over from the previous night but which the day had effaced from my mind. That was how I was reminded of the insect and the mouse. However, it was very quickly obvious that the comparison with these small animals would not do, because I soon realized that whatever was moving deep inside my bandages *was answering to my own will.* It was just as though a tiny hand here and a little foot there were now and then emerging from my two stumps and endowed with the power of movement and feeling. The emergences were intermittent and followed by more or less protracted withdrawals. I am reminded of the hermit crabs we used to catch among the rocks by St. Brigitte's. Put the shell down on the sand and after a few minutes you would see a bundle of legs, pincers and antennae emerge and unfold themselves, grope about to establish the lay of the land, only fold up again and vanish at the slightest alarm. In the same way, out of the swollen, red caves of my stumps, fragile limbs are timidly emerging on exploratory excursions that do not, as yet, extend beyond the limits of my bandages.

Méline had a very strange surprise for me this morning.

Whereabouts in the back of a cupboard did she find those binoculars, the Gemini binoculars given us as a present by the agency we made those little advertising films for? That episode from our childhood has remained clear in my memory as though I had been aware from the beginning that it was packed with significance and destined for future mysteries.

When I had learned how to hold and focus the binoculars with only my right hand, I scanned the view, the beach of the Ile des Hébihens, the mussel beds of Saint-Jacut and the rocks by the Pointe du Chevet, where I followed the tiny hooded figures of some spearfishers. But I soon realized that I was being very unadventurous with them and that there was more to be got out of the binoculars than merely being able to see two miles away as if it were two hundred yards.

When I had done sweeping the horizon, I lowered my sights to my own garden, where Méline was raking up dead leaves. She must have been about thirty yards away and I saw her as if it were two. The difference in close-up was not at all the same as in the case of the spearfishers at the Chevet. They, whether two hundred yards or two miles away, were still way beyond my reach, out of touch if not out of sight. While Méline, who to begin with was well out of reach physically, was brought by the glasses so close as to be right *within* my sphere. And the irony of the situation was that although she was now only two yards away from me—within speaking, almost within touching distance —I, for my part, was still thirty yards away from her. This one-sidedness could be seen clearly by her face, which was concentrated on things and tasks unconnected with me, locked in a circle from which I was excluded. Thanks to the glasses, I was bending on Méline a remote, piercing, inquisitorial eye, the eye of God, in short, and for the first time I was experiencing an *alienating light* overcome, reversed, requited.

But in another moment I had gone beyond that commonplace alternative, that wholly human and subjective means of revenge, steeped in emotions and resentments. The eye of God, all right, but it has always seemed to me that the divine eminence was only really intact when faced with the innocence of nature and the natural elements, and that it lost something of its purity in contact with men. So in the end it was on the garden itself and on the grass in particular that I turned my instrument of hyper-awareness. How surprised I was to discover, as I let my godlike eye penetrate the mass of growing plants, that this reversal of the alienating light whose effects I had just noted in Méline's face enabled me to see the grass and flowers with an incomparable clarity and brilliance. It did not take me long to perceive that the composition of the lawn varied from place to place, and especially in one rather damp corner not far from the sandy edge of the cliff, and on a chalky hump we used to ride down on our bicycles next to the plowed fields which bounded the garden to the east. I got Méline to bring me the big book of grasses with the colored engravings which had belonged to Maria-Barbara's grandfather—my maternal great-grandfather—and to my intense delight was able to pick out of the confused mass of new growth all kinds of species listed there, clovers, white and purple, bird's-foot trefoil, sweet vernal grass, dogstail and smooth-stalked meadow grass, yellow oat grass and burnet, and elsewhere meadow soft grass, fescue, bromegrass, couch, timothy grass, rye grass, cocksfoot and foxtail, and away in the marshy patch, ranunculi, sedge and bullrushes. And every plant stood out from the grassy background with wonderful clarity, stems, umbels, cymes, panicles, stamens and bracts detailed with almost uncanny precision and delicacy. The most observant botanist with legs and arms to walk about his garden and handle his plants could not have seen so much and so clearly with the naked eye.

The work of creation which is proceeding in my two stumps derives from the Japanese miniature gardens. Gemini has just raised the lawns of La Cassine from the status of a tea garden—for strolling about and talking—to that of a Zen garden on which only the eyes may rest. But at Nara my profane eyes saw nothing in the Zen gardens but a blank page—the expanse of raked sand, the two rocks, the skeletal tree were clearly nothing but a virgin stave awaiting the notes of the melody. After the ritual mutilations of Berlin, I am no longer the profane being I was, and the emptiness has been replaced by a magnificent superfluity.

I laid down my binoculars with happy confidence. Certainly I shall never again walk in that garden of our childhood, that special place in which we played, but from now on I can know it and possess it more intimately by my invalid's eyes alone, and I know that knowledge will go on from strength to strength.

That was when my left hand protruded beyond my bandages for the first time.

Sickness, pain, disability, by depriving our lives of a measure of autonomy may perhaps confer on us a more direct access to our environment. A person who is bedridden is tied to one spot, but has he not by that very fact myriad roots and nerve endings going down into that spot which the healthy man, always on the move, can never suspect? An invalid lives a sedentary life with a matchless intensity. I remember Urs Kraus and his "rich space." So rich that in it a man finds himself involved in an infinite number of contradictions so that he can no longer clear himself enough room to move. My disability is changing me into a tree. From now on I have branches in the air and roots in the ground.

This morning my joints are creaking painfully, my stumps are shrinking and my muscles on the verge of cramp.

This is because, for the first time this year, the country awoke to a dressing of hoarfrost, while a northeasterly wind has been tearing the leaves wholesale from the trees. Autumn seems to be turning to winter, but I know from experience—and my whole body, electrified by the sudden cold snap, confirms it—that it is only a false alarm, the autumn is only pretending to go and will return again soon and settle in for a while.

When Méline came in just now pushing the tea trolley ahead of her, I trembled with fear and flung myself backward so that I am still shaking all over with the shock. This was because for the past two hours my left leg—the unseen, amputated one—had been oozing out of the bandages, the sheets, and the bed and dangling onto the floor of the room. I was rather enjoying myself, pushing the limp, invasive member, naked yet sensitive, further and further, to the wall, then to the door, and I was just wondering whether I could manage to turn the handle with my toes.

That was when Méline burst in with her tea trolley and her clumsy shoes and all but trod on my leg. I shall have to get her accustomed to knocking and not coming in until I have pulled myself together.

Interestingly, while my leg was invading the room, my left arm had withdrawn completely into its bandages and my hand, while it had not actually disappeared, was no bigger than a snowdrop bud beneath the gauze. Must I assume a balance between my leg and my arm so that one is bound to shrink as the other grows, or is this only a temporary phase due to my lack of "maturity"?

Another new discovery. I have just connected two sources of hyperawareness. Through the binoculars, I had spotted a colony of mushrooms under an old oak tree. They were lycoperdons, the puffballs we used to play with, squeezing them to make the little cloud of brown dust spurt out. I spent a long time studying the thick, velvety stalk and round, milk-white head covered with tiny pimples of the largest member of the colony in Gemini's unearthly light.

It was then I felt certain that I was also *touching* the mushroom. Indubitably, I was not merely seeing that rounded surface, granular and slightly warm, I was brushing it with my fingertips, and the same with the cool earth and the dew-laden grass which formed the background to my lycoperdon. My left hand was there also, it had moved forward of its own accord at the end of an arm some ten or twelve yards long to arrive at the point at which my eye met the little white mushroom.

But then my left leg had vanished, melted away, swallowed up by its stump! It was as though my right side were not yet strong enough to launch the whole of my left at once upon the conquest of the world and was experimenting, sending out now an arm, now a leg, until it could do better.

I can see now that in the dark night of my pain I identified my missing arm and leg confusedly with my lost brother. And it is quite true that whenever any loved person leaves us they inflict a kind of amputation. It is a part of ourselves which goes and is dead to us thereafter. Life may go on but we have been maimed, and nothing will ever be the same again.

But there is a mystery and a miracle attaching to twinship, and the vanished twin always lives on in a way in the dispaired brother who remains.

I know it, this left side of mine which moves, wriggles and pushes out prodigious extensions into my room, into the garden and soon perhaps into the sky and sea. *It is Jean,* now become a part of his identical brother, Runaway Jean, Jean the Nomad, Jean the Inveterate Traveler.

The truth is that in our great journey we were acting out in an imperfect, clumsy, almost laughable fashion—in short, in a twinless way—what is a profound truth, the very basis of twinship. We ran after one another, like a policeman after a thief, like actors in a comic film, unaware that in so doing we were conforming to the ultimate formula of Bep: dispaired twinship = ubiquity.

After losing my twin, I had to run from Venice to Djerba, from Djerba to Reykjavík, from there to Nara, to Vancouver, to Montreal. I might have run a lot further, since my dispaired twinship required me to be *everywhere.* But that journey was only a parody of a secret vocation, and it was to lead me underneath the Berlin wall for the sole purpose of undergoing the ritual mutilations necessary for me to accede to a different kind of ubiquity. And Jean's inexplicable disappearance was only the other face of that sacrifice.

A small child builds up a world by reconciling his visual, auditory, tactile and other senses among themselves. Once an object has become permanently associated with a particular shape, color, noise or taste, then it is finished and thrown back into the environment.

I am engaged in a similar activity. The bubble of increasing size which I inflate about myself, the increasingly far-reaching explorations of my left side, the surrealistic images revealed to me by Gemini, all these things merge into one another, making

my bed the center of a sphere of sensitivity which grows in di-
ameter from day to day.

The ceiling of uniform gray cloud that stretched from one horizon to the other thins, as though worn away by the little breeze
off the land, and turns to translucent marble, letting the blue sky
filter through. Then the marble cracks, but regularly, into rectangular shapes, and becomes instead a paving with the gaps between growing wider and wider and brighter and brighter.

An extended soul. That, truly, was the privilege of identical
twins who sustain between them a pattern of ideas, feelings, and
sensations as rich as an oriental carpet. Whereas the non-twin
soul crouches, huddled in a dark corner, full of shameful secrets,
like a handkerchief screwed up in the bottom of a pocket.

We played this extension between us all through our childhood. Then we stretched it out to the size of the whole world,
but in a clumsy, ignorant way, on our journey, embroidering it
with exotic, cosmopolitan motifs. It is important to keep this
worldwide dimension, but also to restore to it the regularity and
secrecy of our childhood hopscotch. After cosmopolitan, it must
become cosmic.

The sky this morning was as limpid and clear as a diamond.
Even so, a sensation like the tickling of a razor blade, with thin,
deep cuts, like a foil quivering painfully inside my thigh, fore-
cast a change. Indeed, the sky was streaked with fragile fila-
ments, with silken tendrils, with icy crystals hanging like lusters
at incredible altitudes. Then the crystalline silk thickened and became ermine, angora, merino, and my stomach sank into its soft,
fleecy welcome. At last the main body of cloud appeared, a solemn procession, massive and rounded, splendid and matrimonial
—yes, matrimonial, for I saw two figures that I knew, joined together and radiant with happiness and goodness. Edouard and
Maria-Barbara, holding hands, were advancing to meet the sun,
and the beneficent power of those two deities was so intense that
the whole earth smiled at their passing. And as my left side mingled joyously with the procession and was lost in the luminous,

snow-white mazes of those great beings, my right side stayed
huddled on its couch, weeping for sweetness and nostalgia.

The procession passed on into the glorious east and all day
long I saw its cloudy train roll by, a whole host of attendants,
great and small, gregarious and fantastical, a succession of
shapes, hints, ideas and futile dreams.

All day long the mildness of an Indian summer set the fallow
trees singing in a green sky and an occasional breath of wind
lifted a rusty leaf or two in passing. Then everything fell silent.
The heat no longer radiated from the sun but surged out of the
clouds in waves of electricity. A leaden chaos, topped by brilliant summits, bulbous, burgeoning hillocks, started rolling toward me from the far horizon, rolled along my foot and up my
ankle and my thigh. A last breach opened in the citadel of cloud
and out of it a spear of light fell and shattered in a phosphorescent pool, hot, almost blazing on the gray sea, but I did not
even start to flinch away from its searing touch because I knew it
would not last and night would come down on it again. And indeed the luminous breach went out and the chaos extended over
everything, enveloping me in its electric waves. The garden was
submerged in darkness except for a mass of goldenrod, the
spikes of which were shimmering with an inexplicable
brightness. Gemini informed me that it was caused by swarms of
moths who had come to plunder the yellow flowers. So moths,
too, are given to plunder, and by night, of course? Why not?
Having discovered this little secret of nature, I felt all down my
left arm the brushing of innumerable downy silver wings.

Then the great wrath of the storm thundered in my breast and
my tears began streaming down the windows on the veranda.
My grief, which had begun with rumblings away on the horizon,
burst out in a shattering clamor over the whole Bay of Arguenon.
It had ceased to be a secret wound concealed under a bandage,
endlessly suppurating. My anger set the sky on fire and projected
lightning images of anguish on it: Maria-Barbara thrust into the
German army truck, Alexandre lying stabbed on the docks at
Casablanca, Edouard wandering from camp to hospital with pictures of our lost mother hung around his neck, Jean fleeing

ahead of me across the prairie, the red, slithering jaws of the
Berlin tunnel closing slowly, a whole passionate indictment of
fate, of life, of everything. While all this time my right side
hardly moved, lying flat in bed, stricken with terror, my left side
was shaking the earth and sky, like Samson shaking the pillars of
the temple of Dagon in his rage. Then, carried away by its
anger, it stretched away southward, calling on the moorlands of
Corseul and the great lakes of Jugon and Beaulieu to witness its
misery. Then the rain fell, heavy, calming, assuaging, just the
thing to release the tension, to soothe my unhappiness and fill
my barren, lonely night with watery murmurings and stealthy
kisses.

Has it always been like this, or is it the effect of my new life?
There is an extraordinary harmony between my human *tempo*
and the rhythm of meteorological events. While the stories that
physics, geology and astronomy have to tell us remain wholly
alien, either because they develop so terribly slowly or because
their phenomena occur at such vertiginous speed, the meteors
live at exactly the same pace as ourselves. They are ordered—as
human life is ordered—by the succession of night and day and by
the seasonal round. A cloud forms in the sky, like an image in my
brain, the wind blows as I breathe, a rainbow spans the heavens
in the time it takes my heart to become reconciled to life, the
summer glides by like the passing of the holidays.

And that is fortunate, for otherwise I do not see how my right
side—which Méline washes and feeds—could still serve as the
rootstock—buried and soiled, yet indispensable—for my left side,
extended over the sea like a great, sensitive wing.

The moon unveils her round face and hoots like an owl. The
offshore breeze leaps on and tangles the branches of the silver
birches and shakes off a handful of drips to patter on the sand.
The sea's phosphorescent lip breaks, retreats and froths over
again. A red planet winks at the flashing buoy—also red—which
marks the entrance to the harbor of the Guildo. I can hear the
grass browsing on the rotting humus in the hollows and the tin-

kling footsteps of the stars traversing the vault of heaven from east to west.

Everything is a sign, a dialogue, a conclave. Sky, earth and sea are talking together and each pursues its own monologue. Here I have found the answer to the question I was asking myself on the eve of the Icelandic Pentecost. And this answer is magnificently simple: just as twinship has its own language—cryptophasia—so has dispaired twinship. Being endowed with ubiquity, the dispaired cryptophone hears the voices of all things like the voice of his own moods. What to the non-twin is only the murmur of the blood, the beating of the heart, a cough, a belch, a stomach rumble becomes the song of the whole world to the dispaired cryptophone. Because the geminate speech, intended only for one other person, having lost its pair is thenceforth addressed to wind, sand and stars. What was most private becomes universal. A whisper is raised to the power of divinity.

The poverty of meteorology which understands the life of the skies only from without and presumes to reduce it to clockwork. The way the weather has of continually giving the lie to his forecasts does not deter the meteorologist in his stupid obstinacy one little bit. I know this now that the skies have become my brain: there are more things in them than can be contained in the head of a scientist.

The sky is an organic whole possessing a life of its own, in direct relation to the earth and the seas. Mists, snows, sunshine, frosts, dog days and aurora borealis are all developed freely by this great body according to an internal logic of its own. The scientist lacks one dimension necessary to understand this, the very one which has entered into me, connecting my extended left side to my maimed right one.

Henceforth, I am a flag flapping in the wind. Its right side may be held captive by the wooden staff, the left side floats free, all its fabric quivering and straining under the buffeting of the meteors.

In the past three days, winter, pure and sterile, has imposed its clarity on all things. My left side is made of glass and metal and is resting a long way off on two anticyclones, one situated off northeastern France, the other off the southwest of England. Until this morning, these two Arctic fortresses—glacis of still, cold air—were stoutly withstanding the onslaughts of the Atlantic currents moving in to fill a deep depression rather more than twelve hundred miles to the west of Ireland.

But I can feel that one of them—the more exposed, the one off Cornwall—is surrendering to the warm air, is breaking up and teetering on the edge of the gulf of low pressure. I foresee that it will fall and be pillaged by the moist maritime winds. Never mind! There will be no rise in temperature, the air will retain its still, crystalline transparency, for the other fortress, the Flemish one, remains impregnable, strong in a high-pressure area of 1,021 millibars. It is directing a calm, clear flow of dry, freezing wind toward me, sweeping the sea and the woods until they shine. Yet the covering of snow on the fields is thinning and the clods of black earth left by the plow can be seen poking through. This is because the sun is bright and keen and is causing the snow to evaporate *without thawing*. A transparent, rainbow mist trembles above drifts of hard, unbroken snow. The snow is vaporizing without melting, without running, without softening.

This is called sublimation.